Tro:

or

The Old In and Out. Of Love.

by

Russell Bittner

"You can drive the devil out of your garden, but you will find him again in the garden of your son."

Heinrich Pestalozzi

FOREWORD

Many nights when undrawn to the living,
   I have gone to the graveyard instead,
And sought out my truth among ashes,
   And for beauty, lain down with the dead.

In the stillness of many a midnight,
   I have warmed to their wakening sound,
The impassioned and scorned and unliving
   Who speak to my heart from the ground.

"In the Stillness of Many," by Tom Merrill

Most secrets perish and are buried with the dead—and so, remain captive to the soil. I know: I live hard by a cemetery. The grounds—except on holidays, birthdays and anniversaries—are hushed and only occasionally tremble. I've long suspected this trembling to be the issue of a certain kind of secret that will simply not be hushed; that even the dead whisper discreetly among themselves, those whispers accumulating until they acquire the force of rumor; and that the rumors of the dead, circulating through hollows and caverns and catacombs below the hushed surface of well-groomed cemetery grounds, then seek exit, like a dark geyser.

It is at the moment of eruption that a secret becomes a legacy and begins to travel and traffic among the more energetic—if less discreet—living. Its ultimate object is actualization, resolution and a final, *final* resting place. In its journey, it knows no rest, no peace, no mercy. Meanwhile, the living—always eager to bear witness to injury, destruction and annihilation—become its willing coachmen.

Restless that legacy may be, but also tenacious. Legacies ride steerage across generations like a recessive gene or a shy bacillus—or simply, in our time, as digits across the Internet. Wind-borne, water-borne, blood-borne or Net-borne, legacies are eager fellow travelers in a constant, unerring, exacting search for actualization, resolution and rest.

This is the story of one such legacy in search of a final resting place. Of a legacy that began its last voyage—its *pre*-history—in an obscure Scandinavian village and then crossed an ocean by jetliner in a time when jetliners were still a novelty. It came to rest temporarily, and hardly by accident, in the city of New York only a few, short decades before the close of the second millennium. By cunning and wit, it found means to travel and traffic among the living, to wreak its small havoc of injury, destruction and annihilation towards a certain, inevitable culmination in the spring of the year 2003. But then to find its final, *final* resting place eleven years later in that same obscure Scandinavian village.

New York—this hard nipple of the New World. In lush times and mean, it's a city under siege, as much from within as from without—hence chaffed, even bloody; alternatively calloused and to all appearances, unfeeling. And yet, for all of the bluster and confidence it exudes, New York is finally just one long swath of concrete and asphalt, none of which feels pain or delight, exaltation or misery, surfeit or hunger.

And what of its inhabitants? The more fortunate are laid to rest in cemeteries like the one I live hard by. The others? Consigned to a potter's field where rest remains as elusive in death as it had in life.

Yes, this is the story of one legacy. But it's also the story of a pair of inhabitants who go out as they came in: naked, simple, and penniless. Before they pass on from this piece of Earth, however—from this island with its unending arcade of opportunity, amusement, temptation, seduction and entrapment—we will come to understand how two minor players on such an extraordinary stage came out of opposite wings, created and met in their own center, and then, their hour up, withdrew into their respective wings and disappeared.

Manhattan at the beginning of the twenty-first century is a place of possible lights, at all times competing with other lights for brightness, sometimes winning for a second or even a minute—but then just as easily extinguished or outshone by another competing light. Manhattan is never a place without light. The only matter of interest is: whose light tonight? And for how long?

Chapter 1

Late winter, 1992

*P*hilosophy, he thought to himself, *is a better friend to* Schmutz *than to light.* He thought this not as he considered the discipline, but rather as he looked around at the windows, ceiling and floors of the classroom in which he now sat—waiting not only for a buzzer at the end of the hour, but also for a conclusion to the drone issuing from the lectern directly in front of him. Hegel was the matter at hand. Consequently, he framed his thought in German rather than in Yiddish. His more immediate *hier und jetzt* ("here and now") was not the abstract metaphysical discipline, but rather the edifice that housed the weary weight of it.

The end came. The drone ceased. He stood up and walked out of Philosophy Hall and across the quad towards the subway entrance at 116th and Broadway. As he walked, he heaved heavy eyes towards a logic-free heaven, then let them drift back down to Earth where he found nothing of Quine's quiddities to help him as he spied her slipping out of Lewisohn. He carried a well-thumbed Schopenhauer—*leisure* reading. She, he saw, carried only herself and a sheaf of papers, though both exceedingly well.

He continued walking towards the subway—watching, then sensing, that her footsteps might now be nudging the continents towards some sublime, quixotic shift. As they emerged from under the arches, he saw a limo standing in a **No Standing** zone. Her driver also stood—beside an open back door. She ducked down to enter and caught her mink on the handle. A few papers went flying. He picked one up; recognized the comely shape of verse; read the header and the first two lines:

"They Know I Did It"

In turns, we're heir to nightmares—
and so, debauched of dreams;

He paused as he considered what he might've just stumbled upon: another Sappho-in-the-making; a masked poetess.

Masked, in-the-making, and in mink—hence, a minx he thought as he gave the piece back with a single word of acknowledgment—"Provocative"—and accidentally touched her glove in the hand-off. She thanked him soundlessly with only a flicker of her lips, though eyes—and not just a little—aided and abetted.

The quad lay behind him; the MTA in front. A turnstile to any torch show in Manhattan or its four outlying boroughs was his for the pushing. Until, that is, he caught the scent of something like perfume; heard a sound on concrete no sneaker could make; glanced back and understood, in a second, how even heathens could hosanna when touched by an angel on a pair of heels piled four inches high.

He pretended to fumble with his transit card. Fumbling at his age was first blush, second nature. Pretending? He still lacked the catechism for it. She, meanwhile, stood at the kiosk attempting to purchase a subway token. *An opportunity*, he thought—as purchasing subway tokens was clearly no part of her paradigm. And then it suddenly fell upon him like spring rain: perhaps she was no better at pretending than he was. One thing was crystal clear, however: fumbling was not her forte.

"Fuck it!" he pretended to say as he turned away from the turnstile and started out towards the exit stairway on the opposite side of Broadway.

"*Fandens også!*" ("Fuck it!") was the bouillabaisse of sounds he heard her whisper as he saw a hand slip back through mink and drop the two bills—though he would've known nothing of the syllables, much less of the sexy little accent. Lights on this scene in any case went to dark as he hit the exit.

When he came back up and turned the corner, it was to a set of sun's rays retiring over Riverside. She came up after him. At street-level, she claimed her turf with a single stiletto heel while perusing the panorama—real lighthouse-like. Sending a beacon out in search of lost sailors, however, was not her *shtick:* she was more accustomed to being the Siren—or maybe even the shoal—on which they crashed. The clean-up? Somebody else's problem.

She finally saw him walking down 116th in the direction of the park. She studied his walk—then mimicked it—shredding the space between them like the blades of a scissor as she walked. He leaned up against the wall of a building, attempted to light a cigarette. She leaned up against her own piece of wall, took out her own cigarette. As he flicked at something frantically, she slipped out a Dunhill 18-carat gold-enameled, pressed down gently on the lever and let the electrons do the heavy lifting.

She inhaled, then let the smoke flow back out. *Charming as church bells chiming 'Glory Borealis'* he thought as he caught her exhalation out of the corner of his eye. He, she noticed, was still flicking—and so, she advanced upon him and extended the Dunhill. He looked briefly into a pair of cool emerald greens, then back at the lighter; cupped his hands 'round while letting one thumb rest an instant upon her glove; took the fire and inhaled.

"Thanks," he said.

"*Pas de quoi,*" ("Don't mention it") she answered.

He stumbled—but only for an instant. "*Vous êtes—?*" ("You're—?")

"Just teasing," she sniffed.

She put the cigarette between her lips and inhaled, let the smoke stream back out through flaring nostrils. *Gentle as a riptide,* he thought, his brain now just a commotion of mad molecules. *Beautiful* and *Baudelairean*—he barely managed, suddenly a bashful mass of feet and no mouth.

She, in the meantime, grew bored—and glanced down at his tome: **The Fourfold Root of the Principle of Sufficient Reason**. *Perhaps*—she thought—*I could throw him a starter kit.*

"How many squares would a square root wreck if a square root wrecked for a reason?"

He looked up at her. *Not only beautiful,* he thought, *but—.*

They both exhaled simultaneously. *Perfect timing,* she thought. *Much better than sufficient reason.*

For the next minute, they exchanged only smoke and stares. He then dropped his cigarette and stamped it out. She dropped hers, kicked it in his direction. He looked down; got a fix on its location; looked back up as he squashed it. Lids dropped like final curtains on a pair of prominent cheekbones, Danish-cut. *The time for dallying,* he thought, *is done.*

"Wanna chuck wood?" he asked.

"Sure," she said. "Let's chuck."

He grabbed her hand and moved. The sun, still pampering the Palisades just across the Hudson, ceased to serve as escort.

At Riverside, he sought a shady spot. *Moonbeams can be murder on a mink*, he thought. He found a maple, looked for moths—spotted a pair and motioned for them to scram—then probed for rough before nudging her back against it. The curtsy of her coat against the maple suggested there was no rough; her own sigh confirmed it.

"Tell me—" he said.

"Show me," she countered. The stop, he thought, was drop-dead glottal.

He reached in under her coat as she rotated; let his hand rise slowly along the inside of a thigh; felt a tremor, paused, waited till it had subsided, then eased his hand on up until it met with an impasse of pure silk.

He was Marco Polo—but also Kepler, Copernicus and Galileo. He'd found the road to China, but was about to blow it off for a date with the Milky Way.

Like a pirate on a picnic, he pulled the silk aside, unzipped and slipped in with a simple prayer. It was already too late to recant. He'd surely fry—but had the rest of his life and *then* some to contemplate how hot the coals. He bowed his head to the nape of her neck, found tiny hairs with his lips, inhaled, and flicked the salt of her skin with the tip of his tongue.

The sight, smell, feel and taste of her sent his synapses into overdrive, while his cortex collapsed in a smooth smolder. She'd burned her way in—and the memory, he knew, would stick to him like a brand.

Chapter 2

Spring, 2003—eleven years later

He grabbed his scarf—long, black, woolen; and his jacket—old, brown, leather; picked up his camera; opened the door; then made a quick survey to ensure the burners were off, all lights turned out. For a man of modest means, living in a studio apartment in the East Village of New York City in the year 2003, an assessment of his material impact upon the world didn't require much more than a backwards glance.

He closed and locked the door, then bounded down the steps to the street, camera strap hung over his shoulder. As he ran, he tied a loose knot in his scarf, just snug enough to cover the front of his neck against the wind.

The knot was indicative—loose, casual, but suggesting a certain caution—as was his name: Kit. Casual, but also quick and alert. His nickname, really. "A boy burning bright," his mother had often said to him when he'd been but a toddler—yet still a raging sparkle in her eye. "My little Blakey in the night."

"Charles" was his real name. "Charles Wesley Addison IV" of Radnor, Pennsylvania. But who—she'd thought—should have to go through life with such a handle? Tradition carried some weight with the Addison clan; and so, he'd been given his father's name—even if Sixties-chastened in his father's case to "Charlie III." Charlie's father's name? "Charles Jr.," of course, albeit GI-cropped to "Chas." Only the original Charles Wesley Addison, who'd been old New York Republican clear down to his knees, had kept his first name firmly knickerbockered in "Charles."

Kit's mother, in any case, was damned well not going to saddle her son with 'Charles' or 'Wesley.' And so, 'Kit' it became and 'Kit' it stayed clear through his early years, his teens, and finally on into adulthood.

Today was the epitome of brisk: clear skies, bright sun. A day, Kit thought, he should capture in pictures. As photography was how he made his living, this particular May 21st was one he'd decided he needed to bag. Days like this didn't come often, and he wasn't going to burn it in a dark room, in a library, in a movie theater, or even in some woman's bed. Today, he was going out with his only weapon—his only means to an end—to hunt for the only game he cared to bag: pictures.

He headed west towards the "N" or "R" line to take him uptown to 23rd Street, Madison Square. A quick stop at his studio to pick up gear, then back on the same line to take him north to 59th Street, Columbus Circle—and the southwest corner entrance to Central Park. Maybe he'd change to an express train at 34th, maybe not; he didn't care. Five minutes with the one; eight to nine with the other. The faster he got there, the better. Light was everything to a photographer. And twilight—morning *or* evening—the best.

At the intersection of Third Avenue and St. Marks Place—Cooper Square—he ignored the pedestrian signal and headed out over the zebra. Halfway across, he noticed an oncoming car moving faster than he'd calculated, and which was heading south along the avenue. The car braked, the driver hit the horn, and Kit jumped forward. His camera bag stayed and struck the car's headlight.

"Fuck!" he said in a well-tempered Pennsylvania whisper, inspecting first the outside of the bag, then carefully removing the camera.

The car came to a halt at the other end of the grid and pulled over to the curb. The driver jumped out and rushed to Kit's side. He assessed the situation, saw at a glance that Kit hadn't been hurt, then turned his eyes to the object of Kit's attention.

"Any damage?" he asked as he leaned in over Kit's shoulder. Kit looked up. He instantly liked this man. Most drivers would've blamed the pedestrian, but this man didn't. This man ignored any assignment of responsibility and focused on possible consequences. Kit smiled at him.

"Nah. You've just helped to clean the lens a bit. Good as new. Better. From here out, I dare say it'll learn to mind where and how it walks in the future."

"If there's any damage, any at all, we'll pay to have it fixed."

We? Kit glanced for the first time at the car and at the license plate—a plate of few digits—then noticed a head and a bob of straight auburn hair against the headrest just inside the rear window. "Don't even *think* about it," he said, again smiling. At that moment, the passenger's window motored slowly down. The figure inside—Kit could now make out that it was a woman—contorted just slightly as her head turned and slipped out to look at both of them.

"Ron, is there a problem?" she asked loud enough to be heard over the din of traffic, but with nothing in her tone to suggest more than a perfunctory concern.

"None, ma'am," her driver shouted back.

"Then perhaps we could once again get underway?" It was half-question, half-order. Kit didn't miss the inflection in her voice or the double message behind it. At the same time, he took a moment to study her face: a bit severe in the bone structure and no longer fresh, yet remarkable in some indefinable way. If anyone had later asked him for a description based on this single visual check, he might've said "becoming."

"Becoming" was the kind of word that came naturally to Kit.

She made an equally quick assessment—first of his camera, as it was the object of most immediate concern. She knew cameras, and she knew this one, even at twenty-five yards off. He was clearly no amateur. A cursory second assessment—but now of him—told her that he was also, if professional, probably not yet in his prime. Too young, too slovenly dressed—though slovenly-dressed passed for bohemian in this part of town, and bohemian passed for artsy. Bohemian could mean anything: rich *or* poor. There was no way, then, to make an assessment of his wealth or of his success; hence, no reason for her to have an interest in his welfare—past, present *or* future.

She looked at him more carefully from the neck up. If a man could be called gorgeous, he was that. Not pretty, not a pretty boy by anyone's definition. He was simply extremely good-looking—and masculine to the core. Chestnut-colored hair, slightly wavy; high cheekbones, but not too pronounced; straight, white teeth—she'd seen them in the rear-view mirror when he'd smiled at Ron. From this distance, she couldn't make out his eye color—nor, in the loose clothes he was wearing, could she make out any of his other body parts. He was reasonably tall, slender and compact. That much was clear.

She ducked her head back inside the car, at which point her driver offered an officious tip to the cap he wasn't wearing. *Probably something atavistic*, Kit thought. *Comes with the territory, if not directly with the job description.* Kit just as perfunctorily returned the gesture in the form of a mock military salute and a third smile.

The driver turned, walked back to the car, got in. As he put the limo into gear, then moved it slowly out into traffic, the woman glanced again back through the window and saw that Kit was busy rearranging his camera bag and already stepping up to the curb at Astor Place in the direction of Fourth Avenue. The car, driver and woman continued south to a destination known only to them.

Chapter 3

K it descended into the subway at Eighth and Broadway just as an "R" train arrived at the platform. The noise of its arrival was deafening, the cars packed. He waited patiently to the side as several passengers got off, then edged his way in and found little more than breathing space. To the extent he was able, he looked around for interesting faces or situations. Today, however, there was apparently nothing of note. And so, he studied the ads over the subway seats—some well done; most, just cheap rip-offs of someone else's creative efforts. With little of interest to look at and nothing to read, Kit was happy the trip to 23rd Street would be quick.

He was out and back up to street-level within minutes, then walked four blocks south from Madison Square to his studio located near the corner of 19th Street and Fifth Avenue.

The neighborhood was home to bibliophiles and photographers alike. For their mutual benefit, daily and throughout the day, droves of drop-dead gorgeous women descended—if already successful—from cars driving down from the Upper East Side or in from Westchester County. Others ascended—if just starting out or only of catalog beauty—on foot from the Lower East Side or from subways coming in from Brooklyn, Queens, the Bronx or New Jersey. He'd never heard of a model from Staten Island, but he'd been in the business for only ten years. He figured almost anything was possible in the fashion world: 'anything' might even one day include a lovely from Staten Island.

Kit knew that few of these women had grown up on the Upper East Side or in any of New York's five boroughs for that matter. The supermodels might be from Stockholm, Milan, Paris or Tokyo—even, on rare occasions, from somewhere like Boise. They looked like a masterfully stirred martini of genes, nutrition and personal hygiene. Education didn't necessarily figure into the mix, though some of them had an extra olive or onion's worth of that, too. They promoted their bodies and their faces quite simply because they could. Nobody forced them to—though in Kit's experience, very few could've managed on brains alone. If they were at least street-smart, or had a good manager, they might have a few years' run and never *ever* have to work a titty-bar, the street, or a hotel room by the hour. They could simply retire on their savings and dividends—or land themselves a part-time gig as a trophy wife, hang out the rest of the time with the girls at the club playing cards or just trying on a tan.

If they weren't smart, didn't have a good manager, or simply liked to burn or snort through the cash, well, then—it might be another story altogether, and usually not a very pretty one. From New York on a jet stream to L. A. or Vegas. To Atlantic City or points on an even less desirable compass if nature or bad habits had been unusually swift—then off to Miami, to one of the lesser Keys, or simply off the end of some isolated pier as soon as younger, fresher recruits could be hired, saddled and giddie-upped off to profits.

In any case, life on the modeling circuit was not gracious. You cut through it like a knife and claimed victory, or it cut through you and eventually cut you out. There were no mercy medals, veterans hospitals or quiet retirement homes for those who'd been scarred in battle. Battered hearts were the fashion model's equivalent of the soldier's Purple Heart. But unlike a war hero's medal, a Hallmark paean to a model's freeze-dried heart wasn't something that might find a spot on the mantle back home in Hoboken or even in the family's annual Christmas card. A model's Miss Lonelyhearts secret simply died—and died with her alone.

Kit was up the stairs to the first floor studio and in. The room already stirred as production jocks, make-up artists and a whole crew of personal assistants readied the set for a shoot. He was happy to know it wasn't *his* shoot today; he had more interesting things in mind than beautiful faces and bodies. He was here only to pick up film and an extra couple of lenses.

Mission accomplished, he headed back towards the front door. A step or two away from a quick exit, he was stopped by the arrival of a model. It was easy to spot them—even without make-up: glassy-eyed, flawless teeth and hair, usually tall—though not always—and casually dressed in designer skimp-ware. This one was no exception. He let her pass like a will-o'-the-wisp; ran down the stairs taking two or three steps at a time, then walked out of the building and back to the subway.

When he arrived at Columbus Circle and came up to ground level, he passed by a familiar scene on the way into the park: camera lights and production people; oceans of cable; big vans parked along Central Park West. *Probably a film shoot or maybe just a TV commercial*, he thought. In any case, he was no more interested in their activity than he was in the pigeons hustling about underfoot for breakfast crumbs.

He walked into the park and headed in the direction of The Mall and Poets' Walk.

Just as Kit was entering the park seventeen blocks further north, limo, driver and woman arrived at midtown from an earlier errand.

"Thank you, Ron. I'll see you again this evening at the usual time."

Ron reached up to tip his imaginary cap. The gesture was automatic with or without a cap, which she'd long ago given him the option of wearing—or not—as he saw fit. The woman collected her coat tightly against her, then flung a purse-strap over her shoulder as she made her way from limo to the front door of one of Manhattan's more modest midtown skyscrapers several blocks west of Grand Central Terminal. She was about to enter the building through revolving doors when two suits simultaneously opened adjacent doors to let her pass. She gave them a token nod and swept through, then continued straight on to the elevator. When she arrived, the elevator doors opened almost as if by remote control. She entered and pushed the button for the top floor.

Seconds later, the same doors opened again to another pair of glass doors fifteen feet across the foyer. She pushed one open and walked through.

"Good morning, Daneka."

Daneka nodded and smiled. "Morning, Susan." The receptionist handed her a small stack of phone messages—something of an anachronism in this day and time, but Daneka had insisted upon it when she'd taken the position. No voicemail, no cell phones, no beepers. She liked to do things face-to-face—occasionally by telephone when face-to-face wasn't an option or it didn't matter. But with the telephone, she couldn't see what she needed to know; she could only hear what the other party *wanted* her to hear. Daneka liked to engage all of her senses with people when they mattered in any way to her well-being— which was to say, she liked to understand the other party's motives. She understood that people only seldom revealed their true motives in language—perhaps because she was an expert at concealing her own. But her real talent lay in being able to decipher others' motives within seconds if she could just see their bodies talk. Once she had her read of them, she could control them and bend their motives to serve her own.

It was rare that something didn't become immediately clear to her, or that she didn't get what she wanted. Her position at work certainly allowed her to expect obedience, though she never commanded it. By virtue of her wealth and status in the neighborhood, she could count on others' respect, though it was not in her nature to cajole or coerce. She simply won. She won obedience from the one, obeisance from the other—even from perfect strangers—because she knew how to watch, how to listen, how to interpret, when to bend. Quite simply, she knew what made people tick. And she applied her knowledge with the skill of an expert watchmaker, first in tinkering with—then in winding—their clocks.

"Morning, Kay," she announced with a well-manicured smile the moment she entered the reception area to her office and saw her Personal Assistant.

"Morning, Daneka." Kay returned an equally well-polished smile.

Daneka walked to her office on the other side of a pair of heavy oak doors leading off from the far corner of the reception area, then to the coat closet to hang up her coat, then to her desk. She glanced at a single portrait mounted in an antique walnut frame sitting on the desk, opened her calendar, picked up the phone and dialed a number by heart. Two brief rings later, the other end picked up.

"Hello, darling. Yes, I just arrived." Daneka's speech was precise, slow. Then, following a pause during which she stared again at the picture—"As we agreed, I'll bring dinner at seven"—followed by another, longer pause. "Okay. I love you, too. Play well." She hung up the phone and studied her calendar: first meeting in five minutes. Easy enough—just a *pro forma* approval.

When Kit arrived at The Mall, he noted that the light was exceptional. In an hour, it would be too late—too much glare. But now, the light and shadows were still soft—perfect for what he had in mind, and he liked *perfect*. He dropped the legs on his tripod and inserted a roll of film before mounting his camera, then stepped back to study the view.

This, for Kit, was play. He liked bodies and faces, but they were work—unless he was shooting with a telephoto lens, the subject entirely unaware and unself-conscious. Babies and toddlers were sometimes fun, even good. Models *had* to be good. They had to deal with the camera—if not as friend or lover—then at least as provider.

The camera, itself, was entirely indifferent—however much people liked to insist otherwise. Kit knew better. He knew it was largely the work of the photographer, only sometimes shared by the subject. When both were working well together, he might turn an entire roll into a bonanza.

Efficiency: he liked it in his work; he didn't care about it while at play. And today, at least for the next sixty minutes, was playtime.

Daneka looked up when she heard a soft rap on her office door and smiled at Robert as he walked in, file in hand. She came out from behind her desk, greeted him with a firm handshake, then led him by the elbow to a worktable where he could spread out photos and text.

She liked physical contact, knew that most other people liked it too, and consequently used it whenever she could—first to put people at ease, then to allow them to open up.

As their brief meeting came to a close, and after she'd given the approval she'd known she would give even before Robert came to her with the lay-out, Daneka invited him to lunch.

Chapter 4

Robert, her Art Director, was not by nature a nervous type. His work was excellent; his attitude towards peers, subordinates and Daneka, beyond reproach. But a boss's invitation to lunch could always be read in a variety of ways.

Daneka noted his consternation and gently laughed to put him at ease. "No, Robert, nothing like that. I simply thought we could have lunch. We haven't in a long time, you know. And the truth is, I need your advice on something. My treat, your brains—fair enough? Or have you already got a better date?"

Daneka could be coy when it served her purposes. She knew that no subordinate would turn down an opportunity to get social with the boss, much less the further opportunity to provide advice at that same boss's invitation. Coyness, as a tool, had served her well over the years—and so, she'd mastered it. When a woman was in every respect as charismatic as Daneka, that woman could afford to be whimsically coy.

"Deal! And no. No better date. No dates at all, as a matter of fact. What time works for you?"

"Shall we say one o'clock?"

"Perfect. See you then," Robert said as he turned and walked out.

Daneka walked back to her desk, then sat down to think through how best to deal with the next meeting. This one represented a series of problems—or at least a problem and a series of possible outcomes—and she needed to think through ramifications and solutions before her 11:15 appointment arrived.

When Robert knocked again at Daneka's office door promptly at one o'clock, it was empty. He wondered for a moment whether she'd forgotten about their lunch date, but decided to wait and see if perhaps she'd merely stepped out.

He walked to the far end of her office and looked around. With floor-to-ceiling windows on two sides, Daneka's space occupied the corner of the building. Her windows looked down immediately out over Times Square to the west, over billboards and miscellaneous buildings—and eventually the Empire State Building—to the south. Not so long before, she could also have seen the tops of the World Trade Center towers half an island distant. Now, the tallest structure in sight was once again the Empire State building.

Just as Robert was contemplating this change in the cityscape, he heard the toilet flush in Daneka's private bathroom and realized where she was. He felt awkward and embarrassed at being this close to his boss at a private moment—even if there was a wall separating them—and quickly returned to the front door, eager to give the impression he'd just arrived.

An instant later, Daneka opened the bathroom door and walked out. She grabbed her coat and purse, then Robert's arm.

"What little den of iniquity are you taking me to today?" she asked, fluttering her eyelashes.

Robert blushed, as she knew he would. He was such an easy read—a truly uncomplicated character. Also, a solid family man with a wife as demure in presence and voice as Daneka was commanding.

"I hadn't really considered. I'm sorry. I thought maybe you had something in mind."

"I did and do. Oysters. I'm in the mood for romance and oysters. Sweep me off my feet and onto a plate of oysters, Leander. Sprinkle me with diced onions and a bit of citrus. Then shower me with vinaigrette—but just don't lose your way." They both laughed as they walked onto the elevator, even if Robert had *no* idea what she was referring to. Within a matter of seconds, they were out of the building.

At the Oyster Bar & Grill under Grand Central Terminal, Daneka let Robert play host. He dealt with the Maître d', led her to the table by *her* elbow, let her first enter the banquette and seat herself. He ordered for both of them—as if this were a first date and she were looking for instruction. When their oysters came—hers, Maine Blue Point; his, Long Island—she moved them on from small talk.

"Robert, I need a photographer. Very discreet. Very quiet. Someone who can do the job—probably a couple of hours at most—and who I can count on to deliver. Soup to nuts, and without any grief in between."

"I guess using a staff photographer is out of the question?"

"I'm afraid so for this particular shoot."

"Well, I can consult my Rolodex," he said. And then, jokingly, "Or you could buy a copy of the *Village Voice*. Photographers come in all shapes, sizes and persuasions in the *Voice*."

Daneka snickered. She hadn't looked at *The Voice* in almost twenty years—not because she had anything against it; on the contrary. *The Village Voice* and *The Nation* had once been her regular reading material. Twenty years earlier, she would've considered the magazine of which she was presently the Managing Editor to be irrelevant. But then she'd finished college, J-school, a stint as intern at *Mother Jones*, and had decided she might actually like to own some furniture. The desire for a few creature comforts—not to mention her own raw talent—had brought her to where she was now.

"Okay. Let me know what you come up with. I'll take it from there."

"Will do."

They continued lunch, talked about Robert's family, talked about work, then adjourned to walk back to the office. On the way up the stairs from the great hall at Grand Central, Daneka stopped in at Hudson News and bought a copy of *The Voice*. Robert smiled conspiratorially; she winked back.

They separated at the elevator. She walked to her office, stopping briefly to inquire whether Kay had had a pleasant lunch. It turned out that yes, Kay had had a *very* pleasant lunch with her fiancé. From the way Kay held her hand in front of her mouth while answering, Daneka suspected she had probably also had a glass or two of something marginally at odds with company policy. Daneka chuckled inwardly at Kay's tiny indiscretion. The brief memory of a lunchtime indiscretion or two of her own—when she'd been Kay's age and on lunch break from a dead end job—flashed through her mind.

Daneka walked through the door into her office, took off her coat and flung it over the back of the couch. She laid *The Voice* out on her desk, leafed through the first few pages out of curiosity to see what had become of it in the intervening twenty years, then immediately turned to the classifieds. She found a listing for photographers just under **Personals**, couldn't resist scanning some of the ads and giggling quietly to herself. Her eyes fell upon one announcement in particular, and her giggle promptly turned to grit. She read it word by acrid word, and a scowl formed at the corners of her mouth. In revulsion, she hastily turned the page back to the listings for photographers and scanned the length of the page. Nothing jumped out at her, however, until she read one listing from a photographer who appeared to specialize in portraits and landscapes. Curious, she thought, to find an ad for a landscape photographer in the *Village Voice*, especially on the flip side of some of the more exotic personal ads she'd just seen. Either he didn't know his market, or he must think that readers of *The Voice* in Litchfield County might actually go in for some gardening when not otherwise engaged in grunge.

She dialed the number listed at the bottom of the ad. After three rings, she got a machine, left a message and hung up. She then put the paper away, decided to see what Robert might be able to propose, and turned her attention to the messages Kay had left for her.

Kit walked through the door of his studio.

With the shoot in Central Park behind him, he'd decided to walk back to the office along the Avenue of the Americas and stop in at a diner for lunch. He knew he had a shoot scheduled for mid-afternoon and that he might first have to prep a bit. He now checked his computer screen—sure enough, the shoot was scheduled to start in half an hour. Something for *Vogue*. Lingerie. *'Could be interesting,'* he thought to himself. But 'interesting' in this case didn't apply to the lingerie or to the model. 'Interesting' applied to the lighting schemes he'd already begun to devise.

At precisely three-thirty, a tall brunette walked through the door of the studio. She knew she'd find the make-up girl ready and waiting, and stopped at the front desk only long enough to ask directions to the Green Room.

Kit finished his prep, set up his tripod and mounted his camera—all by five minutes to four. At two minutes to four, the brunette appeared on the set and promptly dropped her robe. She was wearing a pair of sky-blue teddies and a bra to match. Kit noted the perfect symmetry of her breasts; the expanse of flawless, bronzed skin between her breasts and the wings of her pelvis; her navel; the gentle musculature of her abdomen; the perfect pitch of her buttocks; legs that clearly understood the mandate of regular visits to a treadmill. He just as quickly noticed, as she lay down on the plastic tarp, that his lighting-scheme needed some adjustment—and so, he turned his eyes from flesh to floodlights.

To get a good read on exposure, he'd have to position his meter at various focal points around and over his subject. He consequently took readings for foreground and background, then placed the same meter within half an inch of the model's breasts, stomach and pubis. She didn't flinch, and he didn't register anything more exciting than the slight jump of the needle when the light reflecting off her body changed a point or two of candle power. It was all just routine, he knew as he adjusted the lights and moved back to his camera.

"Okay, guys 'n' dolls. Ready to rock 'n' roll when you are."

Chapter 5

She was a pro, and the whole thing was over in an hour. Immediately following the shoot, Kit retired to his cubical where he noticed the message light blinking on his telephone.

The message was brief, to the point and clear. No whine, no rising inflection at the end of each sentence to suggest that this woman was anything less than absolutely certain of her ground, of herself, and of her right to invade some stranger's electronic space with her voice in order to leave a message. He decided to call back immediately.

"Daneka Sørensen's office," an unfamiliar voice greeted him at the end of two rings. That same voice gave the 'r' in Sørensen the full glottal force of the Danish 'r'—and the 'ø,' its own peculiarly *un*English sound. Kit suspected it might be to inform callers that Daneka was not just *another* executive.

"Charles Addison returning Ms. Sorensen's call." Kit always used his proper first name if he didn't already know the caller. At the same time, he wasn't about to attempt awkward-sounding vowels or consonants even if he, too, was fairly certain he could manage both.

"One moment, please," the unfamiliar voice said—followed by a pause.

"Daneka Sørensen," a marginally more familiar voice announced into the receiver an instant later.

Kit was surprised. She apparently hadn't been given his identity. That, or she wasn't letting on—wasn't going to give him that comfort for nothing. "This is Charles Addison returning your call, Ms. Sorenson."

Daneka appreciated—whoever this person was—that he had the good sense not to take certain liberties too quickly and too easily. He was formal, brief, and to the point. He wasn't trying to schmooze in preparation for a quick sale. Good thing, as she wasn't yet in the mood to buy.

"Mr. Addison, I saw your ad in the—" Daneka paused a split second and considered:

to give away that she'd found his ad in *The Voice* might also give him the wrong impression—might make her sound like easy prey "—newspaper. I'm looking for a photographer."

"You're a model? Looking for head-shots?"

Daneka laughed. To Kit's ears, her laugh was like the tinkle of ice cubes against fine crystal. "Not exactly. But if you've got a miracle cure or maybe even a magic wand, we should talk."

"Nope. Sorry. 'Can't help you there. I wouldn't know beauty from beast if they both came through the same door with instructions for dummies on how to distinguish."

Daneka liked his light, self-effacing manner. He was clearly not one of those high-fashion photogs who wouldn't risk his precious lens or reputation on anything or anyone less than a perfect princess. She also liked the tone of his voice and his pacing: economical without being stingy. He wasn't holding anything back, but he wasn't trying to drown her in words, either. On first impression, she liked him just fine.

"Would you like to come by the studio one day this week?" Kit asked.

"I'd love to," she lied. "But this week is tough. Could we rendezvous at my place? Say, on Friday?"

Kit consulted his electronic calendar. As he did so, he asked as if to confirm: "Is your place in town?" He had a shoot scheduled for the morning, but was free from noon on. "What time did you have in mind?" he asked again before he'd received an answer to his first question.

"Yes. East Side. Ninety-sixth street, between Madison and Park. Say, six o'clock?"

"Six works for me." Kit logged the time into his calendar next to the date, May 24.

"Let's confirm the morning of, if that's okay," Daneka suggested.

That was the second time she'd used the first-person plural pronoun in the space of only a few sentences, Kit noted. In the first instance, the "we" clearly did *not* include a willingness to inconvenience herself by traveling to his place of work. Instead, he'd have to travel a considerable distance north while she'd stay put. In the second instance, Kit knew *she* wouldn't have to remember or make the call. Rather, he was certain someone else would handle that obligation for her.

"Very good. I look forward to it." Kit waited a couple of beats before realizing that Daneka had already hung up. "Well," he said to himself. "Guess we're all business, aren't we, Ms. Sorenson. Short, sweet and to the point."

What Kit didn't yet realize was that he was already beginning to mimic her speech.

Chapter 6

The following Friday afternoon, Kit came up out of the subway at Lexington and 96th street and headed west towards Central Park. At the next pedestrian crossing, he looked south into the wide and untroubled expanse of four lanes divided by a well-manicured median strip—a Park Avenue parade of summer flowers. Both southbound and northbound lanes at that moment were a twilight blush of taxis. None rushed—no need: limousines and service cars stood patiently at attention. Some private residence, some psychiatrist's office, some little love-nest would shortly flush out a passenger to some other less-idyllic, some other less-maniacally-manicured, some other decidedly-less-docile destination on the island where well-manicured could trounce even well-bred.

He glanced northward to see Park Avenue dip down into the bowels of Harlem. A block north of where he stood, the grassy median disappeared almost as if the city had simply run out of seasonal plants and an appropriate place to put them. He spotted a few taxis, most of them rushing southward, but no limousines or service cars—also, plenty of stragglers and loiterers, none of whom seemed to have specific appointments they might now be running off to.

He realized he was standing at an unmarked border: no border police, no customs gate or officials, no need to produce a passport—but a border-crossing nonetheless. Those loitering above it knew as well as those bustling below that this border was as well-defined by rights, privileges and obligations as any Checkpoint Charlie between two opposing regimes; that any intent to cross in either direction would be immediate cause for suspicion.

When the pedestrian light turned green, Kit crossed the four lanes of Park Avenue and stepped up onto the far curb. Only then did he first catch sight of the red awning and the liveried doorman. Lettering for "The Fitzgerald" stood out in bold gold against the Burgundy-colored cloth of the awning. As he approached the building, he noticed that "The Fitzgerald" stood over the breast pocket of the attendant whose coat, apparently, had been cut from the same color—if not precisely from the same cloth.

Kit ascended the few stairs to the lobby where he was met by a second gatekeeper—this one greeting him with a mixture of skepticism and deference. "13-A, please, to see Ms. Sorensen."

"She expecting you?"

"She is."

"Name"?

"I believe we just covered that."

"No. *Your* name."

"Addison." Kit decided in that instant that he, too, could play this game of telegraph if that's what the situation called for. It occurred to him that the closer one attempted to get to a private residence inside any given catacomb of private residences on the Upper East Side, the more truculent the gatekeeper. It came with the turf, pure and simple.

This second doorman appeared to be consulting some internal directory behind his console as he picked up a telephone handset and slowly dialed a number. He occasionally glanced up, though never above the level of Kit's chin.

"Hello? Yes, there's a gentleman here—a Mister?"

"Addison."

"A Mr. Addison to see Ms. Sorensen… Uh-huh… Yes, I will." He hung up and looked Kit in the eye for the first time since Kit's arrival. "Mrs. Sorensen is expecting you. 13-A." Kit was grateful that a least one other human being in this woman's world was not trying to assault him with odd-sounding vowels and consonants.

Kit looked back at the doorman, blinked, and wondered what it might mean to a man to be reduced to a function like this and yet have to call it a profession. To have no other purpose in life than to repeat, filter, confirm or deny information. To create nothing in the process, but simply to stand in the way until a pretender could be politely removed, side-stepped or ordered to step aside.

Kit walked to the elevator; closed the doors; pressed the button marked "13." The cabin was paneled, top to bottom, in a rich mahogany. A large, gilt-framed mirror hung on the back wall. The ascent was remarkably swift, he thought, for a pre-war building.

He stepped out on the thirteenth floor into low incandescent light, then walked to the door marked 13-A. On the wall immediately to the right of the door hung a crystal sconce with a meticulously arranged display of fresh-cut flowers, recently misted. He rang the doorbell.

Thirty seconds later, he heard someone lift a chain and turn a knob. A short, squat

- 23 -

woman subsequently greeted him from the other side of the open door.

"*Señor* Addison?"

"*¡Él mismo!*" ("The very same.") Kit answered without hesitation. She smiled broadly, honestly, unguardedly—*like a happy mix of papaya and mango*, Kit thought, and he returned the smile in kind.

"Please, come in."

"Thank you, I will."

"*Señora* Sorensen coming. One moment, please. You like coffee?"

"Please. That would be lovely."

"How you take?"

"With milk and sugar, please."

She looked puzzled. Perhaps he'd spoken too quickly. He tried again—not wanting to offend, but also wanting to ease the communication. "*Con leche y azucar.*" ("With milk and sugar.")

"Coffee coming. With milk and sugar," she said easily.

Kit could never quite understand this game with Hispanics in New York. If ever he asked for something in English, they might shake their heads or answer in Spanish. If he then asked again in Spanish, they'd answer back in English. It was never malicious or rude; it simply was what it was.

Kit stepped into the living room and began to study the interior with a photographer's eye. Immediately to his left, a baby grand piano, with musical scores of Bach and Chopin sitting conspicuously to suggest either the presence of a classical pianist, or else the presence of someone who wanted visitors to *believe* that Bach and Chopin had a place in this household. He had no way of knowing which. At the far end of the room, two sofas and an armchair covered in damask bordered what looked to be a very serious rug. Kit was not an expert in rugs—and so, he merely ventured that this one might actually be an Aubusson. Casually throwing an Aubusson on the living room floor for someone to warm his heels on was conspicuous spending beyond mere ostentation. Either money meant nothing, or the *appearance* that money meant nothing meant everything. He studied the floor-length curtains that matched the cover of one side table. Both were done in a tasteful print, meticulously coordinated with the rest of the interior. The ensemble suggested an obsession with studied refinement. In fact, everything about the living room—and the dining room adjoining it through French doors—suggested a carefully constructed refinement and an obsession with appearances.

Kit felt slightly nauseous—as if he were not in a home so much as in a *salon*. This was not a living room; it was a presentation room. He wondered about children and whether any lived here; tried to imagine how, if there were any, they, too, would've been treated like presentation pieces—allowed to sit in the living room only if their clothes coordinated suitably with the surroundings; would otherwise be restricted to their own bedrooms or to anywhere *but* this room.

The lighting was low, apparently to produce the correct effect. Assorted pieces of art stood around the room, strategically placed. The walls, too, displayed their share of art—all carefully presented in frames that wouldn't have been out of place on the walls of a museum. Even their arrangement, Kit thought, might've been accomplished with calipers. Each hung precisely aligned with its fellows, not a millimeter out of place, not one of them giving evidence of a displacement caused by any more than a cursory glance from a safe distance across the room.

As there was still no sound of anyone's imminent arrival to greet him, he moved closer to the sofas enclosing the Aubusson—also to the coffee table upon it. He noticed a couple of crystal candlesticks much too casually placed to have found themselves in that position by accident, and wondered what, in terms of time and study, their precise placement had cost—and who had paid that price. Then, of course, there were the obligatory books: Scandinavian interior design; French country houses; a visual feast on the gardens of Spain; and finally, another pictorial compendium on Shaker furniture.

A glance at the books arrayed on the coffee table led Kit's eyes to examine the contents of the bookcases. There were several in the living room and in the adjoining dining room although, if there was any order to the books they held, he couldn't discern it—not alphabetical, not chronological, not arranged by subject matter or category. But then, upon closer inspection, he noticed there was simply no *reason* for order. The books didn't belong to a reader; they belonged to a displayer of books, for books' sake—*libri gratia librum* ('books for the sake of books'), he thought to himself ironically. They suggested no particular interest in literature or history, philosophy or psychology, not even in art, music or cuisine. The only thread Kit could discern in the entire collection was a kind of haphazard reflection of the owner's own eclectic tastes in brief acquaintances or fashionable opinions. He pulled one book at random from the shelf. The spine creaked as he opened it—suggesting it had never been looked at, much less read—although he noted that the author had signed it with a dedication inside the front cover. He put it back immediately without reading the dedication.

His eye next fell upon a stack of CD's piled beneath a side table and next to a boom box. *Surely*, he reflected, *with a baby grand in one corner of the room and an expensive rug lying on the floor, this can't be the extent of her musical investment.*

Kit was beginning to feel uncomfortable with his survey. None of this was any of his business. He was here on an errand, nothing more. And however one person might choose to spend her time, money and attention was really not his affair. All he could conclude at this moment—as he had always suspected of most people who'd learned to define themselves by their acquisitions—was that life and the living of it for her must be almost unendurably wretched, however much appearances might belie the fact. To have to pander to others' judgments; to be enslaved to a kind of competition of good taste; to deprive oneself of the privilege of unstudied relaxation—maybe even abandon—in one's own home—*this* was the barest root of poverty. How would the owner of such a home ever sleep soundly, since sleep was necessarily beyond her control? Worse, how could the *children* in such a home—if there were any—feel anything but frigid sterility?

At that moment, the woman who'd greeted him at the front door reappeared with a cup of coffee, a sugar bowl and creamer, and laid them all out on the coffee table.

"*Señor* Addison," she said quite simply. "His coffee."

"Thank you very much," Kit replied. He then extended his hand. "Please, the name's Kit."

"*Sí, Señor. Con mucho gusto.*" ("Yes, Sir. It's a pleasure.")

"And your name?" Kit asked.

"Estrella. My name is Estrella."

'*Star*,' Kit translated to himself a name he hadn't heard in years—a name that immediately conjured up warm memories of a former Spanish lover. His reverie was interrupted by the sound of someone else's footsteps arriving from just out of his field of vision.

She approached from across the room with an outstretched hand. Kit lifted his arm and took her hand, then let her dictate the contour and force of the grasp—which was full, firm and warm, though hardly overbearing. She would, he thought in that instant, be a fair partner—in work, in play, in love. "Mrs.— or is it *Miss* Sorenson?" he asked, as if there were any question about this woman's identity.

"Neither," she answered. "Please just call me 'Daneka.'" She smiled and looked him in the eye.

"Daneka, then," he answered, returning her smile and meeting her glance just as directly. Eye contact upon making a person's acquaintance was always a test, and Kit had been in the adult world long enough to understand its significance. Eye contact was an unwritten ritual, fraught with dangers, but also with possibilities. It could spark a friendship or a love affair in an instant. It could strike a bargain or cement a deal in as little time. It could just as easily result in a still-birth to any of these. And so, he knew he would hold her stare and her hand for as long as *she* felt it to be necessary to satisfy *her* definition of the gambit.

Daneka was the first to withdraw her hand and break eye contact. As far as she was concerned, the terms of engagement had been defined, communicated and accepted to her satisfaction. Kit was equally satisfied. This visual acquaintance confirmed what he'd been led to expect on the basis of his first and only telephone conversation with her.

"Please, sit down," she suggested.

As he took a seat on one of the two adjoining sofas—quite intentionally at the end closest to the sofa in front of which Daneka was still standing—she sat down on the other, also at the end closest to *his* sofa. Their knees were close enough to touch if either of them cared to. Kit took advantage of the momentary gap in their first oral exchange to study Daneka. She was clearly a few years older than he, although it was impossible to say by how many. Deference to her would've come naturally to him on the basis of that fact alone—never mind that his upbringing had taught him to always defer to a woman. What's more, pragmatism had always dictated to him the necessity, under most circumstances, of deferring to a client and to that client's wishes. He knew he was at liberty to politely ignore the woman or to pass on the client. But he was also sufficiently socialized to know he should resort to such a course neither too abruptly nor too rudely.

In this case, however, no such decision weighed on him. He was, quite simply, captivated by her beauty, her charm and her presence. He thought to himself in that instant he'd never met a more *feminine* woman. She carried herself as naturally as a candle carries a flame.

"I see that Estrella has brought you a coffee," she said. This was the first indication to Kit since he'd spoken to her from his office five days earlier that American English was not her native tongue. However many cups of coffee she might've had in her life as a coffee-drinker, however many on the continent of North America, she'd apparently not gained a foothold on this particular native idiom. He found it enchanting.

"Yes, she did. And an excellent one at that!" Kit added mock-pompously.

Daneka appeared to be quite pleased with her housekeeper's performance—pleased, too, at Kit's satisfaction. The truth is, she liked to see and be surrounded by satisfied people—most especially, when she had it within her power to be the engineer of their satisfaction.

As Kit and Daneka exchanged pleasantries, it occurred to each of them almost simultaneously that the other was not a total stranger. Neither could've said with any authority why this was so—much less, what exactly might've given rise to the sensation. And yet, each of them somehow sensed it.

Knees nearly touched. But knees were not noses. "Tell me about your work, Kit."

She may not have absorbed the idiom for a single portion of coffee, Kit thought to himself, *but she has clearly spent enough time on these shores to know to dispense with the formality of titles and last names. Also, to cut to the chase when the matter at hand is business.* "You know, of course, that I'm a photographer. Otherwise, you wouldn't have invited me here."

"Oh, but I might've invited you here just to get a better look," she said, bending her neck at a certain angle and lowering her gaze to the floor.

Kit was instantly smitten, though he didn't know precisely why. He was simply too inexperienced a soldier in the war of the sexes to know any better. This rudimentary gesture, however unconscious on her part, was to him the equivalent of an entire armada, and he was already preparing terms of surrender.

As he gazed at the line of Daneka's neck, the diminutive curve of it, he saw perfect beauty. To him, a neck was the thing that defined a woman's beauty. Other men might favor breasts or buttocks, thighs or stomachs. Hair, of course, had historical precedent. Eyes might be the window to the soul, but to whose soul? You gaze into another's eyes and think you know that person. The reality? You merely get to know yourself a little better through them and through their reflection, if there *is* a discernible reflection. The moment that reflection dies is the moment you first begin to know what you're *really* made of.

But a neck? Kit followed the wave of Daneka's neck and imagined, just beneath the skin, the tension. He wondered for a second how practiced that *tensor maximus* was in achieving this precise gesture. He couldn't possibly have known that it was *extremely* practiced—that it had reached the point of an automatic reflex—except when Daneka might choose to withdraw it from her repertoire—as she could withdraw many things. Still, there was for the moment something in it of Michelangelo's *Pietà*. The downcast eyes—in this instance, certainly not in mourning or grief, but rather suggestive of modesty and humility. Perhaps, in the end, they were the same anyway—grief and humility, mourning and modesty—but Kit was not religious or philosophical and he had only a layman's knowledge of human psychology. He was a photographer with a fine, intuitive sense of beauty, nothing more. He was an æsthete—not by education, but by birthright. It was as if he'd been born with an innate sense of how objects and space belonged together and to each other; of how to create visual harmony between them; of what was genuine or artificial, and of what was not.

In his ignorance, Kit now had but one thought and wish: that he could, with impunity, put his lips to the nape of that neck and explore it as uninitiated fingers might explore Braille: letter by syllable, by word, by thought—to learn its secret.

In the meantime, Daneka had been studying Kit from a certain distance as if she, a predator, were studying the movements of her prey. She quite liked this specimen of a male. There was nothing devious or mischievous either in his behavior or in his language. He appeared to be something of an *ingenue*—if she could apply that epithet to a man. In any case, there was no question of his masculinity. He simply didn't wear it on his sleeve.

She glanced down at his arms and hands. They were, like the lines of his face, both graceful and strong. He had the aspect of an artist, but the physique of an athlete; at least, those parts of his physique that were visible—and these were limited to his head, neck, arms and hands. She wondered what it would take to get his clothes off so that she could inspect the rest of him. She wondered whether he would be easy, aggressive, technical, fanciful or playful. She couldn't imagine that he would be dull, selfish or boastful. Men put together like Kit never were. They didn't have to hunt; they were hunted. And so, they could afford to be selective and patient.

The truth is, Daneka had known a great many men. She'd honed an instinct over the years as she'd moved in and out of men's beds, in and out of men's lives. She'd logged a great many hours in the so-called act of love—a number of them in the mere act of fucking—and she knew practically at first glance whom she could trust and whom she couldn't.

She decided—tentatively—that Kit was one of those she could. Moreover, she had in that instant an almost overwhelming desire to take him to bed in order to prove the accuracy of her instinct. She also knew, however, that this desire could wait. He wasn't going anywhere, and neither was she. It, she and he could all wait.

"When can we see your studio?" she asked.

"Whenever you'd like."

"Actually, and for reasons I'll make clear to you when the time is right, I'd rather have you do the shoot in your apartment. Would that be a problem?"

"No, not at all. I've got a portable light pack at home. Depending upon what you want me to shoot, it may be enough. What—or *who*—is it, anyway, you want me to shoot?"

"All in good time, Mr. Addison. All in good time," she said through a smile, but also in a way that suggested to Kit she was going to want to manage every aspect of the project. The mystery both of her and of the project left him feeling a bit off kilter—but it was a feeling he decided he could live with for a few more days.

"Shall we say next Sunday?" she asked.

"The day after tomorrow, or a week from this coming Sunday?" he asked, already unhappy at the thought of a long wait between this first meeting and the next one.

"No, no," she laughed. "You might forget me in ten days. I meant the day after tomorrow."

Kit kept, to himself, the signs of an incipient passion on the prowl. "Very good," he tossed off easily, as if to suggest that yes, maybe he *could* forget her in ten days. "Does early afternoon work for you?"

"Early afternoon is perfect," she answered. Say, one-ish?"

He was about to answer her suggestion with a confirmation, but suddenly lost his train of thought while staring at her face. Groping for something—anything, really—to get the conversation back on track and not allow this first, brief meeting to come to an end, he looked down at his feet.

"By the way, I was admiring your rug when I first came in. I'm afraid I can't quite identify its provenance."

"Oh, that," she said rather too haphazardly, even as Kit thought he detected a certain pleasure at his observation of it and now at his question. "It's an Aubuisson. I picked it up at practically a yard-sale price. I thought it might complement the décor."

"Really?" Kit was intrigued. "Then you like junk sales?" He was already beginning to assemble a short list of things they might have in common—even if the pronunciation of this particular rug wasn't one of them. Daneka, in the meantime, registered Kit's misinterpretation and welcomed the opportunity to correct him.

"No, it wasn't a *junk* sale, precisely. I got it at auction. I don't remember exactly what I paid for it, but I think it was in the neighborhood of $40,000, plus or minus." The slight smugness of her smile played havoc with her attempts at nonchalance.

Kit's feet instinctively rose up off the rug. He was dumbstruck. The equivalent amount of money would've paid his rent for three years, would've kept entire families in New York alive for as long, would've maintained a small African village for probably much longer. Not to mention the hidden cost, on average, of a pair of child's eyes for every such hand-woven rug. And his goddamned shoes were on it! No less, the stain of his mispronunciation. Certainly—he made a quick mental note—the authority of someone who could afford to throw forty grand down on a foot-warmer outweighed any dilettante's knowledge he might possess on the subject of rugs.

Daneka had already risen from the sofa and was extending a hand. Kit extended his own, which she grasped warmly. Unusual in his experience, she continued to hold onto it as

- 31 -

she led him to the front door. He wondered whether this was some European custom he was unacquainted with, or whether she had simply forgotten—or was too befuddled—to drop his hand. In any case, he relished these extra few seconds of physical contact with her and was in no rush to withdraw his hand from hers.

Daneka, meanwhile, knew *exactly* the effect she was producing. Kit would've felt predictably awkward walking the length of the room with his right arm crossing his own body in order to maintain the parting handshake which she had launched and was holding fast to. Daneka didn't wish to discomfort him precisely. But she did wish him to be slightly off balance—and to fix the memory of these last few seconds in his head, at least until Sunday afternoon.

The fact is, Kit would not forget those few seconds—or the preceding ten or fifteen minutes—for the rest of his life.

Chapter 7

U ntil today, Kit hadn't been in the least self-conscious about the condition of his apartment, the scarcity of material comforts he had to offer, or the condition of the neighborhood. He'd always quite liked the dirt, the garbage and the noise. But he'd also never entertained anyone quite like Daneka before.

For the first time in months, he dedicated an entire Sunday morning to cleaning. He pulled the bed sheets from his bed, bundled them together with everything else that could possibly be machine-washed, and took it all down to Louie's Laundromat. He next decided to put his apartment in order, first vacuuming, then concluding with a mop and bucket of soapy water. He even took Windex and paper towels to the windows, which he hadn't touched in years since the skylight provided him with all the natural light he needed.

With only his laundry left to pick up at noon, he stripped and took a shower.

Fifteen minutes later, he put on a clean pair of jeans, sandals, and a long-sleeved black T-shirt, brushed his hair, picked up his wallet, and prepared to set out to retrieve his laundry—although not before grabbing a bottle of white wine from beneath his worktable and putting it on ice. He didn't know exactly where any of this was going, but he wanted to be ready.

At ten minutes to one, Daneka's taxi pulled up at the corner of Third Avenue and St. Marks Place, where she told the driver to stop, then paid him and slipped out. She'd already decided she wanted to walk the last few blocks in this neighborhood she hadn't visited in well over a decade.

She found, to her amazement, that much of what she remembered of the East Village had remained unchanged. Sure, there were already signs of Starbucks-creep in excess. But otherwise, the Orpheum and all of the old landmarks were still there, as nonchalant and constant as the heat and smells of summer that would soon settle in like swamp muck and remain until late September.

A gentle but persistent breeze blew on this particular late-spring afternoon. Perhaps too eager in her anticipation of warmer days, Daneka had dressed for summer. A cotton dress, cut low in the front, hugged her waist and stopped just above the knee. Black high heels, topaz earrings and—slightly out of sight—matching panties completed the ensemble.

Otherwise, nothing. No stockings, no bra, no other jewelry. Both men and women stopped whatever they were engaged in to admire her as she passed, which she did with the ease and elegance of a mid-size leisure craft at full sail. Her dress billowed out occasionally as the wind took hold along the vertical seam, secured at her waist by an invisible tie. The material, practically weightless and no match for whimsical breezes, at times hugged and caressed the rounded flesh of her breasts, thighs and buttocks, only to spring loose and flap open, as if in answer to the unspoken wishes of this ad hoc crowd of gawkers. For the few minutes she needed to cover the distance to Kit's front door from where the taxi had dropped her off, Daneka owned the street. Walkers, strollers, gawkers, runners, bikers, roller-bladers—even those just hanging out on the stoop and caught up in the act of bartering stories or drawing pictures in the air—she owned them all. And she commanded their attention as if by magic wand, but without even once having to wave it.

When she finally crossed over First Avenue and arrived at number 111 just short of Thompson Square, she saw that he lived in a brownstone quite common to the skylines of both Manhattan and Brooklyn. To one side, Jenny's Café; to the other, Tatiana's—a consignment café, of all things. She giggled soundlessly as she wondered whether Kit was in any way consigned to this Tatiana. She looked across the street: St. Dymphnas. Apostrophes, she noted, were decidedly an afterthought in this neighborhood, though "EAT ME!"—just two doors down—was anything but.

She noted the entablature, which, from street-level, appeared to be of genuine oak—unusual for this part of town—and counted the stories: five, with an accommodating stone stoop and generously-proportioned windows, if not exactly floor-to-ceiling. She couldn't yet know whether Kit's apartment looked out onto the street, or back onto a courtyard, but she guessed that a photographer would've demanded something with plenty of natural light.

Daneka mounted the six steps of the stoop and looked for Kit's name on the tenant registry. She found it—as well as a pushbutton located adjacent to the number twelve—which suggested the top floor and a good view of both the street and the space behind the building. Here, where nothing rose over five stories, his apartment wouldn't be lost in the shadows of taller tenement or office buildings. Instead, he'd have a clear shot at the stars at night—and, at dawn, a panorama of dark, rain-soaked, and age-stained water towers standing like blackened scabs against the sky.

It was just past one o'clock when she pressed the button next to his name. After a couple of seconds, she heard a buzzer in response to her own original signal, also the electronic release of the bolt on the front door, leaving it open for her to walk through. She ignored the double signal, waited a few seconds, then pressed the button a second time. Again, an answering buzzer—which she again ignored as she crossed her arms and turned towards the street. A buzzer sounded a third time. She ignored it. Like birds calling to each other, one buzzer might respond in length and tone to the other in carefully choreographed timing and syncopation—until one or the other simply *didn't*. And then the other might try another or a third time, hoping for an answer. But if no answer came, the first caller always had a couple or three options: desist; call another candidate; or fly over and join the second caller on the same branch for a little avian *tête-à-tête*.

Kit was no bird, but he got the idea. He opened the door to his apartment and bounded down the five sets of stairs to ground level. When he reached the front door, he threw it open and greeted Daneka like a happy puppy.

"Why didn't you come on up?" he asked ingenuously, never thinking for a moment that on his Lower East Side turf, Daneka might still be operating according to her own Upper East Side protocol. She ignored his question, forced a smile and extended a hand.

"I just *love* it here. It's so…campus-like!" she said.

Kit's smile collapsed as if the puppy in him had just been slapped for a too-eager puddle in the middle of the floor. "Nice to see you here at last," was the best wool sock he could now drop at her feet. The tremors of anticipation he'd allowed himself to enjoy since their meeting Friday afternoon suddenly faded into foolishness. The cleaning? The wine in the fridge? What *had* he been thinking, anyway? She wasn't a fucking client; she was merely a prospect—and he, to her, a random vendor with a service to offer. Which she could take or leave at will, from him or from anybody else with a camera and enough spare change to place an ad in the paper. *Goddamn it!* Kit thought and inhaled deeply. He needed to keep in mind who he was, who *she* was, and what this was really all about.

"It's a few flights up. Sorry, no elevator," he mumbled as he held the door open for her to pass through—which she did, though without any word of acknowledgment.

"Yes, I figured that twelve would be on the top floor. Nor did I really expect to find an elevator." They were stuck in a conversational cul-de-sac. Kit tried to maneuver out with a gesture, indicating that she should precede him up the stairs.

As she climbed just a few feet ahead of him, Kit registered the clickety-clack of her heels on the tin planks of the staircase. At the same time, he noticed how the muscles in her calves flexed and rose each time the tip of her shoe touched down upon a plank and pushed off again. The tautness of those muscles continued right up her leg and then disappeared beneath her skirt. Yes, she was a client—or, more to the point—she might *become* a client. But that fact didn't keep her from being gorgeous.

When they reached the fifth floor where Kit had left the door to his apartment slightly ajar, Daneka walked straight through. Once inside, she glanced around in a businesslike manner and noted the skylight. The fact didn't surprise her. She offered no comment, but simply seemed to take it all in in one cursory inspection. She then got right down to business.

"Where's your set?"

"I make it. 'Depends on the subject—or the product, really. What you want to do with it. What you want to project. How you want to position the product against what your competition is offering."

"There's no competition. It's not a question of product positioning."

Kit's eyebrows arched as the next word out of his mouth trailed off into a long ellipsis. "O-k-a-y."

"We're not talking *product*. We're talking person. She's not pushing anything, just as I'm not. What I have in mind is more in the way of portraiture." Daneka swiveled on one heel and looked Kit straight in the eye. "Do you do portraits, Kit?"

The walls of Kit's apartment were fairly covered with his work, much of it award-winning material. Most of the work was portraiture—in some cases, just a headshot; in others, full-body. He chose to ignore that she didn't care to comment on his work, or simply didn't see it. In either case, her lack of acknowledgment confirmed what he'd suspected when he'd first seen the artwork on the walls of her own apartment: for her, art was ornament.

"Head and shoulders only, Ms. Sorenson?" he asked in a deadpan tone of voice.

"No. Full-body."

"I might have to practice," he answered, with just the hint of a smirk in his voice.

"Can I use your little boy's room?" she asked, as if this request somehow followed naturally from her previous declaration.

"Of course," Kit answered as he gestured in the direction of his bathroom. "Right behind you."

Daneka looked over her shoulder and visually located the bathroom door. She walked to it, opened it, stepped inside and closed it, all in one fluid motion. Kit went to the kitchenette to get a glass of water. As he passed the counter, his eyes fell upon an open pack of cigarettes. He took one out and put it between his lips. He then opened the freezer door and extracted a handful of ice cubes while he reached, with the other hand, for a water glass. He dumped the ice cubes into the glass and turned on the tap water. He was about to fill his glass when he remembered his host's duties, then reached for a second glass and a second handful of ice cubes. He was filling both when Daneka stepped out of the bathroom. Although he had his back to her in that instant, he heard the bathroom door close.

"A glass of water?" he asked.

"Sure. Why not." It wasn't really a question.

Kit filled both glasses, set them down next to the sink, wiped his hands on a dishrag, and lit his cigarette. Only then did he turn around—blowing the smoke out in one, long, dumfounded stream.

Daneka was standing in front of him, unencumbered except by the topaz. Earrings, that is.

"Let's practice, shall we?" It was neither request nor command. But no matter, as Kit needed neither to be cajoled nor prompted. Still less did he need to be told or shown what to do. He simply needed to revise this visual image enough in his mind to decide for himself what *she* might consider an appropriate course of action. He stood with the cigarette hanging out of his mouth. In the fifteen steps she needed to get from where she'd been standing to the kitchenette, her eyes never left his.

Kit handed Daneka the glass of water; stepped around her; went to his worktable;

picked up his camera. He removed the lens guard and inserted a roll of black and white film. He put the camera back down on the workbench and went for his light kit, which he then set up at one end of the sofa-bed—the only piece of furniture he owned that he felt might be suitable for this job. He plugged in the light, experimented with several filters until he'd found the right one, closed the automatic door on the skylight, pulled the curtains on all of the windows in the apartment, and took out his light meter. Only then did he turn back to Daneka to indicate that he was ready for her.

"Your casting couch, Kit?"

Kit ignored the comment. *No rose without thorns*, he thought. "Something to drink before we get started?" he asked.

"But you just gave me this," she said, holding up the glass of water.

"I know. What I meant was—."

"I know what you meant. And the answer is 'sure.' Why not. It's Sunday."

Kit went to the refrigerator, took out the bottle of wine, put it on the counter, and rummaged around in the drawer for his corkscrew—a little mermaid with the tail leading off into the coils of the screw.

"*Den lille havfrue,*" ("The little Mermaid") Daneka murmured as she peered down at the corkscrew. "How cute."

He cut off the top of the metallic cap, inserted the corkscrew into the cork, worked the screw down into it. The little mermaid's arm provided him with the necessary leverage to pull the cork, the mermaid's hand fitting snugly onto the glass lip of the bottle. He pulled slowly and carefully. The cork came out in one, smooth motion. He opened the cabinet over the sink and took down a wine glass—a single glass—which he filled to three-quarters.

"Not joining me, Kit?" she asked as he handed her the wine glass.

"Never when I'm working," he answered, letting only the corners of his mouth suggest that he might be just a tad amused.

"Then I suppose we should get to work," Daneka answered in a tone like stiff parchment as she walked over to his sofa-bed. She lay down on it as if this were how she made her living. He moved his light meter over her with his full concentration fixed on the work. He took three readings over her body, one behind the sofa, then adjusted the light accordingly. It was perfect—as was she.

Kit couldn't remember when he had last felt more moved by a human subject than by a landscape. Normally indifferent—or at least immune—to any sexual thoughts about his professional subjects for as long as he was working a gig, something was happening to him he couldn't account for—and so, he allowed himself to look at her as 'woman' rather than as 'subject' or 'client.'

"Give me a couple of seconds, will you? To think about positions," he lied.

"Oh, so *that's* what this is all about. I thought maybe you *liked* what you were looking at," she said, letting her declaration sound like a pout.

"Never when I'm working," Kit answered dryly.

He started at the top of her head. Auburn hair, thick, cut short. He suspected her hair would smell of lilacs, even on a bad day. The forehead high, one particularly prominent tributary of the superficial temporal veins pulsing from hairline to eyebrow along the right temple. Eyebrows sparse, same color as her hair. Eyes like tiny almonds, but the color of olives. Nose slightly pinched, but straight, with a fine pair of nostrils for flaring, he imagined. Lips rich, not too abundant, not in the least puffed. An unusually square chin for a woman. In any case, the architecture of it was consistent with that of her cheekbones. One ear was visible as Daneka's hair fell to either side—large and a bit out of proportion with her other facial characteristics, he thought. Still, he would gratefully spend an hour at each, nibbling like a nervous squirrel over sunflower seeds.

Her neck was nothing less than a pedestal, and with muscles and tendons as voluptuously phrased as anything Rodin might have cared to carve in marble.

Kit followed the lines in her neck down along her clavicle, out to her shoulder, all the way down her arm to the backside of her palm and out to the ends of her fingers. He noted that she had visible biceps, even with her arm in a relaxed position. The fingers at the ends of those arms were long, narrow, prematurely lined and wrinkled. Perhaps too much paperwork over the years, or too much exposure to the sun—both leading to dry and chapped skin. He looked especially at her ring finger and wondered whether it had ever supported the weight of a wedding band.

His eyes crawled back up the underside of her arms—delicately veined, the pale blue lines visible through taught skin—to her armpit, not visible.

Daneka, perhaps bored with his apparent passivity, had closed her eyes. Her breathing was low and regular. Kit thought she might actually have fallen asleep, which he was thankful for: it would allow him to slow down.

He looked at her face once again. Good, solid lines around the eyes and mouth. A woman who slept soundly and laughed a great deal. He liked her. He liked her laugh. He imagined he would like sleeping next to her.

He next looked at both of her breasts. Large, he thought, for such a petite woman. She couldn't possibly weigh more than one hundred thirty pounds, and was probably no more than five-foot-seven even in heels. Yes, her breasts were large, but well proportioned—and for a woman of her age, unusually youthful. Clearly, she'd never nursed. He wondered whether she'd already succumbed to science—they were *that* perfect. A pity, he thought, if she had.

He let his eyes for a moment study her aureoles and nipples: a bit darker than the skin surrounding them, but not by much—and small, tight, compact. His glance sank slowly to her breastplate and abdomen. No paunch. A few lines, perhaps, and skin not quite so taught as it might be on a younger woman. But otherwise gently curving, like dunes surrounding the slight cavity of her navel.

From there, his eyes danced back and forth lightly across the wings of her pelvis as if dusting for fingerprints. It was pronounced, perhaps because her stomach was flat, and it stood out in bold relief against the shallow cave of her abdomen. His eyes entered that cave and found her pubis. The hair on it was the same texture, color and delicacy as the hair on her head. The pubic bone itself was quite pronounced, her lips invisible. He moved his head to within inches of her pubis in order to find her animal smell. It was—as he discovered when he next moved his head the length of her torso up to her armpit and neck—consistent, warm and feminine. His own nostrils flared as he turned off all other senses and absorbed her smell.

After a moment, he opened his eyes again and continued his survey. The curve of her thigh, long and gentle, like that of a clam shell, terminated in the abrupt knot of a knee-cap, then continued on down in a slightly less dramatic parenthesis that was her calf. Hers were long legs, Kit decided: a gymnast's legs—long and well-proportioned to hold the weight of a moderately petite woman. The curve descended from her calf muscle in a quick dip at her anklebone. Her feet were small, the toes like little marshmallows on skewers. He wondered whether he would ever suck on those toes....

As if his thoughts had entered some forbidden realm and bumped noisily up against her own, Daneka stirred, then opened her eyes.

"Do you think maybe we could start sometime today?" she asked.

"Yes. Today. Now, as a matter of fact."

"Good. I was beginning to wonder whether you might have lost interest."

Kit didn't answer. He simply made one last adjustment to his backlight; took the cover off his lens; set his options and focus. He then stepped away from the camera, knelt down next to Daneka and began to 'talk the talk.'

"Try to forget I'm even here. Ignore both me and the camera, if you can."

"I've had tougher challenges."

"And I'll try to compensate with shutter speed for the brightness of your congeniality."

"Kit, it's just a shoot. I mean, it's not as if we're creating art here. Or making love."

"True. But it wouldn't hurt for you to warm up a bit to the camera, if not to me. That's what makes for the magic, you know."

"All right," she sighed heavily, making no pretense of an effort to hide her annoyance. "Let me put on my happy face." Daneka fluttered her eyelashes half a dozen times, pinched her cheeks, and pasted on a smile.

Kit snapped his first shot. "Are you always this gracious, or is it just the spring that brings out your robin?" he asked in a monotone.

"Chirp-chirp."

Kit took a second. "Nice!"

She tried hard to suppress a smile. "I'm glad you think so."

"Maybe you're a natural."

"Posing for a picture, Kit, is not poetry." He took a third and fourth shot.

"No? What is it, then?" Daneka arched her eyebrows, and Kit took three more shots in quick succession. "Nice," he said again.

"Posing, Kit. Just posing."

"Hung up on phonics, are we?" Kit muttered dryly into the lens. He snapped again. Daneka paused for an instant, then rolled on her back and threw her arms and legs into the air. Her laugh was like a whimsical spring breeze as it rolled over him, and he stepped back from the camera to bask in its warmth.

The humor of their exchange exhausted, Daneka lowered her limbs back to the sofa-bed, from where she turned her head and looked straight at him. Kit returned her stare. He thought he could decipher, for the first time, a kind of appreciation—and it delighted him.

"You know what *Schadenfreude* is, Kit?"

"I have a notion," he answered.

"Something tells me it's your stock in trade—as much as that camera."

"Nah. I'm a curmudgeon of the first order, don't get me wrong. But it's not others' pain and suffering I get a kick out of. It's my own. My own irreconcilability with the world."

"I like curmudgeons," she said simply. "I try to take one to bed every chance I get. They're restful."

"Be a bane to a Dane," Kit stated flatly.

Irony settled on Daneka's lips. "Don't be dis*dane*ful."

"What are you talking about? It would never occur to me to be disdainful of you, a possibly rich, beautiful and topaz-tipsy client."

"No, I said dis*dane*ful. I'm a Dane. Don't *dis* me." They shared a moment of silence during which Kit registered the pun, and then they both laughed. "You're good for my word power, Kit. I haven't been this charged since my freshman year in college."

"Nor I since I took my first Polaroid."

"Do you sometimes like to play, Kit?"

"Never when I'm working."

"And do you ever *not* work?" she asked.

"Only when I'm playing," he answered. Daneka's hair had fallen over her face once again, but she made no effort to put it back in place. Kit stepped around in front of his camera and reached out to tuck it back behind her ear. As he did so, she grabbed his wrist and looked directly at him.

"Are we playing or working now, Kit?" she asked him.

Kit turned serious. "I believe we're still working."

"I'm tired of working."

Kit looked hard into her eyes. "Then tell me what it is you want. I can be everything you want. Or nothing. It's entirely up to you. But you have to tell me."

Daneka had been under the lights and in a battle of wits for almost half an hour and had, she noticed as she brushed her finger over her upper lip, begun to perspire.

"Excuse me." She stood up and went directly to the bathroom. When he heard the shower, Kit decided to lie down for a moment and simply breathe in the smell she'd left behind. He stripped down to his boxers and threw his clothes into a pile next to the worktable, then shut his eyes momentarily to rest them. Unfortunately, the stress of preparing for her arrival and trying to keep up with her had taken a toll on him, too. He was fast asleep within seconds.

When Daneka eventually emerged from the bathroom, patting herself with a towel, she saw Kit in the spot she'd vacated only moments earlier. She took a minute to study him, then went to his camera. She took it off the tripod; exposed the remaining frames in the roll; removed the roll and put it on Kit's worktable; inserted a new roll and then approached the sofa-bed. Looking through the lens into his face, Daneka made a few adjustments to the focus, then put the camera back down. She next went around behind Kit and adjusted the backlight to give his face better visibility, then came back to the camera, picked up his light meter, and held it just in front of his face. She made one last adjustment for exposure, moved to within a couple of feet of her subject, and took the shot.

Daneka exposed the remaining frames as she went back to the bathroom to get her clothes. She dressed, came back out to his worktable with the camera, removed the film, dropped it into her purse, and put the camera back down. She then took one last long look at Kit and left his apartment.

Chapter 8

I t was already dusk when Kit awoke from a sleep that had carried him over the precipice and deep into a ravine of no dreams. The first thing he noticed when he awoke was the smell of Daneka on the sofa-bed. The next thing he noticed was her absence.

He jumped up and went to the bathroom: nothing. He walked around his apartment looking for some evidence of her, some remnant, however fleeting or illusory: nothing. He went to the front door; opened it; looked down the hall; stepped out and peered down the stairwell: nothing. It was as if she'd never been present.

Had she been present?

He went to his worktable. His stomach growled, and it occurred to him that he hadn't eaten in twenty-four hours. He saw his clothes in a heap on the floor next to the worktable and realized for the first time that he wasn't even dressed. He stood at his worktable fumbling around in the near dark for something—he wasn't sure for what, exactly—until it occurred to him that he simply couldn't see. He turned on a light and saw, on the table, a single roll of film.

He picked up the roll and went to his darkroom where he loaded it onto a reel, then poured chemical baths out into three tanks. He first submerged the roll into the developer, next into the stop, and finally into the fixer. He then put the film under running water for thirty minutes, ran it through a pair of squeegee tongs, attached it to weighted metal clips, and hung it up to dry.

He now had cat's eyes, a cat's fever, and a cat's nighttime touch—and so, decided to forego making contact prints or a test strip as he was simply too eager to get directly to his enlargements.

One by one, Kit withdrew the finished prints, shook off the last bits of chemical, and immersed them in his washing tank where they sat for an hour under running water. He then set to work drying them one by one under a flatbed drier. He calculated he wouldn't have enough tabletop space to lay them all out, and that he'd have to restore the clothesline he sometimes ran across his apartment for just this purpose. He walked to his closet, fingered around frantically, found nothing. He then went to the kitchen, looked under the sink, and rummaged some more. Finally, he found what he was looking for, took the clothesline out to his living room, and strung it up—then returned to his dark room and grabbed the stack of prints.

As he hung the photos up, he began to see something he hadn't seen face to face with Daneka, nor even through his lens. Yes, there was beauty, poise and confidence, even command. But the camera, or the black and white film—he wasn't sure which—revealed darker caverns behind eyes that were in some frames, coy; in others, boisterous. It was as if he were looking down through a pool into a cave: in one moment the water serene; in the next, stirred, troubled and raucous. At the far end of it, a den of horrors, a bone yard, a reliquary in which lay the battered and broken remains of other lives, possibly of former lovers. Hers were not peaceful eyes. Rather, they were anxious, solicitous, imploring even, though apparently fighting the impulse to implore, as if she might desire to share some burden, but were too proud—or at least too jealous of her privacy—to grant space to a confidant. If eyes were a window on the soul, then her soul was a ship going down, and whose captain would more willingly sacrifice vessel, cargo and crew than admit to a miscalculation.

Kit extended an index finger and touched the eyes one print at a time. Slowly, gently, like a child dabbling in finger paint, he probed the contours of each socket, looking to shape the darker hues and shadows into some language that would speak to him and divulge certain secrets. But prints were dumb, two-dimensional things and would reveal nothing.

Had they been corporeal, he would've wanted in that instant to sooth and give them comfort, to extract whatever private agony lay behind them. But these were prints, photographs, a mere recording of a bit of anatomy belonging to someone he still believed had been in his apartment not even two hours earlier, yet about whom he knew nothing except the topography of her body.

What are the mathematics of love? Who can guess at a calculus of attraction? What theory can begin to explain how and why the seeds of a self-destructive obsession are dispersed, take root, and prosper? What science or logic can ever make clear why one body is drawn to another, is slowly taken captive by another, is ultimately enslaved by another, and consequently cedes the entire privilege of its existence to the other?

In the few minutes Kit stood before the various black and white images of Daneka that hung from a simple clothesline strung from one corner of his apartment to the other, it was as if his body chemistry were undergoing an alteration that was far more than merely hormonal. The transformation was in fact fundamental, primordial, primal.

Chapter 9

Kit dressed, opened the door to his apartment, slammed it shut and bolted down the stairs, then ran out into the street and hailed the first available taxi. Five minutes later, he entered his studio, walked past the elevator, climbed the stairs, opened the door and headed in the direction of his cubicle. It then occurred to him that navigation might be easier with an overhead light, and he turned one on.

Halfway down the hallway, he heard grunts and giggles from one of the sets, peeked in and saw a colleague with a pair of the previous workweek's models. They were not, he noted, playing Parcheesi.

Once at his cubicle, Kit booted up his computer and silently cursed the seconds it took to laboriously push digits and code through its circuitry. When the desktop screen finally came into view, he located his electronic address book, double-clicked to open it, then waited a few more impatient seconds for it to appear. In this era of lightening-fast digital communications, it seemed that each time he needed something elementary—something as simple as a telephone number—he had to slog through mud to get to it.

When his address book finally appeared on the screen, he located Daneka's number, dialed it, and waited what seemed like another long minute for the connection. Finally, it came. The phone—he assumed—at her end, was ringing. Once, twice, three times, four times—then came an answering machine with her voice. *Fuck! Where could she be?* The voice was courteous, if standoffish. No name; just a number and a brief instruction: "Leave a message. I'll get back."

Kit talked into the receiver as if he were trying to reach across the connection, through her answering machine, and back out the other end to grab somebody, some *body*, and make it respond. "Daneka, please pick up. We need to talk." Pause. No, *she* didn't necessarily need to talk. *He* did. What he needed in this instant was to bring her to his same level of urgency, to *his* same need. "Daneka, please. Can we talk? I have your pictures. But I need to show you. I need to know—." Electronic beeps interrupted his message. The conversation was at an end. He'd had his say. And that say was his last—at least for now.

Meanwhile, Daneka had listened passively to the ring, had glanced at the Caller ID screen on her telephone, had vaguely recognized the number as one she'd seen on a previous occasion, and had continued dressing. When she heard the end of her own greeting, she turned up the volume and listened to Kit's voice.

And how, you might ask, did it strike her? As impassioned? As plaintive? Or merely as desperate? She wasn't sure. She sat down on the edge of the bed to listen more carefully, to decipher and decode the voice *behind* the voice, as she knew only too well how to do. It was a voice she recognized, already grown slightly sweet to her ear and nicely masculine. Almost commanding, but still containing too much desperation to be truly attractive. Yes, she decided: it sounded desperate. And desperate people were simply not the company she wished to keep—at least not now. She listened to the remainder of the message and decided not to touch the receiver.

As she heard "I need to know—" she stood up from the bed and smoothed down the tiny wrinkle in her lap. *Silk is so amenable to suggestion,* she thought. Especially if it was cut properly and sat on curves that allowed it to fall in just that way the woman within might intend that it should fall.

The message ended. She picked up the receiver and dialed a number. The phone rang twice at the other end. She said one word in Danish as cue, then continued in English. "Yes, darling. I'll be there in twenty minutes. Of course I'm bringing dinner."

She hung up, walked slowly to the front of the apartment, paused and glanced around in quiet admiration of her material accomplishment, then opened the door and turned out the light. She closed the self-locking door—no need to double-bolt (as this was a building with a twenty-four-hour doorman and tight security)—and called the elevator. When it arrived, she entered, pushed "G," and descended. As the door opened at ground level a few seconds later, she inhaled and let her breasts swell against the soft material, then walked out of the elevator and past the doorman, who rushed to the front door and opened it in time for her to pass through without having to break stride.

Daneka walked unescorted the few steps to her always waiting, always obedient, never desperate or grumbling car and driver. Ron held the rear door open and tipped his imaginary cap. "Evening, ma'am."

A brilliant spring evening spilled over Manhattan—a rare combination of setting sun,

Canadian air, absence of most of the island's population—consequently, an absence of traffic and horns and trundles and general dyspepsia—leading one to think there could be no better place on the planet.

Let them have their corn fields or olive groves! To sit and glide down Park Avenue in a limousine towards Grand Central Terminal; to view a succession of traffic lights clip on, clip off like so many smart soldiers saluting; to hear the occasional rumble of the subway beneath the pavement; to watch young couples unpacking their weekend haul of newly-acquired antiques from Westchester or Bucks County along with their bored, tired, ornery progeny—already quislings-in-waiting to the cause of their parents' supercilious claim of old money—this was sublimity to Daneka.

Unfortunately, there was one lesson Daneka hadn't learned in all the years she'd lived in New York. Nothing in old Denmark could've prepared her for old, established New York. Not so old, certainly, as her fishy old Denmark. But jealously old and established enough to spot an overly ambitious upstart—a pretender whose only purchase on this particular piece of real estate lay in the easy money that could be made in the manic Nineties.

Money in Manhattan in the Nineties was, for many, as fluid as the rivers that surrounded it. Almost anyone could make money—bundles of it, in fact. Quick wealth was not an accomplishment—and less still, a true indicator of achievement. Real achievement, at least in the eyes of established New York, was measured by what one could accomplish without money; also, by dredging oneself up from the South Bronx, Jamaica or Bushwick—from the Bowery even—but then only if one were willing to dredge, drag and haul *others* up. Achievement in New York was a communal affair. This was not *old* York. This was *new* York. And established New York was still about extending a helping hand—even if a very often white-gloved and blue-veined hand—to a less privileged world.

The sun might set over Manhattan as it might set over Mt. Kilimanjaro, over Lake Titicacca, over the Khyber Pass. But only over Manhattan did it set in reflections of gold for which there were capital assets to match. Hence, only in Manhattan could one feel that gliding down rain-splashed, garlanded Park Avenue in a service car was somehow more exceptional, more deserved, more appropriate than pounding dry earth into dust from the back of an elephant or throwing a hand-sewn fishnet from the back of a hand-made skiff. And while the tenant of each might feel entitled to passage in his or her own chosen vessel, Daneka would shortly learn that she was the least entitled of all.

Kit was almost ten years younger than she. In a culture that gave a genteel nod to money, but which ultimately paid servile homage only to youth, she was at a serious disadvantage. Moreover, Kit was old-world America, while Daneka—even if old-world Europe—was only very new-world America. Kit's modest means were an elective, a course already chosen in his youth when he'd looked around and realized how much of a price wealth exacted. Daneka's claim to wealth was borrowed from a new world still willing to be tutored by a more knowledgeable old world—though for how much longer, no one was really willing or able to say.

"Evening, Ron. Downtown, please."

Chapter 10

E arly next morning, Kit rolled over and looked at the clock, blinked his eyes a few times and looked again. It was already 10:50 a.m. *Jesus!* Monday morning, and he'd overslept. In the same instant, he realized he had a shoot scheduled to start in fifteen minutes. As he quickly dressed, he picked up the phone, dialed his work number, got Rachel on the phone and explained his predicament. She told him everything was set: no problem; they'd wait.

"But please hurry, Kit. You know she's already on the clock. And what this one gets paid by the hour would keep me in cookies for a year."

Even as Kit tried frantically to pull on pants, shirt and shoes all at once, his eyes fell upon the photographs of Daneka. He went rigid and could no longer find his shoelaces or buttons. Against the clock and against his will, his fingers reached out for the prints. Every second counted now if he were to have any chance of getting to his studio on time, yet he couldn't pull his hands or eyes away. He looked at the prints slowly, one at a time, over and over again. This trance was broken only when he heard, through the window, the ringing of church bells somewhere in the neighborhood to remind him eleven times over that the hour of his appointment had arrived; that he was already at some time and distance from keeping it; and that he was still not moving in the right direction.

He dropped the prints and ran the few feet to his apartment door, opened and slammed it shut in one motion. Down the stairs, out onto the sidewalk, up to the Fourteenth Street subway entrance and through the turnstile. As he leaped down the staircase to the waiting cross-town "L," he heard the warning bell and saw the doors begin to shut. He took the last five steps in one bound and sprinted off in the direction of a closing door. A young woman of Daneka's approximate height and build, with hair of the same cut and color, had apparently just realized this was her stop. She jumped up from where she'd been sitting and pried the doors open to squeeze herself out. At the same time, her action allowed Kit to slip in.

The same woman walked off hurriedly in the direction of the exit. As she started up the staircase, the conductor released the brakes, and the train moved forward. Kit stared at the back of the woman's head, moving his face from window to window as the train moved, trying to identify her. Of course it couldn't be Daneka—and yet, the resemblance was uncanny.

The "L" arrived at the transfer station. He was the first out, ran to meet the approaching uptown train, and walked in as soon as the doors opened. He was lucky today: the connections were perfect; trains seemed to be running without their usual delays. One quick subway sprint up the West Side to the Twenty-third Street station, and he was out, up the stairs to street level, half a block west, and up another set of stairs.

He opened the door of the studio to Rachel's smirk. Slightly ironic, slightly scolding, her look greeted him with notice of his tardiness. But she liked Kit; he was one of the good ones—and so, she'd taken pains to cover for him. Too bad he was—. What was it? Oh yeah. He was *old*.

"I'm sorry. I—."

"Don't be," she answered. "Britney doesn't know the difference. I told her you were, like, all caught up in her book and couldn't tear yourself away. Like, that you're normally all business and right on time, ya know? But, like, with you—and here I think to myself *Britney!* And so I says to her, 'One look at your book and he gets, like, all weak in the knees.' Britney looks back at me and gets, like, all doe-eyed."

Kit looked at Rachel in utter confusion.

"Guess you had to be there," she said.

Sometimes, Kit thought, the shift between his generation and this one was truly tectonic. "Britney," he said. "Is that her name?"

"Ohmygod! You *old* people! Like, you really don't know who Britney Spears is?"

"Oh, *that* Britney. Yeah, sure. I know who she is. Listen. Do me another favor, will ya, please?"

"Is there pizza at the end of that 'please'?"

"Sure. With pepperonis?" Kit smiled. GenXers might appear to be nomads even to his generation—he was now thinking—but they'd somehow never lost the talents of all the generations of camel-traders before them. "Would you buy me five more minutes of, uh,

Britney's indulgence?"

"Yup. Pepperonis. I'm not really sure what you mean by 'indulgence.' But if you, like, need to jerk off or something, I'll buy you some time."

Although he sometimes found it rude even to his own ears, Kit liked the mock-ghetto bluntness of white-skinned Gen Xers. Their identification with their black peers was some kind of new democracy in the making. Of course, he knew it was only a matter of time and years before it would be bleached out of all but the most hardcore of them by the reality of children, credit card bills, and the life-style to which they would ultimately come to believe they were entitled.

The same had happened with the 1960s generation—he knew that from having eavesdropped on some of his parents' conversations. Revolutions and emancipations were great while you were a comfortably well-off college kid. But when college was over, so was the party. Meanwhile, most of your black boy- and girl-toys of a season all went back into the box, back to the *real* ghetto. Had anything *fundamentally* changed in the U. S. in the last half of the twentieth century? Well, the rich had certainly gotten richer and more powerful, the poor clearly poorer and more disenfranchised. There was micro-brewed beer and Starbuck's for the elite; PBR and the same old Maxwell House for the poor. Their only common ground was tattoos, though the body parts and parlors remained on very different, very separate maps.

"Thanks. Tell me later what you want on your pizza if it's more than just pepperonis."

Kit went to his cubicle, picked up the phone and dialed Daneka's number. It rang once, twice. He frowned and prepared himself for her machine. Instead, a voice answered.

"Daneka! When can I see you?"

"I don't know."

"What is it?" Kit sensed distance.

"Well, darling, I'm on my way to the airport. I'm off to Europe."

"Excuse me?" Kit's ear momentarily registered the 'darling,' but it was the rest of her message that stunned him when he heard the sound of a suitcase being snapped shut somewhere behind the voice. "To the airport?" Where are you going?" He'd vaguely registered the "Europe," but the distance it suggested had bounced off his brain like a bead of water off a red-hot skillet. "When will you be back? What is it you *do* for a living, anyway?" The questions were falling out of him like spilled coffee beans in spite of his best efforts to sound merely curious.

She heard the tone of panic and decided she liked it. "I travel," she laughed—and hung up.

Once downstairs and with her luggage already piled into the trunk, Daneka gave instructions. "To JFK, Ron, but first, a quick trip to Carnegie Hill Photo to drop off a roll of film.

Ron drove her around the corner and two short blocks up Madison Avenue to the photo shop. She opened the door as soon as he'd pulled up to the curb. Out stepped a sheer, black-stockinged leg—exposed almost to the crotch as the flap of her dress fell away for not more than a second—that terminated in a good two and a half inches of black spike heel. Daneka never dressed for comfort when she flew internationally. She dressed for opportunity, for adventure, maybe even for attack. Transatlantic flights in the direction of Europe—except when she took the Concorde—always included an abbreviated night. Just long enough, just anonymous enough, to realize a fantasy or two if the right candidate presented him- or herself. And even the Concorde had a deliciously roomy and comfortable tabletop in its W.C. She knew; she'd tried it a time or two—and not to powder her nose. She sometimes wondered whether some of those who'd shared that high-wire act with her— tycoons and power brokers from downtown, maybe a Hollywood star or two—ever contemplated those same electric moments as they now lay domestically, routinely, boringly beside their Annettes or Mary Janes discussing the kids, their careers, and taxes.

She walked up to the clerk, smiled perfunctorily and placed the roll on the counter. "One frame only. The rest are blanks. Matte finish. And give me an eight-by-ten enlargement with borders, will you?" The clerk was pleased. This customer clearly knew what she wanted, and it seemed to him that she probably also got it more often than not.

"Thursday all right with you, ma'am?" he asked as he tore off and handed her the order stub.

"I'll pick it up in ten days or so. Thanks." She dropped the stub into her purse, turned, and walked back out to where Ron was waiting beside an open door.

"Which airline today, Miss Sorenson?" he asked.

"BA."

Ron made a half-hearted gesture to tip the cap he wasn't wearing.

Chapter 11

That evening, Kit finished work later than usual and decided to take a walk. Instead of heading out to the East Village, he turned north. He didn't know exactly why; nor did he know where he was going. But he knew that only one thing awaited him at home, and that he could no longer be content with a two-dimensional facsimile. It wasn't excitement or diversion he wanted; it wasn't even sex. Sex he could've had easily and with only minor prompting following that day's shoot. This particular "Britney"—as Rachel had so aptly called her—was clearly as ready, willing *and* entitled as any model he'd ever shot. But he was not. He was caught—and, once caught, his affections leaned in only one direction.

Presently, the object of those affections was literally sky-high somewhere out over the Atlantic.

Kit looked up from where he stood. Walking north up Sixth Avenue and still only in the twenties, his view was unobstructed by skyscrapers. The surrounding buildings were uninteresting—many of them sweatshops or wholesale houses to the fashion or interior design industries, none over four or five stories, and not one having anything to distinguish itself from its neighbor.

A lifetime contains perhaps eighty springs. For reasons that have nothing to do with the season itself, the first twenty-five and the last twenty-five don't really count. The mind is either too innocent or too feeble—in any case, too preoccupied—to notice. That leaves only thirty that really matter.

A warm spring evening in any urban setting transforms many women in the same way that estrus transforms other female mammals on the plain, on the steppe, in the swamp, even in the sea. In the case of urban mammals, the most obvious signal is in their dress. And while one might easily attribute this to the change in temperature, it's not the case that all women change their signals with the arrival of spring. Only those who are receptive do.

In the case of a New York urban setting, skirts generally shoot up like kites, while blouses forget buttons like yesterday's news.

Kit wondered for an instant how Daneka would've chosen to dress before heading out to the airport. He just as quickly concluded that—like her temperament—she would've dressed conservatively.

Chapter 12

The next ten days in Kit's life were indistinguishable from any other ten days except in one respect: his daily call to Daneka's answering machine. This machine always picked up after the same four rings and always delivered the same message, followed by the same four beeps. Kit felt each time as if he were shouting down into a crypt.

As he returned home each evening after the same mundane work with the same stunningly beautiful women and with nothing more than the spare, clinking change of a camera shutter in his mental purse, he suspected he'd become merely another urban drone. Day succeeded day with an identical call to the same machine, message and beeps.

The photographs of Daneka provided the only relief to his routine. At the end of every day, at the conclusion of his last session of dozens if not hundreds of takes of faces and bodies he knew would capture the fantasies of millions of men—if not immediately in print, then in virtually unlimited digital variation—Kit returned to his apartment to gaze at a string of simple black and white photographs hanging from a clothesline.

As he walked the length of that clothesline, he couldn't honestly say whether it was Daneka he admired or his own work. One thing, however, was certain: a certain pair of eyes had captured and caged him, and there was no getting out or past them.

Kit recognized that his obsession and most of Daneka's allure lay in her eyes—or rather, hidden in caverns behind those eyes. To find that allure, then uncover it, he'd first have to gain her trust. Once uncovered, he'd have to maintain that trust and mine it, bit by bit. It would no doubt be a painful excavation. She'd have to expose herself, her motives, her ambition, her history in order to convince him—if she even cared to convince him—that she was worth the effort. The question remained, of course: Was *he* worth the effort?

Kit bumped up against his worktable, saw the boxes of two-day old Chinese take-out food and chop sticks with bits of two-day old rice still clinging to the tips, and served himself dinner.

The following day, for a change, he had a gig in California. Some super chick who went by the name of 'Alise' (which rhymed, according to the tabloids, with 'bee's knees'—which she clearly thought she was). He'd seen pictures, even a video, of the famous tattoo: the Kanji-and-flowers body art that sashayed across her lower back each time she'd flex first one, then the other buttock—teasing but also mocking the conventions of the modeling world. Yeah, nice gluteals—and rounder than those of most of the gamin-hipped models he'd photographed.

It was a good gig, all expenses paid. A couple of hours in the studio, then free time. No doubt she'd offer him a blowjob—California lite fare—but he wouldn't be interested. What he wanted was elsewhere—a five- or six-hour sunrise before his own. A sun that rose three hours after *that*—even if on a nicely rounded ass attached at the other end to a pair of puckered pouty lips—held no particle of allure.

Chapter 13

He flew to California as scheduled; did the shoot; saw the famous tattoo. So much Japanese hullabaloo about nothing. So *typically* Californian.

They finished up before noon, local time—*no* time, as far as Kit was concerned. *His* time was Eastern Standard. And just now, also Greenwich Mean. He took his rental car and drove north. He had the rest of the day to kill before his red-eye back home. *Might as well shoot something worthwhile,* he thought—and the Redwoods were, to his way of thinking, eminently worthwhile.

Just outside of Sebastopol, he found them. But with them, he also found trailers, junk-heaps, the refuse of a civilization run amuck. Thousand-year-old Redwoods—living shrines as far as he was concerned—and in their midst, Bubba and his collection of junk, his rusted-out Camaro on cinder blocks, his out-of-control dogs. *What a fucked-up state of affairs!*

He spotted a clearing—almost storybook—and braked. Trunks like giants' thighs. Moss-covered turf beneath like so many *montis veneris* covered in emerald pubic hair. Here was something he couldn't find back East—not anywhere, not anyhow, not in the thousand years or more it would take to replicate it. Here was a small piece of paradise.

He pulled over to the shoulder, parked, grabbed his camera and got out. Nothing but silence, the Redwoods and the moss. He walked in reverently, as if approaching a shrine, found the angle, and shot. Light and shadow. Green upon green upon green.

This is perfection, he thought. He could never sell it. Sell it? Fuck! He could never even begin to convey to anyone else—back East, out West, anywhere in between—what it was all about. These shots were for him alone, or maybe for his grandchildren. Scrapbook material—when, most likely, Redwoods would already be part of the heap.

He moved in close to the base of one in particular—moss and mushrooms making quiet music—and then he looked up. A swath of lichen caught the bit of sunlight able to penetrate the heavy shoulders of Redwood boughs and push on through. It reflected back the stubborn light like a pale lover's plea—weak, plaintive, yet persistent.

Kit dropped his camera and looked at the lichen. *This is it!* This was the thing he could bring back to her. This was the one thing—at least to *him*—that would mean what words couldn't possibly convey.

"Diamonds are a girl's best friend" was a jingle he knew well enough—as was "diamonds are forever." But to Kit, diamonds were just old, dead things. And far from being 'forever,' they frequently found their way into the dusty jaws of jewelry boxes; through the last-prayer doors of pawn shops; down without grace into toilet bowls; out and down, thoroughly down, to the bottom-muck of some indifferent river where 'forever' meant truly forever.

Lichens, on the other hand, were both old—ancient, really—and alive. To give a woman a lichen was to give her the promise of forever *and* life. This was what a lichen meant to Kit: "love for as long as the two of us are alive." And when they were no longer, the lichen would still continue on in someone else's life as a reminder.

He peeled off the piece of bark with its lichen blanket and bagged it. Whatever else he might've found through his lens, he had his prize for Daneka. He wanted desperately to call her, pulled out his cell phone and dialed her number. It would, he knew, already be early evening on the East Coast.

Back in New York, Daneka had returned from Europe only moments earlier. The front door still stood open. Her luggage stood around her like so many impatient minions. But she was more interested in something else: the picture she now held in a pair of hands as greedy as those of any baby on a bender with a tit. It was the first thought she'd had coming off the plane. Actually, it was something she'd anticipated and thought about for the duration of her trip back over the Atlantic. She was coming home to someone, to some *one*, for the first time in years, and the thought of it had made her almost giddy with anticipation.

She'd already bought a frame in Europe and retrieved the picture on the way home from the airport. Unpacking her bags was not the first thing that occurred to her when she stepped into her apartment. Instead, she took the picture out of its envelope and gazed at it. This black and white facsimile of Kit corresponded perfectly with the mental image she'd carried around in her head for the ten long days she'd been away. This, she realized, was a man she could fall in love with—*head over heels* in love. She laughed out loud as she thought of the hundreds of hackneyed stories she'd allowed her magazine to publish over the years. And now she, herself, was about to become one of those clichés. She took a deep breath: *Not so fast, girl. Not so easy.*

Who was this man, anyway? What power did he have that no one before him had had? And why he? Why now? She focused on his face, lips and eyelids. They were indeed fine features. There was strength in the cheeks, chin and jaw-line, but his eyebrows and eyelashes, and the wave of his hair, were almost feminine by contrast. She looked hard at his features—as if, by staring long enough, she might be able to plumb their depth and strength of character and purpose.

This man, she decided in that instant, could be her equal. He might lack her ambition. To her, photography was at worst a reckless hobby, at best a minor art form. And from the little she knew of him, he seemed to be perfectly content to live and let live from the proceeds of his minor art. But right now, she was prepared to accept this artist in spite of his minor ambition and to throw herself at his feet—while throwing all of her worldly goods out the window.

She put the photograph down on the bed; removed the glass from the frame; took it into the kitchen to clean. Then, holding the edges between the palms of her hands, she walked back to the bedroom, re-inserted the glass into the frame and laid in the picture, cardboard inserts and back panel. She locked the panel in place, flipped the frame over, and gazed once more at the image of Kit before placing his eight-by-ten likeness next to her bed. She was still gazing when she heard the phone ring. After three rings she picked up, still not taking her eyes off the photograph.

"Hello."

"Hello, Daneka?"

"Yes. Who's this?"

"Kit."

"Say again?"

"Kit. You do—. Do you remember?"

"Well, not really. What can I do for you?"

Kit dropped to the forest floor like a bag of wet flour. She had effectively knocked the emotional wind out of him and made him feel, once again, like a mere vendor—and so he cut his reply to her measure. "I have your photos. I'd like to deliver them."

"Can't you send them up by messenger?"

"No!" he said emphatically.

"*Excuse* me?"

"No, I don't think so. For one thing, I'm not in New York."

Now it was Daneka's turn to feel distressed. She'd counted on being able to see him that same evening. She had to fight to keep the tone of her voice neutral, measured, blasé even. "Indeed. A little R&R in the country?" she asked as she unconsciously began to scratch her wrist.

"No, I'm in California. I'm on a shoot." The news hit her like a bullet. California was not even remotely in the neighborhood.

"Well, isn't that a shame. Perhaps you could FedEx them to me."

"No! They need me. I mean, they need my annotation, my explanation—. Oh, damn it all! I want to see you."

Daneka smiled. First at Kit through the receiver, then at his picture. She'd won. She'd gotten him to make the first confession. "Well, I don't know—."

"Daneka, *you* need me." There. It was out.

Daneka pulled the receiver away from her ear, stiffened, and looked at it as if the instrument itself were giving offense. There was clearly too much presumption in his statement, and she intended to let him know it in the newer, stiffer tone of voice she adopted when she returned the receiver to her ear and spoke into the mouthpiece. "Ex*cuse* me?"

"Yes. You need me. To explain the photographs. It's what I do. I'm a photographer."

She found the explanation adequate. The presumption had been impersonal— strictly professional. "I have an idea," she said. "Let's meet sometime for dinner. When do you think you might be coming back?" she asked as she resumed scratching her wrist.

"Tonight. I'm coming back on the red-eye tonight."

"Well, there's no rush, of course."

"Yes, there is! For me at least. What about tomorrow night?"

"Let me check my calendar first." Daneka laid the receiver down on the bed and strolled into the kitchen, where she poured herself a glass of water and drank it—very slowly. She returned to her bedroom and picked up the receiver. "You're in luck."

Kit sighed audibly in relief. "What did you have in mind?"

"A place I know in Central Park. The Boathouse. Do you know it?"

"I do. It's a bit beyond my budget. But if you want to establish yourself as an account, I'll be happy to expense it."

"Forget the account. I'm paying. Be there at seven." She was finished with her end of the conversation and about to hang up, then briefly reconsidered: 'conciliatory' wouldn't hurt either of them. "Okay?"

Kit felt resurrected, reincarnated even. For ten days he'd been walking in circles. Tomorrow night, finally, he was going to set back out on a straight course. "Okay. At seven."

She hung up. He hung up. She picked up his picture again and smiled, then kissed him full on his black and white mouth.

Chapter 14

Kit arrived at a point just west of the Boathouse at half past six—well before sunset, but at an hour when the spring sky looked like a teenager primping for her first date. The various species of viburnum were in full bloom, and the surrounding air almost seemed to vibrate with their young smells.

He found a space along the bank of the lake; pulled out his tripod and adjusted the legs so as to compensate for the uneven ground; mounted his camera and attached a telephoto lens. He was confident Daneka wouldn't be looking for him at this angle and that he could execute his shot in complete anonymity as she arrived. This was what he needed now: to see her unrehearsed, not in complete control for a change, maybe even a little anxious during those moments when she might have to sit alone.

It will do her good to wait for a change, he mused.

At two minutes till seven, he saw a car pull up to the curb at about fifty yards from the entrance to the restaurant. Rather unusual, he thought, since private cars generally weren't allowed on this particular stretch of road at this hour. A liveried driver got out and opened the back door. Kit watched as a figure emerged, limb by limb, from the dark interior. Both legs first stepped out, knees together, the heels of a woman's shoes meeting the pavement at the same instant. It was Daneka—he could see that at once even from a distance. He noted she was wearing the shoes she'd worn at the time of her visit to his apartment almost two weeks earlier. Was this a portent or merely a coincidence? Would a mere click of the heels see her disappear from view as mysteriously as she'd disappeared that first time?

He suddenly wondered whether he'd underestimated her reach, overestimated his potential for meeting it even halfway. The thought made him feel once again awkward and insecure. What was he doing, anyway, with this camera and tripod? What did he hope to accomplish? This wasn't any part of their *deal*.

At the same time, he considered: he'd seen her apartment; he'd reached a preliminary judgment about her need for others' approval—even in her private space. What

- 65 -

did this say about *her?* Why then should *he* be feeling insecure?

Kit bent down; turned the camera and lens in her direction; brought her into focus. He watched as Daneka extended a hand to her driver, asking him with this gesture to help her shift her weight forward, up and out of the car in one graceful movement. As she did, the folds of her dress fell like a long, fond caress. She was wearing another summer dress, a simple wrap-around held together only at the waist, the hem falling to just above the knee. The color was somewhere between pale yellow and carnival cream, and Kit could make out through his lens a timid floral print—lavender or larkspur, perhaps some rare variant or cultivar of salvia—he couldn't be certain at this distance. He focused hard on the print and opened his shutter for a shot.

Although her driver's back was to the camera, the movement of Daneka's lips suggested an exchange of words. She then smiled before he closed her door again and slipped back into his driver's seat.

Daneka turned towards the restaurant and walked up the stone path, careful not to catch a heel between pavers. The heads of men and women alike turned and lingered. Her mystique was like a web under perpetual construction and reconstruction, and she was the spider weaving only what nature's endowment had bequeathed her. Her dowry was the object of every woman's secret ambition, the object of every man's concupiscence.

In other, former civilizations, gazes would necessarily have been lowered, would've made do with glancing only at the *shadow* cast by such a woman. But those were different times, different civilizations, different mores. In the present, the distinction between sacred and profane, private and public, personal and communal had vanished; finer distinctions had all been leveled in the great new gold rush to celebrity.

Seemingly indifferent to it all, Daneka continued towards the reception area. Kit took several shots of her in untroubled transit from curbside to dockside as the maître d'—obligingly, protectively, almost possessively—accompanied her down through the throng of hungry, curious, envious, lascivious faces to a table next to the lake. When that same maître d' seated her at a flattering angle to the water's edge, Kit noted Daneka's gesture to him—still present, still hovering, still obliging—followed by his nod, followed immediately by a lighted match and then a lighted candle.

The sun still hadn't set. No other candles in the restaurant had yet been lit. But

Daneka asked for—then got—her candle. The light from it and from a setting sun would give her face and upper body just the kind of nimbus that she knew would deflect Kit's attention from the difference in their ages. No matter how many anonymous heads she was able to turn, no matter how many unspoken but clearly obvious desires she was able to elicit, an older woman's wisdom informed her that familiarity would slowly diminish any infatuation Kit might feel at the burgeoning of their relationship. This evening, this dinner—this moment sliced out from all that would follow—was her opportunity to enchant him with her beauty and make him oblivious of what by nature's own conventions was unnatural. She wanted him blind: blind to other women, blind to any possibility of exit, blind to those events and choices in her past that had first informed, then molded, then finally hardened her character into what it was today.

A waiter approached—a too-eager and too-gallant Prince Charming—to take her drink order. From what Kit could see of the abrupt change in the waiter's demeanor, Daneka didn't hesitate to re-order his agenda. Her nod said 'Yes, bring a drink'—and then she named one. The waiter-prince wandered off, his charm rebuffed to a slightly duller sheen. In the meantime, Kit had moved his focus in as tight as he could on Daneka's face and shoulders, front-lit by the candle and the setting sun behind him. As he was about to take another shot, he saw her raise a hand to her shoulder, then push her dress to one side and begin to massage what appeared through his lens to be a bruise. *Probably the result of a minor collision with something falling out of the overhead rack*, he reasoned. The attendants were always warning of in-flight shifts in overhead baggage….

She looked down at the bruise and winced. Kit had the look and the strained curvature of her neck muscles in tight focus as he snapped his final shot. A look of minor pain on a beautiful face, he thought, gave him a portrait as perfect as he might ever hope to achieve.

Kit disassembled the tripod and retired his lens to his camera bag. Not twenty feet from where he stood was a rowboat. He grabbed his gear and walked over to it, then looked for an attendant—but none was present. He climbed in, found a pair of oars lying at the bottom of the boat and began to row towards the restaurant, then reversed his position in the boat so as to be able to watch Daneka as he rowed. The newer position might've been awkward, but he managed it without difficulty as he watched the waiter set a flute of champagne down in front of her. As she raised the flute to take a sip, her eyes looked out over the water and found Kit for the first time. He was still at some distance, but close enough for her to allow just the hint of a smile as she put the flute to her lips.

He answered with his own quiet smile. As successive pushes of Kit's oars decreased the distance between them, each held the other locked in a stare.

When he finally landed at the dock, he extended a hand. Daneka emptied her glass, stood up from the table and descended the few steps to his waiting rowboat. Kit steadied her as she stepped down and in, then settled her at the stern. At that moment, the waiter reappeared with menus and handed one to each of them. Their menus remained closed and their eyes remained fixed—but not on the menus. Daneka was the first to order. She asked for a bottle of *Veuve Cliquot* and a dozen oysters.

"No, make that two dozen. And some fruit—peaches, nectarines, plums." And then, barely above a whisper, "and a banana."

Kit looked hard at her and then ordered a second bottle of the same champagne and a dozen strawberries. "No," he said, smiling mischievously. "For me, *Grande Dame* and two dozen strawberries. No bananas—instead, some pomegranates and figs." He broke his stare at Daneka long enough to look up and ask whether the waiter could bring their order by gondola. The young man announced that well, yes... maybe he could... but that, well... it might be a problem ... other customers, and... Kit looked at Daneka. "Don't worry. We'll make it worth your while," he announced grandly. The waiter returned an ingratiating bow and smile; retired his pen and order pad to his shirt pocket; was about to walk off when Daneka asked him to dismiss her driver for the evening.

Kit pushed back from the dock with an oar. Daneka, facing him, sat in the stern. He rowed slowly away from the restaurant while she leaned over the transom and trailed a single finger in the water.

"Tell me about yourself, Kit," she said. "Tell me about your early years, your first memories, about growing up, about when you realized you wanted to become a photographer. Or if not a photographer, an artist. Tell me how and why you came to be what and who you are today. All of it. Tell me about your siblings, your parents. Tell me why your friends are your friends, why your enemies are your enemies. And then tell me what you look for in a woman, in a mate." She smiled ironically. "In the love of your life."

"How long have you got," Kit asked, a little surprised at such a tall order, but also skeptical she would have the patience or stamina to sit through all of it.

"We've got the evening and the night. I'm not going anywhere. Besides, we're marooned out here. I can't swim in these clothes, and I'm not yet ready to take them off." She watched for a blush, but none appeared. She liked that.

"Not yet," he said—more of a statement than a question.

"Not yet," she answered, neither a tease nor a challenge. Kit knew she would take them off when she was damned good and ready to take them off—just as she had done once before in his apartment. This time, however, he wouldn't be falling asleep.

"And if I tell you everything, absolutely everything about me, will you grant me the same favor in return?" he asked.

"Maybe," she teased.

"Maybe?"

"Well, my story has a few twists and turns. Most of them happy, mind you. But just the same, a few twists and turns."

"Twists and turns?"

"Like my birthplace. You know, I suppose, that I wasn't born in this country."

"I would never have guessed it."

Daneka feigned a look of hurt. "Is it *that* obvious?"

"Your language is a bit *too* perfect for you to be home-grown. Your accent is—. Well, let's just call it 'finishing school,' shall we? You're very precise with *both* your consonants and your vowels. And I can almost hear the punctuation."

"Oh, but that's because I'm reading *Eats Shoots & Leaves*," Daneka said, barely able to suppress a snicker.

"Excuse me?"

"*Eats Shoots & Leaves*, Daneka repeated. "Or, if you prefer, *Eats* comma *Shoots & Leaves*. I picked it up in London a couple of days ago. It's all the rage over there, or didn't you know?"

"No. I had no idea. But I'm not in the book business, remember? What's it about?"

"The quest for perfect punctuation. Maybe that's why you hear it in my sentences."

"Uh-huh. Punctuation. Fascinating!"

"Yes. It is, actually. As a matter of fact, I've been flirting with a little story myself. For the British market, mind you. Brits get worked up about punctuation the way Americans get worked up about pornography. You're both voyeuristic to the teeth. Brits just have a more refined sense of where to look—as in, between the lines and after an ellipsis. I suspect, somewhere down below their stiff upper lips, they also get worked up about sex from time to time. Otherwise, they'd have a *real* problem—as in no population to punctuate. And no punctuation to populate."

Kit considered her logic; liked the sound of it; allowed himself a small smile. "And so your story—?" He left the question deliberately open-ended.

"—Would use only punctuation marks."

"Uh-huh."

"If I had a piece of paper and a pen, I could sketch it out for you right now. But since I don't, I'll have to tell it to you through dialogue. Of course, less is more, you know, where storytelling is concerned. My *written* story will take up only half a page, top to bottom, and a couple of spaces, left to right, at the left-hand margin of that page. You'll be able to read it in ten seconds. It'll be something like cuneiform or hieroglyphics. It's the future of writing, Kit—at least magazine writing—and much cheaper. It'll accomplish the same thing where readers are concerned, but leave far more space for advertising. If only we could do the same thing with photographs…"

Kit was not at all sure he grasped her concept. He naturally understood visuals better than words. But he also understood words much better than naked punctuation marks. And he certainly didn't care for her ruminations on the future of photography.

"Okay. So, shoot. Or eat. Or leave."

"Why, I thought you'd never ask!"

Daneka sat back in the rowboat, arched her neck and head dramatically, and declaimed. "My title is 'Prurient Punctuation.' I think it needs some more pizzaz, but that's the working title for now."

Kit was so mesmerized by her face, gestures and voice, he lost the sense of the first few lines and had to mentally recoup them before he could begin to grasp the sense of her narrative.

'"Would you?' she whispered into his ear like a brooding question mark.'

'Would I what?' he asked nonchalantly, his beady, black eyes staring back at her like a colon.

'Would you, you know, like to do it?' she sniffed again, still apparently brooding interrogatively.

The colon exploded into a pair of bullet points. A bit of saliva squeezed out and hung from his lip like a semi-colon. 'Yes, I think so—' he answered, sounding to her ear distinctly like a double em dash.

She reached down between his legs. The double em stood suddenly at attention. 'Yes, let's!' he whispered back, now sounding and looking more like a proper exclamation point.

'Hmmmm,' she sighed into his ear. Suddenly feeling Iberian, she inverted, letting her sigh trail off like an ellipsis within easy reach of his exclamation. '¿Shall we…?'

'Oh, God, yes! Let's!!!' he exclaimed. As she gazed in admiration she couldn't believe the size of it. That, or she was seeing his exclamation in triplicate.

He took the length of a paragraph break to study her legs from close up, his eyes once again an upright colon: those legs were, he decided, a delicious pair of parentheses, at the apex of which aired an asterisk. He visualized himself between them and inside it, but then paused, comma-like. Formerly colon-eyes became ##. 'But you're—' The exclamatory in him floundered back down to the fluke of a double em.

'Yes,' she said, two tildes hovering here gravely, there acutely, over a pair of accents. I'm in medias res. It's called a period.'

He looked again—pausing between double ems—at her asterisk resting atop perfect parentheses. It blushed bright red like a squishy ampersand. The parentheses stiffened into brackets.

She bolted upright and exchanged Iberian impulse for a proper
English point of interrogation. 'You now don't want...?'
'Full stop.' The British Puritan in him had spoken."

Her declamation at an end, Daneka looked down at Kit—somewhat sheepishly, he thought. He still wasn't sure what to think about the story, but the delivery had enchanted him. She was an enchantress—pure and simple. His chin had been resting on his hands throughout her recitation. He extended the tips of his fingers and soundlessly applauded. Whatever it may have lacked in volume, his gesture made up for in spirit. She smiled in obvious delight and mock-bowed.

A closer assessment of her story didn't really matter to either of them. What mattered to him was that he'd gotten her to reveal a part of herself—his real strategy. What mattered to her—for once, in the absence of any strategy whatsoever—was that she'd allowed herself to be spontaneous, unselfconscious, a girl again, and that he'd listened to her without motive— without anything to gain or lose—and apparently liked her.

Barely three-quarters of an hour had passed, and yet they'd moved to a point with each other that many married couples never achieve in a lifetime. As both of them were contemplating the same fact, their waiter arrived, as ordered.

The gondolier pulled up alongside their rowboat, and the waiter stepped from one boat into the other. The two men then worked together: one handed over; the other set out: tablecloth, napkins, silverware, ice bucket, flutes, two bottles of champagne, fruit basket, and a plate each of strawberries and oysters. The waiter moved to hand Kit the check. Daneka intercepted it, added a gratuity and signed it, then handed it back. As she reached into her purse for a twenty for the gondolier, the waiter couldn't help sneaking a glance at the tip—nor could he suppress the smile that announced his satisfaction. He bowed formally to Daneka and announced she had only to call: he was hers for the duration of their stay. He'd even brought along a crystal dinner bell for the purpose, which he now placed on the table. As the waiter prepared to exit the rowboat, he glanced once more at Daneka, then at Kit—neither of whom was paying him any attention—then stepped stiffly out of the rowboat and nodded to the gondolier by way of signal to return to the restaurant. The gondola swung out and away from the rowboat in the direction of the Boathouse. The gondolier, money already pocketed, began to hum an Italian folk tune that Kit knew had more of Cagliari in it than of Torcello. *So much for Venetian spectacle*, Kit thought—but kept the thought to himself.

Chapter 15

As Kit became absorbed in opening one of the champagne bottles, Daneka studied him and wondered where he—and the champagne—would take them. He filled the two flutes, handed one to her and raised his own.

"To the future of stories and story-telling," he said. "And to those who tell them, however they tell them. May they be half as good as you were, and it was."

Daneka clinked his glass and lowered her eyes in coy acknowledgment of the compliment. When she looked back up, he had already speared an oyster, and now held the fork in front of her lips. She started to reach for it; stopped herself; opened her mouth instead; let her tongue creep out over her lower lip. Kit put the fork into her mouth and slid the oyster off onto her tongue. She curled it back, then let it slide down her throat. It had been cold only a second earlier on her tongue; as it reached her stomach, however, some other part of her felt a sudden flush.

Kit speared another with the same intent. As he reached up to put this second oyster on her tongue, she gently pushed his arm down with one hand and reached with the other for a strawberry. Holding onto it by the stem, she raised it to her mouth; puckered out her lips and wrapped them around the fruit; chased it slowly back out with her tongue; then turned it around and placed it between Kit's lips. He bit down slowly and separated flesh from stem.

A second flush flared up where the first had flared just seconds earlier, and her legs parted—though by not more than an inch or two. The reaction was involuntary—like a muscle spasm—though by no means against her will.

Kit's reaction when he'd first placed the quivering flesh of the oyster on her tongue had escalated of its own accord as he next watched her caress the strawberry with her lips and tongue, only then to put it into *his* mouth—and his heart and mind began to race. As her legs crept apart, however, and as his gaze was drawn to that part of her, his eyes caught sight of her panties, but not of the flush beneath them. His reaction was as plain to him inside his jeans as it was to Daneka outside of them.

They were now staring openly at each other, but it was, for once, not into each other's eyes. They were two adults fast approaching middle age, and yet each felt the relentless, gravitational pull of hormones even stronger at this moment than the gravity that kept them seated in their rowboat; kept the rowboat floating on the lake; kept the lake puddled in its granite island—that island clinging to a continent; kept that continent anchored to a planet; and kept that planet tethered by the same invisible force to a solar system.

Kit and Daneka were merely two creatures. Except to themselves, the strength of hormonal attraction between them was negligible. Had some anti-gravitational force been accidentally unleashed in the universe to rival the strength of that attraction, however, all would've been reduced to chaos.

There was still the small matter of twenty-two oysters and as many strawberries, not to mention a bottle and a half of champagne and an assortment of fruit—all of which it was not in their nature to waste. Besides, they were adults; they still needed to get to know each other—before, that is, they got to know each other. And so, they settled back and did what adults do first: they talked.

Once she started, it all came out: her birth, her upbringing, her education, her ambitions, her early frustrations, her persistence, and the later rewards—perhaps because of that persistence. In short: how Daneka had become Daneka. It sounded to Kit like an H. C. Andersen fairytale—the more he heard, the more he wanted to hear—and the enthusiasm in his eyes served her story-telling like rich fuel. He felt he could go on listening to her for hours, if only she'd let him. But she wouldn't. Now it was his turn to tell.

The sun had already slipped below the peaks of the apartment buildings along Central Park West when Kit began. The wait staff at the Boathouse, like mate-hungry fireflies on a late-summer evening, moved in a quiet hum around the floor of the restaurant touching Bics and Smart Lites to willing candle wicks. One after the other, these tiny tabletop lighthouses responded until the whole scene, viewed from Kit's perspective in the rowboat, more closely resembled the idyllic backyard of his youth than it did a simple commercial venture in the biggest natural playground in North America's busiest city. As Kit reveled for a moment in a kind of fast-forward newsreel of his youth—and particularly in the part of it spent in his own backyard—he felt Daneka move up behind him and drop her arm down across his chest. She laid her head on his shoulder, and he could almost smell memories of freshly mown grass in her hair. She had the brute beauty of *Brugmansia* and the scent of *Syringa*—and she reduced him in that moment to a buzzing bumblebee.

The arm laid across his chest felt like his mother's arm securing him in the swing or on the monkey bars as he'd try ever bolder, higher ventures—the same mother who'd not once discouraged him from testing and pushing his own limits, and who'd also kept an arm of security around or just in front of him to rescue him from his inevitable falls. As a result, Kit had learned to move cautiously but steadily forward, testing and then taking each new step, each new plot of land, each new challenge in life that play—and then work—put before him. Recklessness such as most of his peers had engaged in at one time or another never became for him a necessity or even a temptation. He simply took life; tried it on; kept the bits that made sense; discarded the rest.

They exhausted the first bottle and Kit opened the second. They'd long since consumed their provision of oysters and strawberries, and even of the additional pieces of fruit. There remained only a few more flutes' worth of champagne in the second bottle. Kit's and Daneka's contentment—with each other, but also with their surroundings—could not have been more complete. All of their appetites but one had been satisfied.

As their rowboat drifted around a bend in the lake towards the Rumble and out of view of the Boathouse, Kit felt Daneka unbutton the top two buttons of his shirt and slip her hand inside. Her fingers lay quietly for an instant just below his collar bone, then slowly began to caress his chest, shoulder and arm muscles. He first heard, then felt, the gradually increasing pace of her breathing as she appeared, almost trancelike, to enter into a state of self-induced excitement. He wanted to slow her down; to take her face into his hands and study it and her eyes, line by line; to trace the length of each tiny line with his lips. But this time, she wouldn't be stopped. Her breathing had become almost a rasp as she brought her hand back outside of his shirt in search of the remaining buttons. These she undid rapidly, then pulled his shirt up and out of his pants.

Her mouth took over the territory her hand had only recently explored, and her lips and tongue moved down across his chest and stomach. As she opened her mouth wide to take in a portion of the skin covering his abdominal muscles, she reached down between his legs. It was clear to both of them that Kit's thoughts had moved on from a swing and monkey bars. As soon as she felt him, Daneka's rasp became a low moan. She moved her hand up to his belt buckle and undid it blindly, expertly, with an economy of gesture. With the same economy, she pulled his zipper down to its base, then slipped her hand inside the opening of his shorts.

As she felt him for the first time without the medium of cloth between his skin and hers, her moan became a quiet growl. She released the skin over his stomach from between her lips and teeth and moved her head down between his legs. She grasped the his penis with one hand and placed it between her lips. With the other hand, she reached down between Kit's body and hers, found one of the two ties holding the upper and lower folds of her dress together—and pulled it. The upper portion of her dress sprang loose and she attempted to wriggle out, apparently not wanting to release him from her grip and mouth.

Kit reached down and pushed the material off her shoulders and halfway down her back. He pulled one arm free from its sleeve, took the hand from his penis and freed the other arm. He then reached around in back and unsnapped her bra, letting it drop to the bottom of the boat. As her breasts came into full view and she felt her nipples brush up against the rough material of Kit's pant leg, she growled louder, then opened her lips and slid her mouth down the entire length of him.

Their boat had long since drifted away from the Rumble, out and under the ironwork span of Bow Bridge and into open water, yet both were completely oblivious of their surroundings. A thousand pairs of eyes might be watching them—if not from the Boathouse, which was now out of view, then from the banks of the lake or through binoculars or telescopes from any of the taller buildings along Central Park West. And still they remained indifferent, caring only for this tiny, private universe of sensation—their own tempest in their own teacup—in which each of them by turns riotously, by turns languorously, bathed.

Kit could easily have come in an instant and Daneka would not have objected. Something in him suspected that she reveled in her ability to hold a man entirely captive in this simple act in which she maintained complete control over pleasure or pain, ecstasy or agony, maybe even over life or death. He suspected she could emasculate a man or destroy his self-esteem instantly if she cared to; at least, that she could reduce all of his earthly aspirations to one focused burst of energy of which she alone would be the recipient.

He suspected, moreover, that she no doubt sensed his straining towards that burst, and that she would know precisely how she might dispose of it—and of him—if that were ultimately her wish.

Kit, however, had other intentions. He wished neither to control nor to be controlled, neither to dominate nor to be dominated. He took her head gently in both hands and lifted it to meet his own. He then kissed her as he'd never kissed another woman—and knew, in that instant, that he would never, *ever* kiss another woman again.

Daneka was momentarily taken aback. The timing of the kiss itself surprised her almost as much as the deep desire behind it. It was not simple lust—far from it. This was the kiss of someone who sought far more than a quick fuck, no matter how ready she was to give it. She felt herself reacting in a way that seemed entirely foreign to her, even disconcerting. For the first time in as long as she could remember, she was not the agent, the motor, the initiator. Rather, she was on the receiving end of something that threatened to overwhelm her, to deprive her of absolute control of the act and its outcome, and it both frightened and seduced her into a state of mind in which she visualized this, her body, as no longer entirely her own.

She wanted a second kiss and moved one hand up to the back of his head, grabbed his hair and pushed his mouth against hers again. This time, she reciprocated—but without fear or hesitation. She kissed him in a way that seemed to mimic the kiss he'd just given her, though with nothing imitative in its or her intent. Her reciprocity served only to increase the depth of his desire—and his, in turn, hers; and then his; and then hers again—until it seemed as if they might engulf each other in this single, ferocious act, like tigers chasing their own tails and slowly churning, turning, burning into butter.

Kit was not particularly strong or robust, and Daneka weighed a good deal more than a feather—or even a lightweight ballerina. But he managed, somehow, to place one arm beneath her hips, lift her feet slightly up into the air, and then grab a seat cushion with the other free hand. She held onto his neck with both arms as he bent over and laid her down on the bottom of the boat. As he reached for a second seat cushion and placed it where her head would lie, she reached down and inserted both thumbs inside her panties, pushed them down over her thighs, knees and ankles, and kicked them off. She then pulled up her dress so that she was bare from her navel up, and bare from the same point down—except for the halo of a silk dress around her waist.

Kit looked up at the plate of strawberries and discovered that one remained. He took it, put it between Daneka's legs, then pushed it into her and rotated it slowly. She stared at him as he then pulled it back out, brought it first up to his mouth and bit off all but the stem. He chewed a couple or three times and then swallowed. Daneka's lids lowered like stage curtains, then raised themselves up again as if hoping for an encore.

As Kit slowly descended over her, she reached up inside his shirt and embraced his bare back with her arms. His chest met her nipples, and then came down gently onto her own chest at the same instant at which the tip of him touched and then easily came to rest inside the moist creases of her. This was indeed that moment of anticipation above all other earthly delights; that moment of sweetest urgency; that moment of voluntary submission when one being only too willingly gives him- or herself over to the other in a contract without restraint or penalty or reprisal, into delirious and delicious human bondage. This was precisely that moment when neither is master, neither slave, but when each is beholden only and entirely to the other for the fulfillment of a promise, the exact outcome and proportions of which neither can anticipate, as there exists no precedent between any two bodies that can yield more than a crude facsimile of the precise experience of any two others.

It was Daneka who initiated by raising her knees to either side of Kit's hips, signaling to him that the sweet anticipation had become intolerable. Already supporting most of his weight on his knees and elbows, Kit raised his hips slightly, slid himself down and entered her. As he slowly and easily penetrated her to his full length, she closed her eyes and gave herself over completely to the nervous sense of purpose with which she was now filled.

As Daneka luxuriated in the sensation of having Kit inside her, and for the few, brief seconds in which they would continue in this state of complete immobility, she involuntarily and without reflection whispered a single monosyllable into his ear, yet drew it out as a virtuoso cellist might draw out a single note with his expert bow: "*Ja*," she breathed.

It was the first Danish word Kit would learn—and the only one he would never forget.

Most likely, they both started to twitch simultaneously—although neither of them was in the least distressed by the other's apparent sense of impatience with their previous state of suspension. After a period of somewhat less than a minute, a natural rhythm started between them. It took only seconds more before they both realized, without the need to acknowledge it one to the other, that both their fit and their individual rhythms in coitus were perfectly complementary. Consequently, it was not all that many more seconds before both reached a climax in which, had one been notably stronger-boned or the other notably weaker-boned, one of the two might've been hurt.

They then collapsed together in a complete and unmolested calm.

Chapter 16

It was only minutes later that Kit, perhaps because of the state of near-ecstatic oblivion into which they'd slipped, noticed their position on the lake. Their boat had drifted out of sight and out of earshot of all but the most determined of voyeurs, had there been any around whose obsession might carry them to the brink of discovery and humiliation. The boat had come to rest under a natural bower of dense, leafy green—a copse of willows, Kit thought, as the sad susurration of bright green leaves and slender catkins now called up something in him he could only vaguely identify as portentous.

It made no sense—this seed of a doubt—particularly now, when they'd finally concluded what Kit could only think of as a mad chase, a game of emotional tag in which one would pause in the other's presence just long enough to touch and run again. It wasn't the conquest he savored as he glanced down at Daneka, who appeared to be fast asleep; rather, it was the fact of their perfect communion. In all the years and all the sex with all the partners he'd ever had, no woman had ever taken hold of him like this one.

Kit kept one arm beneath her neck, but moved off and to the side of her as carefully as if he were cradling an infant. He let his gaze wander reverently over her body, starting from her toes and working up to her ankles, her knees, her thighs, her abdomen, her breasts, her arms and shoulders, her neck, and finally her face. Kit had slept with many beautiful women—with women whose bodies were in every conventional sense as close to perfect as humans in the fickle world of fashion might be defined. And yet….

Daneka's body was far from any such ideal, and Kit's professional eye wouldn't allow him to pretend otherwise. Whatever nutritional and hygienic privilege she had profited from, however favorable her genetic endowment, however much money or science she'd been able to apply, age and gravity were doing their inexorable work. They would never relinquish their day-to-day, hour-to-hour labor of pulling the body towards the grave.

She was probably not more than a decade older than he, and yet that decade of difference was the crucial midpoint in a physical career in which he was still gaining, while she was already losing, even if her wane was only barely perceptible—and then, only to his trained photographer's eye. And yet, he didn't care. If she'd allow it, this was the woman he wanted to spend the rest of his life with. This was the human being he would gladly nurse through old age, and upon whose death he, too, would gladly expire. This was the one mortal in whose coil he would, for as long or as short as his earthly existence might ultimately prove to be, happily lose his own. As much as he might deplore the hackneyed sound of it, Kit realized in this instant he'd found his soul mate.

And yet, this seed of doubt wouldn't allow him the thrill of his discovery without a certain misgiving. Something nagged at him, stuck in his brain like a hook and wouldn't let go. Was it just his self-doubt, or was there a mystery to this woman that he'd discover only over time, if at all?

His eyes left Daneka and looked up. Their boat had drifted, though he hadn't even registered the movement in his reverie. They were once again moving out towards the middle of the lake, and Kit could feel just the hint of a summer breeze as it pushed them further away from the bank. Daneka trembled. With his free arm, Kit made an effort to cover her naked body against the chill, but the effort awakened her, and she abruptly sat up.

"Where—? What are we—?" As she became fully conscious first of Kit's presence, then of her state of undress, the expression of quiet bliss that Daneka had carried in her sleep turned rapidly into one of business, then of annoyance, and finally of scorn. Kit didn't know whether that scorn was directed at him or at herself. He didn't have time to find out.

"Take me back, please," she ordered.

Kit looked at her as if he were suddenly face to face with a stranger—as if what they'd concluded only half an hour earlier had taken place elsewhere, many miles away from this boat and this lake. Could she have forgotten already? Or worse, could she have been transported into some *other* consciousness in which none of this had even registered?

He was at once frightened and humiliated.

"Back to *what?*" he asked. Either of them could see at a glance that the Boathouse was closed and that no one was still milling about. The restaurant was entirely dark but for one low beam emanating from what Kit supposed was the kitchen—hence, probably an overnight light to discourage burglars and vagrants. Their surroundings, too, were entirely dark except for street lamps burning at intervals of twenty-five yards along the road leading through the park from the entrance at Central Park South and Seventh Avenue, on past the restaurant, and then back up and out through Cedar Hill.

"Back to what?" he repeated. "You can't walk out of here now. Not at this hour, not alone."

Daneka dismissed him with a look of disdain. "I know what I'm doing. Take me back to the restaurant," she commanded again.

As Kit picked up and then set the oars into their rowlocks in order to bring the two of them back to the Boathouse, Daneka rearranged her dress to conceal what only moments earlier had been fully exposed to him and to anyone who cared to look. In a matter of a few, quick hand movements, she was once again covered and presentable, and no one except Kit—though even he was beginning to wonder—could've guessed that this staid couple had undertaken anything more exotic than a quiet moonlit cruise in order to escape the bustle of the restaurant.

They rowed to the dock in silence. Once there, Kit stood up to lend Daneka a hand in getting out of the rowboat. She ignored his offer, stepped out unaided, and proceeded up through the terrace and out towards the restaurant entrance.

"Wait!" Kit shouted after her.

Daneka's only acknowledgment of his command was a spartan wave back over her shoulder. She didn't turn; she didn't pause; she simply lifted her hand, rotated her wrist, and let her fingers drop to her palm. Once. As she made her way along the brick walkway leading from the restaurant to the street, a limousine appeared out of nowhere and stopped at the curb. Kit recognized it immediately, even at a distance. He also recognized the driver, who opened his door and got out just as Daneka was approaching the end of the walkway, then opened the rear door of the car to let her in. He closed her door almost soundlessly, climbed back into the front seat, closed his door just as soundlessly, and slowly pulled away from the curb.

But for the steady glow of the streetlamps, Kit's view was presently limited to two red taillights pulling off into the darkness and then vanishing around the bend in the park road. Unknown to him, Daneka had issued only a one-word command to her driver as soon as he'd put the car into gear and glanced up into his rearview mirror for directions.

"Downtown," she'd said.

At this hour, he didn't need to ask which side of downtown.

Chapter 17

It was past midnight when Kit came up out of the subway at Eighth Street and Broadway. Though the end of a workweek, weariness didn't dampen the spirit or energy of any of the sidewalk revelers on the street. Quite to the contrary. In the city that mythically never sleeps, this much could be said about the East Village: however many thousands of nightlights might be turning out at this very moment sixty, seventy, eighty blocks to the north, no windows were going dark here just yet.

When Kit finally reached his apartment building, he found two young men and an even younger woman sitting on the stoop. He excused himself as he nodded, indicating that he wished to get past them and up to the front door. The men returned blank stares as if they either couldn't fathom what he might want or resented his intrusion into their space. The woman, however, stood up and stepped aside, clearing the way for Kit to ascend. At the same time, she gave him a smile that suggested she might be persuaded to join him if he were prepared to give her even half a smile in return. Kit smiled back, but it was not an invitation. Rather, his was a smile of simple gratitude that she'd chosen courtesy over confrontation. As he made his way past the two men and reached the step on which the woman was standing, he leaned down slightly and whispered "Thanks!" into an assortment of metallic baubles nesting comfortably on her ear. He felt suddenly old—until, that is, she quickly turned her face towards his, looked into his eyes, brought her arm up and ran an index finger and black lacquered fingernail the length of his jaw from ear to chin.

"Any time," she said, and flashed a set of perfectly straight white teeth that belied the condition of gothic decadence she might otherwise have liked to convey with her make-up, wardrobe and collection of metal jewelry.

That which we call a woman by any other name would smell as sweet, Kit thought to himself as he inserted his key into the front door and stepped through, chuckling at his own trivial paraphrasing of Shakespeare, yet also grateful for the truth of his paraphrasis.

He bounded up five flights of stairs to his apartment, moved by a force he couldn't yet understand, but knowing at least that he needed something, some answer, some clue—

and that maybe he could find that clue if he looked in the right place. He put his gear away; went to the refrigerator for a beer; popped it open; took out a Lucky and lit up; then leaned back against the kitchen counter to think.

In a moment, it came to him. He sat down at his computer and logged on. He thought he might find something through Google—some possible roadmap perhaps—and typed in her name. What he retrieved in a matter of seconds was several thousand listings. He scrolled down the first page, then the second, and indeed all of the English-language entries were clearly about *this* Daneka Sørensen. The same name appeared as the subject— or at least as part of the article—in a number of Danish-language entries as well, but Kit couldn't even begin to decipher the subject matter of any of them. He opened a couple of the English-language entries and learned that she was the Managing Editor of a well-known fashion magazine; that she was on the board of a number of other publishing companies; and that she served as a senior member of several industry-related organizations. *Busy girl*, Kit thought to himself and wondered if this fact might have something to do with the distance she now apparently wanted to keep.

He quickly dispelled that thought, however, as a non-starter. Sport fucking was not something a woman in Daneka's position would've risked. Moreover, there'd been a moment that evening when he was certain he was more than sheer amusement to her. It had been a fleeting moment, but it was there—and he was absolutely certain of it and of his own not insignificant part in it.

He decided to try a different tact, combining "Sørensen" and "Rønne"—her birthplace and the location of her childhood as he'd learned only this same evening—to see what the combination might yield. This second attempt at Google got him half a dozen entries, but they were all in Danish. There were, in fact, several entries for "Sørensen," but only a couple that combined that same last name with "Daneka." He found something that looked official—possibly a government document—and was able to identify what looked to him to be a date of birth. It also placed the last-known residence of this particular Daneka Sørensen as New York, and the date of her arrival in the U. S. as a little over two decades earlier. Kit was fairly certain he was looking at data that corresponded to *his* Daneka Sørensen.

There was a name and date of birth for someone, Kit decided, who would likely be her mother: "Dagmar," *née* "Kristiansen," apparently still alive and well in Rønne. Next to the entry for 'Father' was the name "Poul Urik Sørensen," deceased—with a day, month and year of death. Kit made a quick calculation and arrived at the astonishing conclusion that Daneka's father would've died at the age of only thirty-five. He then looked again at Daneka's date of birth, made a second quick calculation, and realized she would've been a mere child—sixteen, in fact—when her father's death occurred.

While there might be some perfectly natural cause for this, Kit couldn't figure it out. He decided to move the document to AltaVista for a Babel Fish translation, where he copied it into the appropriate pop-up screen and settled back for the result.

Five or ten seconds later, it was there on his screen. While the translated document was largely Pidgin English, one fact was unmistakable in its brutal clarity: Daneka's father had committed suicide, leaving behind a wife, also aged thirty-five, and a single child—a daughter, aged sixteen.

Kit sat back in his chair and reached for another cigarette. This was disturbing news, as suicides always are. But the most disturbing aspect of it—at least to Kit—was Daneka's clear omission of the fact. They didn't yet know each other well; even Kit would admit that. But they knew each other well enough, Kit felt, for her not to have omitted something as significant as the suicide of a parent at an age when she would've been particularly vulnerable and impressionable.

Far from solving the mystery of Daneka Sørensen, this new information only compounded it. He needed to get to the bottom of it and he needed to get there *now*.

Kit scrambled around among the papers and bits of paper on his worktable until he found Daneka's phone number. In spite of the lateness of the hour, he dialed the number—only to get her answering machine at the other end. He waited out the length of her greeting, hoping she might pick up the receiver. But he waited in vain.

"Daneka, it's me. Kit. I'm coming up. Now." Kit glanced at his watch. "I don't care what time it is. I'm coming."

Kit hung up the receiver, threw on his jacket and ran out of his apartment, not even bothering to lock the door. As he arrived downstairs at the entrance to his apartment building, he noticed that the three transient squatters had left. He was thankful there'd be no need to negotiate passage once again up or down his own front stoop.

A cab was dropping off a pair of haggard-looking passengers directly in front of his building. Kit held the door open as they climbed out. He stepped in, closed the door, and gave the driver Daneka's address. He then rolled down his window to clear out the residual stench of alcohol.

As the cab started up along Park Avenue South, Kit noticed a few stragglers hanging out on street corners, apparently negotiating with some of the hookers for one last snack before dawn and the start of a dumb, domestic weekend. Other than these few pedestrians, the avenue at this hour was largely owned by other taxis and an occasional garbage truck. This was the only hour of every twenty-four that could be called a true friend to deep sleep; the only break between nighttime bluster and daytime commotion; the last hour before dawn and the start of that thing for which New York existed and which, over the years, was turning its slabs of granite into bars of gold; the thing, in short, for which the city was *always* open, even on weekends: business.

Chapter 18

Kit arrived at Daneka's building on Ninety-sixth Street; paid the fare, jumped out of the cab and entered the building. As he started to make his way directly to the elevator to ascend to Daneka's apartment, the doorman stopped him.

Kit knew that doormen who worked the night shift were not paid for their graciousness or charm. They were paid to do a simple job: to stand between rude intruders from the outside and supposedly comfortable, sound sleepers on the inside. The likelihood that someone from the outside would rudely intrude on a supposedly sound sleeper on the inside was negligible at best—but more for want of genuinely sound sleepers than of would-be intruders. Still, those who worked the night shift knew their purpose: they represented, to the one, an obstacle; to the other, the pretense of security. And so, they maintained that delicate sense of equilibrium on which New York's more privileged population depended in order to maintain all of its entitlements—even if one of those entitlements was *not* sound sleep.

As Kit now learned when he announced his errand, doormen who work the night shift were also compensated for another thing—namely, to know precisely the nighttime habits of the residents of those buildings whose security they were paid to maintain, and to keep that knowledge to themselves. In this case, the doorman had no choice but to inform Kit that Daneka was just then not at home, as Kit was already present in the lobby of her building and within striking distance of the elevator to her apartment. That, however, was as much information as he felt compelled to offer.

Momentarily struck dumb by the news, Kit resolved nevertheless to hold his ground. He found a seat in the lobby that he intended to occupy for as long as it might take to unravel this newest mystery—yet one more in an ever-lengthening string of mysteries.

"Would you happen to know at what time she stepped out?" he asked after an appropriate length of time had elapsed.

"I didn't say she stepped out," the doorman replied, but without so much as a glance in Kit's direction to acknowledge his continued presence.

"Would you then happen to know at what time she's due back?" Kit next tried.

"Did I say she was due back?" This time, the question to his question came back to him like some unannounced—and necessarily unwelcome—offering from a pigeon perched directly overhead. Kit decided to let it slide.

"No, I don't suppose you did." Kit opted once again for silence and resolved to keep it, painfully if necessary, for as long as it might take to make this doorman uneasy with the awkwardness of it. He didn't have long to wait.

"Look, Mister. I don't know what your business is with Miss Sorensen. Never mind the hour. Most people—at least those who work for a living—are in bed right about this time," he said with a distinct sneer.

"I see," Kit said. "Well, now. Since I know for a fact that Ms. Sorensen *has* a job, that fact would suggest to me that she is indeed in bed." Then, however, and quite out of character: "and since you're obviously still up at this hour, I guess you don't. Have a *real* job, that is."

It was cheap and Kit knew it. But the *man* in the doorman fell for it.

"I make it my business to know who's in bed and who ain't. I make it my business to know who comes and who goes after a certain hour. I can usually tell, if they come back before I clock out, whether they've been out to walk the dog, or—" and here the doorman's sneer put on its best Sunday smile "—whether they've been out walkin' the dog. Miss Sorensen has a dog. He's a very *old* dog. Old dogs don't move as fast as young dogs. Sometimes, he just takes a little longer. And so does she. Am I making myself clear?"

"Crystal," Kit answered. "In that case, I'm sure you and she won't mind if I just wait here until her old dog finishes his business."

"Not in the least. We do everything we can to make our guests feel comfortable. Are you feeling comfortable, Mr.—?"

"Addison. Very."

They had arrived at an impasse, and Kit knew better than to try to improve upon his position. The only option left to him was to wait it out. He reached into his pocket and pulled out a pack of cigarettes. Before he could extract one and light it up, however, the doorman checked him.

"Smoking's not allowed in the building. Ms. Sorenson's—, uh, management's orders." Kit put the pack back in his pocket and responded with an uncharacteristically forced smile.

"In that case, I believe I'll go for a walk. You wouldn't have a problem with my walking and smoking in the park, would you?"

"Park's public space. So far as I know, you're free to do what you like in the park. At least at *this* hour."

Kit stood up and walked out the front door without a further word. He headed a block and a half west to Fifth Avenue, crossed, and walked up past a children's playground. At that hour, there wasn't so much as a squirrel in sight, though Kit knew it would all shortly change. Dawn was about to break—and with it, the solitary and occasional threads of nighttime stirrings would begin to weave themselves into a solid carpet of noise.

This was quiet time—the time of day when the city was not a block as hard as the granite on which it had been built, but was—to a receptive ear, at least—soft, vulnerable, given over to cats on the prowl, a stubborn hack or cough, an isolated siren, the sound of a cab door slamming, a couple grinding, a woman or man moaning alone. Uptown or down—, East Side or West—, it made no difference. This was the weeping hour—the hour at which one might listen and take in the entirety of the human condition in the only way one could reasonably expect to observe and understand it: in small bits and pieces and in the agonies or ecstasies thought to be most private—but which, by the mere fact of an absence of competition for one's attention—were most public.

Between the faint promise of dawn's rose and the consistent Con-Ed glow of lamps that lit his walkway at regular intervals, Kit decided he would wander into the park. To him, at this hour, the opportunity to walk and think in near silence was worth the risk others might judge incautious, even foolhardy. He smiled to himself as he recalled, out of nowhere, what Aldous Huxley had once written: "The problem of the twentieth century will be the problem of silence." How sadly true, he thought—at least for those who "chose" to live in cities. He knew the same could be said of most peoples' "choices." His livelihood depended upon it; and so, he accepted the necessity of living in a place that occasionally thrilled him, but all too often found him indifferent, frustrated or angry. His escape was photography—sometimes no noisier than the click of a shutter. But too often, at least in the background, it was filled with the noise of people. Of nervous people. Of nervous, obsessive, chattering people who felt compelled to fill the void with talk—or, at the very least, with horns.

Whenever human noise became unbearable, Kit would take his camera and flee to the country. If professional obligations kept him city-bound for any length of time, he'd merely escape to one of its parks. It wasn't so much the beauty of rocks, trees and flowers that captivated him as it was their willingness to model in silence. He was human—and a man—and so hardly indifferent to the beauty of humans. In particular, of women. But he adored the silence of landscapes. What's more, the older he got, the more he preferred landscapes and seascapes and *anything* that could relieve him of the chatter, the senseless noise, the burdensome monotony of human social intercourse.

Now, however, there was *this* woman. Nothing she said even remotely resembled chatter. Her speech to his ears was like nothing he'd ever heard. Indeed, her silences were more precious than any silence he'd found in the country or even in the park. What did it mean to find a "soul mate?" Was it merely an accident that he'd found her—and she, him— as it had occurred, or was there really something called 'destiny' or 'fate?' Their physical compatibility certainly had something to do with it. But Kit was not so naïve as to think that the sexual desire he felt for her would maintain, over the long term, anything like its present intensity. Sooner or later, it would wane—as those things were wont to do. What, then, were the other components of his obsession? He stopped dead in his tracks, took out a second cigarette, then chuckled as he finally acknowledged the thing for what it was.

"Yes," he said—completely unaware that he was talking to himself: he was obsessed.

He continued to walk, though more slowly as he pondered the singular state in which he now found himself and to which he'd just given not only a notional—but also an oral—acknowledgment. He next came across a stone park bench. In the thin light of dawn, he could just barely make out the message of a Latin inscription: *Alteri vivas oportet si vis tibi vivere*. "Live for another if you want to live for yourself," he translated to himself out loud, though no longer quite in command of either his Virgil or his Ovid. *An omen?* he wondered.

The sun was just clearing the horizon as Daneka looked east out of her rear car window. "It looks as if we're going to have a lovely day, wouldn't you say, Ron?" she asked her driver.

Ron glanced back through the rearview mirror. "Yes, ma'am. It would appear that way."

They continued in silence as Ron drove up the West Side Highway towards home. When they reached the Ninety-sixth Street exit, he took the off-ramp and headed east across Riverside Drive, West End, Broadway, Amsterdam, Columbus and Central Park West—then through Central Park. Just short of Park Avenue on the other side of the park, he made a U-turn and pulled up in front of The Fitzgerald. The doorman had spotted her car even before Ron had made his U-turn, and now timed his own arrival curbside to coincide with the car's arrival. As soon as the car stopped, he opened Daneka's door. She stepped out and nodded. He noted she was wearing an evening dress that had lost some of its luster. Or crease. Or both. He noted, too, that she looked tired, worn down in some almost imperceptible way, older than when he'd last seen her only a few nights earlier. He knew that she often came home at this hour looking far from rested, but that she could emerge forty-five minutes later in business dress and looking as sharp and fit as any woman half her age.

He kept his thoughts to himself as he preceded her to the front door and opened it so that she might not have to be inconvenienced by a pause. As she stepped out of the car, but before shutting her door, she leaned in towards her driver.

"Have a wonderful weekend, Ron. Hugs to your wife and kids."

"Yes, ma'am. I'll do just that. And thank you."

Daneka walked to the front door and passed through, once again nodding her thanks to the doorman. As she rose the few steps to the lobby area, he informed her that she'd had an early-morning visitor—a familiar-looking young man—who'd come to see her at about four o'clock, and who'd then gone off for a walk in the park while he awaited her return. Daneka grimaced—an indiscretion she wouldn't normally have displayed to her doorman. However, she said nothing to indicate either pique or pleasure. Instead, she entered the elevator and pushed the button to ascend.

Once inside her apartment, she went directly to her answering machine. The message light was blinking and she depressed the playback button. She listened to Kit's message from several hours earlier and hurriedly disrobed, dropping her clothes in a pile on the floor. She then took a quick but very thorough shower.

Daneka emerged from the bathroom, put on a robe and began to towel-dry her hair. She looked at herself in the bathroom mirror, her face then entirely without make-up and her skin slightly shriveled from the hot water. She was not happy with the image staring back at her as her house intercom suddenly began to buzz. She promptly ceased her malignant meditation and walked to her front door to answer the intercom.

"Yes, I understand. Please send him up." She gathered her evening clothes and threw them into an empty bottom drawer, then returned to the bathroom to hang up her towel and retrieve a comb. As the doorbell rang, she started out of her bedroom towards the front door. Only then did she notice that her panties still lay on the floor where she'd originally thrown them. She scooped them up quickly, opened the same bottom drawer to her dresser, pushed them in under her evening clothes—and was careful to close the drawer tightly.

Chapter 19

No sooner had Daneka shut the drawer on her evening clothes than Kit pushed the buzzer at the front door. It was Saturday morning, and Estrella was not at home to answer. With weekends off, she was in the habit of taking the bus to New Jersey the evening before to stay with her family until Sunday evening. And so, in bathrobe, without make-up, and with hair uncombed, Daneka went, herself, to answer.

She threw the bolt and opened the door. Kit stepped through, trying hard—if with little success—to conceal his annoyance. He knew he was still in no position to interrogate her, much less to make demands. But the quiet rage he felt was no less real for the absence of that privilege or possession. As if nothing had taken place between them just hours earlier, Daneka stood before him stone-faced. Kit felt he might as well have been an appliance repairman who'd arrived long before the appointed hour.

"Well, now, Kit. Who knew you were such an early bird? And accustomed to making unsolicited house calls?"

That was it. No smile, no friendly word, no acknowledgment whatsoever of his right to be in her apartment at an hour that *she*, for a change, had not expressly appointed. Daneka turned and walked back to her bedroom, half closing the door behind her as she entered. Kit stood on the same spot where she'd just left him. He felt out of place, as if he'd rung the wrong buzzer. He wondered whether he should simply turn around and walk back out, return to his apartment, take down the photos of Daneka that had haunted him for the better part of two weeks, and try to regain some sense of who he was and of who he'd been before this woman had become such an overwhelming force in his life.

His reverie was interrupted by the distant sound of fingers typing on a computer keyboard. Whatever pique he might've felt just moments earlier suddenly turned to fury. He no longer needed instructions or an invitation from her to sit, to stay, to leave—to do anything at all but follow his own gut. And his gut was now on fire. He stalked back to Daneka's bedroom, threw the door open and found Daneka seated in front of her computer. She'd apparently already forgotten his presence—or was at the very least choosing to ignore it. He walked up to her computer, reached down in back and ripped the power cord out of the wall. Daneka continued to stare at a blank screen, her hands poised in mid-air above the keyboard as if she were waiting out some momentary glitch.

With more strength than even he knew he possessed, Kit lifted Daneka out of her chair and threw her down on the bed. She landed on her back and settled in easily. Slowly—*very* slowly—she undid the terry cloth knot of her bathrobe, then pulled the bathrobe open.

Daneka's intent was clear. As he took off and threw his clothes onto the floor, Kit kept his eyes trained on hers. The transformation would have amused him had he been in any mood for amusement. But in fact it disturbed him—then horrified him. Though still fixed on *his* eyes, hers appeared to be receding to somewhere deep within their sockets. They looked, but didn't see. They were open and informed, but their own internal light was growing more muted by the second. She had simply switched off—or was looking for an alternative power source—and he was now that source.

Still angry, Kit climbed on top of her—looking not to wage war, however, but to re-establish the peace. At the same time, he wanted desperately to find that moment of empyrean communion they'd found the evening before. Daneka apparently wanted something quite different.

"Fuck me," she said. The first time she said it, he was again amused—though with mixed feelings—at her choice of expletive. His amusement rapidly changed into an odd combination of excitement and pain as she began to command over and over again, each time louder: "Fuck me! Fuck me! Fuck me!" Her command was a syringe that drew out his very male adrenaline, and he did exactly as she ordered. At the same time, he was overwhelmed by sadness. He didn't want to fuck her; he wanted to make love to her. She wasn't a sport fuck—but was, instead, the woman he wanted in his bed and next to his side for the rest of his life.

His ears, however, heard something different. His ears heard over and over again: "Fuck me! Fuck me! Fuck me!" He held her immobile. He held her hard: legs back against her chest and, from the knees down, wrapped over his shoulders. He was a mechanical cock, and she was an equally mechanical cunt. Euphemisms now had no more place in Daneka's bed than terry cloth aprons had a place in a slaughterhouse. The more emphatically she repeated her command, the more emphatically he responded.

However much he might've been carried away by lust, Kit was still emotionally engaged enough to want her to come first. He'd been willing to follow her commands in the act itself, but he now wanted her surrender. It was not the male in him that demanded her surrender; it was the partner. He would, ideally, have wished it to be simultaneous. But he knew, too, that simultaneity couldn't be programmed. He wanted her to stand at that bridge and say 'yes,' she would jump—to risk "the little death." He wanted the clear demonstration of a willingness to jump, if only for a couple of seconds, without knowing at the precise moment of commitment whether she'd jump alone or with a partner. The point of launch was high up; from that altitude, the water would be unforgivably hard; "the little death," certain. To suffer it alone would be horrid; to suffer it together, bliss.

Daneka sensed that Kit was just seconds away from coming himself. One little inducement, and she knew she'd have him. "Fuck me *harder!*" she whispered into his ear.

He came.

He came ecstatically, but also with silent tears. She'd won; he'd lost. He would not find a partner this morning. Her response an instant or two later was appropriate, but Kit suspected it was also artificial. There was release in it, but no surrender.

After a few moments, he rolled off. His only desire was to hold her.

Daneka lay on her side with her knees drawn up tight against her abdomen, Kit behind her. He slid his knees up under hers from the rear and wrapped his arms around her. They were as close as they'd just been, less penetration. Her hair, however, still covered her neck. He blew it gently aside, exposing the nape, which he kissed, increasingly softly, over and over again as Daneka purred.

Kit looked up for an instant and saw, for the first time, his framed picture on the night stand next to her bed, then put his lips one last time to the nape of her neck and smiled.

They both fell asleep.

Chapter 20

Was it an hour later, two hours, three hours even when they both awoke in the same position in which they'd drifted off to sleep? Kit didn't know, but it didn't concern him. This was Saturday—and an opportunity to do what came naturally on Saturdays.

Kit kissed the nape of Daneka's neck once again and she—as if on cue—purred once again in response. She then turned around to face him squarely, put her arms around his neck, pried his mouth open with her own, and let the tip of her tongue dance gently over his teeth and gums. As his breathing became shorter, her tongue stopped dancing. She pried his mouth wide open and pushed her tongue in deep and hard as if she wanted to consume him. She then very slowly turned him on his back and slid a leg over him. Not releasing his mouth from hers, she pulled herself on top and straddled his hips, then transferred her weight to her elbows and knees and carefully placed herself at the tip of his erection.

As she pushed her tongue once again into his mouth, she eased her pelvis down. Kit slid easily into her as he pushed her tongue back with his own. She promptly released his mouth and propped herself up on her hands, rearranging the angle of her pelvis once again so that Kit's penetration was complete. She then closed her eyes and began to move her hips slowly back and forth.

He looked up and realized she was in her own world—and that her world, at this point, was at some distance from any world of which he was a part. Her mouth half open, Kit could hear gurgling sounds of which she was clearly oblivious. Daneka issued no commands. She simply moved.

After a few more seconds, she heaved forward; put her face into the pillow next to Kit's head; and screamed. At the same moment, he felt the contraction of her vaginal muscles like a gentle yet firm grip. He came in the same instant with such force, he wondered whether he might actually pass out. He couldn't remember ever having had a more intense orgasm. Nor could he remember ever having had a more urgent and intense desire to declare his love to a woman.

Instead, he simply embraced her as the contractions receded little by little. He sensed she was once again breathing out of her nose—as she'd turned her face towards his and had it wedged up tight against his neck. Eventually, as he began to lose his erection, she slid off and settled down with one arm draped across his chest, one leg across his legs.

Now it was her turn to give his neck a series of little kisses, his turn to purr. This time, however, neither of them fell asleep. After a couple of minutes, Kit turned his face to hers and smiled, then placed a soft kiss on the end of her nose. She smiled back.

"How about a walk in the park?" he asked.

"Hmm. A wonderful idea, darling. *Wonderful!* But how about a quick shower first?"

"Sure, go right ahead."

Daneka stared back at Kit for a long moment. Then, she reached down between her legs, brought her hand back up, smeared the consommé across Kit's chest and grinned broadly.

"I meant for *both* of us," she said with a guttural laugh.

Kit chuckled quietly, got up and stood alongside the bed, then waited for her to climb out. She rose to her knees and came to him, but with no clear intention of leaving the bed. Instead, her head now at the level of his sternum, she put her lips to his chest and opened her mouth. Her tongue left a thin trail of saliva behind as it made its way first from one nipple to the other, then down towards his navel, then further down still.

At seventeen or eighteen—Kit thought to himself—he might've been able to respond to a third challenge in such a short space of time. But at thirty, he figured the best he'd be able to manage was a chuckle of appreciation.

He'd clearly underestimated both his abilities and Daneka's art. There was—as he was already discovering, and much to his pleasant surprise—some kind of magic in her mouth and in what she could do with it. He'd had a second orgasm less than five minutes earlier, but he could already feel the blood moving and resulting in a third erection. With the grace of a cat, Daneka eased her body down and dropped both knees to the floor. At the same time, she turned Kit around on the edge of the bed, pushed his legs apart and moved in between them. Her hands moved up the insides of his thighs. She slipped one hand in under him, then moved an index finger back to a point at which she could begin to tease his anus. The other grasped his penis, which she slowly began to caress back to a state of full erection. Perhaps out of impatience, perhaps out of a desire not to be scrutinized too closely in how she performed her art, she placed her hand on his chest to let him understand she wanted him to lie back and enjoy the ride, though not necessarily the show. He understood, lay back, and closed his eyes.

As he did so, he could feel Daneka rubbing her face, nose, lips and forehead up against him; it was not long before he found himself once again in the state they both wanted him to be in. And *that* state wasn't anywhere west of the Hudson River. The next move was Daneka's, and she made it without hesitation. As he had the previous night, he felt her mouth come down over him—lips as soft ... as other lips.

When at one point Kit had apparently decided he couldn't or wouldn't allow the pleasure of this exercise to be exclusively his—and so, had attempted to interrupt it, Daneka, without breaking stride or contact between her mouth and his penis, set him straight with a word. "Wait," she said—though the final consonant of her one-word command resonated more in Kit's imagination than in his ear.

He indeed waited for perhaps fifteen or twenty more seconds. And then he came, almost as marvelously and as recklessly as he had come the second time that morning.

Daneka allowed her mouth to rest, but didn't move it from the spot until Kit put his hands under her armpits and lifted her up. He turned around with a mischievous grin, placed her exactly where he'd just been, and gently pushed her back down onto the bed. He then put a hand under each of her thighs and began to separate them. She resisted. He pushed a little harder. She continued to resist. He leaned over her and found an ear, began to nibble, and then bit down on her lobe. She squealed. He laughed.

"Don't fight me," he whispered.

He exerted half as much pressure again in separating her legs. She resisted again. He stopped insisting, found the same ear, and blew into it.

"Don't," he whispered.

Again, Kit exerted just a bit of pressure. This time, slowly, Daneka allowed him to push her legs apart and up until they rested against her own chest.

He was now on his knees against the side of the bed, with his face directly over her. She was on her back, legs spread. In the history of variations on sexual positions, there was certainly nothing new about this one. In his personal history of sexual experiences, this was also hardly a novelty. Yet neither of them had been in this position with each other—until now.

Kit understood that this was not a moment to be trifled with. While it might be erotic, the implications were far deeper. He'd already come to the realization that Daneka was not a woman who allowed herself to be easily aroused, much less "manhandled." He knew that if he wanted to keep her, and keep her confidence, he would have to handle her with care.

He gently kissed the insides of her thighs and moved, contrary to Daneka's expectations, in the direction of her knees. He took his time. Each square inch of Daneka's skin was, for Kit, a discovery. He adored everything about this woman: her feel, her smell, her taste. He would gladly have lingered for a week. There was not enough of her—there would *never* be enough of her, he thought to himself—to taste, bit by delicious bit.

He extended her legs straight up and away from her chest and began to explore the backs of her knees with his lips and tongue. Now, however, it was Daneka who grew impatient. She reached down under her legs with both hands and pulled herself open. Kit looked down and had his first glimpse of the true God.

"Please..." she begged, barely rising above the volume of a whisper.

The request was nothing if not superfluous. Kit began a slow trail of kisses back down from her knee and along the inside of her thigh. He found her fingers and took them, one by one, into his mouth. They tasted slightly of her, though not as urgently, not as pungently, as he might've wished.

Kit noticed he was becoming erect yet again as he put his mouth on her and his tongue as far inside as he was able. He could taste her—and he could taste part of *himself* in her. The tip of his nose was up against her clitoris and he moved it slowly back and forth. She responded with muted sounds—like something far below the surface of the ocean—to Kit's tongue as she had previously responded to another part of him. As he repeatedly inserted and withdrew his tongue, he noted her reaction.

Just as he thought his tongue might give out, she pushed herself hard against his mouth and came. The result, to both his ears and his tongue in the same instant, was enough to render him almost giddy. For the first time, he felt he and Daneka were equals:

equally delirious; equally irresponsible; equally in love.

A week? he reconsidered. He could easily have remained in this position through winter.

A few minutes later, Daneka and Kit got up, showered, dressed, and then finally headed out to the park. They found a bench next to the toddlers' playground at the Ninety-sixth Street entrance and sat down. She immediately draped her legs over his, and he reciprocated. From a distance, they might've more closely resembled a mess of noodles or a ball of multi-colored yarn. Mothers and nannies with young children eyed them sometimes curiously, at other times less than curiously—and anything *but* charitably. This very public display of affection might've been marginally acceptable in two teenagers: in two adults of Kit's and Daneka's ages, however, it fell just short of deplorable.

They continued to carry on completely oblivious of their surroundings. They spoke of trivial things, but it was really just the sound of the other's voice that each wanted to hear. *What* they had to say didn't matter in the least. Daneka finally put an end to the chat with a question.

"Kit, darling, what would you say to a trip to Europe together?"

Kit was at once intrigued by the suggestion, but even more by its implications. If he'd still had any reservations about his status in Daneka's mind at that point, her invitation clearly implied that they'd moved beyond a mere client-vendor relationship.

"Did you have a particular time and country or city in mind? Europe's a big place."

Daneka's eyes lit up. "Next week!" We'll leave next Friday night and fly to Paris."

Kit looked back at her and wondered whether she was toying with him. "And just how long did you have in mind?"

"I was thinking two weeks or so. Now listen to me. We'll stay in Paris for a night or two—just long enough to get some sleep and get re-acclimated. Then we'll fly to Lisbon, rent a car, drive to the coast and stay somewhere south for a couple of nights. We'll drive back to Lisbon and grab a flight to Rome. Then rent another car and drive to one of the most exquisite places on Earth—and one of my personal favorites—Positano, on the Gulf of Salerno, just below Naples. Next, but only if you have a real desire to spend some time in the mountains, we'll fly to Austria and drive to some little village in the Alps. All of that should cost us about a week, give or take."

Kit was starry-eyed at the proposition. At the same time, he considered the condition of his bank account, which only slightly—but decidedly—dampened his burst of enthusiasm. Daneka took both of his hands in hers and looked into his eyes.

"And then, darling, we'll fly to Denmark. To Copenhagen, where we'll get a train to the coast. We'll take a ferry across to Bornholm, then rent another car and drive to Rønne so that you can meet my mother. We won't stay long—maybe a couple of hours—and then we'll drive on to Svaneke, where I have my summer place."

Daneka could barely contain her excitement. She pushed Kit's legs off of hers and jumped into his lap, throwing her arms around his neck at the same instant. Kit, himself, was quietly ecstatic—troubled only by the thought of how he was going to finance *his* half of the trip.

"In Svaneke, we'll spend another whole week together. Just the two of us. Oh, Kit, you're going to *love* it there! Trust me!"

Now it was Kit's turn to be businesslike. "Daneka, have you considered whether you can simply walk into your office on Monday and announce that, from Friday and for two weeks, you'll be on vacation?"

Daneka looked at Kit with a twinkle in her eye and teased. "My darling, that's what bosses do. Who do you think is going to object? My P.A.?"

Kit leaned in and planted a kiss on her nose. "You're really serious—."

"Absolutely! And I'm not taking 'no' for an answer!"

Clearly, Kit thought, *this woman knows how to get what she wants.* "Okay, I promise. I'll do what I can. I have no idea at this point what my bookings are for the next few weeks, but I'm sure I can get someone to cover for me."

She gave him a quick hug. "Good! You won't regret it. Think of this trip as an investment, Kit. I know you don't invest. But sometimes, investing in futures is a good strategy. Think of this *"strategically."*

At which point, she leaned down and whispered into Kit's ear: "Now, darling, let's go back to my apartment and hone our tactics."

Chapter 21

The following Friday afternoon, Kit arrived—bags in hand—at The Fitzgerald. Daneka's car stood outside: hood up; hungry for luggage. Kit recognized the driver immediately. He wasn't certain, however, that the recognition was mutual. And so, Kit approached him cautiously.

"I don't know whether Ms. Sorenson mentioned anything to you—" Kit began.

"She did, Sir. I've been expecting you. May I take those?" the driver asked, saluting Kit and then reaching out for his bags.

"Please, allow me," said Kit. No sooner had Kit replied, however, than the driver reached over, took both bags out of his hands and put them into the trunk of the car.

"I don't want to be presump—," Kit began, then stopped himself. "I don't want to make assumptions. But maybe it wouldn't be entirely *in*appropriate for us to get acquaint—. Oh, fuck it! 'Name's Kit.' At this point, Kit extended a hand and coupled it with a smile. I believe we met once before—downtown—over a little fender-bender with my camera?"

"Yes, Sir. I remember the incident," the driver answered, extending a hand and meeting Kit's smile with his own. "I hope you and your camera have come to better terms with zebra crossings," he ventured further, but with a cautious chuckle.

This brief exchange only further confirmed Kit's first thoughts about Daneka's driver. He was a straight shooter, honest, and someone—Kit concluded—whom both he and Daneka could rely upon to be where he said he'd be, when he said he'd be there.

"And please don't call me 'Sir.' The name's Kit. Pure and simple—Kit."

"Yes, Si—. Yes, Kit." They both laughed. "And mine's—."

"I know. 'Ron.' A pleasure finally to meet you, Ron."

The two men exchanged a few more pleasantries. Kit then grabbed one plastic bag and excused himself to go upstairs to retrieve both Daneka and her luggage. As he entered the building, Kit recognized the doorman of a week earlier, even if at a much earlier hour, and concluded in an instant that doormen at The Fitzgerald must work on rotating shifts. He walked past him with only a cursory acknowledgment. The doorman responded with a barely perceptible—yet remarkably deferential—nod of recognition. Kit knew that he had won *this* battle, but thought better than to declare victory in any obvious way. He didn't need to befriend this man; he also didn't need to make of him an enemy. He walked straight on to the elevator, entered, pushed the button for the thirteenth floor and waited for the doors to close.

When he arrived at Daneka's floor, he stepped out and walked directly across a short space of marble to her door, slightly ajar, then stepped in without ringing. At the entrance, he could hear her voice from the bedroom. From the answers without audible questions, and questions without audible answers, he quickly deduced she was on the phone—with whom, he couldn't know. And yet, he also couldn't help hearing—just before he heard the sound of the receiver being returned to its cradle—"I love you, too." The words left him anything but indifferent. However, he decided to store them away for another time and place.

He quickly took his gift of lichen out of the plastic bag and placed it in the center of her coffee table. He then walked back to Daneka's bedroom just as she was stepping away from the phone. She immediately caught sight of him out of the corner of her eye. In that instant, not having seen him in almost six days, she dropped all pretense of formality, ran to him wearing a smile that looked to Kit like pure sunshine, and threw her arms around his neck.

Chapter 22

On the trip out to JFK, Kit and Deneka behaved as if on a prom date—he, the somewhat impetuous but always proper suitor; she, the somewhat demure but easily excitable object of his attentions. He didn't want to ruffle her dress or smear her lipstick; she didn't want to squash his carnation or wrinkle his dinner jacket. And yet, both of them were dying to get rid of dress, lipstick, flower and tux and find somewhere quiet and private where they could simply get naked with each other. There was nothing but energy and happiness and optimism in the car; even Ron felt it. Quiet, obedient Ron. He couldn't recall ever having seen Daneka so unabashedly merry.

As their car reached curbside check-in at the airport, the two were still carrying on like two love-sick teenagers. Some of it, no doubt, was due to the excitement of international travel. But international travel to Daneka was nothing if not banal. She traveled back and forth to Europe the way thousands of people commuted back and forth between Connecticut or New Jersey and New York. Kit, too, had had his share of travel abroad, though none in recent memory. He was naturally excited about Paris and Positano. He knew France and Italy well, yet never tired of visiting. Portugal he knew not at all—and so, the novelty of seeing it for the first time doubled his excitement. Austria and the Alps had once been as familiar to him as his own backyard—while Scandinavia, like Portugal, was a total unknown. To see the sun set at midnight—or maybe not at all—was something he'd wanted to do all of his life. And to see that part of the world in that most peculiar twilight was for the photographer in him nothing if not a dream come true.

They carried their separate thoughts, wishes, anticipations and fears on board with them. They stowed their carry-on luggage in separate overhead bins, but sat down together like Siamese twins. Daneka buckled Kit in with her seatbelt; Kit buckled Daneka in with his. They were locked together by dint of seatbelts, though nothing of the kind was necessary to keep them together practically the entire length of the trip over the Atlantic.

When they arrived the next morning at Charles DeGaulle Airport, they were understandably tired and cramped. And yet, they were about to breathe French air, which—to anyone or anything but a grub—could smell only of one thing: lust.

One *could* debate whether it's the French themselves who put it there. One could just as easily argue that visitors come already well equipped with lustful expectations—and that the French, being French, do their utmost to accommodate those expectations. In either case, it would be foolish to suggest this is merely a country like any other. It's not. It's as civilized a place as can be found on the planet; at the same time, it remains as close to the mythical Garden of Eden as any piece of Earth can aspire to be.

They were through Customs in a matter of minutes and then out the door for a taxi, which they quickly found. Daneka gave the name of the hotel and the address: *Grand Hôtel de Champaigne,* 17 rue Jean Lantier. As they entered the heart of the city, Kit was pleasantly surprised to see that their residence for the next forty-eight hours was on a particularly quiet street almost equidistant from Notre Dame and the Louvre. Daneka told him, though in no way boastfully, that the building dated back to the sixteenth century.

They checked in and were then immediately escorted upstairs to their room. At the far end of that room—a sumptuous appointment even by the most fastidious of standards—stood a canopy bed. Both Daneka and Kit struggled to appear indifferent, almost aloof, to the enticement of it for as long as they had the company of their porter. But nonchalance did not come easily to either of them at this particular moment.

As soon as the porter had deposited their bags and completed his minor preparations for their stay, Daneka tipped him and showed him the door. She closed it gently but firmly, bolted it, then turned around to face Kit across the room. In the seven or eight strides she required to reach the bed, she managed to kick or strip off everything she was wearing but her panties, and then to grab him practically in mid-flight.

Now, lying face to face with her, Kit kicked off his shoes. She then helped him—clumsily, speedily—to get rid of his jacket, shirt, pants and socks. Kit put a hand down to remove his underwear and then hers, but Daneka was too impatient. She urged him on top of her; reached into his shorts with one hand; pulled the crotch of her panties aside with the other; and then guided him carefully in.

Apparently, in the same amount of time it had taken her to get to the bed from the door and strip off most of her clothes, she'd also become so wet that penetration was about as taxing as tutoring a corporate tax attorney in the art of tax evasion. It may've been only a matter of seconds before they both came, then immediately fell asleep.

When Kit awoke several hours later, the sun was just beginning to set. He got up, put on his shorts, and opened a pair of floor-to-ceiling doors leading out to a tiny terrace. A few lights were on here and there like glowworms out on an early-summer-evening scouting party, but there was still enough natural light to allow people to go about their Saturday evening business without recourse to desk lamps or headlights. That—or the French simply preferred to conduct their business and their lives in semi-darkness.

He looked across the street and through a pair of half-open French doors much like the ones he was standing in front of—and noticed a candle burning on one side of the room. As he looked to the right of the doors and through sheer window curtains, he observed two bodies moving rhythmically under a bed sheet. He didn't look away. A woman was on top—that much was clear. What she was on top *of* he couldn't quite discern.

Just as Kit was about to avert his glance, she raised her head and opened her eyes—and seemed to be looking directly up at him. His immediate reaction was embarrassment at having been caught in the act of watching. However, her reaction was anything *but* annoyed or ashamed. Instead, she smiled up at him without once breaking stride, then half sat up on her partner. Her eyes never left Kit's, although his now took in her face, her breasts, her stomach, and just the top of her pubis. As if being a voyeur's object were just what she had longed for to add a bit of zest to her love-making, the woman leaned back on her outstretched arms and raised her knees up in the air. In this more exposed position, she supported her weight on hands and feet to either side of a pair of outstretched legs below her as she raised and lowered herself onto her partner over and over again, each time with increasing urgency.

Kit could now indeed see that her partner was not another woman.

The woman continued to stare at Kit, and he could feel the onset of a second erection. Without realizing the conspicuousness of what he was doing standing in front of a pair of open French doors, Kit reached inside his shorts and grasped his penis, then brought it out into plain view. In that same instant, the woman's eyes lowered almost imperceptibly and her mouth opened. She reached forward with one hand and grasped her partner's arm, then brought his hand to her mouth. Kit saw the mouth move, though he had no idea what she said. But in the next instant, her partner inserted three fingers into the woman's mouth, and she moved her head on those fingers to the same rhythm she moved her body up and down on her partner's body. Her mouth remained fixed on her partner's hand; her eyes, however, on Kit's hand.

The woman lurched violently forward on her partner. Kit saw two arms encircle her tightly. At the same instant, the pair of previously passive legs beneath her bent at the knee. The man's thighs slammed up against the woman's buttocks, and he pushed his pelvis up and into a locked position with hers.

Kit felt no compunction at having witnessed the moment of a simultaneous climax, even if he wasn't a part of it. However, he now had his own excitement to deal with and turned back into the bedroom. Daneka still slept.

Kit walked to the foot of the bed in order to better view and admire her sleeping body. He shook his head, not knowing or even being able to fathom that he would ever tire of looking at it, of touching it, of making love to it. He leaned over, reached up, took hold of her panties, and gently pulled them down and off. His action was enough to stir Daneka, though not enough to wake her. He raised the panties to his nose and sniffed. They contained the evidence of both of them, though it was only her smell he sought. When he found it, he closed his eyes and inhaled.

He then dropped her panties to the floor, gently pushed her legs apart and climbed on top. She was still wet from their earlier love-making, and he entered her easily. As if by instinct—Kit could not yet tell whether she was fully conscious—Daneka raised her legs and encircled his back with them. It was only when she also put her arms around his neck that he knew she was indeed awake.

Whether it was France, the scene he had just witnessed, the time of day and softness of the light, the smell and sounds of Daneka—or some combination of all of these—Kit couldn't have said. All he knew at this moment was that he cared deeply about this woman he was making love to. He dared not yet speak the words, but he certainly felt them. He knew it was only a matter of time until they would find their way from his lips to her ear, this ear into which he breathed, and on which he began to nibble. In return, she made soft cooing sounds and moved her hips below his in perfect syncopation.

They were finding a rhythm together—a lovers' rhythm—and while it might occasionally, even frequently, result in exquisite orgasms for both of them, it would inevitably result in that other thing Kit was not yet ready to openly declare and which had, up until now, been entirely foreign to Daneka. She, however, also now felt it. The resulting confusion between her brain and her body resulted in the predictable—and she began to cry.

With his lips on her ear, Kit felt rather than heard the first, warm tears as they slid down her cheek and onto his. He knew they couldn't possibly be tears of sadness—not at this moment, not in this pool of sensation in which they were both swimming. He maintained the tempo of his love-making, and she reciprocated to every thrust with one of her own. If lust was the fuel of passion, then love—and especially incipient love—was both bellows and damper. As they moved together towards an inevitable climax, Daneka's tears began to flow in a steady stream as she no longer attempted to muffle the sound of her ecstatic weeping. The brute joy of it produced a similar reaction in Kit, and he sensed tears welling up in his own eyes at the same moment. When, a few moments later, they both came, the climax was as much in their heads as between their legs. He put his mouth on hers, and she embraced him with all the strength she possessed. The sheer physical force and pressure of one upon the other spoke the words neither was yet prepared to say.

Thirty minutes later, they both still lay side by side in a tight embrace. The room was dark and filled with evening sounds. They could've remained in that same position until some dire necessity would've reminded them that life did, unfortunately, consist of more than love-making. It was consequently not their will, but the grumbling of their stomachs that signaled to them that there were things to do in Paris other than make love. Daneka was the first to speak, albeit barely above a whisper.

"How about a shower and dinner, darling?"

Kit smiled down at her. "You're on."

They both climbed languorously out of bed and walked to the bathroom. Kit started the water running while Daneka sat down easily and unselfconsciously on the bidet. Kit stepped in behind the curtain—and Daneka, satisfied with her ablutions, then stepped in behind him. For the next fifteen minutes, they ran the water as hot as either of them could stand while they soaped and shampooed each other.

There were more kisses, of course, but no more erections.

When they finally turned off the water and stepped out into the steam-filled bathroom, Daneka regarded the skin of her arms and hands—and noticed, with some consternation, how much older they looked than Kit's. As he towel-dried her from behind, then kissed her shoulders, back and buttocks, then moved down towards her ankles and feet, he was entirely unmindful of the fact. He adored her—quite simply *adored* her.

Kit tenderly and lovingly moved the towel up her ankles and calves to the insides of her knees and then thighs as she obligingly opened her legs. Just as she thought he was finished, she prepared to return the favor. However, she suddenly felt two hands on her, felt them push her buttocks apart, felt warm breath, then a mouth, then a tongue in an area of her body entirely unused to any such sensations.

"Sweet Jesus," she whispered. "The man is insatiable."

She had been quite prepared to finish drying off, get dressed, step outside and find a restaurant, then settle down to dinner and pleasant conversation. Instead, she found herself overwhelmed by a desire she'd not experienced before in a part of her body that had never been part of her consensual sexual repertoire. She couldn't resist the impulse. Unprompted, she spread her legs further, then leaned down and placed her hands on the sink to support the weight of her upper body.

Her mind went blank as she felt Kit's tongue slip into and out of her anus, slide along the length of her perineum and then enter her vagina from the rear. Some of these were nerves that had never been touched except for purposes of hygiene—and then, the touching of them had been her own and quite disinterested. She could not have believed there was yet enough strength left in her body to respond, or that the response would bring further wetness with it. Consequently, her body surprised even her.

She bent over further, as low as she could, and pushed herself up on her toes. Kit reacted as would any male and increased the pace of his tongue thrusts. The accumulation of his saliva and her own natural wetness increased from a slow drip to a steady trickle. Kit swiveled around underneath and put his mouth up against her, then spread her lips with his lips. The tip of his nose nuzzled against her clitoris. Now supporting her upper-body weight against the sink with her chest rather than with her hands, she reached down to either side of it and pulled his head up hard against her.

Her orgasm was long and liquid. The bathroom was filled with the mixed sounds of her barely muffled scream and his lapping sounds as she came into his open mouth. Her orgasm wouldn't stop, but rolled on wave after wave and surge after surge. She reached down and around to his throat and felt the motions of his neck muscles as he swallowed. She thought her climax might know no end, and her legs began to tremble with the exertion of it.

Finally, of course, it did. Her signal, to both of them, was a low, guttural "Oh, God!"

As she pushed back away from the sink and off her toes, she looked down. Kit looked back at her, squeezed into the plumbing like an awkward, but deliriously happy puppy whose chin was a bright red from their mutual exertions.

"So?" he asked as he raised his eyebrows and smiled.

Daneka dropped to her knees and squeezed her arms in through the plumbing and around him. Neither seemed to notice that two rather large bodies were scrunched up together in an impossibly small space and in imminent danger of banging heads and other hard parts against some rather unforgiving lead pipes and porcelain.

"Oh, my darling, my darling, my darling! My love."

She'd said it before either of them could check the impulse. They'd entered new territory and couldn't go back—and both of them realized it in the same instant. It was not *the* three-word declaration, of course. But she'd used the most important word—and now, only the subject and object were missing.

Kit would not be greedy and demand more—not for a while, at least. For the moment, he was ecstatic. And Daneka—in her own way—was, too.

Chapter 23

The next two nights and all of the space in between were filled with bliss: the bliss of young and crazy love; the bliss of sensual delights to their eyes, ears, nose and stomachs; the quiet bliss of just lying or walking side by side. Something in each of them knew that what they were experiencing was a true *folie-à-deux*—but this, after all, was France. Where better to fall under the spell of their own lovesick insanity than in the country whose language had given the world such a singularly apt expression for it?

When they packed their bags Monday morning and headed back out to the airport, it was not entirely without regret for the loss of this first, fresh bloom. They might never again recapture it, but at least they'd had it. Whatever else might befall them in the coming weeks, months and years, they, too, would be able to say: "We'll always have Paris."

As the plane lifted off the ground through a thin fog, both Daneka and Kit looked out over the city with something already bordering on nostalgia. And yet, they each privately knew that other adventures lay before them. In just over two and a half hours, they'd be in Lisbon. From there, by rental car, they'd descend along the coast to the most southwesterly point of all Europe, the Cabo de São Vicente, in the Algarve. Daneka had already done her research from New York; had wanted a place they could have to themselves; had found one and booked it: Villa Sol. With its swimming pool and view of the sea—not to mention a restaurant or two within walking distance—she figured they'd know how to spend their time in agreeable pursuits.

As the plane began to level off high over French soil, Daneka and Kit settled in for the ride. Daneka looked around and noticed that most of their fellow passengers were businesspeople merely en route from someplace to someplace else, with probably little more on their minds than making a deal and heading back home. Were it not for this man and this brief interlude, she knew she'd merely be one of them. These businesspeople were each in their own separate universes—and, at this moment, theirs had nothing to do with hers.

As she contemplated her happiness, a flight attendant approached on her way to the rear of the cabin. She first looked—then smiled—at Daneka as she continued her journey aft. Daneka took the woman's smile as an invitation to request a favor.

"*Mademoiselle, cela vous importerait de me descendre une couverture?*" ("Would you mind passing me a blanket?")

"*Mais pas du tout, Madame.*" The flight attendant promptly opened the overhead bin and took out a blanket. "*Aussi un oreiller?*" ("Not at all. Also a pillow?")

"*Non, merci. La couverture me suffit.* She looked once at Kit, then back up at the attendant and smiled conspiratorially. *J'ai déjà mon propre oreiller,*" she said, looking back at Kit. ("No thanks. A blanket's fine. I already have a pillow.")

The attendant handed her the blanket with a barely perceptible smile. "*Je vois bien.*" ("Yes, I see.")

"*Merci, Mademoiselle.*"

"*Pas de quoi, Madame.*" ("You're welcome, Madame.")

And then to Kit, "I think I'll take a little snooze, darling. 'Mind if I use your lap?"

Kit was surprised. They'd only just crawled out of bed an hour and a half earlier. But he was only too happy to oblige.

Daneka kicked off her shoes, spread the blanket over her and put her head down on Kit's lap. She pulled the blanket up to her chin so that only her head was visible, then slid her hand over Kit's thigh and let it come to rest on his crotch. At the same time, she turned her head to look at him, smiled mischievously, and ran her tongue over her lips. Then, like a spirited child up for a game of hide-and-seek, she snapped the blanket over her head.

Kit leaned his head back, then closed his eyes and reveled in the sensation of Daneka's hand. He couldn't suppress a chuckle when he felt himself responding to her touch. The chuckle turned into an audible laugh when he heard Daneka's muffled voice from beneath the blanket.

"Oh, dear *me*! What have we *here?*"

He swallowed his laugh, however, when he felt her hand reach up to his belt buckle, which she unfastened with ease. He gulped when he felt that same hand take hold of his zipper and pull it down in one easy motion. And he felt the tingle of minor panic when he realized she was reaching into his shorts.

The next thing he felt was Daneka's lips. The only thing keeping him from drifting off at that moment into his own quite separate universe was the tingle of panic. He looked up and saw a flight attendant moving down the aisle with a drink cart. He calculated, at her present dispatch, that it would be no more than a minute or two before she'd be parallel with him and this blanketed mound in his lap.

This may be Air France, Kit thought to himself. *But even Air France has limits.* He looked down at his lap and saw the outline of Daneka's head bobbing up and down under the blanket. He decided in favor of camouflage and quickly lowered his tray-table. He looked down again. The table indeed covered the bobbing blanket, but was, itself, bobbing. He thought maybe a magazine would help and picked one up. It didn't. It simply became another link in the chain of bobbers. Daneka's head had its own motor, and that motor couldn't be stopped. At the same time, the flight attendant had *her* own motor, and it, too, couldn't be stopped. Kit foresaw a collision of wills, and he was sitting right at the point of impact. He froze. The flight attendant pulled up alongside him while his tray-table and magazine continued to bob.

"*Vous désirez quelque chose à boire, Monsieur?*" she asked with perfect French aplomb. ("Would you like something to drink?")

"*Eh bien, oui,*" Kit answered with the most serious tone of nonchalance he could muster. "*Du café, s'il vous plaît. Et un jus d'orange.*" ("Yes, please. Coffee and an orange juice.")

"*Volontiers, Monsieur,*" ("Very well.") the flight attendant answered with no change in tone or expression. The bobbing continued unabated. Kit wondered where she would put the coffee and orange juice, and whether she would finally notice, possibly comment upon, the peculiar air turbulence that had attached itself to Kit's tray-table.

Instead, she poured the coffee into a cup and placed it on her drink cart. She next pulled out a plastic glass and a pitcher of orange juice, then filled the glass and put it down next to the cup.

Without comment or pause, she reached in over Kit and lowered Daneka's tray-table. The flight attendant was close enough that Kit could smell not only her perfume, but also some of her perspiration. She stood back up, picked up the coffee and orange juice, and put them down on Daneka's tray. Kit's tray continued its satanic bob.

Just as Kit thought the ordeal was over, the flight attendant reached under her service cart and pulled out a plastic flute and a split of champagne. In what seemed like one quick motion, she removed the wire and wrapper and popped the cork. She placed bottle and flute on Daneka's tray-table alongside his coffee and orange juice.

With no variation in tone, the flight attendant looked at Kit. *"Pour Madame. Avec nos compliments."* ("For Madame—with our compliments.") She then turned her attention to the passengers opposite Kit and Daneka's seats and proceeded with the same battery of questions.

When they arrived at the airport in Lisbon two hours and thirty-five minutes later, Daneka was indeed asleep, but upright in her seat and with the most self-satisfied of smiles on her lips. She still held an empty champagne flute in her hand, but all other evidence of a late-morning refreshment had long since been removed. The first bump on the tarmac awakened her.

She took one glance out the window, smiled, and then turned to Kit. "Portugal! Be a sweet man-of-war and give me some of your best poison."

Without wasting a word, Kit reached down inside her blouse and grabbed a breast. Daneka's mouth was on his as she answered with an inarticulate growl whose meaning, however, was clear to both of them. After only two or three passes with the tip of his finger, her nipple began to respond, while her low growl conveyed a clear message of appreciation. She took her mouth from his and moved it up to his ear. At the same time, she opened her eyes and caught an equally appreciative stare from across the aisle. *These French,* she thought to herself. *They love to watch almost as much as they love to do.*

Although she could easily have put an end to their very public display, she resolved to enlarge it. With perfect calculation of the consequences, she threw back her shoulders so that a button popped off her blouse and a breast sprang into view. At the same time, she reached down into Kit's pants. The fit was tight, but he instantly, reflexively, sucked in his stomach. Her mouth at Kit's ear, she whispered just loud enough for her neighbor across the aisle to hear.

"How about a little fucky-fucky?"

Kit had been assaulted from too many angles at once to know how to react appropriately. Even if he didn't share Daneka's precise knowledge of the voyeur across the aisle, he was nonetheless no exhibitionist. That Daneka's breast was on display sent the equivalent of fire alarms to his brain. Those alarms quickly put an end to his momentary arousal, and his hands did the rest to return both Daneka and himself to the *status quo ante*.

"Where, in God's name, did *that* come from?" he asked, as much amused as horrified at the inventiveness of her vocabulary.

"Oh, it's not *mine*, darling. I just read it. Last week—in a story I found in *Granta*, by a Ms. Erthal, or Erdview... Erdal, that was it! Jenny Erdal. Called 'Tiger's Ghost'."

"You read *Granta?*" Kit asked, visibly amazed.

"But of *course*, darling. How else am I going to increase my word power?" Daneka said chuckling to herself as she slipped back into her seat and rearranged her blouse less one critical button. The chuckle became an audible laugh as she looked up at Kit, whose blush was almost fire-engine red.

"My *terribly* demure darling," she whispered as she angled her head and mouth back up to nibble at his ear. "But you know something? I happen to disagree with Ms. Erdal on one critical point. I, for one, don't believe for an instant that 'discretion is the better part of ardor'."

She looked over at her erstwhile spectator and noticed that he, while appearing to study the air traffic scene outside his window, had both hands in his lap—as if attempting to keep quiet and firmly in check the happy testament to his voyeurism. *Boys will be boys*, she thought to herself. *Silly little boys. With their even sillier, predictable little toys.*

As their plane taxied to its gate, Daneka and Kit sat together, quiet arm in quiet arm. Kit's blush gradually transmuted into normal flesh tones as his thoughts turned to disembarking, finding luggage, getting a rental car and driving down the coast.

Daneka's thoughts, however, stayed momentarily with this man—this Kit immediately beside her—and with the seemingly unending source of pleasure he'd become in the space of only a few weeks. As she then considered how she, at her age, was still apparently as much a source of pleasure to him, she also felt the pride of her sex. It was wonderful to be a woman. To be able, with the exposure of a body part, not only to hold one man entirely captive, but to arouse the feral desire of another in the same instant. She decided in that instant to try again.

"Wanna coït?"

Kit looked at her and blinked.

"Wanna coït with a poet?"

He *had* understood her correctly. What a word! He'd never heard it before.

"Wanna coït with a poet, man, and bank some doh re ME?"

She was *too* much, Kit thought. He looked at her—bemused by this jewel of a woman who had not only lips to die for, but killer words at their behest. *An empress of blow-jobs with a brain,* he thought to himself. *There's something downright* Baudelairean *about her. But why does that sound so familiar?* he wondered—and continued thinking.

Daneka, believing she'd just been rebuffed, allowed her thoughts to stray beyond her immediate lover. She began to dissociate and wonder which of her body parts and available orifices could hold a number of men captive at any one time and in a way that would render her literally—if not præternaturally— fulfilled. She closed her eyes and drifted off into a contemplation of a score of naked bodies—under, over, at either end of her, writhing like rude snakes in competition for her attention, for her ministrations, for a mere touch of her fingers, her lips, her hair to bring them to—and hold them in—a state of excruciating suspense. And then to watch those for whom she had not enough hands or lips or hair, out of impatience or brute lust, finish off the matter in their own way. This, as they watched her being taken by those more fortunate and aggressive participants who might actively and simultaneously engage both hands and the three portals in which intercourse with her was physically possible.

She noted the sensation between her legs—like tensely roving fingers—as she allowed herself the crude calculation of how many she could actually take on at once. She marveled not only that she could feel what she imagined was real love for this man next to her, but—in the same instant—could count the number of penises or fingers or lips having simultaneous commerce with her mouth, her vagina, her anus. It was not guilt or remorse that caused what felt like an electrical short-circuit to her brain, but rather the sheer overload of inputs as she visualized all of them thrusting vigorously and selfishly to fill her. At the same time, she felt others' hands on her breasts, her thighs, her stomach—grabbing, kneading, squeezing, caressing wherever there was a swath of skin not already occupied by some other hand or mouth or organ of penetration.

And then, there were the spectators—the less fortunate ones who could only watch, but who were an additional gift of pleasure. Her own eyes, she knew, would be wide open watching them as they watched her and her several partners. She would watch these second-tier participants, men and women both, masturbate alone or with each other as all eyes were trained on her body, this object of collective pursuit and conquest. She would only too happily allow the men to cover her with their ejaculate and the women to spread their legs and flush their passions out on her legs, her breasts, her face. Yes, even that. Once the men had emptied themselves onto her, she would welcome the women and their more delicate—if *equally* hungry—lust. She could see a woman's mouth between her legs, licking and swallowing the semen of however many men might have chosen to leave it there. She'd allow another to take her clitoris between her lips. A third to straddle her own face and nose and eyes with a ravenous cunt.

As she felt the momentum of this fantasy carry her slowly to the brink, she realized her own silent vocabulary had easily accepted a cruder, pornographic jargon for which Anglo-Saxon, she felt, was the perfect vehicle. In her mind, she was fucking—and the givers as well as the recipients of that crude passion were cunts, tongue-fucking cunts, hers no less than theirs.

She'd lost track of the number of bodies and organs she'd just entertained when she felt the shudder of her own orgasm. She kept it in silence, however, as one of the flight attendants spoke up over the intercom and welcomed them all to Lisbon.

Kit, she noticed, was ignorant of any of what had just occurred. Her former spectator was also seemingly preoccupied with gathering his belongings in preparation to disembark. She allowed herself a small smile of private knowledge and gave Kit a peck on the cheek. Within a matter of minutes, both of them were calmly out of their seats and standing in line to exit the plane. As they made their way forward, they came abreast of the flight attendant who'd first served them, and who now smiled in a cordial French way.

"*Au revoir, Monsieur, 'dame. Bon séjour au Portugal.*" ("Goodbye, Sir, Madame. Have a pleasant stay in Portugal.")

"*Merci, Mademoiselle. Et bon retour à Paris,*" Kit offered. ("Thank you, Miss. Have a pleasant trip back to Paris.")

"*Merci bien,*" Daneka said simply as she prepared to exit. She then thought again, paused, looked into the attendant's eyes and said with just the hint of a twinkle in her own:

"*C'était un voyage sans pareil.*" ("That was a trip without equal.")

The attendant didn't miss a beat. As she leaned down to give Daneka the French kiss on both cheeks customarily reserved for close friends and family, she said just above a whisper: "*Pour nous* toutes, *Madame, je vous assure. Pour nous* toutes.*" ("For *all* of us [females], I assure you.") Suddenly, Daneka knew: she'd made a spectacle of herself—not just for this one attendant, but for all of the female attendants. None of them could've known, of course, about the additional male spectator—not to mention the myriad of bodies, both male and female, she'd enjoyed in her fantasy. And yet, a blush of shame was about as likely to color her face at this moment as it might a baby's bottom upon its mother's discovery of a few naughty nuggets in that same baby's nappy.

In short, there was none.

Chapter 24

It took them only minutes to retrieve their luggage, find the car rental agency, then get to their car and negotiate their way to the airport exit. As Lisbon was a port city, their journey would be a coastal drive all the way down to Cabo de São Vicente. The weather was perfect as they set out—still relatively cool even by Mediterranean standards. Daneka opened a road map.

"I figure about two, two and a half hours at most. We should be there by late afternoon. But maybe still early enough for a little swim."

Kit squeezed her hand. "You and a pool. It sounds positively primordial!"

Schools were still in session throughout Europe—and so, vacationers were relatively few. In another few weeks, Daneka knew, hoards of Scandinavians and Germans would descend upon Iberia and head straight out to one of several of the more popular coasts of Spain or Portugal. By the end of July, traffic on the peninsula would be bumper-to-bumper on roads like this one. But today, most of the traffic was commercial—and as Portugal was not precisely an economic powerhouse, 'commercial' meant negligible.

Almost exactly two and a half hours later, Kit and Daneka saw the first indication that they'd arrived at their destination. In Portugal's traditional red and green colors, a sign at the outskirts of a tiny seaside village announced Cabo de São Vicente. The view out over the Atlantic was breathtaking. They stopped their car alongside the road just long enough to admire it and to allow Daneka to determine from her own notes the most direct route to their villa.

It was only a matter of minutes before they found Villa Sol. Small by the standards of most European villas—but with a well-manicured lawn—it was certainly adequate for two guests. They parked their car and walked to the front door. The owners had sent instructions on the location of the house-key, and Daneka looked in the appointed spot. She found it and unlocked the front door—and the two of them stepped in.

The villa's interior was as tastefully laid out as the surrounding grounds. Stone floors were set off on a couple of different levels, while rooms were partitioned by solid stone walls with heavy wood baseboards and door frames. The one concession to modernity was the rear wall, which had been replaced with sliding glass doors leading out to an oval-shaped pool.

"Let me go and get the luggage," Kit offered. In the meantime, Daneka, transfixed by the view of the pool and the ocean beyond, opened the glass doors and stepped out. The pool basin had been lined with what must've been several thousand hand-painted tiles. Steps descended down into the pool at one end. Daneka removed her shoes and walked to them. She sat down on the edge of the pool and tested the water with her toes. The temperature was just a few degrees cooler than body temperature. It was simply too tempting.

She was out of her clothes in seconds and into the water. After several days on dry land, the return to a world of water and liquid warmth touching every pore felt like a return to the womb. She closed her eyes and submerged her head so that even the whisper of sea breezes was turned to silence. She concentrated on nothingness, on the absence of all external stimuli except for the caress of the water. After almost a full minute, and when she could no longer hold her breath, she broke the surface of the water and inhaled. She then opened her eyes and wrung the water out of her hair as she refocused on her immediate surroundings.

Kit was standing at the side of the pool smiling as he looked down at his water nymph.

"It, and you, look lovely!" His smile earned a smile in return.

"Darling, why don't you come in? Just leave your clothes there next to mine and come right in." Daneka's suggestion sounded more like a demand than a mere invitation. When Kit didn't immediately respond, she barked in mock anger: "*Subito!*" ("Now!")

Kit stepped out of his clothes and, rather than wade into the water as Daneka had done, dove straight in. He swam around a bit beneath the surface, then approached her from the front and suggested with a nudge to both ankles that he wanted her to open her legs. She obliged and he swam through. When he re-surfaced immediately behind her, he placed his arms on hers and raised them to encircle his neck. Standing in direct contact with her from shoulders to toes, he slowly slid his hands down her cheeks and neck, then down and around her shoulder blades until they met in front and found her breasts.

Daneka bent her head back, searching for Kit's lips. As he gently pinched her nipples, she slid her tongue into his mouth.

Daneka responded eagerly as Kit began to massage her breasts. Starting at the top, he dragged just the tips of his fingers down and over her nipples, then cupped each breast from underneath and gave it a generous massage. He repeated the maneuver until Daneka's chest was heaving, her breasts reaching out to find his hands, her breath hot, honey-sweet— and like a steam-belching locomotive leading a train of kisses now smothering his face.

Kit gently pulled her up, and Daneka placed her feet on his. He then walked both of them to the edge of the pool facing out over the Atlantic.

"Open your eyes, darling," he whispered into her ear.

She did as he'd asked. What they both saw would have impressed even John Turner. The sun was just dipping into the Atlantic at the western horizon. The optical distortion that normally occurs at just this instant—and so diminishes the sun's brilliance as it sets into the ocean—was absent. Kit and Daneka watched it sink like a golden plumb directly into the water. At the same time, the sky overhead gradually changed from orange to bright red—like the petals of an exotic orchid folding back on themselves.

The air already had something of a nip to it, but the fire in the sky and the fire between the two of them made the pool water feel like soup. With Kit's chest still against her back, Daneka pushed up on her toes and reached around to Kit's erection, which she felt sliding down the rift of her buttocks as she pushed up. She took him with one hand and guided him down between her legs and inside her. She then moved the same hand back up behind his neck and joined it to the other to make a necklace of soft flesh. She liked this gentle bondage. She liked being "tied" to his neck and, at the same time, caught between his body and the wall of the pool—and so, rendered captive. Kit did the lifting from behind her, and she accommodated by pushing up on her toes and then settling back down again in an easy *pas de deux*. Little ripples spread out from them across the surface of the pool. Larger ripples of red reached out overhead and gathered the clouds as if plucking tufts of cotton long enough to saturate them with crimson dye, only to spring them free again.

When they finally came, they came quietly—a whispered benediction to a sun now chanting a last, equally quiet song as it sank far out over the western horizon.

Chapter 25

I t was early evening as Kit and Daneka walked along an unpaved road into the village. Occasionally passing other couples or lone pedestrians along the way, they would offer a nod and a smile in exchange for a *"Boa noite"*—*a very fair exchange indeed*, Kit thought. Although Kit didn't know a word of Portuguese, he'd figured he could make do with Spanish if necessary. But he also knew they were at the mercy of the locals—and of English or of some other *lingua franca*—for any serious conversation or assistance. In any case, the spontaneous greetings and friendliness of these evening strollers were a welcome change from New York, and Kit and Daneka slipped easily into that frame of mind peculiar to more experienced world travelers: they simply observed—and adapted their behavior to that of the locals.

The first restaurant that came into view was a small, quiet, homey-looking affair and, as Kit and Daneka were delightfully downwind from it, suggested its presence and its *raison d'être* already from far off.

They entered and waited for a moment just inside the doorway, but no one greeted them. After a short delay, they realized they were supposed to seat themselves—and so, continued into the dining area to find a table. There were plenty—but all of them empty. Kit and Daneka exchanged glances. Then Daneka peeked around a corner and motioned to Kit with an index finger. The restaurant was in fact quite full, although everyone was out in the garden where the mood was quietly celebratory, the view spectacular.

As Kit and Daneka stepped outside, they were greeted by a hostess.

"Boa noite."

"Muy buenas," Kit answered. *"Somos dos para cenar, por favor."* ("Two for dinner, please.")

The hostess smiled and nodded, picked up two menus and started to walk off among the tables. As soon as she realized that Kit and Daneka weren't following, she turned and beckoned to them from a distance. *"Por favor."* Smiles and hand gestures had an easy and certain way of leaping over language barriers. In this case, it further helped that the Portuguese and Spanish expressions were identical. Kit and Daneka walked forward and caught up with their hostess. As she was seating them, Kit took the initiative.

"Una carta de vinos, por favor." ("A wine list, please.") The hostess nodded assent and returned moments later with the wine menu. *"Gracias, Señorita,"* Kit offered as she handed him a thick leather book.

"De nada," she answered, and Kit wondered which language she was answering in. In any case, it was working. He was quite pleased with his ability to communicate up to this point, and he consequently made no effort to repress a little smile of self-satisfaction.

Daneka noticed it immediately. *"¡Vaya caballero!"* ("What a gentleman!") she said, echoing Kit's smile with her own.

"Well, darling, if you *must* know—" Kit let his thought trail off before getting himself into something too deep to get out of quickly and easily. Europe was, after all, Daneka's turf, and he had no intention of challenging her for domain. That said, she seemed to be taking it all quietly in stride, and he was grateful for the indirect compliment.

"And how do you know that I don't speak fluent Portuguese?" she asked without changing the contours of her smile.

"Do you?"

"Maybe. In any case, my Spanish is passable."

"Is it?"

"Of course. How do you think Estrella and I communicate?"

"In Spanish?"

"In *Spanglish*."

"I noticed."

"You did? When?"

"No, I mean I noticed that Estrella's English wasn't, well—"

"I'm sure it's at *least* as good as your Spanish." Kit's smile, hardly smug to begin with, evanesced on the spot. He wondered whether Daneka's vanity had been piqued, or whether she was simply coming to her housekeeper's defense.

"Why do you say that?" he asked.

Daneka laid a comforting hand on Kit's arm. "Just teasing, darling. Your Spanish is really quite impressive. If I were wearing a blindfold, you could easily have fooled me. I'm sure I would've taken you for a native."

Kit was eager to restore the peace. "Go ahead! Hit me with your best *Danglish*."

Daneka guffawed. "Oh, I don't really know that any such thing exists. Danes are much too clever—or perhaps just too self-conscious—for that kind of thing, you know. That's why I advised you the other day not to be dis*dane*ful. It can backfire, darling."

"Really? How?"

"Well, we may be clever and self-conscious. We can also be vicious and vengeful."

Now it was Kit's turn to reach out and put a comforting hand on *Daneka's* arm. "Certainly not *you*," he said in a tone that was half-question, half-declaration, but lacking any hint of clear conviction.

"And worst of all, we can be silent."

"Silent?"

"Uh-huh. It's a Scandinavian thing, that silence. Like ice. Silence that just freezes you out."

"Silence is golden." Kit sounded like a kid. All hint of a former smile abruptly dropped from Daneka's face.

"Not Nordic silence." Suddenly, it was Kit whose expression turned from gently mocking to deadly serious. "Nordic silence is silver, not golden," she continued. "It's like icicles, but without the tinkle. It can last the length of a winter—of a Scandinavian winter. And be just as dark. Or worse—." The conversation was abruptly halted by the arrival of their waiter.

"Boa noite, Senhores. Querem fazer o vosso pedido?" ("Good evening, Sir, Madame. Would you like to order?")

Kit found himself abruptly out of his league, and his face showed it. *"¿Entiende Usted el español, Señor?* ("Do you, Sir, understand Spanish?")

"Naturalmente, Senhor!" ("But of course!")

He was back in the game. *¡Bueno. Pues en este caso, sí, Señor. Estamos listos."* ("Good. In that case, we're ready.") He smiled tentatively at Daneka, hoping he'd not already lost the minor hero status he felt he'd acquired only moments earlier. "Shall I order for you, darling?"

Daneka was suddenly all toothy smile as she handed him her menu. "Sure, *caballero*."

Kit looked carefully at his dinner menu, first under *Aperitivos* and then under *Pratos principais*. The words describing most of the food items looked reasonably familiar. He could wing this and come out of it feeling like a champ. He promptly ordered two items from the "Appetizers" and two from the "Main Course" selections. Then he turned his attention to the wine menu. *Vinho branco* was certainly easy enough to figure out, and *vinho tinto* was almost identical to the Spanish.

"Red or white, darling?"

"White for me, please."

"*Una botella de*—" and here Kit decided to forego the risk of a disastrous pronunciation—and so, simply pointed at the name of the wine he wanted: *Paço de Teixeiró*. The waiter nodded to him with a solemnity Kit chose to interpret as appreciation of his choice.

It was done—as easy as that. Not only had he survived the ordeal; he was relatively certain that both he and Daneka would thoroughly enjoy his selections.

Life was good. Life was abundant. Daneka was smiling—at him, certainly, but also just on principle. The Atlantic opened wide and blue before them. Even the moon was full. No one could've scripted a better scene. And no one, he thought to himself, could've populated that scene with company more to his liking.

He had her, of course, and that would've been enough under any circumstances. But in addition to her, he noticed the other guests were all quietly talking or laughing among themselves. The ceramic sibilance of plates passing over plates on their way to tables blended well with the sibilance of the Portuguese language. The result was euphony. Waiters and an occasional waitress wove in and out of their tables like busy, efficient bees—never loud or unruly, never banging plates or shouting orders to one another; just a pleasant hum of activity and an equally pleasant hum of conversation. He looked at Daneka and then took both of her hands into his and kissed them lightly. As he did so, she looked back at him.

"*Mi caballero. Mi señor.*" she whispered.

Chapter 26

Following a dinner over which they discussed Daneka's work, Kit's work, the state of the world in general, and the state of *their* world in particular, Kit decided to order a couple of glasses of Port and some sliced pears, Stilton and walnuts. He knew the wine wouldn't be a problem, as the waiter would likely bring out a selection for him to choose from, and the labels would, of course, be printed in English. He could ask for the cheese by name—and so, that wouldn't be a problem either. But pears and walnuts? He hoped that Spanish and Portuguese had similar-sounding words for the same thing. If not, he'd have to resort to pen, paper and a sketch. He motioned to the waiter.

"Sim, Senhor?" ("Yes, Sir?")

"¿Le importaría traernos una selección de Portos, por favor?" ("Would you mind bringing us a selection of ports?")

"Concerteza, Senhor." ("But of course, Sir.")

"¿Y tendrían Ustedes unas peras y unas nueces, también un pedazo de queso? ¿Tienen por casualidad Stilton?" ("And would you happen to have some pears, nuts and a piece of cheese? Stilton by chance?")

"Pois claro, Senhor." ("But of course, Sir.")

Once again, Kit believed he'd successfully negotiated his way out of a ticklish situation and was secretly thankful for the similarity between the two languages.

When their waiter returned a few moments later pushing a wine cart and carrying a plate of sliced pears, a plate of walnuts and a third plate of Stilton, Kit was delighted. With a glance, Daneka gave him the equivalent of a pat on the back. Kit selected a sweet white for her, a *Lagrima*, and a Premium Rachel for himself. Once the waiter had poured for both of them, Kit raised his glass. Daneka, in turn, raised hers to meet it.

Looking at her wine and remembering its classification, he offered: "Let there never be tears of sorrow between us. Only of joy."

She understood perfectly. "Never," she repeated, though Kit noted the solemnity of her one-word rejoinder.

He looked hard into Daneka's eyes to try to ascertain for himself whether she'd grasped the intent of his toast. At the same time, he looked for some indication of the sincerity of her confirmation. She didn't flinch. Nor, however, did she spend a further word or gesture to reinforce that confirmation.

Kit had registered a few minutes earlier both the sights and sounds of some activity at the far end of the garden. As he shifted his gaze from Daneka to focus on it, he realized that they were about to be entertained. He counted a trio of musicians as well as a guitar and a couple of other string instruments he couldn't readily identify, but which resembled mandolins or citterns. Kit decided to risk demonstrating his ignorance and asked the waiter if they were in fact mandolins. The waiter corrected him without even a hint of condescension, but rather with obvious admiration and gratitude for a non-native who could even be bothered to ask: he was looking not at mandolins, but at authentic Portuguese guitars.

As the three musicians began to fine-tune their instruments, Kit caught sight of the arrival of a marginally attractive dark-haired woman whom he guessed to be a singer. His guess proved correct. Judging from their dress, Kit surmised that the music would not be some kind of folkloric kitsch—and for that, he was thankful. His knowledge of Portuguese music didn't extend beyond *fados*. And even there, he was on rather shaky ground. He decided to wait and—he was fairly certain—be pleasantly surprised.

His reward came quickly. Apparently, the woman would sing without a microphone—but no matter given the small area of the garden. She signaled to the instrumentalists in their small troupe. They in turn signaled to each other, and the three commenced.

The first sounds came from the Portuguese guitar. A few plucked notes in isolation up and then back down the scale, followed by a strum, at which point the woman raised her head and opened her eyes and mouth. What came out was a sound Kit was sure he'd never heard. What he didn't know was that he'd never hear it again as he was hearing it now. Just as one can never step into the same body of water twice, one can almost never listen to the same piece of music a second time and feel it in precisely the same way.

Cheia de penas,
Cheia de penas me deito...

The din of conversation in the garden dropped like a stone as the guests sat up and fixed their eyes and ears on the singer. She was indeed singing a *fado*, and this woman was a clear mistress of the form. Kit felt the gooseflesh rise on his arms as the mandolin's first notes—then the woman's voice, and finally an unexpected tremolo—entered his ear.

At the same time, he suddenly felt the weight of Daneka's arm upon his arm, the warm breath of her mouth upon his ear, and a sweet cluster of familiar consonants upon that breath as she translated for him:

"Full of sorrow, full of sorrow, I now lie down…"

He looked at her for a moment in astonishment. She smiled demurely, then dropped her head at an angle that had once transfixed him like an arrow. She put a finger to his lips to stop him from stating the obvious. As the woman continued to sing, Daneka continued to translate.

E com mais penas
E com mais penas me levanto…
"And with a deeper sorrow still, I rise up again."

Kit suddenly became aware of a thread drawn tightly between the singer and Daneka. It seemed to him that the dark-haired woman's gaze was directed exclusively at Daneka, that she was holding her stare against all possible assault or interruption from the outside, and that she was singing each word as if it applied to Daneka and Daneka alone.

No meu peito
Já me ficou no meu peito
Este jeito
O jeito de querer tanto…
"In my heart, already in my heart, this sense of loving too much…"

The *fado* had evoked in him a jumble of raw, visual and aural sensations. Kit was hit by another as he felt something warm and wet drop upon his forearm. Daneka was unwittingly wrenching him back into her own reality and out of the tension this other woman had managed to establish between her voice and his ear. He looked at the spot on his arm and realized that the source of the warm and wet sensation was Daneka's eyes. A single tear had run down her cheek and dropped onto his forearm. Still, she continued to translate.

> *Desespero*
>
> *Tenho por meu desespero*
>
> *Dentro de mim*
>
> *Dentro de mim o castigo*
>
> *Eu não te quero*
>
> *Eu digo que não te quero*
>
> *E de noite*
>
> *De noite sonho contigo...*

"Despair. I carry this despair inside of me, as I also carry inside its punishment. I don't love you. I declare that I don't love you. But then at night, I dream of you."

> *Se considero*
>
> *Que um dia hei-de morrer*
>
> *No desepero*
>
> *Que tenho de te não ver*
>
> *Estendo o meu xaile*
>
> *Estendo o meu xaile no chão*
>
> *Estendo o meu xaile*
>
> *E deixo-me adormecer.*

"When I think that one day I, too, will have to die, I do so without regret, never to see you again. I lay my shawl upon the ground, and fall asleep upon it."

> *Se eu soubesse*
>
> *Se eu soubesse que morrendo*
>
> *Tu me havias*
>
> *Tu me havias de chorrar*
>
> *Por uma lágrima*

Por uma lágrima tua
Que alegría
Me deixaria matar.

**"If I knew that you would take me in exchange for a
single tear, how happily I would give you that tear—and
then die."**

No tears of sorrow between them—ever! was the supplication he'd uttered just minutes earlier—to which she'd responded with an affirmation. "Never," she'd said. And already, there was a flood of them.

What ever the grounds, what ever the justification, however *reasonable* her reaction to the music and to the singer, Daneka had been moved to tears. Kit, too, was moved, though not to tears. He was simply moved by the beauty of the sounds emanating from instruments and from one woman's throat.

However troubled by Daneka's tears, he preferred not to read more into this reaction than what he, himself, was feeling: a general melancholy.

He leaned over and softly kissed both of Daneka's eyes in an attempt to lift some of the burden of *her* melancholy. Instead, his effort resulted in the opposite. Between the music and Kit's gesture, it was as if someone, finally, had given her permission to do what she'd been aching to do all of her adult life—to cry, once again, like a child. She took Kit's hands into hers as if they were a well into which she could pour the contents of her eyes and heart, into which those same eyes and heart could scream their open-mouthed, but long-silent anguish. Still soundless, her tears nevertheless started to flow not in isolated droplets, but in rivulets.

Kit put his arms around her. She moved her head from his hands to his chest so as to muffle the sounds of her weeping. He tightened his embrace so as to quiet her convulsions. He realized these were merely stopgap measures—that the source of her pain was something he couldn't possibly touch this night, the next day, maybe ever. But he'd try. If necessary, he'd dedicate his life to finding that source and to helping her through and out of it. He'd already learned to love her in sex and in fun. Now, he realized, he was learning to love her in pain. And this was to him the most delicious love of all.

Chapter 27

The embrace helped—to give her the shoulder she craved at that moment and also to provide her with a shirt to absorb the flow of tears. When she finally looked up at him with wet eyes and a red nose after several minutes, she managed to squeeze out a smile. He squeezed one of his own back out in return.

"Daneka, darling, can we talk about this?" he asked. She allowed herself a couple of last sniffles. He put his hand inside his shirt, bunched some of the material together between thumb and index finger, then put fingers and material to her nose and nodded. "Go ahead. Blow."

With her nose firmly buried in his shirt, Daneka lifted her eyes and looked up into Kit's. He nodded again. She blew.

"Yes and no." Daneka chuckled self-mockingly. "What's that line from *Amazing Grace*? 'I was lost, but now I'm found'?" Kit put out a hand and began to caress the knuckle of one of her fingers with the tip of his own index finger.

"Tell me about the 'lost'," he urged, though with more of request in his voice than of command.

Daneka sighed. "I'm not a little girl anymore, Kit. You and I both know that. I've been around the horn a few times. You and I know that, too. I figured up until a few weeks ago that the last love boat had left port, that I'd missed my chance. Nature is fairly ruthless, you know, where women are concerned. We can keep on in the work world, of course. Or as mothers. At the very least, as providers of some kind of hearth and home to *someone*. But as viable and desirable egg-donors? As candidates for love and romance? Well, that's another story. Love and romance belong to young women. To women who carry fresh eggs, whose fertility is defined and on display in curves that rise and fall in all the right places.

"Men don't look at women of my age except for a raise or a hand-out—or sometimes, just a hand-job." Daneka chuckled again, but it was bile rather than boastfulness that drove the sound from her throat. Kit winced.

"I don't feel old. My desires are every bit as real as they were twenty years ago—maybe even more so. But I can't speak about those desires. I can't put them on a T-shirt and then walk around braless like some rude matinee marquee. Not at my age. I have to get my needs taken care of in some other way." Daneka paused and looked Kit in the eye. "At least I did until a few days ago. Now—?"

Her question, like her glance, hung in the air—as did the second half of the lyric: '…but now I'm found.' Kit wondered whether this was the moment to risk it all and pronounce the three words he'd been thinking almost since the moment they'd first sat knee to knee on two adjoining sofas. He decided it was. "Daneka, I—"

She missed the signal. "*Da quando amo, riesco ad indossare i miei anni: non sono piu' vecchia*," ("When in love, my age no longer shows") she murmured, seemingly out of some parallel universe in which she was traveling quite alone.

"Excuse me?" Kit ducked his head low.

"Nothing. Just something I read a couple of weeks ago inside the wrapper of a Perugina Baci."

"*Bacio.*"

"Huh?"

"You read it on the wrapper of a Perugina 'kiss,' right?"

"Right."

"Then it's one Perugina *bacio.*"

"No. Actually, Kit, it would be one '*bacio perugino*' if we wanted to be grammatically correct. But I was talking *bonbons.*" She glared at him, and it suddenly seemed as if the stars had lost all of their former luster.

Oh, fuck—? Kit floundered for a moment, then resorted to the only pair of words that had, historically, proved redemptive. "Forgive me," he said.

Daneka looked back at him, and the stars—at least in *her* eyes—slowly began to twinkle once again. "It all happened so fast—. I just don't know. You frighten me. *It* frightens me. I want it. I want you. But I don't know how much longer I can keep you."

It was once again Kit's turn to be knocked off balance. Was she being intentionally ambiguous? Did she mean "keep him" in the sense of hold on to him, maintain his interest and his exclusive attention? Did she mean "keep him" as a pet, as a plaything, as a *kept* man? Or did she mean "keep him" until her own interest necessarily dissipated, her own eye began to wander?

He knew the answer to the first and would've been only too eager to make a declaration of love, now and forever. The second possibility was one that had occurred to him and that had already begun to trouble him. He didn't know how he was going to be able to maintain a life-style that came naturally to her—and yet, he wasn't prepared to be kept by any woman, by any human being for that matter. It was simply not in his constitution to be kept.

The third possibility was the one that most troubled him—not just then, but from the start of their relationship, when he'd first seen how easily she could disappear for long stretches at a time. The same if he acted spontaneously—as he had once when he'd arrived at her apartment without appointment and, so far as he knew, with only a few seconds' prior announcement. There was, of course, also the matter of the telephone declaration he'd overheard the afternoon he came to get her for their trip out to JFK. What did it mean? To whom was it addressed? Who *now*, in his place, was sitting at home in front of a computer screen or walking the streets of New York in a daze, obsessing over this same woman? Whoever it was was competition. And yet, Kit didn't wish his same former predicament on anyone—even on a competitor.

"Darling, can we go?" Her question suggested he wouldn't get an answer—at least not now, not at this table. "*Garçom,*" ("Waiter,") she said just loud enough to be heard over the music of another *fado*. Their waiter promptly arrived—and Daneka, this time, addressed him in what sounded to Kit's ears like flawless Portuguese.

"*Sim, Senhora?*"

"*Podia-nos trazer a conta, por favor?*" ("Could you please bring us the check?") she asked, handing over her credit card at the same time.

"*Pois certamente, Senhora.*" ("But of course, Madame.")

"You could have told me, you know," Kit said sheepishly. You could have spared both of us the embarrassment."

"'Embarrassment?'" she asked. "*What* 'embarrassment?' You were doing just fine. I was very proud of you," she said as she reached out and gave Kit's cheek an affectionate pinch. "Nothing you do could ever embarrass me. Trust me. I know."

When their waiter returned with the check, she glanced at it, signed the credit card receipt, then handed the lot of pen, check and receipt back to him after having first torn off her copy and taken back her card. *"Muito obrigado, Senhor. Foi um prazer."* ("Thank you, Sir, very much. It was a pleasure.")

"Nós vê-los-emos outra vez, Senhores?" ("Will we see you again, Madame and Sir?")

"Naturalmente. Talvez já amanhã à noite." ("Surely. Perhaps already as early as tomorrow evening.") Kit and Daneka stood up at the same time. *"Boa noite, Senhor."*

"Boa noite, Senhores. Até amanhã." ("Until tomorrow, then.")

They made their way to the front door and past the hostess, who likewise wished them a pleasant evening. When they walked out of the restaurant, they were greeted by an unobstructed canopy of stars, the equivalent of which Kit, at least, had never seen. He offered his hand, and Daneka took it. They then walked off into darkness, their footpath made clear to them only by moonlight—while their other path, Kit thought to himself—the path of their future—was illuminated by much weaker starlight.

Chapter 28

They walked for a long while in silence. Silence, to Kit's way of thinking, was the real reward of confidence. When two people had a firm enough foundation—whether as lovers or even just as friends—the luxury of walking, eating, standing, or sitting in silence was their just reward. He felt it here under the stars. He wondered if she did, too, and if their separate desires to economize on dialogue were a reflection of that same confidence. Yet he didn't dare ask. To ask would've suggested doubt, and doubt was a thing he wanted none of just now. If they didn't say another word to each other between this moment and their last goodnight kiss, that, to Kit, would be just fine.

As he was about to discover, however, Daneka's train of thought during their walk back to the villa had been running along a quite different track, had been gaining steam along the way, and was about to enter a long, dark tunnel—the first of many tunnels in the coming months until, it would seem to Kit, there were *only* tunnels—long, dark and silent, though none of them suggesting the silence of confidence.

She dropped his hand, and he suddenly felt the weight of it at the end of his arm. At the same time, and although there was nothing in the night air to even hint at an arresting chill, she crossed her arms tightly across her chest as if to ward one off.

"The other day, Kit, when I mentioned *Granta* to you—"

"Yes, I remember. It was during the fli—."

"*Precisely*," Daneka cut in. "Your memory for detail never ceases to amaze me, darling." From the tone, Kit surmised that the next words out of her mouth were not going to comprise a compliment, and that 'darling' was not intended as a term of endearment. She stopped walking and turned to him. "It seemed to surprise you somehow. That I would read it—or even *know* of it, for that matter."

Whatever morning lark of confidence Kit had felt moments earlier fled from him like a bat from a cave. He became uneasy. The memory of his sleuthing about her living room and bookcases the first time he'd visited her apartment was poking around like an unwelcome stranger. It rattled the back door of his conscience, pulled insistently from without as he held tight to the knob from within.

The knob broke apart. The door sprang open. The stranger leered at him. This stranger, Kit discovered, was no stranger at all. He, of necessity, had done commerce with this stranger many times in his adult life—though never, until now, where Daneka was concerned. The stranger was a thing Kit hated in principle and would never have allowed to share even the same air he breathed with Daneka. The stranger was a lie.

"Well, I just didn't … I couldn't … I wasn't prepared to make any assumptions."

"*Assumptions?*" Daneka's eyebrows arched up. "What might you have assumed, or not, about my reading habits?"

"*Granta* isn't every man's choice of a journal, Daneka. That's all I'm trying to say."

"And so I'm *every* man, Kit?"

The moonlight was just bright enough for Kit to see the steel in Daneka's eyes, and he suddenly realized why it was that Ron was chauffeuring Daneka—and not the other way around; why she walked or didn't walk, ate or didn't eat, traveled or didn't travel, when she *wanted* to do these things, and not when others ordered her to do them.

Daneka, too, understood the meaning of silence—especially when it came back to her, head hung low, in answer to a reprimand. She could let someone swim indefinitely in a pool of it, let him thrash about, let him eventually drown if she so chose. But that wasn't her choice now—not here, not with Kit. She let the steel melt. She'd wanted to put him on guard, and she'd succeeded. He'd clearly felt the sting of his error, and he clearly wouldn't forget it for a long time to come—if ever. It was, she felt, time to make a peace offering.

"Darling," she cooed as she sidled up to him and took his arm in both of hers. "I read lots of things. It's my job. Not necessarily cover to cover. For that, I hire readers. I have a roomful of them, and they do nothing all day but leaf through magazines and journals and surf the 'Net looking for good stories. They bring me those stories, maybe four, five, six a week. I read a few paragraphs to see if the story is right for us. If it is, I buy it. Sometimes, if I like it a lot, I may read the whole thing—just for kicks. That was the case with Jennie Erdal's 'Tiger's Ghost.' Besides, I'd just read it the evening before we left New York and had called the next morning to make her an offer. It was still fresh in my mind— especially her wordplay with 'discretion' and 'ardor.' I liked it. And it proved useful to me, as I was sure it one day would."

Kit knew she expected him so say something back, and yet he was frozen. The steel in her eyes had shackled him, had gone straight through his flesh and clamped onto his bones. He marveled at the power of this woman—apparently over all things and people in her life, and now over him. She had him in thrall because she now owned the power to make him lie—or at least bend the truth—so as not to jeopardize this fragile thing between them.

There was no way around it. A lie had entered their relationship, and no matter how piddling, how trivial, how "white," it was there like an indelible spot. He couldn't remove it because he couldn't tell her the truth. He wondered whether this white lie would spawn other little white lies; they always did. Lies were like viruses. Once they'd found a willing host, they'd invariably multiply. Let one little vector through the back door, and soon they'd own every corner and every niche, where they'd quietly propagate themselves into great, hoary multitudes. Soon, what had started out as one little white lie would become a grey mass, squeezing out of corners and niches by virtue of its sheer volume until even the air took on a grey hue. And then, ultimately, the grey would convert to black, and the entire relationship would become one black lie.

Only moments earlier, Kit had been deliriously happy and confident of his future, of *their* future together. Now, however, he felt the first prick of sadness, as if this stranger entering through the back door of his conscience had just slipped up behind him and put the tip of a knife against his back. There was no blood; it was just a pin prick. But the knife was there, and the stranger had no intention of removing it. Ever. And so the pin prick would eventually, through force of lie upon lie, become a gash. From that gash, blood would flow—first in a trickle, then in a torrent. What had started out as a pin prick of sadness would become a torrent of sorrow until, he feared, his body and their love would become a bloodless, lifeless, bootless corpse.

As he'd learned early on in life, Kit knew his only recourse now lay in action—the consequences be damned. He stopped, faced Daneka, looked into her eyes, and spoke the three words neither of them had dared speak to one another until this moment.

"I love you."

He'd broken the dam. He'd set mad fire to a forest of emotions. Flames flared and water poured through; he no longer cared whether he might be consumed by the one or drowned by the other. At this moment, he cared nothing about the fate of the planet; about wars or famine; about melting polar caps; about Portugal; about a full moon over the Atlantic; about *fados* or mandolins; nothing about photography even. If he'd had a wife and children, even they would've meant nothing to him at this instant. Only one thing in all of his known universe meant anything to him right here and now, and that thing was this woman.

Kit couldn't see Daneka's upturned face as it perched on his shoulder, her cheek hard against his, her eyes looking *not* at the guileless gaze of stars peeking out from under the black comfort of heaven, but rather looking out over the western horizon in the direction of New York, where they sought electricity and neon, streetlamps, headlights, marquees—and the cold, self-reflecting adulation of eyeballs acting like mirrors.

Love was complicated. She could speak of it easily enough to her housekeeper, to a neighbor's dog; could say it about a symphony or a painting, about a new purse or another woman's hairdo. But to declare it to a man to whom she was actually *making* love? To say it with real emotion and reciprocal obligations attached? *That* had consequences.

And so, the smile she might otherwise have willed in this instant struggled with years of suppression, of keeping this one single sentiment under strict lock and key in the deepest, darkest dungeon she could find. The result was not tears or even a sigh of happiness at liberation. No attendant *cri d'amour*—still less, a *cri du coeur*—climbed back up out of that dungeon to meet Kit's declaration. Instead, she answered with a voice like a carapace.

"I love you, too, darling."

The vectors were already abuzz in warm and sticky propagation.

Chapter 29

Kit and Daneka, his arm about her waist and hers about his, continued walking once again in silence until they reached their villa. In the hours since they'd first gone out to dinner, the temperature might've fallen by a degree or two at most.

"Kit, what would you say to a little moonlit dip?" Daneka asked as she walked through the front door.

"Dip, did you say, or dollop?" Kit was feeling coy—kittenish, really—and Daneka was clearly up for the game.

"Wisp or wallop, what shall it be?"

"No hanky-panky—okay, Spanky?"

"I'll race you to the pool!" Daneka challenged, shedding most of her clothes en route, but momentarily delayed as she attempted to hop out of her jeans.

"A place where I can drool," Kit growled as he bounded across the living room and lunged out at Daneka from behind. He attempted to grab her where he knew her to be most amply padded, but instead came up with only a handful of panty. Kit's lunge had more behind it than either of them might've expected. Something like a little girl's scream escaped from her throat as Daneka fell to the floor neither in pain nor in fear, but in sheer delight. Her panties tore loose in Kit's hand. She lay on her back, mouth open, legs and arms akimbo.

"Some like it rough," she said, her eyes like tiny flames and her tongue moving slug-like over her upper lip. Kit crawled up on hands and knees between her legs.

"Some lack the stuff," he answered as soon as he'd determined that Daneka had not been hurt by the fall. As he bent his head to let his tongue find hers, Kit felt both of her hands reach down between his legs, unzip his zipper and unbuckle his belt, then reach for his shorts, out of which another part of him was already peeking. She caressed him once, then moved her hands to the material on either side and yanked hard, redering shorts into shreds.

"Tit for tat, darling," she smiled up at him.

"*Tits* for that," Kit said and put his mouth on one of her breasts, licked the nipple a degree or two past ennui, then moved immediately to the other.

Daneka yelped as she scurried out from underneath him, jumped to her feet, and ran out the back door. Kit stood up, stepped out of his jeans and former boxer shorts—now, at best, a dustcloth—and walked to the back door, where he stood for a moment to admire Daneka in the moonlight.

"Some like it clean," she said in a hoarse whisper as she descended slowly into the pool. He walked over to the same set of steps she'd just used to enter, stepped in to find the water at a temperature equal to that of the night air, and slipped into the pool behind her.

"I see what you mean," Kit whispered back.

She'd already drifted off to the middle of the pool. From the position of a semi-crouch she'd taken to immerse everything but her head, she stood up and turned around to face Kit. The water reached just above her navel. Drops ran down from her shoulders to her breasts, which she grasped from below and pushed in his direction. The moonlight bounced off the fleeting drops of water and back into his eyes as he walked slowly across the pool.

"Tits for *that*," she said, indicating with a downward glance in his direction something just below the surface of the water—and of which Kit, himself, was not entirely unaware—if also not entirely in control.

As their bodies met, Kit put his hands under Daneka's armpits and lifted her easily so that her face was on a level with his. She dropped her breasts and put her arms around his neck, pressed her mouth against his and pried open his lips with her own. At the same time, and without need of a prompt, she spread her legs and raised her knees to rest on his haunches. With Daneka willing and able to support her own diminished weight with her arms around his neck and her legs riding on his hips, Kit's hands were free to slip back down under water and find her buttocks. He gently parted them as he brought her lower abdomen into position. The water gave Daneka's body a kind of artificial buoyancy, which allowed Kit to hold her in suspension. With her legs spread to encircle his hips, Kit found Daneka easily and entered her. At the same instant, Daneka pushed her tongue into his mouth. As he let her slide down until he was completely inside her, she just as completely filled his mouth with her tongue.

They remained that way, he in her and she in him, without the merest tease of a motion, for a full minute. Then, as if the wish had been announced by both, to both, and at the same instant—though not even a whisper passed between them—Daneka hoisted herself up, then let herself slide back down in one easy motion. Kit lent the strength of his arms and hands to raise her up and then to brake her slide back down, but this natural rhythm they'd just found seemed to require very little exertion for either of them.

While good arguments can be made for making love on dry land, the most melodious sounds of sex are, even there, all wet ones. It's in water—or in its bodily equivalent—that we conceive. Without a constant supply of water, we die in short order. At death, our private reservoirs begin to drain and run to other livelier, needier bodies. Death—however else it may be described—is ultimately about the absence of water.

Kit and Daneka were at this moment more of water than of flesh. Kit was gloriously surrounded, enveloped, by the warm wetness of Daneka's womb. In almost stylized syncopation, Daneka's tongue poked, prodded and lolled in the warm, wet recesses of his mouth. Their bodies were surrounded by the tepid wetness of the pool water. At a short distance, they could hear waves quietly surging, breaking, then washing up onto the beach. Overhead, stars seemed to swim in a sea of black ink. All was wet, all warm, all life.

Daneka suddenly pulled her tongue from Kit's mouth and put her own mouth next to his ear. Her hands moved from around his neck in a frantic, almost spasmodic dance through his hair. She pushed her belly hard against his and gripped his hips with her legs. Kit first felt her contractions, then heard her long, low sigh of affirmation in his ear. It was enough. His own contractions began to replicate hers; his own sigh to echo her sigh. They were both now swimming in a sea of watery sensation.

Chapter 30

When Kit awoke the following morning, it was not to a warm body next to his, but rather only to the souvenir of it. He loved that the residual warmth and smell of Daneka had remained behind to greet his first waking moment. But a pillow was no substitute for a head, warm sheets no adequate compensation for warmer skin, the familiar perfume of her more intimate parts no acceptable facsimile for the parts themselves. Whatever legerdemain had taken her off and left mere tokens of her behind was an artfulness for which Kit had not the slightest appreciation or understanding. The shock of it brought him immediately to rude consciousness.

He threw back the sheets and jumped out of bed. He first looked in the bathroom. Nothing. He then walked out into the living room. Nothing. He went into the kitchen. Still nothing. The sensation he'd not felt in weeks—namely, when he'd awakened the first time in his apartment in New York to find her gone—came raging back.

He went to the front door, found it locked. Then it suddenly occurred to him: she was probably in the pool again. A woman of Daneka's age didn't—*couldn't*—look like Daneka and maintain her exquisite shape without exercise. He smiled ironically at this residual flicker of separation anxiety, walked to the back door and opened it.

There she was: swimming. She'd been doing laps, apparently, while he'd slept. Sleep was the prerogative of youth; laps were the obligation of creeping age. He, too, would be doing morning laps soon—and doing them, with any luck, right alongside her.

Whether she sensed his presence or decided she'd swum enough, Daneka stopped at the far end of the pool, stood up and took off her goggles. Kit suddenly understood that this was probably routine for her; that she might even have an extra set of travel goggles. He smiled again at his private speculation: what different worlds they lived in!

"Good morning, darling," she called out, only partially out of breath. "Sleep well?"

"Like a rock!" Kit answered.

"How about a little swim for my merman?"

"You mean a little dip like last night's dollop?"

"Well, now," Daneka replied with a throaty guffaw that sounded as much like a threat as a tease. "Whatever my little merman's in the mood for is fine by me. A dip, a dollop, or just a...." Daneka was wearing a one-piece bathing suit—a concession, Kit supposed, to habit or exercise or both. As she slipped the straps of her suit off her shoulders and pulled the material down to her waist, she looked up at Kit with a disingenuous smile.

"Do I hear any interest, or should I pack my things and go to town?"

How can she look this good? he wondered to himself. *How can she look this desirable?* Not just the first time, or even the first few times he'd seen her naked. But over and over again. He wanted her. And the message he was getting from her—a message that left him almost delirious with joy—was that she wanted him, too. He wondered if the two of them should be made illegal.

"Oh, I think you should stay for a bit. I might need a lifeguard," Kit said mock-coquettishly.

"Are we speaking literally or figuratively now, darling? The question was not one Kit was prepared to quibble with so early in the morning. He thought for a moment.

"Well, I think a bit of both, really."

"Huh?" Daneka tilted her head *just so* and began to take little baby steps towards Kit. She eventually reached the side of the pool and mounted the steps to ground level.

She can be monstrously coy when she wants to be, he thought to himself. *And me, she could have in chains. Could have in chains? Has in chains!*

But Kit wasn't quite ready to become anyone's slave—not even Daneka's. For one thing, he was simply too headstrong. For another, he'd worked too hard to become his own master and a slave to no one. He wanted to love—and be loved—now more than ever. But he wanted that love without bondage. He wouldn't lend his soul to anyone; nor would he borrow another's soul. He simply wouldn't do commerce in souls to anyone's advantage or disadvantage, least of all to his own.

As he watched her maneuvering on cat's paws in his direction, head at an angle and breasts exposed, he looked at her with as much love as he thought any man capable of feeling for a woman. But his love, tender feelings—yes, even desire—were not entirely free of a certain sense of wariness and circumspection. He loved her beauty and he loved her charisma. He was also beginning to appreciate both of those attributes with something approaching dread for the enormous power they exerted over him.

She reached him and stopped just short of stepping on his feet; slowly relaxed her neck from its previous tilt; then bent her head up, eyes closed, to put her lips within an inch of his.

"How might I smite thee? Let me count the ways," she said, eyes still closed. She then opened them and fluttered her eyelashes half a dozen times. It was clear to Kit she was about to burst out into a fit of riotous laughter. Just as she'd caught him off guard with her question, he reciprocated by pulling her bathing suit down to her ankles. She obligingly stepped out, hooked it with one foot, and launched it into the garden. Kit then pushed his boxers down to his ankles, stepped out, grabbed Daneka about the waist with both arms, and catapulted them both headfirst into the water.

When they came up for air, Daneka was the first to speak. "Dear, dear, dear! What *shall* we do with you?"

"It's not what you'll do with me, darling, but what I'll do with you!" It was now from Kit's throat that a half-menacing, half-teasing growl issued. Daneka bit her lip in mock terror. She really had no idea what Kit could be up to, but she'd already won a healthy respect both for his imagination and for his willingness to exercise it on her behalf.

Unknown to her, Kit had discovered something the evening before just after they'd first made love in the water. On the side wall, about a foot below the surface of the water, he'd found the hole through which filtered water entered back into the pool. He next discovered that the water flowed in with considerable force. It required little of him to figure out how he might use this artificial force to their mutual advantage. Assuming she'd cooperate, Kit wondered to what degree Daneka might be willing to let herself go without his being part of the mix. He, this time, would remain in complete control of himself—and ultimately, of her. She, he conjectured, would remain in control of nothing—and least of all of herself.

Ms. Sørensen, meet Mr. 'mad, bad and dangerous' Whoopie-jet."

"Show, don't tell, darling," she said as she smiled at him, and Kit had a moment of *déjà entendu.* He turned her around so that she was facing away from him and towards the wall, then lifted her arms and placed her hands behind his neck. He put his own arms around her waist and lifted her just enough so that she could put her feet down on his. Then he began to walk both himself and Daneka towards the wall. When they were close enough to touch it, Kit put his hand out and found the water-jet. It would be better, he knew, than any vibrator. The steady, liquid throb would deliver sensations he couldn't even begin to give her. What's more, they wouldn't stop until *she* wanted them to stop, until she begged him to remove her from the source.

Daneka was still without a clue. From the way she was positioning herself without his prompting, it appeared to Kit she thought he wanted to enter her from behind and make love to her against the side of the pool. To that end, she was slowly arching her back and leaning forward with her hands extended, reaching for something to hold on to. At the same time, she spread her legs to circle Kit's hips from behind and pull him in. But he pushed her legs back down, pulled her torso back up against his chest and repositioned her arms back around his neck. When he began to massage her breasts with his free hands, she craned her neck around to find his ear. Her lips smiled into it as her tongue and teeth found the lobe.

"Ah, yes. Foreplay. Thank you, darling. I'd almost forgotten."

Kit's script for foreplay in this instance lasted little more than a few seconds. He found the hole in the wall again with his finger, grasped Daneka around the waist, lifted her just a couple of inches and pushed her forward. He knew that from his angle he'd be able only to approximate her exact position for maximum effect. But he trusted nature—more precisely, the circuitry between Daneka's clitoris, her cerebellum and the periaqueductal gray of her brain stem, and finally her pectoral muscles to hone in on just the right spot for her to feel the full force of the water—and consequently knew that once she found that source, it wouldn't be her upper thighs or stomach muscles she'd want to oblige with a massage.

He was right in at least part of his assumption. The instant she'd gotten the drift of his plan and felt the liquid throb, she moved to it like a newborn to its mother's tit.

Kit was less correct, however, in the rest of his assumption. He'd figured this magic little stream of water would bring her to a comfortable orgasm—even several, if she wanted—in approximately the time it might take her to achieve the same result through coitus. The principal advantage here, to Kit's way of thinking, was quite simply in the inexhaustibility of the supply, and he was entirely prepared to concede victory to hydrodynamics and electricity.

None of that, however. Daneka clung to the side of the pool as if her body and it were both made of Velcro. Luckily—given not only the increasing duration of her orgasms, but also the increasingly louder celebration of their effects—Kit and Daneka were far enough away from both neighbors and passers-by so as not to startle either group with the sight and sounds of this 'hydro-erotic' *ménage à trois*.

Better reason told Kit he had no good grounds for becoming jealous of a water-jet. And yet, there it was: the damned thing was making a fool of him. In his scheme to have her lose a little bit of self-control, he'd introduced her to a virtual stud whose energy was boundless, whose aim was accurate beyond any known means of calibration, and who would never talk back, need a shave, or expect breakfast. How in God's name was he ever going to compete with *that*? And more to the point, how was he going to detach the woman he loved from this mere gadget?

He didn't have to wonder long about his predicament, however, as she finally collapsed backwards into his arms. He withdrew them both slowly from her fount of euphoria and walked across the bottom of the pool to the steps. Having disqualified his competition, he wondered how he might now remove the smile on her face. They paused— and she kissed him lightly on the lips, her lids only barely open.

"Darling, if you don't mind, I think I'll skip breakfast and take a little nap." She pulled herself up by the handrail, and Kit noticed that her legs were trembling as she picked up a beach towel and disappeared through the back door.

When he walked into the bedroom five minutes later, Daneka appeared to be fast asleep and with a look of perfect contentment fixed on her face. He sat down next to her, then bent down and kissed her forehead. "Hmm…" came back to him.

Kit walked into the kitchen and started preparing a pot of coffee. As the water boiled, he considered what he'd just witnessed. The good news for him was that the water-jet was a lover of only one organ. However efficient it might be in the exercise of its singular talent, it could, in fact, *not* talk back or hold any kind of reasonable conversation. However receptive and responsive her own corresponding organ might be, Daneka had

- 147 -

more than only that one. His salvation, he knew, lay in being able to satisfy the others.

He lit a cigarette and looked out the back window at the pool, then specifically at the location of his competition.

"Loser," he whispered emphatically, then exhaled a long and confident lungful of smoke.

Chapter 31

As Kit sat quietly at the dining room table gazing out over the Atlantic, smoking and drinking his coffee in silence, Daneka slept. This was his first real opportunity to reflect upon the state of their affair—at least its past and present—and also to ruminate upon its future.

The past of it had been turbulent, sexually-charged, flesh getting comfortable with flesh. The electricity between them couldn't last forever—that he knew. But if there was such a thing as finding the perfect mate, no matter how coincidental the circumstances of their first meeting, he felt he'd found his.

The present of it was indeed that—a present, a gift by any reckoning of time, place and opportunity, to explore and become intimately familiar with another human being. Familiarity, he knew, could lead to contempt; it could also head down an alternative road to family. Perhaps the two weren't so mutually exclusive as might appear at first glance. It was, in any case, a risk he was willing to take.

The future of it? In a matter of a few days, he'd meet her mother, would become acquainted with however many members of her extended family were still alive, would feel with his fingers the soil and roots of her earliest years. He longed to know, to the extent possible, the infant, toddler and young girl this woman had once been, and then to reconcile all of that with the mature woman whose life he now wanted to make part of his own. If she showed an equal interest in him and in their future together, he'd willingly take her to Pennsylvania to meet his parents and to sit in the swing of *his* youth—to hear, as he'd heard, his first songs of nature: to smell the same luscious lilacs and feel the same whiplash wind; to know what earthly stuff had informed his child's mind, had made of him the man he'd become, would accompany him for all of his remaining days, and would then prepare him to exit gracefully, manfully and thankfully at the end of those days. Would that future contain her? Would they exit together? If Kit had been a praying man, this would've been his prayer.

Instead, he lit up another cigarette.

At the same instant, Daneka emerged from the bedroom. Kit suddenly became aware of the cloud of smoke he'd created, stood up and opened the back door to clear the air.

"Sorry, darling. I got carried away. I wasn't thinking."

"Oh, nonsense! It doesn't bother me in the least."

"Really?"

"No. In fact, I think it's rather sexy. With *you*, that is. With others, well, they don't have your eyes." Kit ignored the complimentary *non sequitur* as Daneka bent down to kiss first one eyelid, then the other.

"Daneka, my sweet, what would you like to do today?" Daneka moved to the back door and looked out over the ocean. In his minutes-long reverie, Kit had ignored the change in weather. Sun and sky were obscured by a dense fog rolling in like ephemeral, airborne ocean waves. The Atlantic itself, barely visible below, was just one broad carpet of gray except where the waves broke loosely on the beach like frayed ends of the same carpet turned muslin-colored.

"Exactly what we're doing, darling. This and nothing more." She sat down in his lap and laid her head on his shoulder, then met his ear with what sounded to Kit like a sigh of satisfaction.

"Are you happy here, Daneka? With me, I mean."

"My God! Isn't it obvious?"

Kit winced. It had cost him something to ask the question. That she'd answered his question with a question of her own—and that she apparently hadn't wished to look him directly in the eye as she'd asked it—unsettled Kit and gave him pause to wonder whether he was, for her, just a temporary means to an end; a momentary plaything; a brief, entertaining interlude.

"We could stay here, you know. Not in this villa, of course. But somewhere here on the coast. Or elsewhere in Portugal. Or anywhere in Europe, for that matter. I could continue my photography. You could do—. Well, you could continue doing what you do. Remotely. Then just fly over to New York when you needed to. We could lead a simpler life. Just the two of us—and an occasional goat."

Kit had said as much as he wanted or needed to say. He'd laid out the gambit. Now it was now up to Daneka to pick it up or drop it.

"Baaaaaaaaaaah." Daneka smiled.

"That would be a sheep. A goat says 'bauauauauauauauauh'."

"Is that a fact?"

"Yup. I know. I'm a country boy at heart, just trying to woo some big city-girl with my country ways." Daneka looked at Kit for a long moment, her gaze and the thinking behind it inscrutable.

"You say 'bauauauauauauau' and I say 'baaaaaaaaaah.' You say 'skadoodle' and I say 'skadadle.' Let's call the whole thing off!" To the last bit of silly lyric, she added an exasperated sigh and the sweep of one arm, suggesting curt dismissal. Kit didn't know exactly how to interpret the gesture. It could be drama for the sake of drama, or it could be something else, something entirely unconscious—as non-verbal communication all too often was in his experience. She then scrunched up her nose and waved a hand in front of her face to disperse the cloud of smoke. Kit immediately reached out to the ashtray and detached the hot ash from the end of his cigarette. The ash continued to burn. Daneka reached down, grabbed the butt and stamped out the ash—not, Kit thought, without a hint of indignation.

"You didn't answer my question," Kit said.

"Which question?

"About us. Here. Now. About a future for us. Here or elsewhere. A simpler future. A future without the buzz and grind of New York. A future without the bright lights—sure. But also a future of fados, of fandangos—or if not of fandangos, than of flamencos. I don't really give a fat fuck *what* the dance is—or the song. I just want to know about our future."

"Speaking of, wanna?"

"'Wanna what?" Kit's eyebrows descended into a dark "V."

"Wanna fuck? What else?" Daneka's eyebrows mirrored Kit's, but inverted.

"Who's talking about fucking?" Kit asked, visibly annoyed.

"Well, as long as we're on the subject of finances—."

There it was. After all of the physical thrust and parry, all of the wordplay, all of the sweet words and warm tears in response to some of the local folklore, it boiled down to this. Kit smiled inwardly at how a little alliteration could lead like an arrow to a bull's eye—to the *real* issue.

"I'm aware of it," he said. "I've been aware of it since the beginn—."

"No, darling. I didn't mean that." Kit was finally glad for some *real* dialogue between them.

"Yes, you did. In some sense, anyway. And even if you didn't, it's about time we discussed it. I've been aware of it—painfully aware—since the beginning. We live in different worlds, you and I. That doesn't have to stop us, but we can't ignore it."

"Well?" Daneka took a seat opposite him, put both hands on the table and locked her fingers.

"Well, nothing. This trip is clearly over my head. I'll contribute what I can, but only as an investment. That's the best I can do."

"As an *investment?*" she asked, and Kit immediately saw the hard, grey steel replacing the soft, olive green in a pair of eyes he loved even better than his own—or, at least, whose reflection he loved better than his own. As he looked hard at her, he noticed there *was* still a reflection. "My, how quickly we learn!" she said.

He extended both hands across the table and grasped hers. "Yes, darling. As an investment—in us. I'm already way beyond my means on this trip. But it's worth it to me. Every penny of it—and for as long as I may have to work to pay it off. I want to do the job—whatever the job is—that you hired me to do. But you and I both know we're well beyond a mere job at this point. I just don't know, in your mind, where the job ends and something else begins."

"Kit, darling. Let's forget the job for the time being, okay? Let's just enjoy ourselves and worry about that job, *any* job, *mañana.*" Daneka abruptly stood up. The discussion was at an end—at least for her. She turned back around to him. "And as for the cost of this trip, leave it to me. I can expense it."

'I can expense it' was not precisely the answer he'd hoped to receive to his original question. But their interlude was far from over. For now, he'd elicited—and received—a reprieve of sorts. They'd continue. He'd put her on notice that he was, financially at least, not up to the challenge. She'd answered, at least as far as he was concerned, that she understood and would accept the burden for both of them. If finances were the only obstacle, he was certain they could overcome that obstacle.

Kit was still young, naïve, "old world" in the ways of the new world in this new millennium—especially, where the ostentatiously new of old-world-Europe bumped up against the unsuspecting old of new-world-New York. New, old or middling really didn't much matter where New York was concerned. After all, New York wasn't Philadelphia or Boston. New York was a casino where anyone could play. You needed only to have the chips and sufficient chutzpah—and Daneka had more than her fair share of both.

Chapter 32

As the day wore on, it became clear the fog was not going to lift—either over the Atlantic and their particular piece of coastline, or over their last conversation. Fog and finances couldn't—like an under-performing employee—simply be dismissed. And so, both of them were here to stay for a while.

Each time he lit up a cigarette, Kit was careful to move to the back door—or just outside it—so as not to contribute further to the strained atmosphere he felt hanging in the room. This was the first time, indoors or out, that he and Daneka had spent an extended period of time in close physical proximity—yet absent any effort at intimacy. They were a pair of pewter goblets standing opposite one another at either end of a mantel (*pace* both Flaubert and Conrad), beneath which a warm fire should've been crackling. But none crackled—nor even burned. Instead, small bits of unspent log smoldered in silence, each tiny spark of an effort immediately snuffed out by the weight of sighs as heavy as the fog that rolled in over the beach and up to their back door. The villa was theirs to do with as they wished; the bedroom was theirs to do with it whatever they wanted; the bed in the bedroom in the villa was theirs to do with as they knew how; and yet, they did nothing.

Hour by hour, it became more difficult to delineate sky from water, water from beach, beach from dry land, the grey dampness without from the still more grey dampness within. The steady tick-tock of an antique clock hanging just over the dining room table was punctuated only occasionally by chimes marking the quarter-, half- and full-hour.

As seven successive hourly chimes suggested the likelihood of dusk—however invisible—Kit heard Daneka rise from their bed, open and close the bathroom door, then start the shower.

He stood up from his own place of quiet vigil at the dining room table, lit another cigarette and stepped outside. It was indeed beginning to grow dark, or maybe the fog was simply growing more dense. In either case, each time Kit took a drag on his cigarette, the glow from its tip stood out to him in close-up relief against the warning flare of a buoy at some ill-defined distance from the shoreline below: two little bright orange lights surging, then receding, at regular intervals, and one in imitation of the other. He could interpret it as a sign if he wished to—but he didn't. Instead, when he heard the shower stop, he dropped the remainder of his cigarette to the stones below, exhaled in one long, steady stream, and stamped the butt out. The wisp of a *déjà vu* ignited and just as readily self-extinguised with the stamp of his foot—at which point, he returned through the back door, closed it behind him and walked across the dining room floor to the bedroom.

"Evening, darling," Daneka murmured. "Hungry?"

"Quite."

"Shall we go back to the same place?"

"Yes, let's, unless—."

"Unless… What?"

"Well, I doubt that we'll want to sit in the garden tonight. I doubt that *anyone* will want to sit in the garden tonight. It's rather damp outside. Damp and dreary. We could simply stay in. 'Get a fire going. 'Make an evening of it at home."

"At *home*?" Daneka looked at Kit.

"Well, in a manner of speaking, I guess. A temporary home. A home away from home."

"I suppose that home is where the heart is," Daneka answered flatly. "Yes," she added with a bit more enthusiasm. "This *is* home—at least for the moment."

She was looking directly at Kit for the first time in hours. He felt gratitude—even if her last qualifying phrase had left things open-ended once again—and smiled back at her. The fog that had been hanging inside the villa all day seemed instantly to vanish with the smile she returned. She walked to him, a thing of terry cloth from head to toe and without make-up, still wet in places she hadn't yet reached with the towel.

"Forgive me, darling. I've been brooding all day. I don't know why, exactly. Probably the weather."

"That's quite okay," Kit offered. "I haven't been particularly communicative myself. I own—. I'm to blame for at least half of this." Daneka put her arms around Kit's neck and let her towel drop to the floor. She pressed her body up against his, found his mouth with hers, gave him a long, passionate kiss.

Kit felt a tingle grow into a glow. When she finally broke the kiss, she remained with the tip of her nose touching his and looked warmly into his eyes. He felt the first rays of a familiar sun rise back up between them.

"All better now?" she teased. And then, without waiting for an answer, she answered for him in sing-song. "All better now."

Kit stepped back. "Yes. All better now," he mimicked. "Let me make another fire and then take a quick shower before we go. Okay?"

"K," Daneka answered. In the meantime, I'll apply some science. And I think I'll wear a dress tonight. No special occasion. I just feel like it." With that, she picked the towel back up off the floor and continued to dry herself off until Kit interrupted her.

"Let me do that." She surrendered the towel to him and Kit continued to pat her dry. When he reached under her arms to dry her armpits, she obligingly lifted them. Daneka, herself, would've been at a loss to explain why the same action she'd initiated only moments earlier with her own hands should now result in a quite unexpected secondary benefit. She first noticed it in her nipples. That reaction was only further reinforced when Kit reached between her legs, which she opened without hesitation. He easily found the last, cool drops of shower water and removed them with the towel. These, however, were instantly replaced with something just as wet, warm, and decidedly viscous. This internal reaction was quite involuntary—as was her slow rotation and the placement first of her hands, followed by her elbows, on the bed as she bent down from the waist. While keeping her hips high and what was between them fully exposed, she simultaneously spread her legs and rose up on tip toes so as to elevate her hips at best an inch higher. It was something primal, atavistic, simian even, and she felt no shame in it. He was male and highly desirable; she was female and—even *she* felt it—highly desirable. Her body told her this. Her nerves and her blood—and yes, even her endocrine glands—told her the same. At this particular moment, only one thing mattered: copulation. It was the thing for which she'd been made, for which every cell in her body now screamed. If she were forced to confess the truth of it: no matter how much she loved this man and this man alone; no matter how desirable she found him and him alone; no matter … she would've taken any man, any number of men, any men in any confusion or congeries of ways, to satisfy the instinct—the *ur*-drive—to have something of flesh inside her. The only thing that mattered now wanted out in a blinding, raging desire to copulate, to fornicate, to fuck.

Kit dropped the towel. In its place, she felt the caresses of bare fingers as they slid easily back and forth, in and out, gently pinching her swelling parts. She first heard, then smelled, the pungent ripeness of her sex as it oiled his fingers. She next grabbed a pillow and thrust it under her belly as if it might still be possible to elevate and expose herself more than the full extent to which she'd raised herself up only seconds earlier. At some indefinable distance, she heard metallic sounds. They registered, abstractly, as Kit's efforts to undo his belt buckle—but he was far too slow for her. She whipped around, grabbed the end of his belt and yanked it back, tearing a belt loop with the force of her pull. In almost the same motion, Daneka pulled down his zipper, then his jeans and shorts.

She spun back around and re-positioned herself as she'd been seconds earlier. As he entered her, her world went instantly black with his first thrust. She grabbed the other pillow and buried her mouth into it.

For how long she screamed, neither of them had a sufficient presence of mind to calculate. It went on and on, as did the waves of her orgasm. Kit, himself, lasted no more than thirty seconds before he, too, buried *his* face next to hers into the same pillow. At the instant her waves had just begun to abate, he came. She was hit by a second, even more violent orgasm that sent her over the edge and into a *blacker* black, practically into unconsciousness.

Kit settled his full weight on top of her, grabbed both of her hands in his, and stretched them out as if on a rack of the most exquisite torture. She reciprocated with her vaginal muscles, holding him immobile inside her. They lay together in a flesh-lock for five long minutes before Kit pulled out and stood up.

"Did I say something about a fire?" he asked. Daneka turned over slowly, the delicious exhaustion in all of her muscles rendering any real exertion virtually impossible. Even raising her head seemed to be impossibility, though she somehow managed a smile.

"You did, darling. *And* a quick shower. I think we just had a bit of both." The two of them shared a conspiratorial chuckle.

Kit walked into the living room, brushed the spent wood and ashes aside, set down wads of newspaper and a small collection of twigs. Once the fire had taken hold of the paper and kindling, he added a few larger branches. These in turn caught fire, and then he carefully loaded a few logs. He had a good fire burning in no time when he returned to the bedroom. Daneka was lying in the same position in which he'd left her—and with her eyes wide open. Kit noticed the dreamy expression on her face and wondered whether he or their love-making were any part of it. He didn't ask. Instead, he went into the bathroom, turned on the shower and stepped into the stall.

When he stepped back out ten minutes later to dry off, he noticed Daneka through the open bathroom door. She was seated at the vanity applying her make-up and wearing the same dress she'd worn when she'd first come to visit him at his apartment. He loved the dress and he loved her in it. It showed everything about her in all the right places. He might not particularly like that other men's eyes would see the same thing and probably think some of his same thoughts. But so long as she'd take it off for him and him only, what did it really matter? Hers was a body too good to waste on the desert stare of one man's eyes—even *he* knew that. She was a creation of nature that belonged to the entire natural world to ogle, to fantasize about, to imagine in positions he'd happily put her in—as if any other man had sufficient imagination even to conjure up the image of some of those positions.

"Almost ready, Daneka?" he asked. If not, he thought, he'd willingly stand and watch her for another season or two.

She finished applying her lipstick with a flourish; pursed her lips once; put the cap back on and stood up from the vanity. "Yes," she said. "Unless, of course, there's something you'd like me to change."

Kit could see that she was braless and—from the absence of a discernable panty line—wearing nothing else beneath the sheerest of possible materials that could still be called a covering. If he thought she might ever leave home that way except in his company, the knowledge, he knew, would drive him absolutely bonkers. But here? Now? With him present? Why not?

"Not a thing, darling. Just don't lose me—or it might be the last I'll ever see of you!"

Kit quickly put on his jeans and a shirt, then threw on a jacket as concession to the fog and possible chill. He didn't realize that Daneka had been watching him the entire time.

"Grrrrrr," she muttered. "I don't know whether I prefer you *in* clothes or out. Either way, you're a tasty little package! So, don't lose me, either—or even the *sight* of me. I don't want some Portuguese shepherdess herding you off with her flock."

Kit was quietly ecstatic. This was the first time she'd openly acknowledged she liked what she saw. It was also the first time he was allowed to understand that yes, even Daneka could feel something like jealousy and the urge to possess where he was concerned.

Kit stepped up and put his hands on her shoulders. "You, Daneka, are the only shepherdess I've ever wanted and will ever want." He waited—perhaps a beat or two longer than he should have—for a response. There was none.

"Let's go to dinner, shall we?"

Chapter 33

When they reached the same restaurant where they'd dined the evening before, it was as Kit had suspected: plenty of patrons, and all of them indoors. As Kit hesitated—wondering whether he, with his Spanish, or Daneka, with her Portuguese, should take the lead—the same hostess greeted them at the reception desk, this time in flawless English. Kit was dumfounded; Daneka was not. For all of his travels, Kit was still naïvely American and would never *really* know Europeans and their peculiar ways.

Daneka, however, did—as she now proved and would prove over and over again. The previous night, she knew, had simply been a test to determine whether these two voyagers cared enough to make an effort—or whether they, like so many others before and after them, would be content with a group snapshot, a silly trinket or memento, an experience of no account, an empty exploit.

As the hostess led them to a corner table next to one of three ecumenically quiet fireplaces in the main room of the restaurant, all heads swiveled to look at Daneka. Just as she'd once taken command of Kit's street on the Lower East Side on a sunny, early-spring Sunday afternoon in New York, she now took command of a restaurant half a world away. Kit noted familiar faces from the night before, faces that—he would've thought—had taken no notice of them then, nodding, smiling, greeting them as if they were old acquaintances. There was nothing lewd nor lascivious in the men's looks; there was also nothing of envy or jealousy in the looks of their female dinner companions. Rather, both men and women stared openly, like guileless children, as Daneka walked through with Kit. They were curious and appreciative, but they were also respectful. Theirs was a quiet admiration of a natural wonder, of a thing of consummate beauty, of a woman who, in their eyes, was clearly the personification of grace—even if that grace was Nordic rather than Iberian.

Now more wise than vain, Daneka silently registered every glance. She was the sun they'd all longed for behind the fog they'd all lived with—not just that day, but for days and months and years of their lives. She radiated for them not out of vainglory, but out of generosity—and because, quite simply, she could. It was as much a pleasure for her to give light and warmth as it was for them to bathe in it, and there was neither hubris nor condescension in her gait or in her demeanor.

The hostess seated them, though without menus. Before Kit could signal to her, they were surrounded by waiters and even a wine steward who immediately opened a bottle of white and a bottle of red—both of an unknown house and vintage. From the look of the labels and the crusty exterior of the bottle of red, it was clear to Kit that these were no ordinary wines, but something very old and possibly very rare. The wine steward didn't, as would've been the custom under other circumstances, invite Kit to taste the wine. Instead, he taste-tested it himself with his own heavy, silver *tâte-vin* and pronounced it satisfactory not with a word, but with an understated Portuguese nod of approval—following which, he poured both white and red into a pair of glasses he'd set down in front of Kit and Daneka.

Kit and Daneka looked at each other with eyes that registered pure delight—even if Kit's mien still registered the suggestion of a question mark at the end. Just as Kit thought once again that it might be expedient to request menus, a flurry of waiters appeared at their table with small plates of appetizers: olives; sardines; anchovies; raw vegetables; and small slices of hard-ribbed bread baked in rosemary, marjoram, thyme or sage. No fewer than three little dishes of olive oil of ostensibly different grades, consistency and colors took their places among the plates of appetizers. All of this was accomplished without the exchange of a single word—as was each subsequent visit from their wine steward who, over the next couple of hours, never once thought to save himself an extra trip to their table by filling their glasses more than five-eighths full.

As soon as they'd finished their first course, hands appeared almost out of nowhere to chase their plates away. New plates appeared with tiny morsels of grilled fish, octopus, shrimp and squid—and alongside these, ice-packed earthenware tureens of oysters and clams, more shrimp, squid and octopus. There were no fewer than six different sauces ranging from tangy to sublimely sweet—none of them familiar-tasting to either Kit or Daneka, but all of them exquisite. Again—and repeatedly—the wine-steward made a timely visit to their table. Again—and without a whisper—empty plates and dishes were removed.

Both Kit and Daneka were beginning to feel supremely satisfied when a third course arrived. This time, and once again cut into tiny, bite-sized morsels, grilled meats: lamb; beef; goat; veal; venison; partridge; and quail. Additionally, small, white potatoes cut into ovals and sautéed in butter and parsley; broccoli florets and asparagus spears; buttered carrots, more sauces—and all of it delivered to their table in silence.

Kit began to wonder what kind of a tribute would be exacted of them, and whether or not they could pay it. Daneka, however, appeared to take it all in stride, perfectly willing and able to pay whatever price their headwaiter might name. Both of them marveled, to themselves only, that such a nondescript restaurant could provide comparable fare.

At the conclusion of what Kit hoped was their main and final course, hands reappeared, plates disappeared, wine glasses and bottles with them. The wine steward returned with two Port glasses and a bottle he carried like a new-born. He put one glass down in front of each of them, then signaled to the waiters in the background, who promptly arrived with a dish of walnuts, another of almonds, a third of cashews, a fourth of radishes, and a cutting board with at least half a dozen cheeses, some soft and buttery, others hard and scaly. Kit looked at the rinds of the hard cheeses and thought he'd never seen such subtle hues of gray and brown—colors that reflected the earth tones and rocky ridges of the coastline. What he would've given for a light-pack and his camera at this moment! The colors of the rinds and of the cheeses themselves, the Rachel-rich clarity of the Port and, in the background, Daneka in her dress—but also the fire's flames dancing deliciously, deliriously through the transparency of it and around the firmness of her. It would be a portrait of edibles and potables—he smiled to himself—to end all portraits.

As the wait-staff and wine steward withdrew from their table, Kit noted the arrival of the same group of musicians who'd played outside in the garden the night before. He presently had a better opportunity to study them and their instruments close up, and he saw that their instruments were indeed mandolins—if a local variation which he'd not, until the night before, ever seen. The musicians themselves were dressed in a rustic fashion, though without a too-obvious bow to costumes or anything that could be called even remotely folkloric. *They look simply natural,* Kit thought—*like the rinds of the local cheeses.* When *she* finally appeared, Kit could see at a glance why Portuguese women could not claim any of that reputation for oxygen-sucking beauty that some of their other Mediterranean sisters were heir to. There was something a bit too masculine about her, a bit too rough around the edges. Consequently, Kit understood immediately why the men in the room had reacted as they had when Daneka had brushed through. Hers was a beauty—and not only to Kit's eyes—to suck more than air out of a room. If the women hadn't reacted with jealousy or envy, Kit thought, it was only because they lacked a language of comparison, a syntax to give any real definition or meaning to sentiments of jealousy or envy of a beauty like hers.

As if by way of compensation for her lack of physical beauty, however, this woman had a voice whose sound to his ears—and apparently to every other pair of ears present—was a thing that could rival what Daneka's face and body could do to his and their eyes. As she began to sing the same series of *fados* she'd sung the night before, he leaned forward as if reeled in by the same thread Daneka had been tied to the previous night—and now began to hear the sadness that had brought Daneka to tears. He reflected on their love-making of only a couple of hours earlier. And then, as if running the film backwards and in deliciously slow motion, he reflected upon all of their love-making—place, time of day and circumstances—since the first time near the Boathouse. Finally, he reflected upon the first time he'd seen her naked, in his own apartment, and on how he'd studied the curves and contours of her as she slept.

He didn't know—really couldn't distinguish—whether it was these memories, or the music, or some premonition that now saddened him. In any case, when he opened his eyes again several minutes later during a short intermission, he felt dampness on his cheeks and knew that he, like Daneka the night before, had succumbed. When he looked at her, he noted that her eyes, too, were misty, though he saw no evidence of what he'd seen the night before. She'd simply grown inured to the sadness and had let it become a part of her as it had long ago become a part of all of the others seated around them.

"Shall we go, darling?" she asked as she put her hands on his.

"Yes. Let's.

"And shall we leave tomorrow if the fog hasn't lifted?"

Kit nodded. "If that's your wish."

"It is, my darling. I love it here. And I love being here with you. I could be anywhere with you and be happy. But right now, I also desperately need to feel the sun again. There'll be more than enough fog and mist and dreariness in Denmark—trust me."

"Then let's go find that sun. Let's leave tomorrow for Italy."

Daneka bent down and kissed Kit's hands. With eyes closed, she then brought her head back up and kissed him softly on the lips. She opened her eyes, reached up and touched him once on the tip of his nose, then smiled.

"Thank you, darling. I'll never forget you for this."

He hoped she never would. But that was a question only time could answer—and *would* answer, one day, much sooner than either of them might have anticipated.

Chapter 34

D aneka signaled to their headwaiter, who promptly came to the table.

"*Sim, Senhora?*" he asked.

"*A conta, por favor.*" The waiter looked first at Daneka, then turned to Kit.

"*Com sua permissão, Senhor,*" he asked, but without waiting for Kit to give his permission *or* withhold it. He bowed his head, picked up Daneka's hand and put his lips to it. The gesture was pure chivalry. "*Este é o único pagamento que exijo, Senhora.*" ("This, Madame, is the only payment I require.")

Because Daneka was European and knew instinctively how to react, Kit's intercession would've been entirely superfluous. His own mother, he was certain, would've blushed, mumbled something girlishly incoherent, taken out her traveler's cheques or credit card to hide her embarrassment and, in the process, would've likely insulted her host.

Daneka, however, stood up, took the headwaiter's hands in hers, and kissed him once on each cheek. She then walked up to each of the other attending waiters and did the same. Finally, she repeated the gesture with the wine steward, paused an instant, reached down to the *tâte-vin* at the end of its silver chain and brought it to her lips as a parting gesture of respect both for the steward and for the wine.

Kit realized the room had grown respectfully silent during this impromptu ceremony. Without knowing why she was doing what she was doing, those present nevertheless seemed to have a profound admiration for what she did—and for how she did it. As Kit and Daneka walked to the front of the restaurant, Daneka paused once more face to face with the singer and, as she had with the wait staff, took both of the singer's hands in her own.

"*Você tem a voz de um anjo, Sinhorita,*" she said. ("You, Miss, have the voice of an angel.")

"*Muitíssimo obrigado,*" the singer said. "*E você tem um anjo, tem a cara, Senhora.*" ("Thank you very much. And you, Madame, the face of one.")

The two women stood peering into other's eyes for an instant longer, a pair of hands in a pair of hands. Then Daneka disengaged, and Kit and Daneka walked through the reception area and out the front door.

The fog still hung on the night air like a slightly out-of-season winter coat. Daneka, without benefit of an outer garment, huddled down under Kit's protective arm as they walked back to their villa. Just there, where the night sky's foggy fabric had worn momentarily thin, a full moon broke through and illuminated the villa, now within eyesight. A thin trail of blue smoke rose from the chimney and appeared to pay homage to a moon whose cheesily melancholy face sent benevolent beams back down.

As they arrived at the front door, Daneka reached out to open it. Kit, instead, took her hand in his.

"Have I ever told you that I love you?" he asked. "Not just love—but admire, respect, adore … yes, even worship you." This last was something Kit said not in the tone of a lingering question, but with the self-assurance of a full-scale declaration.

Daneka's eyes did not rise to meet Kit's. Anonymous admiration—the stares of strangers and of people who made no claim to her heart, who had no chance of ever entering in, who remained, simply and categorically, admirers—was something Daneka could easily accommodate. The adoration of *one* man, however, was another matter entirely. Worship from that same man was like a bit of foreign matter in the eye, and she reached up unconsciously to find and flush it out before tears might find a way to do the same. There was, of course, nothing in her eye to remove. The gesture had no purpose and no result other than to put an end to Kit's declaration.

"What is it, Daneka?" he asked solicitously—hiding as he did so, his disappointment.

"Oh, it's nothing, Kit. Just a little something—at least it *feels* like something—in my eye." She looked up at him and blinked. "Can you see anything there?" The fact that she'd finally said his name once again in as long as he could remember was like a bandage to the wound she'd just unknowingly—or perhaps knowingly—re-opened.

"Yes, I think I see—." And here, he peered down into her eyes, brought his hand up and pinched thumb and forefinger together as if to pluck something out. "A thorn. Or maybe an entire thorn *bush*. Or maybe even an entire *forest* of thorn bushes."

Daneka laughed. "A forest of thorny, *horny* bushes?" she asked coquettishly.

"Scornfully thorny bushes," Kit answered, then sighed. "Or maybe mournfully horny bushes. It's a little hard to see the horny for the trees in this case. The forest gets lost -

in the thick-thistled understory." Kit's metaphor was not lost on Daneka. She, after all, had brought him to it. She chose not to offer a rejoinder, but instead let it hang in the air as she opened the front door.

And there it hung, all night long, the occasional crackle from the fireplace incapable of doing anything to lighten or puncture or scare it loose from its lurking place. Kit slept fitfully; Daneka, soundly.

At the first sign of dawn, Kit rose and walked out the back door. He figured he had a good hour or two before Daneka would awaken. He descended through the rocks to the beach below. The sky, still grey and fog-laden, joined the sea at the waistline. Further down below the western horizon, Kit knew, if his eyes could've seen far enough to somehow magically follow the curvature of the Earth, he would find—just below ankle-level—New York.

New York on its faster, take-no-prisoners, shit-kicking pair of feet.

He and Daneka could fly halfway around the world. They could find a paradise in Paris, another in Portugal, a third—he was certain—in Italy. And in Denmark? He had no idea—only an inkling, really—that Denmark, too, would prove to be a paradise, even if filled with 'fog and mist and dreariness.' He would take any and all of it now and for the rest of his life—if only he could have her with it. But now he knew. However much of a paradise it might seem to him, it remained too small a pleasure for her.

He knew she loved him. To the extent she was *capable* of loving—and it was becoming progressively, painfully apparent that this was very little—she loved him. But there was something, some *thing* that made it impossible for her to love—him, or probably anyone else for that matter. Of this, he was becoming increasingly certain.

Europe was a continent too small, too intimate, too quiet and full of fog for her to rest easy and remain content on with a sparse regimen of one man and the keening of her own thoughts. She needed the bang, the dash, the glare and glitter of New York to distract her. She needed New York's constant noise, the non-stop assault on ears and eyes, nose and fingers—on every known sense and then on the other unknown, unknowable ones—to distract her from her thoughts, from some long-suppressed memory, from some cosmic collision in a brief history on Earth that had left her caught in a perpetual emotional winter.

For all of her grace and beauty and superlative performance, Kit finally recognized Daneka for who she was: a *trompe-l'œil*. An illusion. A diamond of no carats—or maybe a diamond of countless carats, brilliant in its unremitting radiance, but ultimately dead.

He remembered his gift to her of a lichen and felt suddenly foolish. What could she know—or care about—of a thing that might require half a century to grow to the size of a shirt button? Of a thing that would endure any hardship, that to all appearances existed for the mere sake of existence and needed nothing more than whatever minerals it could squeeze from a rock through the secretion of its own beggarly supply of chemical? And now, it sat on her coffee table—pointless in its persistence, most likely looking to her and to all those who traveled through her living room like a locker-room fungus, the product of bad circulation and a negligent housekeeper, a bit of mildew with green hair.

What he'd seen with a clearer vision the first time he visited her apartment in New York was no accident: the sterile, museum-like, picture-perfect quality of the rooms where photographs and tableaux had been hung for show, but with no love; the books standing on bookshelves like an impeccably dressed Vatican Swiss Guard, their bindings no more stressed by the fly-weight of the material within than by the non-existent threat of a curious-fingered assault from without.

Yes, he now had to concede: she was an Echo to his Narcissus, and one who reflected back to him only the idealized version of himself that he had, until now, blindly, gratefully embraced. He was a photographer and should know better—should know even better than a therapist how to read his subject's exterior in order to understand what lay just below the surface. And yet, he'd never trained his camera on himself—and that was the problem. Instead, he'd looked at Daneka through it; had taken at face value what his camera told him; had pronounced it, and her, beautiful. She was an exquisite *trompe-l'œil*—no mistake about it. And now, he realized, he'd fallen in love, deeply in love, obsessively in love, with an illusion.

He felt like an old man when he climbed the rocks back up to the villa. Upon his arrival, the error of his earlier conjecture struck him dumb. Daneka was up, showered, dressed, made-up and packed. Even his own suitcase was laid out on the bed with all of his things neatly folded and lying next to it. She smiled at him as he came in through the back door. He made what he believed to be an entirely successful attempt to rid his face of any expression that might reveal his struggle of the previous hour.

"Good morning, darling." "'Have a nice walk?"

"I did indeed." And as he looked at her now, possessing all of the radiant beauty of the diamond he'd dismissed only minutes earlier, his mind backed slowly away from thoughts of the lichen as if it were an untouchable—or, at the very least, a thoroughly expendable—piece of frozen tundra.

Chapter 35

Except for the occasional swish of the windshield wipers, they drove north in silence—though by no means an uncomfortable one. Daneka sat directly beside Kit, her head on his shoulder, one hand inside his shirt and resting comfortably against his chest. Their car was greeted now and again by pairs of amber fog lights on cars traveling in the opposite direction. Still less often, Kit had to maneuver his vehicle around a slow-moving tractor. There were no service roads in this area of the country. Everyone— big or small, slow or fast, tourist or farmer—made do with the national road.

When they arrived at the airport, Kit dropped Daneka and their luggage off just outside the international departure lounge, then drove down and around to return the rental car. He found her twenty minutes later at the check-in counter for Alitalia, explaining to the clerk in what seemed to Kit's ear to be fluent Italian the reason for their early departure. The clerk in this case was another woman, and Daneka's charm didn't seem to be working its usual magic. Finally, in exasperation, she asked to speak with the clerk's supervisor.

"What's the problem, Daneka?" Kit asked.

"Oh, she wants us to pay a penalty for early departure. I just refuse, on principle, to pay penalty fees. Either the goddamned plane's got seats or it hasn't. It costs them no more to fly us today than it will tomorrow."

When a smartly dressed, middle-aged man came into view, Daneka's demeanor shifted abruptly from the Janus-face of an annoyed customer to the Janus-face of a woman-in-need-of-a-helping-hand. She was all pained smile and droopy eyelashes when he stepped up to the counter.

"*Buongiorno, Signora. Ci sono problemi?*" ("Is there a problem, Madame?")

Daneka's subsequent spiel left Kit dazzled. Her eyes and eyelashes spoke in fluttered phrases; her hands spoke in fistfuls of anguish and disappointment; her mouth merely gave sounds and punctuation to both. Finally, she paused and—in summation—put both hands together as if in prayer.

"*Può aiutarci, caro Signore?*" ("Can you help us, dear Sir?")

The supervisor mumbled a few words to the clerk; looked down at the tickets;

looked at both Kit's and Daneka's passport photos; tossed Kit's passport aside, but flipped assiduously through every page of Daneka's, looking up from time to time at her but ignoring Kit as if he were an unrelated bit of carry-on luggage.

"*É danese di nascita, Lei?*" ("You're Danish, then, by birth?")

"*Sì, Signore. Nata in Danimarca, ma abito a New York.*" ("Yes. Born in Denmark, though I live in New York.")

"*Peccato,*" ("A pity,") was all he said, and Kit thought to himself that it was no shame *whatsofuckingever* that she lived in New York. What's more, what presumption did this particular peacock take upon himself to suggest otherwise? *Italy—another paradise?* Kit was already having serious misgivings, and they hadn't yet even boarded the plane.

The supervisor made a notation on Daneka's ticket and signed it with a flourish, then handed it to the clerk for re-processing. "*Fatto, Signora.*" ("Done, Madame.")

"*Mille grazie, Signore. É molto gentile!*" ("Many thanks. That was very kind of you!") Daneka gushed. Truth is, the supervisor seemed to be quite satisfied with him*self* and with the end-result of the transaction—and next reached out for Daneka's hand in what Kit suspected was going to be some sort of secret Mediterranean hand-squeeze. *Don't you fucking dare!* was what he thought—though luckily for all of them, he only thought it.

In fact, the handshake—at least that Kit could see—remained professional and insinuated nothing more than the pleasure of doing business. Italian-style. Kit was quite prepared to think long and hard about what it was Italian men knew about Scandinavian women that he obviously didn't know, when the supervisor showed clear signs of exiting the scene.

"*E il mio?*" ("And *mine?*") Kit almost screeched, since both the officious supervisor and Kit's captivating little mermaid-of-a-consort had apparently forgotten that she didn't come without some solid carry-on baggage—namely, him.

The man gave him a quick look, reached down to the second ticket and scribbled his initials. Did he then pick the ticket up and hand it to his clerk? He did not. He simply turned on his heel and marched off.

Bella fucking Italia indeed! Kit thought.

As Kit and Daneka collected their tickets from the female clerk, he gave her a nice, you've-got-a-friend-in-Pennsylvania smile. She ignored Daneka completely and directed her subtle smile—and a warm hand—in return.

"*Buon viaggio*," ("Have a nice trip,") she murmured. Their handshake lingered, and the steamship of Kit's earlier assessment of Italy and things Italian suddenly turned its rudder 180°. As it did so, however, it ran up against Daneka—who was suddenly looking more like a Danish tugboat than like a Danish mermaid.

"Shall we go?" Her question, to him, sounded indeed like the warning blast of just such a tugboat.

"*ArrivederLa, Signorina*," Kit offered the still smiling clerk before releasing her hand. "Yes, Daneka. Let's."

Italy—Kit thought to himself as they walked towards Passport Control and the departure gate for their Lisbon-to-Rome flight—*is going to be one freaking barrel of laughs.*

Chapter 36

The flight from Lisbon to Rome passed without incident—also, however, without repeat of any earlier aerial pleasures. Whether it was the lingering feeling of Lisbon's fog or the malingering memories of their first encounter with Italian machismo, Kit couldn't be certain. In any case, he and Daneka weren't talking. Maybe, he thought, some real sun—or at least some sidewalk serenade to the real thing—would lighten things up.

As their plane began its slow descent into *Fiumicino,* the clouds parted just in time for them to view the Vatican City under a pocket of clear sky. Other landmarks gradually found light and definition in Kit's eyes as the cloud-cover pulled back like a lady's skirt, and snickering sunlight put the "good bits" down below on full display. Shade and shadow, he knew, were essential to love and romance. At the moment, however, he had no use for either. His photographer's eye simply wanted to ogle the cityscape; his middling historian's mind wanted to associate three-dimensional blocks of stone with two-dimensional facsimiles he'd seen in the illustrations of history books; his lover's imagination wanted to revel in the projection of the two of them, in short order, walking hand in hand through tunneled streets and dark alleys of this 'eternal city.' He felt that any commentary would be superfluous.

Daneka clearly felt no compulsion to offer any, either; and so, they descended in silence.

Once inside the airport and through Passport Control, Kit suggested he'd take care of the rental car rather than lose valuable time waiting to collect their luggage and get through Customs. Daneka nodded her approval and announced that she'd call the hotel in Positano to clear their early arrival. They moved their carry-on bags over to a bank of pay phones and agreed to rendezvous there again in twenty minutes.

Exactly nineteen minutes later, they did.

"The hotel's booked for the night," she announced with an abrupt gesture, clearly disappointed with a situation even *she* couldn't amend. "We'll either have to put up here in Rome or move on somewhere down the coast. What's your preference?"

"I'm sorry, Daneka," Kit answered. But he wasn't really; he was delighted. An entire afternoon, evening and night in Rome was a gift of serendipity he hadn't expected—the chance, finally, to walk the streets his parents had walked and talked about, always with a peculiar gleam in their eyes.

"Would you mind terribly staying here in Rome?" he asked.

"No. That's fine. I only wonder where."

Although he'd never studied the language formally, Kit felt that what little he'd picked up from his parents would be sufficient for him to handle booking a hotel room. "Mind if I try?" he asked.

"Not at all," Daneka replied. "I don't really know Rome well enough even to make a suggestion." Kit was happy for once that Daneka's book knowledge—and so, he assumed, her *carnal* knowledge—did not include every city, village and hamlet on the Continent. He was especially happy that it *ex*cluded the capital of this particular Mediterranean country—a city whose historical reputation for debauchery rivaled even that of Berlin and Düsseldorf and rendered what he knew of New York's, in comparison, a kids' version of 'suck-face.'

He started off in the direction of where he thought he might find information, transportation and hotel reservation kiosks, then paused for an instant and looked back.

"Daneka," he half shouted. She seemed to be preoccupied; but hearing his call, she turned around.

"Yes, darling?" And then with a slightly flippant air—perhaps for the benefit of whoever might be listening—"Are you trying to pick me up? You just dropped me off!"

"Oh, nothing in particular," Kit said. But he felt suddenly light-hearted again, grateful for this talent of hers that could remove obstacles between them as quickly as it could erect them.

Kit finally found the airport's hotel reservation desk and took his place in line. During the few minutes he had to wait his turn, he leafed through his mental book of useful Italian phrases. He knew, of course, that he could count on finding at least one person at the desk who spoke English, but his recent experience in Portugal had given him an entirely new perspective on the ancillary benefits of making a little extra effort. He didn't want to make a fool of himself, but he knew he had the accent, and he figured he could make a good stab at the music. The grammar? Let the grammar take care of itself.

When his turn finally came, he stepped up in front of a woman whose beauty, he felt, could easily have gotten catalog work—at the very least—in New York. Here in Rome, however, she was a mere clerk at a hotel reservation desk. He'd already noticed how she'd been strictly business with her previous customer. Suddenly, in his presence, she was all teeth, eyes and lashes that fell around him like a lasso. He let himself be taken in as he glanced down at her name-plate. It perched hallucinogenically atop one of a pair of breasts that—in most counties in the U. S., he mused—local authorities would, at the very least, have restricted to view with a second sign just below her nameplate: NO LOITERING!

"*Buongiorno, Rafaela*," he said grandly. Good Puritan that he was, he announced the name to her face rather than to her name-plate.

"*Buongiorno, Signore!*" she answered gaily—and grateful that a perfect stranger had even bothered to read her name. At the same time, however, she looked more directly at the man standing in front of her—and self-consciously slipped a hand inside her blouse behind the adventitously-lucky name-plate.

"*Cerchiamo una camera per la notte. Un albergo vicino Piazza Campo de' Fiori, si è possibile.*" ("We're looking for a room for the night in the vicinity of the Piazza Campo de' Fiori.")

"*Quanti siete, Signore?*" ("How many of you are there?") she asked as her eyes quickly scanned to the right and left of him to see who 'we' might be. At the same time, Kit noticed that her smile contained not the least hint of condescension to suggest that his efforts were, at least grammatically speaking, in vain.

"*Siamo due, Signora.*" ("Two, Madame.")

"*Signorina,*" ("Miss,") she corrected him. Kit noticed from the glint in her eye that the correction was not a grammatical one. Rather, she was putting him on notice, rutting in one of those subtle ways that *homo sapiens* can rut. He was thankful—though only barely— that his present situation wouldn't allow him to pursue the scent. And opted instead for diplomacy.

"*Scusi, Signorina Rafaela.* ("Excuse me, Miss Rafaela.")

"*Prego,*" she laughed, her laugh the sound of clinking prisms hanging from a bright new chandelier. "*Quanti letti vi servono?*" ("How many beds will you need?") she asked. The gig was up. Kit knew that announcing the number of beds he and Daneka required would quickly move him and Rafaela to end-game.

"*Ce ne serve solo uno, Signorina.*" ("Only one.")

The glint dried up like a gulch, and her eyes disappeared into the deep ravine of her computer. The screen was invisible to Kit as she muttered to herself, though audibly enough for Kit to hear: "*Un albergo vicino Piazza Campo de' Fiori…camera per due persone…un letto…*" Then after only a few seconds, "*Ecco, Signore. Possiamo offrirvi una camera con bagno particolare,* with a queen-sized bed." ("Here we are. We can offer you a room with a private bath.") Kit wondered about the additional information of a "queen-sized bed" offered in very clipped, very *un*Italian consonants.

"That will be perfect, Rafaela. And the price of this *queen-sized* bed for the night?"

"Two hundred and seventy-five euros per couple, per night, for a double room—or four hundred and fifty for a suite," she answered. She was now all business English. "In the *Via dei Cappellari*" she announced as she scribbled the name and address of the hotel down on a piece of paper. "Would you like to pay for it now?"

"Yes, please. And I think we'll make do with the double room. The price of a suite is just too sweet, thank you," Kit added for effect—even as he accepted that his effort was a lost cause. He took out his only credit card and handed it over. The sponge of romance had been wrung dry, and out of it had come only dollars and cents. Time, then, to turn sensible about the whole matter and get back to Daneka.

She handed him pen and receipt. He signed, handed them both back, and retrieved his credit card. He decided to try one final time at a lame bit of gallantry—as chivalry had long since run off with the horses.

"*Mille grazie, Signorina. É stato un piacere.*" ("Many thanks, Miss. It's been a pleasure.")

"*Tutto mio, Signor Addison. Buon viaggio e buon soggiorno! Arrivederci.*" ("Entirely mine, Mr. Addison. Have a pleasant trip and a pleasant stay.") And then, as if the paint of him drying in front of her desk might suddenly begin to peel, she looked around and past him to the next no-one-in-particular, "*Chi viene dopo?*" ("Next in line?")

Kit returned to the baggage claim area in search of Daneka. He saw her at a distance, if barely, as she was surrounded by men looking more like frazzled roosters, and she, the lone—but hardly lonely—hen. Kit eased himself in with an occasional "*Scusate*" so as not to ruffle feathers. This was the only concession to airport culture he cared to make under what he decided were circumstances of strict *transit gloria mundi*—for both of them.

"It's done, Daneka. We have a place in town. We can drive in or take a taxi." At the mention of taxi, the brood of roosters re-frazzled.

Daneka smiled appreciatively, took Kit by the elbow, and led him out to a spot where they could talk. "Darling, why don't we take a couple of night bags, leave the rest in storage, pick all of it and the car up tomorrow morning, and then drive out to Positano from here?"

"Sounds like a plan," he said.

They looked more like two college kids on a Europe-on-five-dollars-a-day tour as they collected their luggage in Baggage Claims, sat down on the floor and began to sort and pack into two bags only the essentials for a one-night stay. At the sight of the two of them floor-bound—and however *un*accustomed to flight—her riot of roosters had flown the coop.

Two bags packed, Kit and Daneka retired the rest to an overnight storage facility, checked in at the car rental agency once again to register the postponement of their departure, then headed out to a taxi stand where they quickly found a car. Kit gave the name and street address of the hotel, and they were off even before he'd had time to close his door. A somewhat harrowing, but appropriately Roman forty-five minutes later through side streets and back alleys, they were standing in front of the hotel. Daneka paid the fare; they registered at the front desk; the porter took their bags; all three then ascended via a cramped elevator smelling of stale cigarette smoke to their floor and room.

This was decidedly not the *Grand Hôtel de Champaigne,* but Rome had not been part of their original itinerary. It would be adequate; it had a bed and a private bathroom—and was, as Kit had noted when they climbed out of their taxi, on a side street leading right up to the Piazza Campo de' Fiori. What's more—as the porter made demonstrably clear to them in the act of flinging open a pair of French doors leading out to a terrace much like the one they'd enjoyed in Paris—their room looked directly out onto that same *piazza.* As far as Kit was concerned—and he hoped, Daneka, too—it was perfect.

Daneka tipped the porter a 5€ note, and he exited gracefully.

"Darling, I'm famished. How about a little stroll and then lunch?"

"Great idea!" Kit answered, eager to get out and have a look around.

"'Give me two minutes in the bathroom, darling?" Daneka asked.

"Certainly. Take your time."

Daneka disappeared behind the bathroom door and Kit unpacked their luggage. He made a quick check of his armpits and decided he and his shirt could ride for a few more hours without tipping to 'offensive.' Daneka re-emerged and picked up her purse. They walked out and locked the door to their room, took the stairs rather than the elevator back down to the lobby, then walked out the front door into bright, midday sunlight.

Chapter 37

The *Piazza Campo de' Fiori* was essentially what he'd expected to find, if somewhat more festive. *Perhaps,* he thought to himself, *the square has a dual personality: all business by day; all romance and intrigue—maybe even mayhem—by night.*

Standing center-ring over the flower and vegetable commerce was the statue of a martyr—of Giordano Bruno, whom Kit could now only vaguely recall as someone who'd challenged the Church, who'd subsequently been condemned by the Inquisition in 1600, and who'd then been promptly torched. Elsewhere on the *piazza,* the brother of Lucrezia Borgia had been poisoned: whether by the very same high priest of celibacy who'd impregnated her or merely by one of the Pope's lackeys, Kit didn't know. Here, too, Caravaggio had served tennis balls—until, that is, *love forty* had led to *ad out*, had led to *love nothing*, and the player of acute artistic sensibilities had bludgeoned his opponent to death with something a little less delicate than a paintbrush.

That was as much history as Kit knew about this particular *piazza.* The more contemporary—and so, to him, far more interesting—history was the one he knew from his parents. They'd been present, off and on, in the Sixties and Seventies to participate in anti-war protests, the first of which had been against the French for their reluctance to leave Algeria and, afterwards, Indochina. The French learned their lesson the hard way, however, and eventually withdrew. The Americans, thinking themselves somehow superior, rushed in to fill the vacuum—and Kit's parents rushed back to Rome to protest not only America's presence in Vietnam, but also Portugal's in Mozambique and Angola. Four years later, Salazar died, and Portugal's colonial empire collapsed. They went to protest, certainly, but also to celebrate the act of protesting. After all, a good march or demonstration sure beat a 9-5 job.

As Kit and Daneka walked among the flower and vegetable stands, he became almost nostalgic for a thing he'd never possessed except by proxy. He considered how little attention his generation had paid to the still-abysmal conditions of most of the rest of the world. Wars, injustice and inhumanity had not stopped or even slowed down; the news of them simply didn't penetrate. All pilgrimages now and for as long as Kit could remember led to celebrity; or if not to celebrity, then to real estate. Burn bright or buy right. Those were the only mantras of raging national debate.

Kit didn't exclude himself from his sweeping condemnation—not by a long shot. He considered how he'd chosen to make a living: by taking pictures of celebrities, or at least of celebrity-like mannequins. When had *he* last participated in a demonstration, volunteered in a soup kitchen, or played father to a fatherless boy for a few hours a week?

Kit suddenly felt the sting of shame. And yet, this wasn't something he could share with the person he cared most about in the world—this woman who walked at his side, but whose commiseration, he suspected, would lead neither of them to a soup kitchen. As if to confirm his suspicions, she grabbed his arm.

"Darling, shall we find a restaurant?"

"I'm sorry, Daneka. You did say you were hungry, didn't you." Kit looked up and saw a sign announcing an eatery called *Osterìa La Carbonara*. It looked inviting enough, and Kit liked that they could eat *al fresco*. He pointed. "Will that one do?"

"Oh, sure, darling. It looks as good as any other."

They walked over and looked among the empty tables for a place to sit. A waiter who'd seen them approaching grabbed two menus. Not knowing in which language to address them, however, he hesitated until Kit provided a handle.

"*Buongiorno, Signore. Siamo due a fare colazione, per piacere.*" ("Two for lunch, please.")

The waiter smiled. "*Buongiorno! Buongiorno! Prego, Signora, Signore*"—and here he gestured with his free hand to an empty table, seated them and handed over a pair of menus. "*Desiderate qualcosa da bere?*" ("Would you like something to drink?")

"*Abbia la gentilezza, Signore, di portarci una carta dei vini.*" ("Please bring us a wine list.")

"*Certo, Signore. Con piacere.*" ("Of course, Sir. It'll be a pleasure.")

So far, it was working splendidly, and Kit was enormously pleased with himself. As for the grammatical errors he was no doubt committing, he didn't care: he was managing, and that was the important thing. He wondered, however, how really fluent Daneka's Italian was, and whether he was yet again making a fool of himself in her eyes. He didn't know how to ask her, and she wasn't giving out clues. She was in this—as in so many things—a complete mystery. Compounding the mystery of her inscrutability was the mystery of his own reluctance to ask the hard questions, to probe beneath the smooth surface of their day-to-day, hour-to-hour intercourse in order to find out who she really was, what she really wanted, what she really thought. He adored her wit. He adored her way with language—not just the words she spoke, but the way she spoke them: her *body* language. And yes, as if he needed to remind himself, he adored in particular the mechanism that made *that* language possible.

But he abhorred the mystery—the part of her she wouldn't reveal to anyone—or perhaps just not to *him*: her disappearances; her extended silences; her total withdrawal when- and however often she felt the need to withdraw. He decided, simply, to broach the subject head-on.

"Daneka, please tell me you don't also speak fluent Italian.".

"Oh, sort of, darling. But you're doing just fine. You don't need any help from me."

Kit was satisfied. He didn't know what to make of the "sort of," but he figured her qualifier would reveal itself to him over the course of the next few days. Besides, the waiter had just returned with the wine list, and Kit now had a more immediate issue to deal with.

They ordered lunch and a bottle of the local red wine. Kit chose something pressed from a combination of Sangiovese and Montepulciano grapes: a wine of no particular account except for the delightful effect his order seemed to produce on the waiter, who appeared to take a special Roman pride in the promotion of anything homegrown—but more to the point, in the promotion of anything that was *not* from Tuscany.

When they finished lunch, Kit ordered a pair of *espressi* and asked for the check. Their waiter's eyebrows suggested disappointment that they were already leaving. Just as quickly, however, the same pair of eyebrows took flight—and their owner with them on equally quick feet—to the kitchen. He returned a few moments later with two glasses and a bottle of grappa in one hand, a single plate—but two forks—of *tiramisù* in the other. He then put down the check in its leather holder next to Kit.

"*Con i complimenti della casa* ("Compliments of the house,"), *Signora, Signore.*"

Already light-headed from the combination of a hot sun and the wine, this unexpected kindness from a no-doubt jaded Roman waiter—not to mention the two additional shots of grappa—all but lifted them off their seats. It was now Daneka's turn to take the lead.

"Mille, mille grazie, carissimo Signore. E' molto gentile!" ("Many, many thanks, dearest Sir. This is very kind of you.")

Kit noted that her accent and cadence were flawless. And yet, it wasn't envy he felt at the discovery: after all, his ear and mouth were quite up to accomplishing the same task with as much authority. Rather, it was an uneasiness, once again, at the mystery. 'Sort of?' What did 'sort of' really mean in Daneka's mouth? Was it simple modesty on her part, or was it meant to diffuse a further inquiry into how, when and under what torrid Tuscan sun she'd learned this language in the first place?

Kit realized he'd just become a victim of his own experience. He knew—and had repeated many times for the benefit of those who might be interested—that the only *real* way to learn a language was in-country, and preferably across a pillow. Years earlier, he'd spent the better part of two years in Madrid not with his head buried in a dictionary or grammar book, but rather on a ravishing Spanish pillow—next to the *real* thing. His lover had had exploration and discovery in her genes. Moreover, she'd proved to be more catholic than Catholic in her tastes. He'd become, as a result, fluent in all things Spanish he cared to be fluent in—even if most of those things had necessarily been limited to the 1st and 2nd Person Singular, Present Tense, of most Spanish verbs.

Kit began to wonder how many languages Daneka spoke—and how many of them she spoke fluently. He remembered that he hadn't seen a single foreign language grammar book or dictionary in her library or bedroom. So much, he thought, for his unique pedagogy as it pertained to the learning of foreign languages.

During the several seconds Kit had been reminiscing about Spain—only then to send his thoughts off on a bumbling quest for the explanation of Daneka's linguistic talents—she'd managed to slip an arm out behind his seat, snatch the leather holder, put her credit card inside it, and deliver the lot under the tablecloth to an amused waiter. She'd also managed to mouth—inaudibly, yet perfectly intelligibly—instructions to that same waiter to add an additional ten points to the fifteen-percent gratuity. He was off and running as she delivered a first forkful of *tiramisù* to Kit's mouth, now pouting as if stuck in the departure lounge of some airport—and in very *un*happy transit between two distinctly undesirable destinations.

"Darling," she said. "You look lost. Take a bite."

By the time the two of them had concluded feeding each other forkfuls of *tiramisù*, their waiter had returned. Daneka signed the receipt, took her copy, and returned the rest. In a parting toast to love, Rome, the *Osterìa La Carbonara,* and the honor of good waiters everywhere, Kit and Daneka raised their glasses and poured the rest of the grappa down each other's throats—but only after their waiter, in tears of gratitude, had snatched a glass off a neighboring table, poured himself a hefty portion, and thrown it down *his* throat.

Embraces all around with cheeky kisses from the waiter to both Daneka and Kit, and they were off—feeling more wobbly than worldly, and in urgent need of some place to lie down and sleep it all off.

Chapter 38

It might otherwise have been a short journey from the *osterìa* to their hotel, but they wanted to savor every step. Between the clip of the cobblestones underfoot and the hammer of the mid-day sun overhead, not to mention the wine and grappa doing time in between, Kit and Daneka somehow managed to bob and weave their way first through the *piazza*—already beginning to thin out as vendors gradually exhausted their one-day provision of flowers, vegetables or fruit; and so, packed themselves, their new supply of cash, and their remaining belongings into small spaces in some means or other of transport and headed, without passion, but also without tumult, back out to the country for an afternoon and evening of unharried domestic quiet far from the congestion of the marketplace—and through the throng of hawkers, buyers, sellers, gawkers, children, babies, *signorinelle* with a plan, *pensionati* without a plan, tourists without a clue, cyclists, ventriloquists, artists, *other* lovers, dancers, necrophiles, necromancers, philosophers, nut-cases: in short, a sampling of the whole human race with its various and crushing thoughts, desires, likes, dislikes, expectations, illusions, delusions, confusions, smells, expectorations, urinations, defecations, vomitus, decrepitude and death—and then rounded the corner into the *Via dei Cappellari*, at which point they spied the front door of their hotel.

Finally free of the crowd, Daneka felt the rush of open space and dropped her guard. As they walked out from between two parked cars into the street at a spot just diagonally opposite the hotel entrance, she craned her neck up to give Kit a kiss on the cheek. At the same instant, a motor scooter approached on her outside flank. The driver navigated his scooter with the precision of a sharpshooter aiming through a scope at a two-inch target a hundred yards off: there was no allowable margin of error between the parked car on his right and Daneka on his left. His accomplice, another even younger kid, rode with one arm circling the driver's waist. With his free arm, the accomplice swooped in like a falcon and snatched Daneka's purse from her shoulder.

The scooter accelerated. It was already thirty yards off before Daneka realized she'd been robbed and then hollered without reserve: *"Al ladro!"* ("Thief!")

There was no need. A pair of shopkeepers at the far end of the street, out for a smoke and a chat, had seen the whole thing, start to finish. As if acting on instinct to a scenario they might've witnessed many times before, they quickly armed themselves with tools of the kind shopkeepers use to roll their awnings up each day at the close of business, then took them in hand like javelins. One of the two men quickly crossed the street to the opposite side. They waited—and when the scooter finally passed by, each thrust his tool, now a weapon, into its spokes. The fine, metal spokes of a kid's motor scooter were no match for the angry iron spikes in the hands of two defenders of a woman's virtue and property. The scooter upended, sending its two occupants off and up, then slid on gracefully and eventually came to a mangled stop. Its two occupants flew through the air like plastic bags scooped up by a sudden draft, and slammed into the rear window of a parked car, shattering it. That same impact likely shattered several of their bones, but the shopkeepers paid no attention to the agony of a pair of young thieves. Instead, their eyes scoured the area for the location of Daneka's purse.

They spotted and retrieved it, then walked the hundred yards from where it had lain to where Daneka stood, and presented their booty. Kit marveled to see the quick transition: just moments earlier, two warriors bent on vengeance if not precisely on murder; now, those same fierce warriors meek and apologetic, as if *they* had committed the crime or had somehow been involved in its perpetration.

Daneka was equally quick to show her gratitude. What she said to them, or they to her, flew by Kit like gibberish. It was, in any case, clear she wanted to offer them something—some token of her appreciation. They refused. They were merely being honorable men, behaving as honorable men should, in times meant to test the mettle of otherwise honorable (note: not *hungry*) men, only to find it lacking.

Eventually they bowed, welcomed both Kit and Daneka to Rome, wished them an enjoyable stay—if possible, without any further such unpleasantness—then shook hands and left. Kit knew his first attention should be to Daneka; after all, she'd been the victim. However, he couldn't get his mind off the two kids.

"Are you all right, Daneka?" he finally asked.

"I thought you'd never ask!" she barked peevishly. It was rare for Daneka to complete a sentence or a question without first making sure that the caboose of 'darling' was firmly attached at the end. Leaving it sidetracked enabled Kit to infer intentional negligence, to toy with the notion of a wreck up ahead—or worse, with a whole terminal of wrecks.

"Look, I know this kind of thing is distressing. I'm sympathetic—really! But I'm also wondering about those two boys. They're probably in bad shape. I need to do something."

"Why do you need to do something about *them*? Why can't you do something about *me* for a change? They're fucking *criminals*, for Christ's sake. They just didn't get away with it this time."

Kit was torn between Daneka's clear yet callous logic and the need, his *personal* need, to help two young kids, however he could, out of a life-threatening situation. As he glanced first at Daneka—apparently at least as angry with him as she'd been, moments earlier, with her two assailants—then up the street to where the halves of two bodies dangled out of the smashed rear window of a parked car, he remained torn. The upshot? He stood motionless, pinioned to the spot by the weight of his indecision.

At the same moment, he saw one of the shopkeepers violently kick the rear bumper of the car out of which the kids' bodies half-hung, and he heard the same man spit out an imprecation: "*Cazzi napoletani!*" ("Fucking Neapolitans!") he cursed, and Kit instantly recognized that other, larger, centuries-old prejudice based on geography alone. They could indeed be gracious, chivalrous—in all manner, perfect gentlemen to a light-skinned woman whose personal sanctuary, whose *private fucking property*, had just been violated. But they could be equally quick, equally ruthless, equally pig-headed, and yes—he allowed himself to draw the comparison—equally *red-necked* in rushing to assign guilt to half the population of an entire country for one act of villainy committed by an isolated pair of individuals. And why? Because those two individuals were obviously poor, probably unskilled, untrained, ill-prepared—and, most obvious of all—darker-skinned.

Kit was as angry as everyone else, but he was angry for his own reasons—none of which had anything to do with Daneka, with the attempted theft, with the apprehension of the two criminals, or with the unfortunate outcome of that apprehension. He was simply angry at the world, at the way it operated, at the persistent and pig-headed *wrongness* of it.

Finally, he channeled anger into action and started off in the direction of the injured boys, though not knowing precisely what he was going to do or how he was going to do it once he got there. Lucky for him, he was saved by the sound of an approaching siren. A

- 186 -

small white car with a roof-mounted beacon and the word *Polizia* printed on the side ripped out of the *Via Giulia* and into the *Via Cappellari,* then screeched to a halt. Two officers in full battledress jumped out. What followed—at least from Kit's perspective—resembled more vaudeville than police action.

Both officers immediately unholstered their guns, then looked to one of the assembled shopkeepers for a clue as to where the miscreants might now be lurking. They then crouched and made their way slowly towards the car whose rear window had, apart from the boys, borne the brunt of the damage in the whole incident. Each carefully unclipped a pair of handcuffs.

What the whole scene lacked, Kit decided, was flares, or at least some kind of high-intensity lighting in case the original siren—and the drama of two cops on the prowl for a pair of world-class terrorists—wasn't sufficiently attention-getting to round up a couple of hundred spectators. In the meantime, Kit thought, these kids were probably bleeding to death.

When the officers finally made it to the back of the car and saw the kids' condition, their first reaction was a clear sense of relief that they, themselves, were not in any danger. Each took out a cigarette and lit up. Kit couldn't hear their conversation. But from their gestures to each other and their occasional glances at the two bodies, and also from their obvious reluctance to retire the handcuffs, Kit could see that law enforcement—apart from a quick cigarette—was still their first priority. They seemed, finally, to reach an accord and divided the boys between them. Each subsequently took his own set of cuffs and clipped one end to "his" boy's ankle and the other end to the car's bumper. They then walked off, Kit noted, in the direction of a *caffè*.

Law enforced. No emergency call. No administration of first aid. No examination of *any* kind to ascertain whether the boys were even still alive. Priorities. First: a cigarette. Second: their personal safety. Third: a cappuccino—maybe even a newspaper.

Kit was on the verge of taking matters into his own hands, whatever it might cost him to challenge the authority of a cop in a foreign country. At that same instant, however, he heard a second siren and saw an ambulance turn the corner and pull up alongside the police car. Three emergency medical personnel jumped out of the ambulance and ran to where the boys were located. All business, they set to work immediately to determine how serious the boys' injuries were. They spoke in hushed, businesslike tones to one another, concerned only with saving a pair of lives that were clearly in jeopardy, and not giving a second thought to the question of whether or not these particular lives were *worth* saving.

Only once they'd made preparations to move the bodies to stretchers did one of the attendants notice the handcuffs. He gave his colleagues a blank, incredulous stare. Kit recognized a few of the expletives, but his Italian wasn't fluent enough to understand and savor how each particular word or phrase condemned first the cops in their private parts, then the cops' mothers in *their* private parts, then various acts between the cops' mothers and a particular shepherd, and finally, similar acts between the same cops' mothers and the shepherd's goats. However, one thing was perfectly clear to him: love and respect between the medical establishment and those responsible for the enforcement of law and order in Rome appeared to be lacking in what the Anglo-Saxon world might like to call, on a good day, vigor—and on a bad day, rigor.

The same attendant went off in search of two of Rome's finest. When the three of them returned moments later, Kit observed the officers' expressions, which more closely resembled those he'd seen on the faces of babies just seconds after they might've dumped a little something into their nappies; the news might not yet have reached others' noses, but it was most assuredly lighting up their own.

The officers unlocked the hand-cuffs. The attendants carefully moved the bodies onto stretchers, then moved the stretchers to the ambulance. The driver of the ambulance swung his vehicle into reverse, turned on his siren, then began to back out onto the *Via Giulia*. In an effort to save whatever small portion of face might yet be salvageable, the two officers moved to the center of the street and brought traffic to a halt so that the ambulance could safely exit.

It did, then left the scene quickly. The officers disappeared back into the *caffè*. The crowd dispersed and went about its business. Only as he turned to walk back to the hotel did Kit notice that Daneka had also ditched the scene.

When he unlocked the door to their hotel room, he saw Daneka standing in front of the French doors, arms crossed over her chest, looking out through thin, lace curtains onto the *piazza* below. She remained standing with her back to him as he closed the door.

"I hope you had a wonderful time, darling." Her tone was frigid, but at least the all-too-familiar caboose was back with the train. Kit wondered how firmly hitched it really was; marveled at how easily she could disconnect and reconnect the 'darling'; wondered, too, about the reliability of train travel with her if she was the only one deciding which cars traveled, which didn't, for how long or short of a journey, and on which pair of tracks.

"I'm sorry, Daneka. Somebody needed to do something for those boys, and I just didn't see anything happening. Turns out, I was wrong. Somebody *had* called the police— and an ambulance. They'll be fine now. I thin—"

"Yes, I'm sure they will be. At least I *hope* so. To rise and strike another day, the poor darlings!"

Kit found her riposte slightly nettling. He noted the tone, but also her use of *the word* in a distinctly *un*affectionate context. He was beginning to hate the sound of it, her careless use of it, her fucking *ab*use of it as she seemed quite willing and able to apply it to everything short of a dishtowel. It was like some kind of *patois* for the jet set. So much of her vocabulary was, to his ear, original, spontaneous, at times even poetic. She could make adjectives dance on tip-toe, invert nouns and verbs like jelly-jointed contortionists, put even simple pronouns on parade in a way that made him want to sit back and applaud. But this other—this affectation that sounded to him like the yip of a nervous poodle—*this* was beginning to stick in his ear. *If only there were a way to disabuse her of—*.

"Darling, I forgive you," she said as she turned around and faced him. "Let's not squabble or quibble. Let's, instead, cuddle."

Case in point. The ear-jerk of her first word was immediately muffled by the mess of crazy quilts in which she dressed the rest of her consonants. The initial zing to his *darling*-weary ear became a mere tickle in the flutter of syllables that followed. He was once again wax; she, once again, flame.

She pushed him to the bed, climbed on top and straddled his hips. "Do me, darl—"

Kit quickly put a finger to her lips. She hushed. With the same hand, he reached between her parted thighs and pulled her panties to one side. She raised up on her legs just enough for him to turn his hand over and pull his zipper down. At the same time, she pulled her dress over her head and flung it across the room, knocking a table-lamp to the floor. He reached around behind her to undo her bra, but fumbled with the snap. She reached up in front and tore the bra off, then threw it in the direction of the table-lamp and dress. In the meantime, her panties had slipped back. He pushed them once again to the side and prepared to enter her, but the soft silk slipped back yet again.

Daneka reached down with both hands, set them in opposition to one another, grabbed the silk and tore. She then took hold of him with one hand, raised her knees off the bed while propping herself up with the other hand, guided the tip of him two or three strokes across the moist petals of her inner labia, and plunged down.

The thunder-cluster of consonants that had served moments earlier to bring them under a common umbrella became, instead, a spring shower of sibilance.

"Yes! Yes! Yes! Yes! YES! YES...." The only variation to Daneka's declaration was in its crescendo, which neither of them made any effort this time to stifle. When she came, seconds later, and he immediately after her, an appreciative street vendor down below paused long enough in his packing to glance up at their open window.

"*Bravi!*" he said, nodding his head in approval.

A satisfied minute later, Daneka climbed off Kit, then turned away from him and curled up in a fetal position. He curled up behind her—placing his knees behind her knees, his stomach against her lower back, one arm over her breasts, and his lips against the nape of her neck, which he kissed progressively more softly until both of them drifted off to sleep.

Chapter 39

Kit awoke several hours later after a long sleep—then crawled carefully out of bed so as not to wake Daneka, who seemed almost to be in a coma. He surveyed the chaos in the room and chuckled, then slipped on a pair of jeans and walked to the French doors and out to the terrace overlooking the *piazza* below.

It was early evening, and nothing in all of Kit's experience had prepared him for the sight of an early-evening Italian sky in late spring. He was a photographer who knew how to create magic with light, shadow, shade and all of the nuances in between. And yet, he was at a loss to name—much less describe—what here and now met his eyes.

The sun had apparently already dipped below the western horizon. In its place, he watched as the promise of another far more subtle visual delight climbed up from the same favonian source behind the thirteenth-, fourteenth- and fifteenth-century residential buildings surrounding the *piazza*. As it passed through filters of dust particles close to the Earth's surface and then feathered out onto billowy cumulous cushions, this refracted light played with a palette of pinks, oranges and reds unlike any Kit had ever seen replicated in a color spectrum.

At the same time, gangs of swallows chased flying insects, when not each other, in funnels up and down and across the *piazza*—a pointillist's portrayal of whirlwinds, occurring and then dissipating just as suddenly and as randomly as they might in the desert or at sea.

At ground-level, he noted activity quite different from what he'd seen earlier that day. Preparations were underway for some form of entertainment or spectacle. If Paris could have its summertime *son et lumière* on the Champs Elysée, and Athens its equivalent at the Acropolis, then Rome, Kit suspected, could certainly accomplish something more on the *Piazza Campo de' Fiori* than mere window dressing for the next day's bit of business. *What luck*—he thought to himself—*that we weren't able to drive directly on to Positano, but instead decided to spend the night here!*

Elaborate scaffolding stood at center stage just behind the statue of Giordano Bruno. To what purpose, Kit still didn't know—and nothing about the scaffolding itself gave him any real indication. It was obviously robust enough to handle something reasonably heavy, but not large enough to accommodate too many of whatever—or whoever—was going to sit or stand upon it.

As he looked to his far right, he saw a flatbed truck arriving through one of the side streets leading into the *piazza*. On it—and surrounding some large, black, solid object that Kit couldn't yet identify—were about a half-dozen young men. As the truck came into clearer focus, he realized the object was a piano—a grand, no less. So *that* was it: a concert of some kind; and if a grand piano, then probably something classical. But looking at the throngs of younger people starting to enter the *piazza,* he somehow doubted it. This might well be the country that had given birth to grand opera, but young people were young people the world over. He didn't suppose that hundreds of young people—though beginning to look more like potential thousands—would come to the center of town on a weekday night to listen to a classical recital.

No, he decided. *It had to be something else. But what?*

Kit dressed quickly but quietly. Daneka was still fast asleep and—he noticed for the first time—snoring. *How delightful!* he thought. *A snoring Danish mermaid.*

He opened and closed the door quietly, walked the couple of flights down to the lobby, then decided to check with Reception to see whether someone might know what it was all about. He approached the desk clerk, who looked up with a cordial smile.

"*Buona sera, Signore,*" Kit said.

"*Buona sera!*" the clerk answered with what Kit thought was slightly more enthusiasm than a mere exchange of greetings should warrant.

"*Mi dica, Signore. Sa che cosa sucede nella piazza stasera?*" ("Tell me, Sir. Do you know what's happening this evening on the piazza?")

"*Ma si, Signore. C'è una dimostrazione contro l'invasione.*" ("But of course, Sir. A demonstration against the invasion.")

"*Contro l'invasione?*" Kit asked. "*Contro che invasione?*" ("Against *what* invasion?")

"*Ma contro l'invasione dell'Iraq. Me ne dispiace.*" ("Against the invasion of Iraq. Sorry.")

Kit couldn't believe his luck. "*Grazie, Signore. Mille grazie!*"

"*Prego.*"

The one night in his entire life he's in Rome—an extraordinary bit of serendipity to begin with—and he's going to bear witness to an antiwar demonstration!

If only I'd brought my camera, he thought wistfully. But no. This evening, his eyes would be his camera. This evening, he'd make himself look and record with his mind and not with film; he'd force himself to remember—then later, when he next saw his parents, to relate—every detail of the drama he was about to witness. This evening, he'd *participate* for a change, and not merely chronicle.

He walked out the front door of the hotel, turned and crossed the thirty feet of cobblestone between the hotel entrance and the *piazza*. He was already being jostled by far more pedestrians than he'd seen in the same place earlier that day, though commerce was not the reason for this human tumult. Their reason was a cause—and one to which Kit subscribed. What they might do if they discovered he carried the passport and spoke the language of the 'enemy' was something he couldn't know. He hoped, if his identity were somehow discovered, they'd be generous enough to overlook his passport and his age and accept his show of solidarity—to accept him, simply, as one of their own.

At the same time, he hoped there'd be no flag-burnings or anti-American sloganeering. Kit deplored patriotic displays no matter what the cause. A part of him actually hated the Fourth of July—its excess and the refuge it afforded every scoundrel to wax bombastic about something for which most had never spent a single drop of sweat, never mind blood. Likewise, he found the mob chorus of "USA! USA!" at international athletic competitions so repugnant, he could no longer even tune in to watch the events on television.

For the same reason, however, he hated to see flag-burnings—whether of his own stars and stripes or of any other country's colors. Flags, he knew, were merely a symbol. But they symbolized the poetry and pain, the hard work and high hopes, of simple people as much as they did the military or economic might (or lack of it) of a nation. He knew it was the simple people—above all the poor people—who were history's waifs. That it was they who'd died defending not a mere flag or a way of life about which they could only dream, but rather the *hope* that some little portion of that dream could one day be theirs; or if not theirs, then their children's—or their children's children's.

In flag-burnings and sloganeering, Kit knew, the mob ignored those people and their dreams. And so, they were twice cursed: once to serve—to become wounded or crippled for life, possibly to die—for a cause and a way of life they could, at best, hope to enjoy the crumbs of; and a second time in being included in the general condemnation—and so, rendered mute, voiceless and every bit as villainous in their graves or in their wheelchairs as those who waged war in their names and who sent them into battle by the truckload.

Now, just a couple of dozen feet away from what was obviously a stage of some kind, Kit looked at the flatbed and thought there were much more worthwhile things one could do with a truck than haul soldiers into battle.

The half-dozen or so young men aboard the flatbed wasted no energy on banter as they prepared to lift the grand piano to the stage. Kit heard *"uno, due, trè"* as they all simultaneously reached under and lifted up, moving the instrument carefully to its recently erected platform. Let the world say what it might about Italian engineering know-how and can-do attitude towards hard work—or lack of, as the case might rather be; in this instance, both were proving to be quite up to the task.

The piano in place, the ad hoc crew of young roustabouts turned its attention to power. Within minutes, they'd jury-rigged an electrical system for microphone and lights that put the stage in sharp relief against the *piazza* that surrounded it, practically invisible in its obscurity as night had indeed descended like a heavy, black curtain over Rome, over the Piazza Campo de' Fiori, and over the demonstrators. Incredible as it seemed to someone who lived in a city where the lights never really went out, and who'd consequently never seen the stars from street-level or even from his rooftop, Kit looked up and saw an entire panorama of them twinkling like little beacons. At the same time, he surveyed the circumference of the *piazza* and remarked, in amazement, that every window had gone dark; that in each stood a candle; that from behind each, in pale reflection of the meager power each candle projected, a face—sometimes two or three or four—looked out in eager anticipation of the spectacle that was about to take place.

This, then, was the romance and the light he'd seen so often in his parents' eyes whenever they'd spoken of *their* Roman moment. And here he was, a generation and thirty-plus years later, about to drink from the same fabled fountain.

Kit felt gooseflesh rise up on his arms. At the same time, he realized—whatever the consequences—that he was stuck. The *piazza* was packed. How they'd all gotten in so quickly was a mystery to him, but he couldn't deny the evidence of it: he was locked in by warm bodies. As he looked from one face to another in the crowd, the names Rafaela,

Laura, Julietta and Beatrice occurred to him again for the first time since his arrival at the airport. He'd never seen so many gorgeous women—*or* men for that matter—in one place at one time.

A bearded, bespectacled—and somewhat less than gorgeous—someone or other ascended the platform and stood in front of the microphone. "Testing, *uno, due, tre,*" he said, and apparently found the volume and clarity entirely satisfactory. Then, for the obvious benefit of some of the old-timers in the crowd, he bellowed: *"Fate attenzione! La CIA ci spia!"* ("Be careful! The CIA's watching us!")

A roar went up in response. It may have been an old Sixties chant, but it had clearly lost none of its power to electrify a crowd. The CIA was always spying on *someone* or other, though in more recent times, rather less effectively. Given the effusiveness of the roar—and Kit detected a great deal of laughter in the mix—maybe even the Italians understood this newer reality.

The speaker droned on for a bit about Irak, about Afghanistan, about Yankee imperialism, about Western imperialism—the usual stuff and fluff of antiwar demonstrations. He introduced a few other bearded somebodies or other who read from the poems of Gabriele D'Annunzio, Alfonso Gatto, and Cesare Pavese; one or two articles from Antonio Gramsci's *Letters from Prison*; translations from Siegfried Sassoon, Wilfred Owen and Rupert Brooke; and finally, but from the lips of a woman Kit thought resembled a jean-clad Greek or Roman goddess more than any mortal he'd ever seen, a couple of the antiwar poems of Giuseppe Ungaretti followed by a rendering, in Italian, of three or four of the love poems of Pablo Neruda. *Leave it to the Italians,* he thought, *to kick off an antiwar demonstration with paeans to love.*

Just as she concluded to rather too-generous applause—at least as much for the visual privilege of her reading as for the aural honor of Ungaretti's and Neruda's writing, Kit was certain—the first bearded, bespectacled somebody returned to the microphone. Now, he informed the crowd, the music would begin, and he had the privilege of introducing two relatively unknown, but—at least in *his* opinion—highly regarded artists. Both carried passports and spoke the language of the 'enemy.' The crowd booed and hissed. But each, he reminded that same crowd, spoke for his own country's opposition to the invasion. The fickle Roman mob cheered. What's more, the speaker insisted, each did it in his own way with music and poetry that was on a par with the best antiwar lyrics ever written. The skeptical crowd remained silent.

The first man to be introduced was as much a mystery to Kit as—he assumed—to most if not all of those present: an Australian by the name of Eric Bogle—a squat man with a bit of a pot belly, and who wore a funny old hat. He was accompanied by an entourage of musicians bearing various kinds of guitars, a cello, a flute, a recorder, a fiddle, a mandolin, an autoharp and a dulcimer. One of them also wore a harmonica around his neck—Dylan-style. Bogle himself carried a banjo and a guitar. He laid the banjo down and stepped up to the microphone to introduce his band.

"*Buona sera, compagni e compagne!*" ("Good evening, comrades!") he started off, his Aussie accent coming through loud and clear in a bumbled attempt at Italian which the crowd quickly warmed up to.

He gave a nod to his band, then started in on a song Kit recognized immediately: *No Man's Land*. The crowd was amazingly respectful, Kit thought, as many around him quietly provided ad hoc translations for the benefit of those who didn't understand enough English to get the gist of the song.

Bogle concluded his first number to enthusiastic applause. He put down his guitar, then picked up his banjo and announced his second number in English: *And The Band Played Waltzing Matilda*. Kit had never heard of it; but by the second stanza, he was mesmerized by the simple lyrics. Once again, many around him served as translators to others. As Bogle approached the conclusion of the song and started in on the more familiar refrain of the original *Waltzing Matilda*, Kit was amazed to hear the crowd sing along with him. A chorus of thousands of peaceful voices could be a moving thing, especially when those voices were singing in a language that was not their own. However much he might've deplored America's part in making English the *de facto lingua franca* of the commercial world, this was one instance in which he felt something approaching pride.

Bogle and his band finished up with a word of thanks. The demonstrators, in return, thanked him with thunderous applause.

The next performer was a tall, wiry American, a man by the name of John McCutcheon. Kit wondered whether the crowd would react with hostility; it did not. Either they'd taken their host's earlier words to heart, or McCutcheon had a reputation here, locally, that would seem to have largely escaped him at home. He also greeted the audience with a cheerful "*Buona sera*" and then introduced his band on fiddle, viola, cello, guitar, mandolin, mandocello, and half a dozen other instruments.

As McCutcheon picked up his guitar and started in, Kit recognized the song instantly as one he'd grown up with: *Christmas in the Trenches.* The melody was hauntingly simple; the accompaniment spare and perfectly attuned to the stripped-down poignancy of the lyrics. As for the song itself, McCutcheon had the perfect voice: deep, unaffected; as clear as well water. Kit felt a tight spot in his chest as he listened. He looked around and saw tears on the cheeks of many of those in his vicinity who were listening with one ear to the singer, the other to a translator. It was a long song, yet no one seemed to tire of it. When McCutcheon concluded as simply as he'd begun, there was a moment of near-perfect silence, followed by the same thunderous applause that had greeted Bogle at the conclusion of *his* performance.

Kit wondered again at his luck: two talented musicians who clearly didn't just happen to be passing through at the same time looking to busk on the sidewalks of Rome. He wondered, too, who could possibly follow them. The demonstration was not yet at an end; that much was clear to him. But how *would* it end?

Kit sensed a bit of a stirring off to the left and behind where he stood. Someone was coming through, and the crowd's enthusiasm for this new arrival was not only audible, but palpable. When he was finally close enough for Kit to see a face, Kit didn't recognize the man—middle-aged, salt and pepper beard and hair, wearing dark-framed glasses, dressed in faded jeans and a loose-fitting shirt. Kit didn't, however, have long to wait.

A chorus of "Antonello! Antonello!" rose from thousands of voices. Kit was beginning to think he was in a dream. *Could it possibly be*—? The man ascended the stage and spoke a few words into the microphone. What he said had the immediate result of quieting the crowd to near silence. He subsequently turned and said a few private words to the emcee, then seated himself at the piano. Opposite him sat a second musician at a synthesizer. The two of them waited a few moments while Bogle, McCutcheon and both of their bands came back up on the stage. Their collective re-appearance—Kit decided—was apparently the substance of whatever the man had just said to the emcee.

The still unidentified artist and his accompanist nodded to each other and smiled in that way musicians have of communicating—especially when they're about to be transported by music. Then the man—this Antonello—lifted his hands to the piano and played a few notes. His partner answered after a few bars in what sounded to Kit like a synthesized hammer dulcimer, or perhaps a mandolin—he couldn't be sure which.

Eventually, the man began to sing.

"Campo de' fiori io non corro più, gli amici di ieri,…"

And then Kit was sure. It was. It was Antonello Venditti! And he was singing the song that took its title from this very *piazza;* the song that had been a rallying cry through the Sixties and Seventies for all kinds of protests; the song that had been the musical equivalent of baby's milk to Kit in his infancy; the song that—no matter how bad their mood, how deep some passing disagreement—had always brought his parents into each other's arms; the song that then stood for them as a reminder of better times, of *bigger* times and *bigger* issues than their temporary disagreement; the song that had, by dint of serendipity, brought Kit to request a room in a hotel overlooking this *piazza* so that he could share all of it, in some way, with Daneka.

"il tempo ha già sconfitto le ombre di un'età.
E gli amori, gli amori, sono proprio veri
e non ho più paura della li-ber-tà."

The tight spot he'd felt in his chest earlier as McCutcheon had sung his song now became a hard knot of emotion. The plaintive melody and lyrics recalling lost, carefree youth and an increasingly uncertain future threatened to overwhelm him as he suddenly felt what it meant to grow older and lose that gift of carefree youth.

As he first remarked how the other musicians, one by one, seemed to be picking up on the melody; as he further remarked that voices around him were starting to sing along with Venditti until the entire *piazza* was one mass of twenty, thirty, forty thousand singing voices; and finally, when he felt arms to either side of him slipping through his and pulling him back and forth in a human wave to the music; it and his resulting emotions no longer *threatened* to overwhelm him: they *did* overwhelm him. As he felt warm tears running unabashedly down his cheeks, he looked at his nearest partners in this wave of human bodies and saw through smiles back to him and mouths rapturously moving to the song's lyrics that their cheeks, too, were covered in rivers of tears.

One of them—a beautiful young girl who'd slipped her arm through his, and who apparently realized that Kit was not Italian, graciously—if unnecessarily and somewhat clumsily—began to translate for him:

> *"Campo de' Fiori: I no longer run among the friends of yesterday.*
> *Time has already conquered the shadows of an age.*
> *Love is now for real, and I'm no longer afraid of freedom."*

Kit already knew that there are episodes in life that you take to the grave—episodes that remind you, in your death rattle, of why it was all worth it, of what it meant to be *really* alive, if only for those few moments. And of why every living thing, from a thousand-year-old Redwood to the ten thousand-year-old lichen that lives upon it, will fight to the death to maintain that life, sometimes against seemingly impossible odds. For Kit, this was one such episode.

> *"Ma i tuoi bambini crescono bene, rubano sempre ma non tradiscono mai.*
> *Oh mai, oh mai.*
> *Campo de' fiori io non corro più, sulle strade di ieri*
> *il tempo ha già sconfitto i soldi di papà,*
> *ma le partite stavolta sono proprio vere*
> *e adesso ho un po' paura per la libertà."*

The young girl next to him continued to translate:

> *"My, but your children grow well.*
> *They may steal, but they never betray.*
> *Never!*

Campo de' Fiori: I no longer run along the roads of yesterday.
Time has already exhausted all of Papa's money;
and so the games this time are for real,
and now I'm a bit anxious about liberty."

Only one thing lacked, and it occurred to him that he hadn't thought about her in an hour. The thing keeping this moment from being a perfect souvenir was that Daneka was not present to share it with him.

"I tuoi bambini io li vedo crescono bene,
rubano sempre ma non tradiscono mai.
Oh mai, oh mai.
Adesso ho un po' paura per la li-ber-tà."

"I see your children growing up well.
They may steal, but they never betray.
Never!
And now, I am a bit anxious about liberty."

He wondered if she still slept, and looked up again at the buildings surrounding the *piazza*. As before, he noticed that all of the windows were dark except for the dim flicker of candles burning in each. He then looked to where he imagined their hotel room to be. Light shown through a single pair of French doors—faintly, behind gauze-like curtains. In dark silhouette behind those same curtains, and in sharp relief against the light behind her, stood a woman. Although the silhouette revealed to him nothing of the face, Kit could make out immediately from her curves, from her height, from the way her hair fell to her shoulders, to whom that silhouette belonged.

She stood, unmoved and unmoving, not part of any wave. Not part of any wave at all, except her own.

Chapter 40

The demonstration concluded without incident. Kit exchanged quick kisses on the cheek with each of his two immediate neighbors. The one who'd just provided him with a translation of Venditti's song let her lips linger a bit longer than mere Continental custom might've dictated, and Kit was acutely aware of it. He was equally aware of her breasts, now pressing against his chest in a way that suggested to him in the afterglow of the demonstration why Rome was called *la città eternal*—but could, just as easily—he mused—be called *la città materna*. With her lingering lips and breasts that seemed to want to ponder where they could best press, she, too, apparently meant to remain eternal—at least in one man's mind.

Her lips strayed from one cheek as he rotated his face to give her the other. Halfway through that rotation, however, they stopped and found *his* lips—and lingered longer.

She was gorgeous, and Kit suddenly felt himself caught in chasm: a hiatus of no happy exit. The woman he loved was not more than two-hundred yards away—nothing in real distance, although he wondered how really far removed they were, one from the other. This other woman, this beautiful stranger, had her lips on his. Roman lips—like rose petals; lips of almost unfathomable fullness; lips that seemed to dissolve, then resolve, blending into his until he felt that his own were merely an obstruction.

He loved Daneka's mouth. He loved what she could do with it and the words that came out of it; the expressiveness of it; occasionally, the wantonness of it. But hers were Scandinavian lips that could be smart, terse, indicative, stentorian, imperative.

These were Roman lips. These lips dwelt in the conditional tense and in the subjunctive mood: What if—? If only—. If one might—. If we could—. The conditional and subjunctive, Kit knew, were a danger zone. He took stock of the situation: he was susceptible at this moment and he knew it. Rome would not have him, not tonight. He broke the kiss.

"*Come ti chiami?*" ("What's your name?") he asked. She let go of his lips, but not of him. Instead, she leaned her lower body harder into his.

Her mouth slipped back from Kit's and found his ear. "*Mi chiamano Afrodite*," she breathed. ("My name is Aphrodite.")

Kit wondered whether he was hallucinating and whether the whole last hour—and now this woman—were merely a dream. This Roman goddess of love could, he knew, easily tempt him into an Elysium of her own making. But he was already in love—and with another woman.

"*Dunque, Afrodite, La ringrazio per tutto*," ("In that case, Aphrodite, I thank you for everything,") Kit said and gently disengaged himself.

Her hampster's pout and withdrawing breasts felt to him, at that moment, like the contents of a canteen poured into the sand before the eyes of a man crawling out of the desert. But Kit had willed it. Just before he let her go, he kissed her softly on the forehead and hoped the gesture would help to remove any shame she might've felt at his rejection.

He made his way back through the dispersing crowd to the hotel, took the elevator up to the fourth floor, unlocked the door and entered. Daneka stood waiting for him with her back to the *piazza*.

"Perhaps now, darling, we can get a little something to eat?" Her mood was neither peevish nor petulant. Apparently, she was just hungry—and now well-rested. Kit was enormously relieved. He was also eager to tell her what he'd just witnessed, to share with her in words what he'd wanted to share with her in person.

"Where shall we go, darling?" He, too, could use the "D-word" once in a while without offending his own ear in its employment. It didn't offend because he meant every endearing letter of it. She was, to him, a darling—and becoming more so by the hour.

"Let's walk a bit, shall we? Perhaps we'll find something over by the river. I want to cross the Tiber at least once in my life and pronounce '*Alea iacta est!*' ('The die is cast!') She said it comic-grandly, and Kit thought he might just fall in love all over again with this daughter of Vikings now quoting Rome's most famous general. He dropped to a knee in mock-homage and took one of her sandaled feet in both hands.

"Allow me to render unto Caesar what is Caesar's."

"*Fiat!*" ("So be it!") she pronounced, at which point Kit bent to her foot and kissed it—once, twice, three times. Her Latin then began to work its ancient wonders. He pushed her gently back onto the bed with no resistance. Instead, she looked up at him inquisitively and with just a bit of a smile on her lips. Kit removed her sandal and replaced it with his mouth. He slid his tongue between two toes, sucked on one and then the other, giving each a long moment and equal attention. Only once he'd sucked on all five did he allow his tongue to move slowly up her ankle.

"And dinner, darling?" Daneka rasped, though her inquiry this time clearly lacked its former urgency.

"Precisely," Kit answered as his mouth and tongue made their devious way up over her calf, behind her knee, then over her kneecap. Without any prompting from him, Daneka was already reaching down to take hold of the hem of her dress. As his head slowly ascended one leg, she began to pull the material up towards her waist, one snail's footstep at a time. Kit, however, was in no rush to get through his first course. He nibbled just above her knee, then moved his head back down to the other foot. Off came the second sandal; on went his mouth. He sucked and licked even more slowly on the other five toes, then began his ascent up her second leg: the ankle; then the calf; then, finally, her knee.

Daneka's breathing sounded like bats fluttering around the ceiling of a cave. Kit noticed as his head moved up between her thighs that her fingers trembled as they bunched and pulled back the material of her dress. He nibbled gently on her thighs. Daneka pulled the material up over her panties, then dropped it and moved her hands up to her chest. Without waiting for him, she slipped her hands inside her dress, then pulled her bra up over her breasts and began to caress them. The caresses were at first almost motherly, but increased in urgency and roughness as Kit's head inched up.

When he finally reached her panties and put his mouth on her, Daneka whimpered, raised her knees and spread her legs so that a foot hung on the edge of either side of the bed. Kit exhaled a long, warm breath. Her response came from deep within, the bloom of which Kit eagerly sucked on from outside her panties. He continued alternately blowing and sucking on the thin material. Her whimper turned into a groan, as she now verged on tears of bittersweet frustration.

Kit had no desire to prolong that frustration another second. He reached up between her thighs with one hand and pushed her panties aside. What greeted his eyes was the thing that seemed to occupy almost all of his waking hours. Those same eyes, he knew, would never see enough of it; his mouth would never grow indifferent to the taste of it; his nose, with its curious memory, could conjure up the smell of it at any instant, awake or asleep, and yet he knew that that nose would welcome every opportunity to renew the memory with a fresh impression.

His fingers moved like foot-soldiers over her *mons*, first teasing the hair, then delicately parting her outer and inner lips to allow entry to his tongue. As he pushed it in, Daneka reached in under her thighs and pulled her legs back to her chest. Kit first peeled off her panties, then grabbed both bed-pillows and pushed them in under Daneka's hips. Her abdomen was now a good six inches off the bed, her legs splayed. He angled his chin in snugly against her perineum and pushed his tongue as far into her as he could—until, with the tip of it, he could just barely sense the presence of her cervix. And then he began— slowly at first, but building momentum—his tongue thrusts. Daneka pulled her thighs tighter against her chest, and Kit could see her strain. He adored how, in complete abandon, she attempted to meet his thrusts with her own. As he sensed that she was only seconds away from orgasm, he quickly reversed their positions and put *his* head on the pillow— which allowed her, in effect, to ride his face.

Another couple of seconds passed by while Daneka regained her rhythm. When they both knew she could no longer hold back, she suddenly reached down and pulled Kit's head into her—pressing down on his mouth with as much strength as she could still muster. Her head fell to the bed and she screamed into the sheets. At the same time, her muscles began to contract, sending the evidence of her euphoria down into Kit's mouth and throat. Each time she contracted, Kit eagerly swallowed. The contractions and swallowing seemed to have no end. Nor did the recklessness of Daneka's screams.

After what seemed to both of them a small eternity, all of it finally subsided. Daneka's screams of passion presently turned into weeping. She moved her head and body down to Kit's and embraced him with a feverish affection that surprised both of them. It seemed to him in these post-orgasmic moments that she simply couldn't get close enough, but instead kept pushing, trying harder to cover every inch of his body with hers. Tears fell furiously as she pressed her head into his neck. Her wailing was like that of an inconsolable child, and Kit didn't know whether to be happy or alarmed.

When Daneka's breathing returned to normal several minutes later, she raised her head and looked directly into Kit's eyes.

"I love you more than my own life," she said. A fresh set of tears began to fall as she contemplated the depths of the emotional abyss into which she had, with this too-hastily made confession, just slipped.

Chapter 41

Kit stood up from the bed and pulled Daneka up with him. He hadn't intended to answer her confession with one of his own, as he really didn't know what to say. Instead, he embraced her, then kissed both her eyes—now slightly puffy and lacking any evidence of the elaborate make-up she'd applied to them while he'd been at the demonstration.

"Let me take a quick shower and then smarten myself with a bit of science, darling. I won't be ten minutes. 'Promise."

"No!" Kit was prepared to stand firm. Daneka looked at him curiously.

"What do you mean, 'no'?"

"I mean 'no!' No shower. No make-up. No anything but what I see right in front of me here and now."

"But Kit, I'm a mess!"

"You're nothing of the kind. I've never seen you more beautiful!" Daneka's look suggested to Kit that she didn't know whether to feel flattered or devastated. "I mean, yes. Of course I have. But there's a raw, uncluttered beauty about you at this moment that I adore—that I want to enjoy now and for the rest of my life."

"But my laugh-lines!" Either Daneka hadn't heard Kit's declaration, or she'd quite intentionally passed right over and around it. "I can't go out like this. People might think I'm your mother."

"Let people think what they fucking well will. You and I know you're nothing of the kind. That's enough for me. Isn't it for you?" Kit suspected he should say something to disabuse her, once and for all, of this nagging discrepancy in their ages. But it was too late; he'd missed the opportunity—and Daneka's pained expression confirmed it.

"Please, darling. At least a little powder."

"Okay. A little."

He sat back down on the bed while Daneka went into the bathroom and half-closed the door behind her. When he heard her turn on the shower, however, he jumped up and pushed the door open.

"*No!* No shower!"

"But darling! I smell—. Oh, I don't know. I think I smell a little—."

"You smell divine. You smell savage. You smell like sex. You're a line of pure nose-candy. No shower."

"May I at least—? You know."

"No you may not! Powder—that's it!"

Daneka chuckled. "Well, darling, it's *your* nose." She turned to the mirror, studied her face for a couple of seconds, then reached into her make-up bag. Kit walked out of the bathroom and sat back down on the bed. Two minutes later, she re-emerged with just enough powder and rouge on her face to highlight her cheeks to bewildering effect. She went to the dresser, pulled open a drawer and took out another pair of panties. Kit jumped off the bed and came up behind her. He took the panties out of her hand and dropped them back into the drawer, then closed it.

"And no panties."

Daneka looked at him for a moment as if he'd gone perfectly mad, then chuckled. "Are you planning on a second course before we even sit down to dinner?"

"Maybe."

Daneka stared hard at Kit as she moved like a leopard to a position directly in front of him. She reached inside his jeans, and Kit felt himself respond immediately to her touch.

"Well, now," she whispered. "Let's not forget that I, too, have an appetite." Kit put his mouth on hers. She responded with her tongue, with a murmur, and with a squeeze. As she dropped her other hand to undo his belt buckle, he reached for it.

"Now stop that! C'mon," he said, taking hold of both of Daneka's wrists. "We have to eat something. We're going to die here if we don't!"

"Yes, I know, darling. But *what* a way to die! One little nibble before we go? Just one little nibble for this naughty nymphet?" she asked as she returned unabashedly with both hands to his belt buckle and zipper.

She had the first undone and the second down before Kit could object. Whatever his head and stomach told him, another part of him was demanding the contrary—and Daneka knew precisely how to answer the call. She dropped to her knees; freed him of his pants and underwear; took him into her mouth. Kit looked down at her—this woman he loved almost to the point of pain—and wondered at his luck. Not only was she brilliant and beautiful, clever and charismatic, seductive and occasionally even seditious; she could also give a blow-job, he imagined, like nobody else on the planet. He watched as her lips worked, crawling steadily and cautiously forward until she had taken in all of him. He knew that many men preferred oral to genital sex. He didn't. Whatever power or dominance the act suggested was not something that moved him. He liked oral sex, but only as titillation, as foreplay, as a preamble to the real thing. And the real thing for Kit was being inside her; his mouth on her mouth; his arms around her, and hers around him.

He knew he could easily have come in that instant. He knew that Daneka would not have objected, and that she would've been delighted to see, once again, how easily she could bring a man to climax. But not now. Later. Tonight. In bed. Inside her—where once again, with luck, he could make her come *with* him.

"Darling," he whispered as he bent down and gently forced her to disengage. "Let's go to supper."

They arrived by elevator at the ground floor and walked across the hotel lobby. At the sight of Daneka, the bell captain wasted no time in stepping up to open the front door for her. Having paused momentarily to pull out a cigarette, Kit trailed her with just enough space to see the bell captain's nostrils flare as she passed by. Kit smiled to himself at the man's unconscious gesture. This vestige, this left-over from a time when *homo sapiens* were not yet *homo sapiens*, when their bodies were still covered with hair, when they freely and spontaneously reacted with their noses not to the chemical concoctions of Revlon or Estée Lauder, but to the natural flower of estrus or the musk of a female's unwashed hind quarters—this, Kit knew, was also human. It took someone like Daneka, however, to make the latent obvious.

They walked arm in arm like young lovers—like young, *Roman* lovers—across the Piazza Campo de' Fiori and turned right into the Via dei Farnesi, then veered briefly left into the Via Giulia and up over the Tiber River onto the Ponte Sisto. Here, as she'd suggested she would, Daneka struck up a grand pose—which, Kit knew, she could only have learned from the movies—and pronounced for any who might've cared to hear: *"Alea iacta est!"* Then she turned to Kit with the look of a gamine. Her finishing-school English, however, belied any secret ambitions she might've had to suggest some mysterious origins in the back-

- 208 -

streets of Araby.

"How *does* one say that in English, darling? I knew once, but I've forgotten. And since almost nobody in New York knows Latin anymore, I never get a chance to refresh my early knowledges.

Kit knew this last flourish was intended for him. He loved it when she was able to poke fun at non-native speakers whose knowledge of English had as much in common with hers as a pyrope might have with a ruby. The twinkle in her eye only confirmed it as she stood, Caesar-like, with her body facing imperiously down the Tiber, but her head and neck strained in Kit's direction. Kit looked at the tendons in that neck. *Exquisite!* he thought to himself. "The die is cast" was all he said, however, as his eyes dined silently on the curvature of that neck. She turned her head again to look downriver and lifted her chin as if to make an historic pronouncement.

"The die, you bastards, is cast!" she pronounced as she pretended to flutter her hand impatiently. "Now make haste to lay waste, before my reign is done!"

Traffic over the bridge did not come to a standstill. In fact, nothing in all of Rome changed one iota of its intentions. But Kit's heart soared. She jerked her head back around, careful not to lose one line of its expression as she looked at him to test the effect of her oratory. Apparently satisfied, she broke into gales of laughter and jumped into his arms.

"Oh, darling, that felt *so* good! Whaddya think? Could I, too, be a Viking princess? Just a little bit of one? Maybe just for tonight?"

Kit wanted to answer with a simple but enthusiastic "Yes! Yes! Yes!" to each of her questions. But the knot in his throat stopped him. Instead, he hugged her passionately, greedily, looked out over her shoulder at this city of lights and domes, of distant laughter and even more distant cathedral bells ringing out the hour, and wondered for how much longer he could—.

They walked on, down off the Ponte Sesto and into Trastevere. It wasn't long before they found a place called the Trattoria da Lucia, walked in and announced their intention to the Maître d'. He greeted them solemnly—as Kit might've expected from a man whose position contrived to inure him to the sight of a beautiful woman. Yet even this Maître d', for all of his self-control, could not defeat an automatic reflex as Daneka stepped up to his desk to ask for a table. Nostrils once again flared at the smell of her sex that now, like some kind of savage perfume, seemed to pervade eve the air of the restaurant. One by one, the faces of both men and women turned in her direction as she and Kit followed the Maître d' back to their table. Kit knew the cause of it. If Daneka did as well, she was giving no hint either of pride or of embarrassment at its effect on the other diners.

The Maître d' chose to seat them in a corner of the *trattoria* as far removed from himself and from the rest of his clientele as possible. He wanted to avert a riot—at least a riot of the senses. He noted that other women in the restaurant were looking conspicuously *un*excited as their male consorts—husbands, lovers, even sons—squirmed in their seats.

She's a fucking aphrodisiac! Kit thought to himself. There was apparently no limit to the effect she could have not only on him, but on every member of his sex who still possessed senses and organs alive enough to react with. But there were limits, he realized—even in Rome; or maybe especially in Rome. In any case, he hoped the two of them would survive this night and get out of town intact. And for the future, he would never again suggest that she walk out into a public space without panties on.

The next hour would prove to be among the most memorable of Kit's life.

Their waiter had to come back four times to get their order. He broke two pencils in the process, yet still managed to get it wrong in the end. Busboys dropped bread, pitchers of water, plates, glasses. The same busboys then broke two brooms in their effort to clean up the mess. A constant stream of visitors walked past their table on the way to the restrooms—sometimes, the same men two or three times. What had been any number of quiet dinner conversations when they'd first entered the *trattoria* turned into brawls. Women yelled at their men; men yelled back at their women, then marched off to the men's room. The few children present may've had no understanding of what was going on, yet they happily contributed their share of bedlam to the general uproar until distraught mothers picked them up and walked out with them. One couple had been unfortunate enough to bring along a baby, who now wailed ceaselessly. At long last, the mother picked the baby up and dropped it like a stone into her husband's lap. She then picked up the check, wrapped it in a soiled diaper and, on her way out of the *trattoria*, flung it at the Maître d'.

The restaurant was verging on hysteria and breakdown. When dessert finally came, Kit felt it expedient to ask for the check.

The waiter came back flustered: he couldn't find the check; there was no check; there was no evidence of their having eaten anything. Kit offered to review with him again what they *had* eaten and let him write out a new check.

At that moment, the Maître d' appeared at their table—a wretched and much older version of the very composed gentleman who'd greeted them upon their arrival. It was very kind of Kit to offer…but there'd be no need…no need at all…compliments of the house, the chef, himself, the entire wait staff. Did they need a taxi? He could have one at the front door in seconds. He knew the man personally. Very dependable—his brother, in fact. 'Would take them anywhere in Rome—anywhere at all.

He'd taken out his cell phone and had already started dialing when Kit told him it wouldn't be necessary, that they could walk back to the hotel. The man visibly withered and seemed to age even further as he stood before Kit and Daneka imploring them to leave with every body part except his mouth, which simply couldn't pronounce the actual words. He was crumbling. His restaurant was crumbling. All of Rome was crumbling before this barbarian invasion.

Daneka went on munching, but Kit recognized that a crisis was at hand. He had no desire to be the cause of another fall of the Roman Empire. He suggested to Daneka they could finish dessert in the hotel. She apparently didn't understand what all the fuss was about or why the rush.

"Trust me, darling," he finally said to her as he took the spoon out of her hand and put it down on her dessert dish. "It'll be better this way."

Kit stood up and pulled Daneka's chair back. The Maître d' looked at him with tears of gratitude; his restaurant might yet be saved thanks to this man. Rome, too. He mumbled words about a "second liberation" as he ushered them out: Daneka, like an unruly puppy on an invisible leash; and Kit—understanding better this man's sense of urgency—and so, coaxing Daneka along from behind. At the door, both received a final *"Grazie, grazie* and *Buona Notte* before the Maître d' closed the door behind them, sat down on the floor and wept tears of salty gratitude.

"What in the world—?" Daneka said, apparently ignorant of the part she'd just played in the near demise of a family business of multiple generations. "My, but these Romans are a lively bunch!"

Kit didn't know whether to laugh or cry. This woman, otherwise and in every instance entirely self-aware and consequently aware of the effect she could have on others, obviously had no clue about the near-chaos she'd just caused—and *not*, this time, exclusively because of the way she looked, but much more because of the way she smelled. He thought, however, that the situation called for discretion.

"I just don't know what got into those people. Do you, darling?" she said to Kit as she looked at him through big, round eyes.

"I don't know either, Daneka. But you know how temperamental Italians are—at least by reputation. Maybe there was something in the food. Or in the wine. Or maybe even in the stars," Kit said as he looked up at the sky, trying valiantly to suppress a guffaw. "You don't suppose there might've been something in the air?" he asked.

"In the air?" Daneka "You mean, like pollen?"

"Well, *related.*

"Related? How *related?*" she asked.

"Well, darling. There's pollen. And then there's the pollen receptor—the pistil or stigma. Surely, you remember enough from botany, or from biology, or from whatever you called it in Denmark at the time you were of an age to study it at school."

"Yes, of course. But I just don't see the connection. Are these pistils, like pollen, in the air? And do they somehow cause people to act a little strange?"

"Could be, could be," Kit lied, allowing himself just the hint of a smile. They were once again on the Ponte Sisto en route back to the hotel. However much the little *Comedia del'arte* they'd just staged was still on his mind, he couldn't ignore the serious beauty surrounding them. Rome suffered from pollution at least as much as any other big city he knew—and yet the stars were clearly visible. The Tiber flowed beneath them on its steady course towards the sea. Buildings that had withstood the ravages of time, of war, of invasions—some of those buildings for over two millennia—greeted his eyes with the same quiet solidity with which they'd greeted the eyes of countless lovers before them and would no doubt greet as many after them. And somehow, it all worked.

Kit knew he and Daneka were two human beings of no consequence, acting out their insignificant parts on an enormous stage that had as little regard for them as it did for any other pair of lovers. And yet, at this instant, their insignificance didn't mean a whit to him. If love and happiness meant anything at all in the universe, if some God—or gods— somewhere were not entirely indifferent to such love, then he had at last found the only thing worth finding—the only thing that gave his life, or *any* life, real purpose and meaning. And he had found it with her.

They walked on and eventually arrived at the hotel. The lobby was quiet except for some late-night activity in the reception area. They took the elevator to the fourth floor, got out, opened the door to their room and turned the light on. They undressed quickly; turned the light back out; got into bed. Before he could even wish her sweet dreams, Kit saw that Daneka had fallen asleep.

"Goodnight, my delectable little Viking princess," he said to her eyelids and kissed them both.

Chapter 42

The next morning, Daneka and Kit rose early, checked out of their hotel, grabbed a taxi to the airport, retrieved their luggage and rental car, then headed out to the *autostrada* in the direction of Naples—and, ultimately, of Positano—albeit in no particular rush. They simply wanted to be out and away from it all: away from the traffic, the noise, the unrelenting thrum of city life.

Positano was located on the Gulf of Salerno at 40.37° north of the equator and just a few tenths of a latitudinal degree south of New York—so, daytime temperatures would likely feel familiar. The summer solstice was fast approaching. These would not be the hottest days of the year by any means—either in Positano *or* in New York. But they'd certainly be warm enough for swimming, for sun-bathing, for taking walks along the beach well into evening.

Kit and Daneka had estimated two hours for the drive if they pushed hard, three hours if they didn't. The key to their roadmap told them this tiny gem of a village by the sea was about one hundred twenty-five miles south of Rome. As they coasted along with other southbound traffic, Kit let his mind wander. Highway travel was highway travel the industrialized world over: one could practically put one's vehicle on autopilot; set the accelerator to 70 or 75 mph; then just go with the flow.

His free associations were temporarily interrupted, however, when he noticed their car rapidly gaining on the rear bumper of a slower-moving truck up ahead. As he approached close enough to read its license plate, Kit identified the telltale first two letters of the truck's registration: PA—Palermo. The truck's exhaust emitted an ugly stream of black smoke, and its rear panel had been gussied up with a pair of nudes. The solid gold silhouettes of two women in provocatively reclining positions faced each other off like some kind of cheap faïence at opposite ends of a fireplace mantle. Poverty, Kit thought to himself, headlined itself in more than kitsch and bad dental care; it could also be noted in the absence of catalytic converters.

He checked his mirror for traffic approaching from the rear: only one car—far behind, its headlights curiously flashing on and off—so, not a problem. He figured he'd need only a few seconds to get past this truck. He set his blinker, accelerated, and moved out into the passing lane just as he caught sight of a portion of the truckdriver's face in the vehicle's exterior side-view mirror. A couple of day's dark, stubby growth highlighted two or three remaining teeth in the gaping "O" of the man's mouth as his eyes bulged and his eyebrows shot up into two panicked crescents.

Kit later confessed to Daneka that he had no recollection of the next few seconds. The longer minutes that followed, however, resulted in feelings of remorse such that, from that day forward, he never again drove a car without hands clenched on the steering wheel in equal parts dread and guilt. If it had been possible, he would never have driven again at all.

As Kit pulled out into the passing lane, the car approaching in the same lane from his rear reacted quickly—but not quickly enough for the speed at which it was traveling. There was too little space between Kit's car and the median for the rapidly approaching vehicle to squeeze through without side-swiping Kit's car in the process. The driver consequently swerved to the right to try to reach and then pass on the shoulder. The low front bumper of his candy apple-red Lamborghini caught the rear bumper of the truck and sent it into a tailspin. Kit braked his own car as the truck swerved in front, struck the center median, then bounced back and flipped over. It rolled several times before spilling its cargo and then bursting into flames. As Kit's car quickly decelerated through 50 mph, leaving a rubber skid mark on the pavement as proof of his effort to avoid colliding with the truck, a detached arm bounced up off the pavement and slammed into his windshield.

In the meantime, the brief handshake of the truck's rear bumper and the front bumper of the much lighter, much faster-traveling Lamborghini had been sufficient to send it gliding off onto the shoulder like a paper plane, where a cement kilometer marker caught it head on. The marker didn't budge; consequently, what had to give was the Lamborghini. The energy of its velocity needed to go somewhere, and a simple kilometer marker—small, yet robust—refused to yield to close to a ton of steel and fiberglass traveling forward at 120 mph.

The car upended and turned somersaults. When it finally came to a rest, it—like the truck a split second earlier—burst into flames, as its gas tank had separated from the vehicle in the enormous expenditure of energy unleashed by the accident, then collided with the cement median. The result was a fireball that engulfed both sides of the highway.

The two occupants of the Lamborghini, apparently not wearing seatbelts, were ejected upon impact with the cement marker. They, like the vehicle itself, instantly became an assortment of unusable spare parts whose market-value would no longer bear scrutiny, much less appraisal. As the Lamborghini's roof detached itself from the car, it took their heads with it. The driver's lower torso had merged with the steering column with the force of the impact—and so, remained behind. The upper half of him, less head, flew like a wet pillow through the air until it collided with the trunk of one of the pine trees lining the *autostrada,* where it now hung from the sharp stub of a dead branch.

The body of his much younger female companion initially suffered none of the indignities of dismemberment except for the loss of itself from the neck up, which part rolled on down the *autostrada* like a knobbly soccer ball until it came to rest several hundred yards away against the median. The rest of her—less one four-inch spike heel that stayed behind and burned with the car—followed for a much shorter distance, leaving a bloody exclamation mark that would not entirely wash away until the season's next torrential rainstorm. Her crumpled torso—like the point in that exclamation mark—would be removed, however, within the hour.

Traffic came to a halt in both directions, but at a safe distance from the flames. People emerged from cars, cell phones in hand in order to call for help. Some of them, whether from an urge to gawk, or simply unlucky in their curiosity, peeked over the median into wreckage and body parts—and vomited. Others, perhaps more hardened by work, by war, or by some calamity of their own making, slowly removed themselves from the scene and walked back to their cars to await the arrival of the police—also, of those personnel whose joyless job it was either to assemble statistics or to clean up the *stuff* of those statistics.

Two hours later, their windshield wiped clean of any evidence of their mishap, Daneka sat in the driver's seat and turned the key in the ignition to start them back up on their journey south. Check-in—she calculated with a sigh of relief—would no longer be an issue, as noon would've come and gone by the time they reached the hotel in Positano.

Kit was beyond calculation of any kind, stuck in a horror he felt *he* had engineered, however unwittingly. Daneka had done her best to convince him otherwise, but her efforts had worked no particular magic in this instance. He remained hard stuck, and no words of consolation could pry him loose.

They rode in silence. Traffic on the *autostrada* eventually began to find its selfsame rhythm—for all, that is, but the driver of one Sicilian truck and the occupants of one candy-apple red Lamborghini. *Their* rhythm was now quite different. *Their* music had stopped altogether. For them, a concern with dental care, kitsch, or catalytic converters—or with the choice of spike heels versus utilitarian flats—would no longer have quite the same urgency.

Chapter 43

By one o'clock, Daneka had managed to navigate the last bit of *autostrada* from Rome on past the chaos of Naples to Salerno, then onto a country road along the southern coast of the peninsula up through Amalfi and on to Positano. This was a two-lane town; she knew that asking directions to the Albergo Casa Albertina was unnecessary, not to say irrelevant. Instead, she drove slowly and conducted her own visual check—as Kit was still in no condition to help out.

She found it—or rather its marker—and parked the car in the white gravel lot just off the road. She vaguely remembered that the hotel itself was situated on a shoulder of the cliff overlooking the gulf. They could carry their baggage down if they cared to; alternatively, they could simply walk down the couple of hundred stone steps to the lobby, then send a porter up for their bags. She opted for the alternative as she thought an unencumbered view of the gulf might help to lift Kit's mood.

"Darling, we're here," she said as she turned off the engine. She said it to him as if to a sleeping child after a long trip home—just a soft nudge to wake him up and get him moving in the direction of bed. Kit, like that same child suddenly stirred from sleep, acknowledged her words with a grunt, then opened his car door, stepped out into the bright sunlight and squinted. She came around the back of the car and took his arm in hers, then walked him to the stone stairway.

They descended together, she leading him by the arm. The view in many respects was spectacularly similar to the one they'd enjoyed from their villa in Cabo de São Vicente, even if they'd now exchanged the Atlantic Ocean for the Tyrrhenian Sea. Kit couldn't tell whether the blues were truly bluer—or merely appeared to be so by contrast with the red he'd seen, in all of *its* many morbid hues, in the course of the previous several hours. In any case, these blues soothed—and little by little, step by step, he emerged from the mental cave into which he'd crawled following the accident.

He knew he might never leave that cave entirely behind, and that he might re-enter and dwell there for periods of time, on and off, for the rest of his life. The cave was now a part of him—every bit as much as the memory of swings and fresh cut grass of his youth; of countless beautiful bodies and faces he'd photographed or made love to, or both, during his later years; of this woman who was still very much a part of his present, but who, he knew, could just as easily and for no fathomable reason become a distant and silent part of his past.

Everything in life was but a moment; a snapshot; an event; and then, eventually, just an entry in one long log of memories—until, of course, through natural cause or sudden accident, the log was lost, the lights grew dim, the memories were deleted.

They reached the lobby of the *Albergo Casa Albertina*. The attendant greeted them effusively—a bit *too* effusively, Kit noted even in his stupor, although he was growing accustomed to this peculiar Italian sense of cordiality. And yet, it seemed to him there was an all-too-easy familiarity between the attendant and Daneka—a subtle undertone lying just beneath and at an odd angle to what one might otherwise expect between hotel host and guest. He suspected she'd been here before. She, after all, had made the reservation, while he'd never even heard of Positano until the day she'd first suggested it as part of their itinerary.

The attendant finally presented them with a pair of room keys and promised to send a porter up to get their bags. Daneka thanked him with a wink. He looked at Kit with the pained expression of an opponent battling the stress of ennui between *en garde* and checkmate, then returned Daneka's wink. It was while walking to their room that Kit decided the time was right to ask the question that had been nagging him.

"Daneka, how did you come to know about this place?"

"Positano? Or this hotel?"

"Both, really."

"Well, it's a long story. For one thing, Luigi Pirandello used to vacation at this house well before it became a hotel. You've heard of him, of course. He wrote a play called *Six Characters in Search of an Author*. I was one of those characters." She said it with a light-hearted laugh and looked sideways at Kit for a response, but he'd missed the joke.

"Oh, darling, don't be ridiculous! He was dead long before I was born—before even my mother was born!" Kit's sigh suggested to Daneka's ear she might find something more than a pout at the end of this line of inquiry. "I was just your average Scandinavian girl," she lied. "After a long winter, all we ever wanted was to see the sun," she lied further. "My parents would bring me here every summer," she lied outrageously. Kit, however, had no way of knowing to what degree—as he really knew nothing about her parents' financial condition during Daneka's youth. What he *did* know, however, was that most Danes, while hardly poor even by Western standards, were not really wealthy, either—at least not wealthy enough, with few exceptions, to summer on the coast of Italy year after year.

"Some summers, we'd spend a month here in Positano. Other summers, a month in Amalfi. You might've noticed it when we drove through on our way here. Still others, we'd spend the time in Sorrento, just across the peninsula on the Gulf of Naples. And if it had been a particularly good year, we'd take a private boat out to the Isle of Capri—which is just across from the Punta Campanella at the tip of the peninsula."

A series of little lies was snowballing into *the big lie.* Kit had been quite prepared to believe her until her mention of Capri. But models talked—on the job and off. He knew about places like Capri and Ibiza from snippets of conversations he'd heard over the years. Supermodels had made the rounds of all of them—their particular brand of finishing school. The occasional beauties from Boise were sent off immediately to ripen their farm-fresh milkiness with a *soupçon* of bacterial culture—usually via Milan or Rome where they could hook up for the week or month with someone who just *happened* to own a yacht, who just *happened* to have some extra time on his hands, who just *happened* not to have that same time—or at least not the inclination—to invite the wife and kiddies along for the cruise.

If Vegas was Disneyland for adults, Kit knew, then Capri and the smallest of the Ballearic Islands, Ibiza—just off the Costa Brava in the Gulf of Valencia—were Disneyland for the decadent. But family vacation spots? Hardly—not even for well-to-do Scandinavian families.

Still, he was in no humor to probe. The accident continued to eat at him. If anything, he wanted to go to sleep; wake up; then find out it had all just been a nightmare.

They arrived at their room, and Daneka unlocked the door. Kit looked around in amazement. If possible, it was even more spectacular than their room at the *Grand Hôtel de Champaigne,* in Paris. Irregular squares of polished stone peeked out from between the more regular rectangles of Persian rugs. The furniture was classic Italian; solid; not a cheap piece in sight—at least not here in the living room. Kit crossed to an open door leading to the bedroom and looked in. More of the same, all of it perfectly coordinated. The bed reminded him of one he'd seen in his youth in the Albert and Victoria Museum in London, and which had once belonged to Henry VIII. He remembered wondering at the time—he was still just a kid, with a kid's understandably limited worldview—whether that particular Henry had needed so many wives because he owned such a large bed, or whether he'd needed such a large bed because he had so many wives. For Kit at the time, serial monogamy was not a working concept. This particular instantiation of 'bedness' in the *Albergo Casa Albertina* also had four heavy columns and a canopy. If the conundrum of four columns on a bed had suggested at least as many wives to his kid's imagination, the utility of those columns implied something quite different to his adult's better-informed imagination—and contained not a splinter of anything Albertian or Victorian; *least* of all, Platonic.

He walked into the bathroom. It was enormous, all marble, with space enough not only for a double sink, stand-up shower, bidet and bathtub, but also for a Jacuzzi. The Jacuzzi, itself, had space enough for four adults, or—but of course—for one very well-off Danish family in its annual celebration of an Italian summer sun.

"What do you think, darling? Do you like it?"

"It's exquisite," Kit said, and now it was *his* turn to lie. The rooms were indeed exquisite—nothing less than—but Kit's eye couldn't look at the furniture and the bathroom amenities without, at the same time, seeing a younger version of Daneka in them. Nor was it the ghost of the *child* he imagined cavorting with the other ghosts of one happy Danish family.

"Do you mind if I lie down and rest?" he asked. "I've got a bit of a headache."

Daneka grimaced. "My poor darling. Yes—by all means, please do. Try to sleep it off while I put our things away. Then, if you feel better, we can go to lunch. Okay?"

"Sure. And thanks."

Kit lay down. He didn't really have a headache; nor was he in the least bit sleepy. He simply wanted to clear his mind of mental images that wouldn't allow him to see this place for what it really was: a small piece of paradise. Whatever it *had* been to Daneka at one time was not for him to question. He'd not been a part of her life then; he was a part of her life now. And the only thing that should matter to him was her happiness—their happiness—now and for as long as he could keep it and her.

The accident was just that—an accident. His part in it had been an unhappy coincidence. He hadn't been careless, ignorant or in violation of the rules of the highway. He'd simply been caught in a blind spot. Life was full of blind spots, of unknowns, of accidents just waiting to happen. If you were cautious, careful, attentive, you could avoid most of them; but not all of them—not all the time.

Kit was cautious. He was also quick and alert. This morning, however, he'd just not been cautious, quick or alert enough.

Chapter 44

When Kit awoke to the sound of a somewhat distant door being closed, it was mid-afternoon. He'd eventually fallen asleep after all, and Daneka at some point had slipped out quietly and closed the bedroom door behind her. He now heard her sandaled feet crossing the living room towards the bedroom. She turned the knob slowly, quietly, then peeked in. Kit looked back at her and blinked.

"Darling, you're awake! Feeling any better?"

"Much, thanks. Where'd you go?"

"I went up for a bite to the terrace restaurant. The view is stupendous! You have to come and see it."

"Wha'd you have?"

"Just a hamburger. You hungry?"

Not only was Kit not hungry; the thought of red meat made him nauseous. "Not particularly. I think I'm really much more in the mood for a walk."

"Wonderful! And a swim?"

"Maybe. In any case, I'd really like to take a walk on the beach if you're up for it."

"Sure! Why don't we put our bathing suits on just in case?"

"Sounds good."

Daneka put on a bikini and a dab or two of sunblock, then stepped back into her sandals. Kit put on his own bathing suit, also a pair of jeans over it and a shirt. If she felt no particular compunction about walking out in a token swatch or three past birthday-suit-naked into a semi-public space, he wouldn't either—at least not on *her* account. His Pennsylvania roots, however, were beholden to a somewhat different sense of propriety where *his* body was concerned.

They left their hotel room and walked out through the lobby, Kit just a couple of paces behind her. A few stray males and one familiar-looking attendant at the reception desk feigned indifference. Kit knew better and so did Daneka. He thought there might be more than just her usual sway as he watched her hips cross the lobby and saunter out to the pool area. Kit held his stare as he nodded to the other males in that way that certain males have of staring and nodding when they're just out for a stroll with a mate in tow. The other stray males and one attendant nodded back in that way that certain males have of acknowledging another male's proprietorship—for at least as long as subject and object are visibly linked.

Kit registered their conditional acknowledgment. At the same time, he made a mental note not to let Daneka out of his sight for as long as there was light—and that light, the province of some sun to radiate it and of some moon to reflect it—in Positano.

He followed Daneka out to the pool deck where there were lots of sunbathers, many of them topless. At a glance, he could see that none of the females present were pre-pubescent. Maybe—he observed to himself with just the hint of a dark chuckle—all of the Scandinavian families were summering in Amalfi this year.

Daneka seemed to know exactly where she was headed—and so, Kit followed. After they'd crossed the pool deck, they found themselves at the entrance to a structure with two doors. Behind one of the doors stood an elevator; behind the other, a cable and empty space. Daneka opened the door leading to the cage-like elevator, then turned to Kit.

"This will take us down to the beach, darling. Down to the Spiaggia delle Sirene. Quite a fetching name, don't you think? 'Beach of the Sirens.' I wonder if we'll see any. If we do, I'll just have to plug up your little ears with beeswax," she cooed to him as she reached up and pinched a lobe.

Kit wondered whether 'fetching' was a left-over from her early English-as-a-second-language school days, or rather from some more recent encounter—hence, whether her unconscious employment of it might suggest the possibility of a British liaison in a not-so-distant Positano past. He decided, in either case, the word could stay exactly where she'd dropped it. 'Fetch' was not a sound that fit easily into his mouth—except when the subject-matter was dogs. Or maybe their training.

Once they'd boarded the elevator, Daneka pushed the "S" button and the elevator began its descent. As they slowly dropped towards the beach, she pointed along the cliffs to a kind of ravine off in the distance.

"It's called the Sentiero degli Dei, she said. "'The Path of the gods.' You know why they call it that?" Daneka was fairly certain he didn't. "That's where the Christians hid during the Muslim invasions of the tenth century. 'The invasion of the Saracens' is what they called it. Nasty and brutish! Brutish and nasty! Not a very pleasant nighttime tale for a child," she said, although there seemed to be more delight than disgust in her pretense of a grimace.

"Indeed," was as much as Kit could offer in return. Yet Daneka apparently didn't hear in the terseness of his two syllables a lack of interest—at least in this case—in historical minutiae. The taurine in her seemed to relish the opportunity to rumble a bit of the china in his closet.

"Yup. Ever wonder why southern Italians are so much darker than northern Italians? Well, sure, the sun certainly has something to do with it. And they are, for the most part, farmers—or at least harvesters or herders. And so, they spend a lot more time outdoors, tending their flocks. But suntans don't travel very well, genetically speaking. Genes do. Whether, as they say, *consensually* or *non-consensually* doesn't really make much of a difference to genes. Moreover, there's only so much hiding you can do, ya know. And seekers generally fare better, over time, than hiders. Saracen seekers especially. Christian hiders especially *not*."

Kit could connect the dots without Daneka's having to take him along by the hand. This was already more of history than he really wanted to know. He looked out at the hillside as it fell away to the sea; it was indeed a little piece of paradise. But even in paradise, hell could find a foothold and flourish. He forced himself to imagine what it would've been like to have to hide, day after day—but most especially, night after night—in paradise: to see the sun rise, and be glad for it; to see the moon rise, and feel terror in every follicle; to have all of the hairs of one's body stand on end, ready for flight at a second's notice and at the merest hint of an approaching torch. As marauders moved through the mountains, Christians would've crouched and waited like lambs before their inevitable slaughter: men, with immediate certainty; women, only after certain other amusements had been exhausted; children and babies, for the sheer fun of it.

Kit wondered how many women would've been compelled to smother their babies into silence—and not stopgap silence—so as not to precipitate quick and easy discovery in paradise. And what of those who couldn't, or who demurred a second too long? Remnants of old, stagnant gene pools would've been dashed onto the rocks below, hurled out into the air and into the sea like bad seed and replaced—how had Daneka put it precisely, if also euphemistically? '*non*-consensually'—by new seed, new genes, an entirely new pool.

Genes were nature at her most brutish. Genes cared nothing for religious distinctions, the purity of races, rising moons or setting suns, hell or paradise—or hell *in* paradise. Genes simply marched forward, *by whatever means possible,* in a relentless quest for survival.

The elevator arrived with a bump. Kit was thankful that something as simple as a funicular vehicle could now deliver him from a reverie that was doing little to improve the view.

Chapter 45

The beach was empty, deserted, not a body in motion in either direction, up or down, for as far as Kit could see. He took Daneka's hand and they strolled, combing the beach for secrets. He wanted to know hers, but neither the waves nor she would give any of them up. They tested the water with their toes, found it chilly and continued walking.

About a half-mile distant from the hotel, they found an old fishing boat, its paint long since sacrificed to age and the elements. Still, it didn't look abandoned—someone had at least taken enough care to turn it over and store the oars underneath.

"Darling, what do you say? How about a little ride? This isn't the Boathouse, and we can't really order up strawberries and champagne. But we can still pretend, can't we?"

"I don't know, Daneka. This boat looks to me like a means to someone's livelihood. For all we know, that someone comes out to fish at this time of day. If he arrives and finds his boat gone, what's he going to tell his wife?"

"He's going to tell her it's gone. And then he'll probably want to gnash his teeth and beat his children or kick the dog. But she'll calm him down and tell him it's probably just been borrowed for a couple of hours by someone—or, more likely, by some *ones*—from the hotel, who will no doubt have the courtesy to leave a few euro notes so she can buy meat. Then he'll be satisfied, she'll be ecstatic, and the kids will eat something other than fish for a change."

She's got it all figured out, Kit thought. *She always does. If there's an explanation to be had that will justify her desire, she'll find it.* "Okay—just so long as one of us first runs back to the hotel for some money."

Daneka smiled, reached into her bikini bottom and withdrew a small stack of bills. "Euro notes. Never leave home without 'em." She looked in both directions and, spotting the thing she wanted, ran over and picked it up. She returned to Kit and the boat with an old tin can. "*Ecco!*" ("Here we are!") She counted out three 1€ notes and slipped them into the can, which she half-buried in the sand in place of the anchor she'd just pulled out.

Together, the two of them turned the boat over and pushed it out to where the waves were just breaking. Daneka let out a little scream as a wave crashed up against her, soaking her backside and resulting in the chill she'd tried so diligently to avoid as well as an abundance of gooseflesh on her arms and legs. Kit snickered, gave her back and shoulders a few brisk rubs, then helped her up into the boat where she sat huddled and shivering. He pushed the boat out until the bottom cleared the sand entirely, jumped in and set the oars.

For the next thirty minutes, Kit rowed in silence. Daneka had long since stopped shivering and now lay stretched out before him. One hand extended out over the bow of the boat and trailed in the water—her index finger, a miniature vessel accompanying their much larger boat, its wake spreading out in tiny imitation of the boat's much larger wake. Even the boat's wake, however, amounted to a barely perceptible demonstration of energy in contrast to the natural surge and flow of the gulf waters surrounding them—enough energy, that is, to move them forward.

The sun, no longer directly overhead, nevertheless radiated with the heft of wrought-iron shackles and reduced Daneka's own occasional expenditure of energy to an occasional upstart movement that swelled with momentary ambition, only to be pulled back down as if beholden to chains. *Is she dreaming?* Kit wondered. Was Daneka in fact hinged to some nightmare whose lurid scenes she was frantically trying to cut and discard like so many outtakes, only to fall back defeated by the hammer of the sun's rays? Her spasmodic gestures and fluttering eyelids suggested as much to Kit's reckoning.

In the meantime, Kit's clothes had begun to feel as welcome to his skin as a ghillie suit. He secured the oars in their rowlocks and let them drop slowly through the water until they reached an almost vertical position. At the same time, he unbuttoned and took off his shirt, then stood up and did the same with his jeans. He looked around, discovered they were well out of sight of any curious eyes not in possession of a pair of binoculars, and considered doing the same with his swimsuit. Was it not less than a month earlier he'd risked even more in plain sight of God-knows-how-many onlookers in and around Central Park? Funny, he thought, how lust could so cavalierly remove all obstacles, all caution, in a body's headlong pursuit of it—while here and now, only a few weeks later, 'headlong' easily catered to the consideration of consequences. For the time being, he decided, he could live with this swimsuit.

He looked at Daneka and thought back to the woman he'd seen lying before him in a very similar rowboat, under a willow, on the edge of the Rumble. It was the same person—or was it? The same body—or was it? The same heart and mind in the same body of the same person. Or were they? Whatever changes that body, heart and mind might've undergone in the space of a few short weeks would be subtle enough to elude detection. Or would they? He wondered whether she'd still feel the same desire; whether she'd react to his kiss, here and now, as she'd reacted that first night; whether, if he abruptly invaded her sleep, her dreams—her nightmares even—by taking her without warning, she'd welcome that spontaneous penetration as she'd welcomed the others.

He looked down and marveled at how something as silent as a rumination, like a traffic cop of the senses, could direct the flow of blood in his body to a part that now commanded it—and thereby willy-nilly reverse an earlier decision. He dropped his swimsuit to his ankles and stepped out. As he stood over Daneka's outstretched body wondering how he could remove, without disturbing her sleep at the same time, the little bit of cloth remaining between his questions and the answer to those questions, her lids receded—as if on cue—just enough to let him catch a glimpse of some of the sclera of her eyeballs. Was she awake, then, after all? Or had some strange telepathy allowed her to see into his mind, all the while maintaining the newsreel of her thoughts, memories and fantasies running on a different energy source than that which fed her REM sleep?

He smiled down at her to check her response: nothing. It occurred to him that the brief movement of her eyelids more closely resembled those of a lizard or a snake—or of any reptile whose occasional need for sleep would still not defeat an instinctive circumspection of every *thing* and every *body* in its immediate vicinity. Perhaps he, too, fell into that category where Daneka was concerned. Perhaps, to her, he was ultimately nothing more than prey or predator. And yes—perhaps, to him, there was some scintilla of the reptilian that lurked behind all of the other more obviously mammalian aspects of her. It was something he hadn't wanted to consider. It was something he'd always preferred not to consider where *any* human being was concerned. And yet, experience had taught him over the years that many of his species were indeed more reptilian than mammalian. It was the thing that gave New York—unique among the cities he'd known throughout his life—the feel of the desert at night. No matter how well lit, no matter how full of bustle and obvious life, fangs or a quick, lethal sting might lurk beneath any rock, around any corner, at the end of the block, even in the next cubicle.

As Kit was about to rouse her from whatever demi-stupor she apparently still languished in, her next sequence of movements hit him with the force of a coil and quick strike—and then slowly injected its venom into his mind. With one hand, Daneka reached up and pushed her bikini top off; with the other, she reached down into the thin thread of material covering her pubis. The one hand was roughly squeezing her own nipples, its fingernails clawing her breasts and leaving the evidence behind in clearly delineated red streaks. The greedy ministrations of the second hand in almost no time became rougher, greedier and faster under the cloth of her bikini bottom. A grimace crossed Daneka's face. Whether it was from the self-inflicted pain or from the self-induced pleasure was a distinction Kit preferred not to consider. What was obvious to him—and *painfully* so in a way that no erotic experience in his life had ever quite prepared him—was that he was not a player in any part of this scenario. The fantasy *or* memory (he had to concede the possibility) that was driving Daneka inexorably towards frenzy was empty of his participation except as a sorry spectator. He had never felt more pathetic, more redundant, more alone—in his life.

If there was still any doubt in Kit's mind as to whether she was flying entirely without him in the trapeze of this autoerotic act, Daneka promptly put an end to his speculation. As the tempo and violence of her onanism increased, she consciously or unconsciously added language and an imperative voice to it. What he'd heard out of her mouth the first time they'd made love in her apartment, he now realized, was no hallucination. If she'd been speaking in tongues at the time, this particular *patois* was yet another language in which she was clearly quite fluent.

She delivered, seemingly to the air, hard-edged commands in a particular version of Anglo-Saxon Kit thought the preserve of porn. Her consonants were all percussion, no melody, and she bit off and spit out each imprecation as if it were a piece of gristle. Her climax to come was one he had no desire to witness. The traffic cop of his senses had long since redirected the blood-flow elsewhere—mostly, Kit realized, to a brain on fire and in desperate need of a dousing, of a drenching, of total submersion.

He jumped into the water with no thought for how cold it might be or for what he might find—or for what might find him—swimming around down below. He closed his eyes and tried to block out the memory of what he'd just witnessed—as if, by shutting them tightly enough, he might simply squeeze the memory out and let it merge with the salty darkness surrounding him. He remained in this state of suspended agitation for what might've been close to a full minute. Then, however, his lungs suggested to him that enough was enough.

He broke the surface of the water and inhaled sharply. The boat had drifted only a few yards off from where he was now treading water. He paddled his way over to it and hoisted himself up. Daneka, he noted, was stern-faced as she gripped both oars.

"Let's go back" was as much as he'd get from her for the next several hours.

She rowed them to the beach. Together, they hauled the boat back up to its former landing, turned it over, placed the oars underneath, then re-inserted the anchor into its former nest after having first removed the tin can, which Kit handed to Daneka.

She removed the three 1€ notes and stuffed them back into her bikini bottom, then threw the tin can in the general direction of where she'd originally found it.

They walked back to the hotel in silence; ascended by elevator in silence; walked through the hotel lobby to their room in silence; opened the door in silence.

"I believe I'll lie down for a while," Daneka finally announced. Then, without waiting for Kit's acknowledgment, she walked to the bedroom, took off her bikini and slipped in under the covers. Kit remained dressed, but followed her into the bedroom and climbed in next to her. In answer to his fully-clothed proximity, Daneka turned on her side and towards the wall, brought her knees up against her belly, dragged a pillow down to her chest and hugged it. Her neck, he noted from his position behind her, was bent over the pillow. The slenderness of it, the gorgeous white expanse of it, lay before him like an altar. He bent his head down and kissed it gently—once, twice, three times.

Daneka moved away from Kit's kisses and in the direction of the wall.

After a moment of further silence and a distance that he felt was growing inexorably between them at a speed Kit didn't even care to consider, he got up off the bed, walked out of the bedroom, quietly closed the door behind him and sat down to write Daneka a note, less salutation: "I've gone for a walk. I'll be back before dark. Kit."

He left their hotel room, then walked back through the lobby and out through the pool area. This time, he took no notice of whether those lying around the pool were male or female, pre- or post-pubescent, with or without a bikini top. He found the elevator to the beach and descended, then began a walk along the shore that would take him several miles around the perimeter of the gulf, all of the remaining daylight hours, and—in his head—three thousand miles across the Mediterranean Sea and the Atlantic Ocean to a tiny island off the coast of New Jersey.

Chapter 46

By the time Kit returned to the stretch of beach just below the albergo, the moon had risen up over the gulf. Until that moment, he'd never seen a larger and more beautiful moon than that over Manhattan in late September or early October. Each year, as if en route to an annual cotillion ball, it would rise towards sunset—towards summerset—in a pale orange of such sensuality that no camera could capture it, no set of eyes see enough of it, no set of words describe it more honorably than to call it by its given name: Harvest Moon.

This evening, however, Manhattan's Harvest Moon would find a tough competitor and a real contender for the crown. The color of this moon was not pale orange, but roseate, and it was every bit as shapely as the competition three thousand miles to the west. Moreover, it was the gossamer gown of this moon high-stepping in reflection off the Gulf of Salerno—rather than pushing, shoving, kicking its way out from behind the roughneck silhouette of Queens—that imbued it with a grace no upstart Harvest Moon of Manhattan could hope to contend with.

Tiny waves broke in muted applause along the shore, sending up their silver spray like handfuls of pocket-change. Who would wear the crown at *this* particular cotillion ball was clearly not in dispute.

Kit easily found the elevator in the moonlight, stepped inside and ascended to the level of the hotel. He walked out across the pool deck—deserted except for one couple stretched out on one of the chaises longues and in the throes of something he preferred not to know anything more about—then proceeded through the hotel lobby and out. When he reached their room, he unlocked the door, then closed it and walked across to the bedroom. As he was about to enter, Daneka put down her make-up and stood up from her vanity table.

"Good evening, darling. Nice walk?" She had addressed him directly with her voice; her eyes, however, presently looked everywhere else but at him.

"Yes, thank you."

"And thank *you*, by the way, for the note." Kit looked at Daneka in the hope that she'd at least reciprocate with a glance. She didn't. His stare, however, brought him tangential rewards: he noticed her dress—one he'd not seen before—as sheer a material and subtle a pattern as any he could recall on the models in the innumerable high-fashion shows he'd shot over the years. To say she was stunning in it, Kit thought, would simply concede the poverty of his own vocabulary; to describe her using *any* English word, he imagined, would simply highlight the poverty of the language. The moon he'd just seen might well be the belle of the ball, but even that moon, he felt, would run for cloud-cover if Daneka were to appear before it.

She was beyond beautiful, beyond regal, beyond—if possible—even perfection. Hyperbole as homage in this case was no better than chump change. What nature and a bit of science had given this woman was, Kit decided in that instant, a singular endowment and only to be repeated at the risk of impoverishing the gene pool for the rest of the species. *Do other men see her as I do?* he wondered. *If not, why not? If so, how can they get on with their lives, their work, their wives, their mistresses—and not thrash about in the night, at least in their dreams, in search of this extra-ordinary thing that I possess in the flesh, but which for them is destined to remain an ever-elusive* Fata Morgana?

"I believe I'll go up to the terrace for a cocktail and wait for you there, darling. Is that okay with you?"

It wasn't. The last thing Kit wanted was to allow her out of his sight. But he knew bondage was not his prerogative. Risk: he'd have to learn to live with it if he wanted this woman to remain in his life, and if he wanted to remain in hers.

"Of course. I'll be up shortly."

As Daneka made her way out of the bedroom and across to the front door of their hotel room without so much as a wave, Kit thought the best he could hope for would be low light on the terrace—too low to reveal to the other guests the body and face of the goddess who was now sitting among them. He put the unpleasant thought out of his mind, took off his clothes and jumped into the shower; followed the shower with a shave; put on a clean set of clothes; brushed his hair and teeth; and then left the room.

When he arrived at the terrace, his eyes easily found Daneka seated at the end of a row of tables and just next to the balcony. The choice had clearly been hers as there were a number of other, empty tables between her own and the next occupied table. She sat—Kit noted briefly and thankfully—absorbed in quiet contemplation of the moon rather than busied in some effort to broadcast her presence. In a kind of lunar *noblesse oblige*, the moon's reflected rays—together with the light of one candle on the table in front of her—seemed to pick out Daneka's face for particular encomium. The re-reflected light played charitably on lines she might otherwise not have wished to reveal in public had she been any less self-absorbed.

He approached her table and she looked up.

"Hello, darling. Hungry?"

"Not terribly, though I can certainly eat a little something. You?"

"Famished!" At that same instant, a waiter who'd apparently taken note of Kit's arrival approached their table.

"*É arrivato,*" ("He's arrived.") he said to Daneka as if to confirm the obvious. And then, looking at Kit, "*Buona sera, Signore.*"

"*Buona sera,*" Kit returned. "*Portici, per piacere—*" ("Please bring us—") but the waiter had already anticipated Kit's request and presented both him and Daneka with a menu, laid a wine list down on the table, then launched into a recitation of that evening's specials. He subsequently bowed in proper, waiterly fashion and withdrew for a few minutes to give them an opportunity to decide.

After an appropriate silence of a couple of minutes, Daneka looked up over her menu. "What are you in the mood for, darling?"

"I'm in the mood for love," Kit intoned—but his attempt at levity floundered like a singed moth to the ground. "If I understand correctly what I'm reading, they have a number of seafood specials. I think I'll get the *frutti di mare*. And you?"

"I'm feeling like meat tonight. I think I could eat half a cow if they brought me one." At that moment, the waiter returned to their table.

"*Signora, Signore, avete fatto una scelta?*" ("Have you decided?")

Kit ordered the seafood platter for himself, a steak for Daneka. "*Al sangue*" ("Rare") she offered in anticipation of the waiter's question as to how she wanted it cooked.

"*Va bene. E da bere?*" ("Very good. And to drink?")

Daneka ordered a glass of one of the local reds for herself while Kit looked through the wine list. He ultimately opted for a white from Sardinia and ordered an entire bottle.

The waiter nodded, collected the menus and wine list and retired from their table.

Kit may well have felt the need for conversation, but Daneka apparently did not. She continued to stare at the moon, interrupting her contemplation only occasionally to take a sip from her glass of white wine.

The waiter returned to their table several minutes later with Daneka's glass of red and Kit's bottle of white, which he then opened and poured for Kit to sample. He did and nodded his approval, at which point the waiter filled his glass and withdrew once again. Kit picked it up and held it out midway across the table.

"To you." Daneka picked up her own, brought it out to meet his, and clinked.

"And to you." She took a sip, set it back down on the table, then returned her gaze to the moon. Kit took out a cigarette and lit it up.

"So——" he ventured, but without having first considered what other little bejeweled parts of speech he might pack into this treasure chest of an oration that would pique the pleasure of her curiosity. Kit's poor planning left Daneka demonstrably unmoved. She'd been staring at the moon for twenty minutes in stone-cold silence; she might be quite willing and able, Kit realized with some chagrin, to stare at it in silence for another twenty—even if slightly stonier, slightly colder. At one point, she waved her hand in front of her face, suggesting that the smoke from Kit's cigarette was getting to where it was decidedly unwanted. Kit quickly re-positioned his hand so as to send the smoke off in some other direction. Unfortunately, his cigarette seemed to have a will of its own, and that will took the smoke directly back into Daneka's face. She waved again. He stubbed his cigarette out and moved the ashtray to the next table.

The silence that ensued between them suggested to his mind that they might as well have been put into invisible, adjoining, soundproof cabins. Kit emptied his glass and poured himself another. He wanted a second cigarette, but the memory and small comfort of the previous one discouraged him from risking what he feared might be taken as effrontery. He was almost certain she'd used the word 'sexy' not ten days earlier to describe the habit—at least where he was the *habitué*—but maybe she'd been speaking contextually. And yes, a thing or two had occurred since then to measurably alter the contextual landscape.

Or maybe he'd heard 'smoking' when she'd really meant 'drinking.' He emptied his second glass and poured himself a third, hoping to ingratiate himself with her maybe just enough to trade comments on the weather. She turned towards him and looked not into his eyes, but at his wineglass as Kit poured some of the guilt-ridden contents of the bottle into it. No, he surmised from the icicles gathering under her stare: 'drinking' was apparently also not what she'd meant to say.

As the wine bottle was already somewhere between half- and dangerously close to empty, Kit considered taking a break until dinner arrived. He decided he might as well join Daneka in her admiration of the moon. Wolves, after all, stared at the moon. Wolves were also monogamous. They and he might have a lot in common. He could try howling, but he was afraid the gesture might be lost on the locals.

Kit was just beginning to consider how subtle and sublime a thing like solitary confinement must be—at least to the mind of a prison warden—when the waiter arrived with their dinners and interrupted Kit's reverie. *Food!* he thought. *She'd admitted, after all, to being famished. Maybe food will restore her energy and their camaraderie....*

"*Buon appetito!*" the waiter offered as he set their plates down in front of them.

"*Grazie, Signore*," Kit answered.

"*L'appetito vien mangiando*," Daneka suggested with a wink.*

"*Eh, sì. Certo, Signora!*" their waiter offered together with a belly-laugh.

Famished? Kit reconsidered. So 'famished' she had no problem turning a proverb into a pun in someone else's language. Perhaps food wasn't the answer either.

The waiter retired from their table once again as Kit and Daneka set about the business of eating. She ate with gusto, Kit noticed, almost as if red meat were an exotic, foreign dish. He wondered where the appetite came from, then remembered the afternoon's singular maritime exercises. The memory and the sight of the unbridled carnivore in Daneka slowly produced an unpleasant surfeit in Kit as he began to put the two together. He retired his knife and fork and reached for his wineglass. Maybe alcohol would help him forget.

Daneka continued to eat in silence.

At long last, she finished, looked up, and noticed that Kit's plate was still half full.

"Darling, you didn't like what you ordered?"

---

* Rough equivalent in English: "**The more you get, the more you want.**" The English-language calque would be "**Appetite comes with eating.**"

"I liked it all right. I just—. Well, I guess I wasn't really that hungry." It was a sort of conversation, he thought—or, at least, the start of one.

"Don't you want to finish?" she asked. The tone of her question was genuinely solicitous, Kit thought, if also a bit condescending. She asked it as if she were speaking to a young child at home in bed with the flu.

"No, Daneka. I think I've had enough." Daneka signaled to their waiter that they were finished, then ordered a couple of *espressi*.

"*Ed una grappa, per favore,*" Kit quickly added.

"*Solamente una?*" ("Only one?") the waiter looked first at Kit, then at Daneka.

"None for me," she answered with a dismissive wave, sufficient to make her will known with or without the English accompaniment.

Their table cleared and the waiter gone, Daneka reached across the table and took both of Kit's hands into hers as if they hadn't just spent an hour together in almost total silence—as if nothing of that afternoon had happened to put her to sleep, alone, and him in desperate need of separation, distance, and a long walk to find both. Kit was nonplussed, absolutely flummoxed by the turnabout. At the same time, he was grateful for the contact and didn't dare risk putting any of it to the test of a simple question: *why?*

"Darling, what would you say to amending our travel plans somewhat?" Kit wondered with a sharp pang whether she intended to abort their trip, call it quits, head home.

"What did you have in mind?" he asked tentatively. She caressed his hands with hers and moved in closer. At that moment, the waiter reappeared with their coffee and Kit's grappa. Daneka removed her hands from Kit's and settled back into her chair. The waiter set tiny cups down in front of each, a single *pousse-café* glass in front of Kit. Daneka waited until he'd finished, then leaned back in, put her hands once again on Kit's and continued.

"Would you mind terribly if we skipped the Alps altogether and went straight to Denmark?" she asked. "I want so much to show you my little place in Svaneke."

If it wouldn't have been altogether inappropriate and unbefitting—and probably, to boot, shocked Daneka right out of her sandals—Kit would've howled. He would've howled at the moon for its beauty; he would've howled for the release of tension and mystery and incertitude; he would've howled out of gratitude for the splinter she'd just removed from his heart and for the implicit suggestion of monogamy she'd put in its place; he would've howled out of pure joy for the fact of life, here and now, with this woman. But he didn't. Instead, he kept it all inside and did the best he knew how to keep the quiet elation out of his voice and eyes when he answered, though not without first having to look away and clear his throat: "Of course we can, darling."

Kit called for the check. While they waited for it to arrive, Daneka explained once again, in animated detail, and exactly as she'd once done on a certain park bench in Central Park, how they'd first fly to Copenhagen; would then take the train to the coast and, from there, a ferry to the island of Bornholm in the Baltic Sea where they could rent a car and drive to her little cottage in the village of Svaneke on the eastern coast and just across the island from Rønne, her birthplace, where her mother still lived and whom they could visit the next day if they weren't too tired; but if they were too tired, they could sleep in and visit her only the following day … it was a very short drive, and her mother spoke excellent English … Rønne, too, was a charming village as Kit would see with his own eyes—if only he'd brought along his camera!—and then they could return to Svaneke and sleep and make love and sleep some more and then make love some more … she would even bake some of her favorite Danish pastries for their afternoon teas—they would, of course, have tea every afternoon, and it was *so* much better than English tea, as he would shortly find out for himself—and although she might have to make daily trips across the island to see her mother, Kit could stay behind and garden or read or take long walks or just sleep, if he wanted to—until she returned—when she'd then crawl back into bed with him and make some more love.

As their waiter approached to give Kit the check, Daneka intercepted it, laid her credit card on top and handed it back. Did this sound like a reasonable plan?—she wanted to know—and asked the question with the guilelessness of one child asking another would he mind terribly a bit of chocolate sauce with his vanilla ice cream.

Kit looked at her and wondered whether there were physical limits to how much one person could love another without simply exploding. He was considering that he might be on the brink when their waiter re-appeared with the check and Daneka's credit card. She made a quick calculation and signed the receipt. From the look on the waiter's face as he picked it up, she'd calculated very generously on his behalf.

- 239 -

"*Mille grazie, Signora,*" he said and bowed as Kit and Daneka pushed back their chairs.

"*A Lei, Signore,*" ("Thank *you,* Sir,") they answered together.

They walked back to their room in silence, but it was once again the silence of bliss, harmony and momentarily requited love. Kit unlocked the door, shut and locked it behind them while Daneka went to the bedroom and opened the curtains. The moon, now much higher in the sky, was still round and bright and poured its beams in through the window like a silver dust storm. When Kit finally stood in front of her, having already stepped out of his shoes and socks, she unbuttoned his shirt and threw it to the floor, promptly followed by his pants and shorts. She then reached in, found the two tiny hooks that held her dress together and unlatched them. Kit stared in amazement as her dress fell open and he realized that it— and her sandals—had been the only thing between her and another possible riot in yet another restaurant. She dropped it to the floor without a further thought.

They climbed into bed together. Within seconds, and at her bidding, Kit was inside her. He pushed her legs back down until they lay flat on the bed, then gripped them from the outside with his own two. In this position, and with their arms tightly around each other, they fell asleep. Nothing of this full-body embrace would change for the next eight hours.

Chapter 47

When Kit awakened the next morning and found Daneka beneath him and still fast asleep, the sight of her came to him as if in a dream. He realized he'd lain atop and inside her the entire night; that she'd supported his weight without so much as a sigh; that she, like a velvet vice-grip, had held and kept him erect for eight hours; and that he wanted nothing more in the world at this instant than to come. It wasn't love—that, even he would've conceded. It was lust. *Pure* lust. From the inertia of a sustained, but unspent physical excitement he would derive impetus; from impetus, energy; from energy, thrust; at the peak of his thrust, release—and then, once again, quiet inertia.

He twitched once, twice, inside her. The second call was briefly answered with a contraction. He twitched three more times in quick succession. The answer this time was immediate and unmistakable. Daneka's brain might still be asleep, but another part of her was wide awake thanks to Kit's reveille. He felt her muscles seize him. At the same time, he felt the first liquid tendrils of a warm bath wash over him, suggestive of a tentative, mounting excitement. He raised himself up on elbows and toes and began, slowly, to back out of her. In response, her muscles attempted to grasp him tighter in order to deny him an exit. Whatever unconscious desire might be motivating one part of her to contract, to grasp, to clamp down on this thing she sought for comfort or for partnership, that same part couldn't escape the machinations of an endocrine system that seemed to be waging something of a counter-insurgency.

Kit was all but out of her when Daneka's head, atop a pillow, finally reconnoitered with her vagina—a desert away by tactical calculations. Her eyes opened wide and sent word of a losing position back to a still-dosing brain. Sleepy synapses sprang to attention and dispatched a message to the muscles of her legs, which in turn called for reinforcement from hip and knee joints. Her legs shot out and scaled Kit's back in one bound, where they locked in tight defense just above his waist.

Daneka recruited her vaginal muscles in an all-out, last-ditch effort to hold her ground. Kit called a halt to his retreat. Front lines eyeballed front lines. And then Kit's synapses bugled a thirsty charge. He lunged forward until he was stopped by her cervix. Daneka's reaction was a sharp intake of breath, followed by an equally thirsty counter-charge.

For the next five minutes, juggernaut met juggernaut under an already broiling southern Italian sun whose rays streamed in through the window as if conspiring to do *both* armies in. The previous night's wine poured out of them and onto the bed sheets like the blood of battle. Above the waist, mouths and hands traded attack for counter-attack in well-coordinated kisses, gropes, squeezes, scratches, pounding, kneading and pleading. Below the waist, grunts on the front lines did bare-knuckled combat in a salty swamp.

Just as the battle was about to be decided in delirious favor of both combatants, Kit pushed himself up on his hands so as to bring his pelvis tightly up against Daneka's. She, in turn, arched her back, grasped both legs just below the knees and pulled them up against her chest. They met in a silent scream of rapture, like two pieces of marble at odd angles to one other, yet indistinguishably, inseparably joined at midpoint.

A few seconds later, they *did* separate—then collapsed. What 'Elysium' best describes—the few minutes before, the seconds of, or the few minutes thereafter—is something that neither was in any humor to debate. They were spent, deliciously spent, and that was all that mattered. After an interlude, Kit was the first to speak.

"*Veni. Vidi. Vici*—though not necessarily in that order," he pronounced to the ceiling in lame grandeur. At that instant, and out of his peripheral vision, he caught sight of a single index finger. Its wag in mid-air suggested that unilateral victory was not precisely his to claim.

"*Venimus. Vidimus. Vicimus.*" ("*We* came. *We* saw. *We* conquered.") Daneka corrected with a woman's willingness to include even the adversary in victory. Kit chuckled. Daneka took his chuckle as a bugle call, sprang up and straddled him.

"Re-match, darling? *Quid pro quo?* Me, topsy-turvy? You all bottomsy?" she asked with just the hint of a challenge in her voice. "Say 'hello' to one little mermaid," Daneka teased as she pinned Kit's arms back against the bed and brought her breasts down to within easy reach of his tongue and lips. He obliged with a nuzzle, a lick and a quick kiss to each.

His intentions had been purely playful. Daneka's might've been the same. Whether fortunate or unfortunate for both, his little play produced an unexpected reaction. Daneka returned the first breast to his mouth, and he took it in greedily. The first breast and nipple satisfied, she gave him the second—for which he showed an equal enthusiasm. He looked

- 242 -

up into her face and saw her watching him. His greed was clearly exciting her. The tip of her tongue on her own lips mimicked Kit's as he hop-scotched first across one breast and then across the other. Her excitement—her unconscious mimicry—in turn produced an instantaneous reaction in him, which she now felt prowling about between her legs.

She released his arms. But some indefinable pleasure in her domination, however benign, kept them where they lay. Maintaining her crouched position, Daneka slid—as if oiled—down his thigh until her chest was directly over his pelvis, then reached up with both hands and bunched her breasts around his tentative erection. With her tongue, and by means of some contortion Kit wouldn't have thought possible, she alternatively licked her own nipples and the tip of him.

Just seconds earlier, one part of him had been tentative—but that part was tentative no longer. He propped his head up on a pillow and watched her intently as she masturbated him with her breasts. From time to time, she reached between her legs, paused for a few seconds as she closed her eyes, then brought her hand back up and smeared both him and her breasts with a fresh effusion.

The liquid sounds and sight of her should've been enough to bring him to an easy climax, but they weren't. His greed exceeded the simple desire of an ejaculation. He wanted her capitulation, her total resignation. And if language was the key, he'd use it—even *her* language.

Kit reached down under her armpits and dragged her—still crouching—forward until her head was level with his. He then blew the hair aside from her ear, leaned forward, and whispered:

"I wanna fuck you. Fuck you hard. I want your cunt to take my cock—"

Daneka's reaction cut him short and rendered any further language superfluous. As she raised her upper body up off of his, he looked up at her eyes. They'd gone blank; had receded immediately into her *other* world. At the same time, she reached down between her legs with both hands, grabbed him with one, spread herself open with the other, and plunged down with a vengeance.

She rode him—even Kit could've found no more delicate way to describe it. With her head thrown back and her hands clutching the headboard for support, she rode him—into one, two, three successive orgasms. He'd only recently climaxed with her, and it would be a while before he could come again. But she, with her magic, managed to keep him erect. Occasionally, as she continued her inexorable humping, she'd sense he might be losing his erection. When she did, she wasted no time. Without altering her rhythm or her angle, she'd bend down close to his ear and whisper:

"Fuck me ...fuck me ...fuck my ravenous cunt!"

It was fuel for both their fires. He'd regain his erection and she'd continue to ride. She had a fourth, then a fifth, until he finally rose up against her and they climaxed simultaneously. The faint, warm sensation of him shooting up inside caused her to bang the headboard first with her fists, then with her head. She grimaced in pain, but still she banged. Tears streamed down her cheeks. Tears became sobs. Sobs became one prolonged wail.

Kit grabbed her wrists while she struggled against him. He let go of her wrists and encircled her with both his arms, pulling her in with a straitjacket embrace. She struggled harder to get free, all the while sobbing, wailing, transferring her blows from the headboard to his chest. Kit became frightened: this struggle was unnatural. She was possessed by something, and that something seethed in her like a coil of angry snakes—as much beyond his control as beyond hers. If he were unable to tap into and break this possession, he feared she might do one or both of them some real damage. Not physical damage—he had too tight a hold on her to let that happen—but emotional damage.

He realized he'd just crossed over with her—not only that he'd accompanied her into that netherworld of which he'd already caught a horrid glimpse twice before—but that he, with clear intention, had led her there; had taken her by the hand and dragged her over at a moment when they were both vulnerable, both defeated by an adversary neither was even remotely equipped to contend with, much less defeat. He'd led her to the brink, and then pushed her over and jumped in after. Together, they'd fallen headlong and tumbled to a place to which Kit would otherwise never have ventured. His rejection, until this moment, was born *not* out of fear or repugnance, nor even out of a lack of curiosity. He knew what humanity was capable of. He'd read history, had surfed the 'Net, had read up on everything from self-flagellation to the ecstatic rituals of the Хлысты. That which was simply too hideous to describe or display in either was still available to his imagination—and his imagination, he knew, could unlock *all* doors.

There were those who thrived on orgiastic sex, and Kit knew it. There were those who'd work their way through bodies and orifices until there were no more to be had—searching, always searching, for some other, newer sensation. There were those for whom multiple partners, group sex, simultaneous penetration in as many ways and in as many places as humanly possible was simply yesterday's news—who then sought some higher—or lower—form of sensation through pain and degradation, whether inflicted upon others or upon themselves. He knew this, too. There were those for whom no beauty was too pure, no age or relation inviolable, no principle unbreakable. Kit had seen first-hand, heard about, or allowed himself to imagine everything from chicken fucks to snuff films.

Love, he also knew, was generous. For love—and, in particular, for the love of this woman—he would travel to any depths, would tolerate any decadence, would suffer humiliation, even emotional evisceration. He would do any and all of this out of love for her—provided she would come out with him at the other end, made whole again, and never glance back.

He wondered whether Denmark would hold some clue, some key to the door she kept shut; whether the solution to the mystery of Daneka lay in Denmark, and whether he was about to find it; and whether, in finding it, she'd allow him to lead her back out the other end—for all time—to become, finally, his true soul mate.

Chapter 48

She was now calm and composed—her breathing, regular; her heartbeat, steady. Much to Kit's chagrin, however, the incident would not prove to be an epiphany. In preference to reflection, Daneka chose the nearest, quickest exit: humor. With a low chuckle, she turned only her head towards him, too exhausted to move any other body part.

"Now, *that's* what I call a breakfast of champions!"

However keen his disappointment, even Kit knew that trading quips was far less likely to lead to conflict than would a forced introspection. They had a plane to catch, a continent to cross, and a thousand tiny tasks to attend to first. Introspection, he reasoned conveniently, could wait.

"Or maybe of *champignons*," he answered—a smirk just catching the corners of his mouth.

Daneka tweaked his nose. "You're *my* little *champignon*! Shower, darling? Together?"

"The pair that showers together, flares together," Kit deadpanned.

"Oh, no, no!" she corrected. "The pair that showers together, *flowers* together. We're in full bloom, darling, or hadn't you noticed?" She tweaked his nose again, slid off the bed and walked into the bathroom. Kit sat up and watched her through the door as she bent over to adjust the hot and cold water faucets. The sight of her from behind provoked in him that same instinctive desire that is provoked in the male of every species when his eyes trip accidentally upon a view from the rear of a female bending over. But no—not now, not again, he reasoned: they had a plane to catch.

They showered together in businesslike fashion, but took a child's delight in soaping each other. Daneka's expert technique with the suds facilitated yet another demonstration of Kit's remarkable resiliency. Once she'd rinsed off the soap, she dropped down on both knees to relieve his renewed excitation.

They lost another five minutes: he, somewhere in paradise; she, in enough water to drown half a dozen good men—as Kit had neglected to turn the shower nozzle away from her slightly upturned face, while she adamantly refused to interrupt the task at hand—or at mouth, as it were.

They dried off; shaved whatever each felt needed shaving; brushed their teeth and hair. Kit suggested he'd go up to the front office to check them out and settle the bill.

"Sounds fine, darling, but the bill's already been paid. I did that from New York before we left," she said to him through the medium of the bathroom mirror, in the reflection of which she was beginning to apply her make-up.

"Uh-huh. Then I owe you one."

"For the room, darling, or for the shower?" she asked. Kit noticed a glint in her eye and just the merest curtsy of laugh-lines in her reflection.

"For both."

"Well, now, if you're absolutely going to insist… You know, of course, that it's an hour and a half from Naples to Milan—and then just over two hours from Milan to Copenhagen. Since neither of us fancies cards, and since I can't think of a single good book I'd like to curl up with, and since I absolutely *abhor* silly jokes… Well, then, you may just have to devise something a little different." Her eyebrows arched and she blinked several times in quick succession as if to suggest that the matter was quite settled—unless, of course, Kit still had doubts as to how he might fulfill his obligation.

He had nothing of the kind.

When Kit returned to their room several minutes later, she'd done it all: dressed; re-arranged their flight reservations and car rental for a drop-off in Naples; packed their bags; even arranged for a porter—who was just now knocking at the door—to take their bags up to the car. And she'd done all of it in as much time as it had taken him to walk to the hotel lobby, pick up a receipt for a bill she'd already paid, and walk back to their room.

What is there this woman can't do? he wondered.

Moreover, they'd not *once* spoken about her job—the thing, Kit assumed, that took up most of her waking hours in New York, and at which she was clearly a star. The fact that she hadn't made a single telephone call back to the office suggested to him either that she had things so well under control she could afford to let it all run on autopilot, or that she was simply so self-confident, she knew whatever needed her attention could, and would, wait.

He suspected that most men in her position and with comparable responsibilities would be frantic with worry at this point as to how the company and its business could possibly survive without them; alternatively, that they'd be bored silly without fires to start—which they could then heroically put out; without procedures to devise, administer, tinker with, then discard and replace with new ones; without ceremonies and meetings to attend, business lords and ladies to flatter, lackeys and adversaries to browbeat, berate, cajole, coerce, undermine—in short, to do the stuff of "work" while the real work went on elsewhere.

What, then, is she doing with me? he thought to himself.

He suddenly noticed she wasn't dressed in her usual way, and that her make-up was—he wasn't sure how else to put it—stark. The outfit she'd chosen could hardly be described as 'sexy' or 'glamorous.' He even wondered how it had come to share the same wardrobe with everything else he'd ever seen her in. It was, in a word, homespun. Her hair, too, was arranged in a way that made her look almost girlish. One of the most beautiful women he'd ever seen—with a sense of fashion, style and fit that made everything she wore look custom-tailored—now presented herself like a peasant who'd never set foot outside her own village.

And then it dawned on him: she was going home. However much life had changed her between then and now, however *sophisticated* and urbane she'd become in the ways of the world and in how to effectively manage her life and the people in it, she was now—at least in dress and demeanor—deferring to something more primitive, more rudimentary. It was, Kit thought, almost as if she were regressing; and yet, he wouldn't have thought it possible that a woman of Daneka's accomplishments and abilities would, under any circumstances or for any*one*, regress.

As they drove to the airport just north of the Gulf of Naples, she was bubbly and even hoydenish; she spoke unselfconsciously, without reserve or restraint, and also without artifice—and her enthusiasm became infectious. However much he loved Italy and knew he could've stayed for weeks, months, maybe forever, Kit was now looking forward to Denmark in a way he had once, as a small boy, looked forward to Christmas.

The drive from Positano to Capodichino Airport was relatively short. They found the airport; found the rental car return; dropped off the car; collected their baggage; checked in; proceeded to their departure gate; waited a brief twenty-five minutes; then boarded for the first leg of their flight. Within minutes, they were airborne.

Kit had forgotten neither his obligation nor his promise to fulfill it. At the same time, something about this particular flight felt distinctly *un*erotic. Naples to Milan was domestic: perhaps that was it. In duration and distance, the flight felt like New York City to Buffalo; Miami to Tallahassee; Los Angeles to Sacramento. It could've been that. But Daneka also felt different to him. She sat with her purse in her lap, her knees pressed together, her feet flat on the floor. When she wasn't peering out the window, she was checking her watch.

They remained silent. An hour and a half later and right on schedule, they landed in Milan.

Chapter 49

A t Malpensa Airport, they made their way easily from their arrival gate, through Customs, and on into the international lounge, where they found their departure gate and settled in to await their boarding call. The Italian Customs officials, Kit noted with some amusement, had been distinctly uninterested in Daneka. Whether it was her lack of make-up in combination with the peasant plainness of her dress or rather the boisterous presence of a group—just behind them as he and Daneka came through—of tall, blond, scantily-dressed and strikingly good-looking girls in their late teens or early twenties, Kit couldn't be certain. What he *could* be certain of, however, was that Daneka had also registered their presence. From the unguarded and Danishly disdainful expression she wore on her face, it was clear to Kit she wasn't feeling any particular solidarity with this group of Nordic sisters.

"*Swedes!*" she hissed and nudged him forward towards the waiting lounge before promptly collecting both their passports from an official whose attention was clearly focused elsewhere—and so, who hadn't even bothered to compare the portraits in their documents with the faces of the two people standing in front of him.

They found a couple of empty seats and sat down. Other passengers continued to stream into the lounge alone or in pairs, occasionally in families, and Kit began to wonder what had become of the girls. He announced his intention to wander over to the smoking section to have a cigarette. Daneka simply nodded.

Apart from wanting to satisfy his curiosity, Kit had had another thought that was now directing his feet to the duty-free shopping area. While en route, he passed by Customs and noticed that the girls were still there. Other passengers were being waved through with barely a glance, much less an inspection of their carry-on luggage. The girls' bags and knapsacks, by contrast, seemed to be under intense scrutiny. Kit wondered ironically what weapons the Customs officials might be looking for as they *satyrically* emptied out the contents: thongs, bikinis, underwear—even birth control paraphernalia—all the while exchanging smiles with the girls and quips with their colleagues. One in particular appeared to have enough command of English to use it with the girls, all of whom had no problem responding to him—or even trading quips with one another—in English. The official then provided translations for his colleagues, whose chortles and smirks told Kit whatever part of the story wasn't directly audible.

He eventually found what looked like a well-stocked shop; went first to the cigarette section where, not finding his beloved Lucky Strikes, he at least found non-filter Camels—and grabbed a carton. He next went looking among the selection of champagnes for a bottle of *Veuve Cliquot;* found it and took two; thought about Daneka's mother and went looking among the bottles of port; found a twenty-year-old tawny and took it; made his way to the register, presented his boarding pass and paid for all of it with his credit card. In five minutes, he was on his way back to their departure gate via the smoking section, where he spent another five minutes in quiet gratitude for Italy's *laissez-faire* attitude in the matter of certain personal vices. A country in which smokers and non-smokers could comfortably co-exist was, Kit thought, one he could get easily used to.

As he passed once again by Customs on his way back to their gate, he saw the same group of girls he'd seen twice before. Their mood seemed to be striking an uncomfortable balance between dour and tense as the charade of baggage inspection began to impinge upon the less frivolous, less fanciful fact of airline schedules and final departure calls. Youth and beauty had their privileges, Kit thought, but also their price. He suspected the ordeal would continue right up until the final, nervous minute, but that even Italian Customs officials would then have to defer to a flight schedule and let the girls get to their gate.

He spotted Daneka, already in line to board, and made his way forward to join her. "I bought a little something for your mother—also for us," he said as he opened the top of his shopping bag and showed her the contents.

"You're an absolute *darling,* darling," she said and pinched his cheek. They walked down the inflated, wormlike umbilical cord joining building to jet. Until that moment, Kit had ignored—and not thought to ask—what airline they were flying to Copenhagen. He now did.

"Why, SAS, darling—but of course!" Daneka answered as if there were simply no reason to consider any other.

As they prepared to enter the aircraft itself, Kit got his first look at what, he supposed, gave Scandinavia its particular fame; also of what—if she were any indication of the bounty to come once they landed in Denmark—promised to be eye-candy as deliciously vanilla as her Italian counterparts had been deliciously chocolate. 'Judicious' took precedence over 'delicious,' however, and he resolved to keep his saccharine metaphors to himself. The flight attendant looked at Kit briefly, then looked at Daneka. Whether the attendant's thoughts in that instant mulled into metaphor or simply into calculation, Kit couldn't determine. However, she did seem to reach some personal decision with regard to Daneka—on the basis of what, exactly, Kit couldn't even begin to guess—and addressed her in what Kit supposed was Danish.

"*God morgon!*" she said. "*Får jag be om biljetterna, tack.*" ("Morning. May I see your tickets, please?")

"*Javisst,*" ("Of course.") Daneka answered—Kit supposed—for them both. And although his head told him there was absolutely nothing extraordinary about the fact that she'd be perfectly at ease in her own language, he still couldn't help marveling at the miracle of it, and of her, speaking in sounds he couldn't even begin to decipher.

With a gesture, the flight attendant pointed them in the direction of the aisle at the further side of the cabin. "*Här borta är det.*" ("Just over there.")

"*Tack så mycket,*" Daneka again answered for them both. ("Thanks very much.")

It was only after they'd managed to stow their carry-on luggage and get buckled in that Kit allowed himself to express his quiet admiration, practically bubbling over since he'd heard her utter her first syllable. "So *that's* Danish. It's beautiful! And you're beautiful speaking it!"

Still settling in, Daneka looked at Kit as if over the rims of a pair of ill-fitting glasses. "That wasn't Danish, darling."

Kit stared at Daneka in complete befuddlement. She took a moment to savor her easy conquest, buckled her seatbelt and straightened out her dress, then turned back to him and pretended to look once again over the rims of the same pair of ill-fitting glasses. "That was Swedish."

He blinked. "Swedish? You also speak Swedish?" Then, after a slight pause, and before getting the obvious answer to a senseless question: "But why were the two of you speaking in Swedish?"

Daneka might've blushed with pride had it not all been so obvious. "Danes have no choice in the matter, Kit. Nor, by the way, do Finns, Norwegians or Icelanders. Swedish, darling, is the first language of Scandinavia—and the language we all learn even before we learn English. If you ask the Swedes, by the way, they'll tell you it's not the first, but the *only* language of Scandinavia—so why should the rest of us even bother with our own silly little dialects?"

Kit was beginning to suspect that Swedes and all things Swedish were not so perfectly popular as he'd always assumed—at least not among a certain subset of Danes. His suspicions were only further confirmed as the giddy group of girls they'd recently left behind came bouncing down the aisle towards their seats somewhere in the rear of the plane. Daneka acknowledged their presence by taking a sudden and intense interest in the tarmac outside her window—more particularly, in the heat waves rising up from it. Not wishing Kit to be deprived of the spectacle, she gently but firmly took his face in her hand and steered his gaze *out*.

"Isn't it fascinating, darling, how the heat seems to make the air almost boil! I don't know that I've ever seen something so marvelous, have you?"

Yes, Kit thought—but thought it only to himself. *Probably no fewer than ten thousand times in my life.* He also remembered having been stoned once—and so fascinated by the itinerary of a slug across a windowpane that he'd watched it for almost an hour. The spectacle of the slug—by contrast with the simmering of heat waves on this tarmac—had been fireworks.

"Yes, darling. It's absolutely *riveting.*" Slightly more riveting, of course, was the parade of young legs, hips and breasts walking just past his shoulder and which made his sockets scream with the strain of peripheral vision as he pretended to stare directly at the tarmac. "Riveting!"

"Well," Daneka said with a huff. "I'm glad we agree on *something!*"

The girls, meanwhile, had passed on and out of even his peripheral vision. Kit reflected: however close his bladder might come to bursting during the next two hours and five minutes aloft, he might do better to abjure a trip to the toilet.

The captain's voice came over the intercom and droned on as captains' voices the world over tend to do. "*Mina damer och herrar...*" ("Ladies and gentlemen...") Kit listened, academically, to the length of his address. The language had its sing-song charm, no doubt

- 253 -

about it. But he decided on the spot he preferred it out of a woman's mouth—as he did most foreign languages. He was about to ask Daneka for a translation when he noticed that several of his fellow male passengers were chuckling. Daneka, he observed at the same time, was turning a bright shade of red. From the ruthlessness with which she pursed her lips, Kit suspected it was not embarrassment she was feeling, but something a bit more visceral. He opted for discretion.

The captain paused momentarily, and Kit thought he'd finished. Then, however, the same voice came back over the public address system in English. The news he delivered was anything but extraordinary: a welcome on board; crew members by name; tentative departure and arrival times; weather conditions at ten thousand meters. *So what's the big deal?* Kit wondered. Then, in a slightly clumsier English because the vocabulary for it was not canned and had not been repeated with minor variations three or four times a day over the course of twenty years, the captain extended a special welcome to a group of young ladies on their way back to university, in Uppsala, who'd apparently represented Sweden—and "rather amply," he added, though 'amply' sounded to Kit's ear more like 'apple-y'—in Milan's annual wet T-shirt competition.

Unfortunately for Kit's clear comprehension, but quite fortunately for his cynical sense of humor, the captain's reach with English-language metaphors greatly exceeded his grasp. He (the captain) wanted to say, in conclusion, that 'it had been his privilege to personally attend the competition, and that he could assure all present, and especially the young ladies, that no flag had left the event unfurled, no stone unturned.' As for 'the lassies'—and here Kit suddenly had a vision of bare-breasted collies—'they'd displayed their very best for God, King and country.' He then suggested that the same country that had given a solid piece of Swedish engineering to the world and had had the temerity to call it a 'Volvo' was a country that would, no doubt, find a way to commemorate these lovely ladies' accomplishments with an engineering feat of equally *extrapopalonius* finesse—or something to that effect.

"Thank you, ladies and gentlemen for flying SAS, and have a nice day."

Have a nice day indeed! Kit thought as he caught a glimpse of Daneka out of the corner of his eye and saw that she was no more amused by the English translation than she'd been by the original address in Swedish. He kept his comments to himself and prepared to enjoy another quiet flight.

Unfortunately, however, the captain had neglected to turn off the public address system, and the entire cabin could hear his ongoing conversation in the cockpit. It was in Swedish; and so, Kit caught none of it. He could, however, deduce from the snickers and occasional guffaws from several of the passengers around him—male *and* female, he noted, though Daneka was decidedly not among them—that the content was probably rather burlesque. At one point, former snickers and occasional guffaws became a general uproar. Just then, a flight attendant whom Kit hadn't seen up until that moment went running past him up the aisle and in the direction of the cockpit. He caught only a glimpse of rather nicely curved calf muscles and a skirt bouncing to mid-thigh as she ran. The last thing he heard before the address system went dead was the voice of a woman—perhaps an octave or two higher and several decibels louder than he would've thought appropriate for collegial discourse.

Kit now knew the sound of panic in Swedish. Too bad. He'd just then been thinking what a fun country this Sweden might be. *So why are we going to Denmark?* he mused.

The plane shuddered slightly as it began to roll away from the gate, taxied out and, without a minute's delay, went full-throttle down the runway and took off. *Ciao, Milano.*

The Alps—first the Italian, then the Swiss—were in plain view as their plane climbed up to a cruising altitude often thousand meters. *It would've been nice*—Kit thought momentarily—*to spend some time with Daneka at an Alpine resort. Different—very different.* He would've been on more familiar, less dangerous, turf—less exotic, too—as the mountains might've made introspection easier. Mountains could do that: could make one feel small, insignificant, more inclined to take one's own measure against the immensity of natural phenomena. The sea could do it, too; but not a mere gulf—and certainly not a gulf as small and safe as the Gulf of Sorrento.

Their plane climbed steadily and then broke through the clouds into a clear blue sky. At the same time, any further view of the ground beneath them was lost to the nearly opaque cloud-cover that was as much a part of Europe as castles, fine wine and hand kisses.

Art, architecture, music, literature, philosophy—the whole gamut of Western culture, Kit mused—were not so much the result of any particular European genius as the result of an inhospitable European climate. Give someone—boy *or* man—a sunny day, and he'd go outside to play or fish. Give him grey skies and any form of precipitation, and he'd naturally stay inside to paint a picture; design a building; compose a sonata; write a story; contemplate and discourse upon phenomena and epiphenomena—or simply comment upon the logic or illogic of it all. Europe was a grand continent, Kit mused. But no one should short the role of shitty climate in its grandeur.

His gaze and thoughts reverse-zoomed back into the cabin and to the contemplation of their present micro-climate. By virtue of a shiny, winged tube now zipping through airspace, he was about to exchange, in a matter of only a couple of hours, the birthplace of the Renaissance for a country whose principal claims to fame were the Vikings, Copernicus, Tycho Brache, H. C. Andersen, mountains of surplus butter, and a personal income tax structure that could twist Bulldogs into Pekingese—or pretzels.

He knew, too, that the Danes had behaved nobly in the second world war—much more nobly, in fact, than had the rest of the civilized world—including, for too long, his own 'last, best hope'; that Hitler had dismissed Denmark as "the little country" and had squashed it like an afterthought with his *Wehrmacht;* but that simple Danish farmers, by their simple Danish example, had demonstrated why French art, German philosophy and Italian *opera buffa* were as expendable—and as flammable—as the contents of a hot-air balloon.

He appraised this woman sitting next to him; pondered her genesis; wondered—dressed as she was—whether she, too, was the daughter of simple, yet noble, Danish farmers. If so, would her parents even have been born before the end of WWII? He tried to remember what he'd found out the night in New York he'd Googled to her name, but he couldn't remember the exact dates. By quick calculation, he decided it was unlikely.

Kit remained absorbed in his thoughts—and Daneka in hers—for the next ninety minutes. Then, with only a short while to go before the start of their descent, he decided to broach one of the many topics that had been troubling him for the several weeks he'd known her.

"Daneka?"

"Yes, darling."

"Tell me about your family."

Her face seemed to light up at the prospect. "You'll see for yourself soon enough."

"I know I will. But tell me anyway. You haven't mentioned brothers or sisters."

"There weren't any. I was an only lonely child." She raised her hands and eyes in pretend self-pity.

"Right. And your parents?"

"Only parents. Only lonely parents of an only lonely child."

The charade, Kit thought, was wearing thin. "*Dan*eka!" He gave the first syllable of her name an extra pounce; she clearly, *finally*, understood the weight of it.

"Oh. Sorry, darling."

"That's okay. I'm patient."

She reached over to him and pinched his cheek. "I know. That's what I love about you."

"Your parents?"

Daneka sighed. "I haven't seen my mother in over a year. She's a simple but good woman. Strong. Quite 'here and now,' although her 'now' is sixty-plus. She still lives in the same house I was born in. In which *she* was born—in 1941."

Kit made another quick mental calculation. If Daneka's mother had been born in 1941, and this was 2003, she would be sixty-two. But Daneka had been born in 1960—which meant that her mother would've been only nineteen when Daneka was born and eighteen when Daneka was conceived. So how old when she married? Denmark, Kit knew, was a progressive country. But then, perhaps Denmark's progress had been made only very much *after* the second world war had ended....

"And Germany invaded Denmark in what year?"

"1940. It was all over in a couple of days.

What a happy coincidence, Kit mused. Germany invades Denmark; the next year, Daneka's mother is born. He wondered whether the conception was an act of celebration, of defiance, or simply the result of a spontaneous romp for lack of any easy butter to churn.

"I didn't really get to know my grandparents. They all died shortly after the invasion. Not by a firing squad or anything as dramatic as that. Just died. Maybe of despondency."

"But if they all died, who took care of your mother?"

For as long as he'd known her, Daneka had always been ready with a quick answer.

This time, however, she wasn't. She hovered over the question like a bee buzzing around an uncertain flower, apparently struggling to form the first word of an answer, but then closing her mouth again each time and withdrawing into silence.

"Daneka?"

"I guess I don't really know. I never asked and she never offered." Again, she paused. "I'm frankly a little ashamed to admit I never really thought about it until now."

Kit put a hand on top of hers, pressed four fingers down between her fingers and wrapped his thumb around her thumb. "I understand. We all sometimes get a little too absorbed in our own lives to think about the lives of others—ironically, and most especially, about the lives of our parents."

Daneka remained pensive for another long moment. Then, more to herself than to Kit: *"God!* To think I never even asked her—."

Kit took her hand in both of his and leaned down. "It's not too late, you know. Perhaps this trip is a bit of felicitous serendipity. Perhaps you were meant to have this opportunity to get to know the *woman* in the mother you once had, and not just the mother."

Another long moment of silence, following which Daneka looked into Kit's eyes. "Perhaps you're right." It was the last thing she said before the captain announced their imminent arrival in Copenhagen. Kit took notice of how she'd once again quite effectively eluded the subject of her father.

Chapter 50

Denmark—as far as the eye could see—appeared to be fog-bound. This came as no surprise to Daneka, though Kit was certainly sorry to be deprived of a clear aerial view in this, his first glimpse of a Nordic country. He looked around and noted the expressions of most of his fellow travelers: like the weather outside their window, they'd turned stern and grey. Those same passengers—he'd *also* noted from time to time during their flight north—had been consuming alcohol like candy. Full bladders, he conjectured, would explain the unusually heavy foot traffic back to the lavatories. For every couple or three passengers who disappeared to the rear of the plane, however, only one seemed to return—and that one was almost always a woman.

Kit craned his neck; glanced back; was somehow not surprised to see a small congregation in tipsy attendance at what he imagined to be the location of the wet-shirt set. He suspected their conversation and thoughts at this instant would not be on Heidegger, Husserl, Hegel, or even on Kierkegaard, but rather on the *smörgåsbord* of tasties just beyond morally and ethically—not to say legally—acceptable reach to all but the most jaded. Then again, maybe he was merely imputing to the workings of other men's minds the peculiar gear work of his own—a grinding of wheels and cogs that rarely rested from the calibration, data-entry and cataloguing of women's faces and bodies—not to mention his penchant for always thinking of them as edibles. Maybe these people really *were* discussing Kierkegaard.

In any case, he'd never know. The captain's voice—now tied, it seemed to Kit, to a considerably more sober frame of mind than the one in which that same captain had first greeted them—came over the public address system to ask all passengers to kindly return to their seats, buckle up and prepare for landing.

The captain's request seemed to rouse Daneka from her brooding, and the sound of her voice spared Kit any further contemplation of his own sorry feet of clay.

"Now once we get our baggage, darling, we'll go directly downstairs and grab a train to Øresundsbroen, then take a high-speed ferry via Ystad to Bornholm—you know, the island I told you about. You'll be happy to know, by the way, that Ystad is in Sweden. The ferry actually lands at Rønne—you know, where my mother lives. But I think I'd rather get a car and drive directly to Svaneke if you don't mind. It's located on the other side of the

- 259 -

island, and it's where I have my little cottage. We can visit my mother tomorrow. It's only ninety-two kilometers from Copenhagen to Rønne, by the way, and shouldn't take us more than about an hour and a half once we board the train. Sound like a plan?"

"Sounds like a plan," Kit said. He was eager to meet Daneka's mother, but he first wanted to get acclimated, to get a sense of his surroundings, to get a feel for "the little country" and its people—even if just by observation—before he'd actually meet one of them.

Their plane landed with the grace of a water bird: its pilot was obviously adept—at least at piloting. Kit and Daneka disembarked with the other passengers, passed through the distinctly businesslike—albeit cordial—affair of Danish Customs and made their way to the Baggage Claims area. Kit expected to see a bevy of buxom blonds blow through at any moment. His repeated glances belied the attitude of idle curiosity he was otherwise trying hard to project.

"Sorry, darling. That plane is taking your pretties directly on to Stockholm. You'll just have to make do with Danish and coffee today."

"*My* pretties?" Kit asked with a disingenuousness even he found off-putting. Was he so transparent? Or was she—in addition to everything else—also præternaturally intuitive? And this "Danish and coffee." Was it a clear reference to what he'd always believed was a private penchant? How could she possibly know about *that*? He chose silence over denial as the better of the two strategies.

"*Qui tacet consentit,* ("Silence gives consent,") darling," Daneka said through lips that seemed to Kit at that moment to be made of Roman marble—the old, cold kind. "Don't forget—Latin is *also* one of my languages. She reached up and put a hand on Kit's shoulder. If she meant the gesture to be consoling, the tone in her voice was instead condescending. "So go ahead and dally, darling. Just don't deny it. And *don't* do it in my presence."

Kit reached for a cigarette.

"Sorry, darling. This isn't Italy. You'll have to step outside for that fag."

She'd just added banishment to scorn and condescension, and he suddenly remembered their earlier conversation in the restaurant that first night in Portugal. "We can also be vicious and vengeful," she'd warned. The waiter had interrupted her as she was about to explain how 'vicious' and 'vengeful' might ultimately evolve into a severe Scandinavian silence.

As he dropped the pack of cigarettes back into his pocket, he shuddered. He'd only just set foot in Scandinavia—in summer, no less—moments earlier. And yet the chill of it, and the chill of her, felt like the dead of winter.

Chapter 51

They collected their bags. Kit renounced his cigarette and followed Daneka down one level to the train station, where she purchased two round-trip tickets from an automat that spelled out **København<—>Rønne**.

While she was busy with the purchase, Kit looked around and was suitably impressed with what he saw. For all of New York's inane efforts to implement and operate an effective "train to the plane," someone might've thought to ask the Danes how to do it properly. Their achievement looked to him like the work of master craftsmen—even if in miniature. Directions in both Danish and English were clear, concise, and color-coordinated so that even travelers who were neither Danish- nor English-speaking could, with some ingenuity, manage to find their way about. The platforms were uncluttered; the tracks, clean. Except for occasional announcements over the public address system, the noise-level rarely exceeded that of a dentist's office. Whenever announcements were made, they were clear, intelligible, and given in both Danish and English.

When trains arrived, people wishing to board stepped aside and waited patiently until the last exiting passengers had stepped out. In several instances, those waiting on the platform to depart would first help other, elderly or overburdened passengers—and would then, and *only* then, board themselves. Even the trains were quiet: they entered and exited the station quietly; their doors opened and closed quietly. 'Quiet' seemed to be—if not the signature feature of the whole operation—then at least a significant consideration in its design.

France, Portugal and Italy were civilized countries—there was no question in Kit's mind about that. But in Denmark—at least in this train station, in this city, at this moment—he was discovering an entirely different way in which a country might call itself civilized: *quietly* civilized.

Kit and Daneka boarded their train when it arrived, and Daneka found their reserved seats. They stowed their luggage in the overhead racks, and Daneka insisted that Kit take the window seat. As the train slowly pulled out of the underground station and up into muted daylight, she slipped her arm through his and gave him a quick kiss on the cheek.

"Peace, darling. Let's leave Sweden at the airport and just blame your little *lapsus* on

Stockholm Syndrome, shall we? Strange things happen to people when they're taken hostage. The girls were cute—I'll give you that—but they were girls. More to the point, they were *Swedish* girls. And you want to be very careful where Swedish girls are concerned."

"Swedish girls are somehow different from other girls?" Kit asked.

"Well, you know I hate to generalize—except when I like to generalize. Yes, they're different."

"How so?"

"They feel superior and entitled. They're opportunistic. And so, they rely on their good looks to get just about anything they want—the good-looking ones, that is. I realize that even Sweden has its share of homelies, but they become doctors or chemists."

"Sounds to me like a lot of the women on the Upper East Side. And like almost all of the women I work with—I mean the ones I shoot."

"Yes. Supermodels and Swedish pretties have a lot in common. But there's a difference. Models have to work at it. If they don't, they fall out of a job and just as quickly fall out of fashion. Swedish pretties just look around for the next party, crash it, then hone in on the money."

"It still sounds to me like most of the models I've known over the years."

"Except that your models are making their own money. Modelling may not be a terribly noble cause, but it's a job. More glamorous than most, I'll grant you, but a job nevertheless—with hours and appointments to keep, clients to please, personalities to mollify, and hours of sleep to log."

Kit chuckled. "Sleep?"

"Yes—and another point at which models and your Swedish pretties part ways. Models actually have to sleep if they intend to remain models. Alone. Not around. And not with two or three guys at the same time. Okay, so they may dally from time to time."

Daneka's show of teeth with this last comment struck Kit as more nudge than smile. "But if they're smart, they'll dally serially—and carefully. You're average Swedish ducky can't even spell 'serially,' much less keep up with the sexual math of it. In any case, not where there's good cash to be had—the old-fashioned way."

"I guess I'd never really thought about it." Kit paused, then looked again at Daneka.

"Is there anything you actually like about Sweden?"

"Yes, of course. I like Swedish men—for the most part. Not the jerks who fly planes, of course. And I like Stockholm tremendously. It's a beautiful city—much more beautiful than Copenhagen in fact. There's really only one problem with it."

"And what's that?"

"It's full of Swedes."

Kit smiled.

"No, it's true! In the summer, when most of the women have left for the beaches of Spain or Italy or Greece, it's a beautiful city. It's really the *only* city—with Amsterdam perhaps—that I find tolerable in the summer."

At her mention of Amsterdam, Kit turned nostalgic. Whatever was or wasn't true about Stockholm and Swedish women, Amsterdam—and Dutch women—held a special place in both his heart and memory.

Of the cities he'd known and loved in his life—Paris, London, Rome; Madrid and Barcelona; Athens, Vienna, St. Petersburg; and of course, New York, at least in the spring and fall—none of them held a real candle to Amsterdam. Nor could the women of any of the others—whether home-grown or imported—compete with the women of Holland, and especially with those of Amsterdam. The beauty of Dutch women on the streets of Amsterdam was obvious. Part of it was no doubt in the genes; the other part, in their diet and reliance on bicycles or feet for locomotion.

But there was something else about Dutch women—something, it seemed to Kit, that they and they alone possessed: a modesty; almost a timidity; in any case, a seemingly complete unawareness of what nature and a high standard of living had given them. He'd never done a shoot with a girl from Staten Island; he'd also never shot one from Holland. And yet he, personally, had seen it in Amsterdam in one face after another—on the streets; in cafés; on playgrounds with young children; on bicycles everywhere. If the fashion world hadn't yet found out about Dutch beauty, he thought, so much the better. That particular beauty would remain unseen by the world at large and would consequently also remain unselfconscious and uncorrupted.

"Darling, you seem preoccupied. What is it? Have I sullied some boyhood fantasy of yours about Swedish girls? Were you also once curious yellow about everything that sounded like 'Volvo?' I'm so sorry."

Kit chucked. "Sorry?"

"Look. I know something about advertising. Swedish sexuality is as strong a brand as Mercedes, Coca-Cola and Marlboro. Unfortunately, it's also little more than a rumor."

Kit smiled. He knew she was right. Sexiness and sensuality were no more a birthright—the product of a passport or a function of geography—than freckles. And yet, there was something about those women from the Deep South….

"Can we talk some more about your parents? Tell me about your father," he said.

Daneka seemed reluctant to answer. Following a long pause and a sigh, however, she clasped her hands together and started in.

"My mother never really said much about him. I don't know how well she knew him, to be quite honest. He was a farmer—like most Danes at the time. He worked hard from dawn till dusk. Read little. Never left the island—not even to visit Copenhagen. Went to church every Sunday—and then died, as I told you earlier, shortly after the German invasion."

Kit suddenly realized that Daneka had misinterpreted his question—whether intentionally or unintentionally, he couldn't be certain. "Are you talking about your father or your grandfather?"

"My grandfather, of course. My mother's father. *Min morfar*," she said to be precise, at least in her own mind. "Isn't that what you were asking?"

"No. Not at all. I asked about your *father*. *Your* father." Kit was perplexed. This wasn't a question of vocabulary. This was a genuine—what had she called it?—*lapsus*.

Then, after another too obvious pause, she recommenced. "Well, there's not really much to tell. Besides, we're almost halfway to Øresundsbroen, and you haven't looked out the window even once. I know that Denmark's not Italy or Portugal, but it does have its own little charm. You could spend just a minute or two pretending to admire it, darling. For my sake?"

"Daneka."

"Yes, darling?"

"Tell me about your father. *Your* father."

This time, she didn't hesitate.

"We were not particularly close. What else would you like to know?"

If Kit had been slightly perplexed a moment earlier, he was now entirely nonplussed. *Not particularly close?* Did she really think he'd be satisfied with that summation of a relationship with the second most important person in her life—at least up to her tenth or eleventh birthday? Did she intend to conceal from Kit what he already knew had happened to her father? And, at an age—her age—when that same father's decision to make a too-hasty exit could've meant only one thing to an impressionable child just entering adolescence? This was troubling. Either she was too ashamed to talk about it, didn't think their relationship secure or significant enough to risk introducing it, or—most troubling of all—was simply catering to denial.

Kit had been loath until now to confront her on any of what had bothered him since they'd first met: her extended absences without explanation; the "I love you, too" he'd heard at the tail-end of a telephone conversation just before they'd left for JFK; whatever it was that had *really* brought her to tears after their first simultaneous orgasm. But also that first night in Cabo de São Vicente, at the restaurant, the result of lyrics, or of the music, or of a voice, or of all three; and, of course, some of the less savory aspects of her sexuality—how it seemed to him that, the rougher it got, the more responsive she became. All of that could wait. This, however, could not.

He was about to confess to his late-night date with Google when the conductor entered their car. "*Goddag. Må jeg se billetterne.*" ("Tickets, please.") Daneka promptly presented their tickets. She appeared to be grateful for the reprieve and in no particular rush to continue the conversation she felt she'd adequately concluded—at least to *her* satisfaction. As the conductor approached the two of them, she greeted him with a smile.

"*Goddag. Du kunne vel ikke fortælle mig, hvornår vi kommer til Øresundsbroen?*" ("Can you please tell me at what time we're scheduled to arrive in Øresundsbroen?")

"*Jo, naturligvis. Vi ankommer til tiden—klokken 15.10.*" ("Yes, of course. At 3:10.")

"*Og færgen til Bornholm sejler klokken 15.30?*" ("And the ferry sails for Bornholm at 3:30?")

"*Lige et øjeblik ….*" The conductor withdrew a schedule of departures and arrivals from his rear pants pocket and consulted it. He found the page he was looking for, then ran his finger down it until he arrived at the answer to Daneka's question. "*Det er rigtigt—*

klokken 15.30." ("Let me see…Right. 3:30.")

"Tusind tak," ("Many thanks,") she said.

"Det var så lidt." ("You're welcome.") He looked briefly at her; then at Kit; then added with a smile, *"God tur. Og god ferie!"* ("Have a nice trip—and a pleasant holiday!")

So, this *is Danish,* Kit thought. It certainly resembled Swedish—to some degree or another—but the two languages were so utterly foreign-sounding to his ear, he really couldn't distinguish one from the other. He would've liked to spend some time discussing the distinctions with Daneka, but he now had a more urgent matter to sound her out on.

"Daneka, I have to tell you something."

"What is it, darling? That my Danish also sounds too 'finishing-school?'" she asked with an edge to her voice, which—Kit suspected—had more to do with her anticipation of his intent to continue their earlier discussion than with any possible criticism of a language he knew nothing about.

The confession didn't come easily to him, and he got off to a clumsy start. "A couple of weeks ago—. I don't remember the exact night. You were in Europe. I missed you. I was curious—." He paused.

"Yes, darling. *Do* please go on."

"I Googled."

"You Googled."

"I Googled."

"Well, I hope it was fun, this Googling. Tell me. Did you Google all by yourself, or did you Google with a partner? It doesn't take two to Google. It's not like the tango. But it's certainly much more entertaining *à deux—zu zweit—*than *tout seul."* ("as a pair than all alone").

She was not smiling. French might've been an attempt at humor; German was not. *Schadenfreude* was the only other German he'd ever heard her use—once, in his apartment, when they were first getting to know each other. German in her mouth was not the stuff of poetry. There were too many other connotations. She used it here—and he suspected she would use it elsewhere—like a hammer.

"Let's cut the shit, shall we?" Kit was surprised to hear his temper escalate in response to hers.

"Yes, please. Let's. You Googled. And?"

"I Googled to your name."

"To my name. With or without the 'ø'?"

He ignored the sarcasm. "To find out who you were. What you did. Where you came from."

Daneka glared back at him. For the first time, the laugh lines around her eyes betrayed the difference in their ages. He suspected, under the circumstances, she'd had to work to keep her rage under control. However, one thing was clear: she didn't like snoops. Her magazine might have a gossip column or two, but Daneka didn't like having any of that kind of spotlight turned directly on her.

Another thing also now became clear to Kit. Under pressure, she didn't withdraw, much less crumble. She recouped. Arms now carefully resting at her sides, hands clasped in her lap, neck and head straight up, a slight forward lean—he could see it all in a carefully controlled posture. The ensemble suggested she was poised for a counter-attack behind a carefully managed barricade. The kind and quantity of ammunition behind that barricade was information she wasn't about to reveal to a potential assailant—and Kit, although this had hardly been his intent, now felt as if he were on the offensive.

"And?" she said.

"And so, I know about his suicide," Kit said as he extended a hand to cover hers.

"What about it?" she said as she quickly withdrew both hands and crossed her arms over her chest.

If Kit had thought that modulating the tone of his voice would serve to convey sympathy, empathy, a shared *anything*—anything, that is, but a wish to do battle with her— he'd sadly overestimated his own authority.

"I know that he killed himself when you were only fifteen. I know that the pain of losing a parent at that age—by whatever cause, but particularly by suicide—would leave most people crippled for—."

"You don't know shit, Kit!"

Her pronouncement all but knocked the wind out of him; but he, too, quickly recouped. "All right then. Tell me."

Daneka took a long moment to compose herself. She was not in the habit of taking commands from anyone, least of all from Kit. She'd answer when she was damned well ready to answer. Until then, she'd maintain her composure—and maintain, too, total control of the situation. She stared at him long enough to make him blink.

"If you must know, my father was a moody man. 'Depressed' is a more accurate way to describe him—at least for as long as I was on Earth. His death was just a logical conclusion to a sorry life."

Logical conclusion to a sorry life? Kit stared at her in amazement. *Is* that *how a child describes the suicide*—a word, he noted, she'd carefully avoided—*of her own father?*

"Let me tell you something else. In high school. Another boy. A schoolmate. A boy from elsewhere in the village. Months earlier, he'd also lost a father. He came to me when he heard. One day, before the start of school, I didn't know what he wanted. I wasn't interested in what he wanted. As far as I was concerned, we had nothing in common. He mumbled something. I told him to shut up and go away. I wanted to read my book. He never tried again."

Kit looked at Daneka. She'd maintained perfect control and had said everything she intended to say. The case, for her, was closed.

He shifted his gaze, looked out and studied the landscape for a long moment. The panorama reminded him of Lancaster County: frothy fat, piebald cows lounging in tessellated fields of chartreuse or civette green; the occasional russet-stained tractor; the still more occasional sorrel- or umber-colored farmhouse; next to each, a vertical grain silo standing tall, its aluminum top hat straining for an occasional caress of the sun's rays. Kit looked at it all through the glaucous grey filter of dew or fog or mist—or maybe of a light rain—which collected on the pane, spread out in odd, wind-painted patterns, then simply blew off, dropped to the tracks, and disappeared.

He turned to Daneka. "It's beautiful, your Denmark."

She said nothing, ignored his remark, and continued to stare out of her half of the same window.

Chapter 52

Their train arrived at 15:09:50—ten seconds earlier than predicted by both conductor and schedule. Denmark was, Kit suspected, one of those countries in which punctuality mattered. He and Daneka hauled down their luggage from the overhead racks, descended to the station platform and walked towards the wharf.

Their ferry to the island of Bornholm stood ready, its hold taking on passengers on foot—like them—as well as others in cars or trucks. Kit looked at license plates as he and Daneka walked along the line of waiting vehicles. The telltale "S," "DK," and less frequent "D" or "N" told him the likely nationality of each vehicle's occupants. He tried to catch snippets of conversation as they walked past open windows. It was easy enough whenever they'd come across a "D." As with Americans—Kit thought—the lever for volume control with Germans always seemed to be broken. With "S," "DK" and "N," however, the task was trickier. Swedes, Danes and Norwegians tended to say little. When they did, they spoke in clipped, quiet syllables. What's more, all of it—to Kit's ear—was simply inscrutable.

Kit and Daneka made their way up the gangplank of the *Villum Clausen* —their ferry—towards the main passenger deck. Just ahead of them, and by unhappy coincidence, trundled an American family—or at least the semblance of an American family—an older woman with two adolescent children: the one, a gangly girl with pale skin and straight, blond hair; the other, a much darker-skinned boy, Polynesian-looking, with an attitude problem. *His* hair—sleek, black—peeked out defiantly from under a baseball cap, which he wore 'ghetto-style' with the bill to the rear. The woman was attractive, Kit thought. Remarkably tight body and a quietly stunning face, if also ageing a little less than gracefully. The lines seemed to come from some hidden strain, at least one source of which Kit was about to discover.

As the family entered the enclosed main passenger deck, the boy announced his presence in plain English. "It smells like *shit* in here!" he shouted for the benefit of any receptive ears within a hundred yards. He then tossed his knapsack in front of the most accessible banquette and sat down—on the knapsack, that is, rather than on the banquette. "Christian!" the woman all but shouted, though with a curious French inflection. American children, Kit knew, came in all shapes, sizes and attitudes; their names, however, weren't subject to nasalization except by way of affectation. Maybe, he thought, affectation was another source of this woman's strain.

Wearing earphones attached to a CD player, the girl took a seat on the same banquette and stared off into space. She was certainly pleasant enough looking, and neither her demeanor nor her behavior gave the least offense. She might one day, Kit thought, turn into a real beauty. He just wasn't sure on which planet.

"Get up off the floor, take your cap off and sit down here like a human being for a change!" the woman ordered. The boy ignored her. Apparently exasperated, she snatched the knapsack out from underneath him. His bottom hit the floor with a thud.

"God*damn* it!" he said, injecting a few extra decibels for the benefit of ears beyond the hundred-yard perimeter of his earlier exclamation.

"Watch your mouth," the mother squeezed out under her breath and with rather too much control. The boy's mouth, Kit surmised, might just be a third source of this woman's strain. In any case, she was losing the fight. *She probably lost the entire cause years earlier,* Kit thought. *She just doesn't know it yet.*

Kit nudged Daneka along in an effort to get as far away from this bunch as possible. After they'd moved on a few steps, Kit caught one last exclamation: *"Skit också!"* ("Ah, shit!") He turned around. The woman lowered her eyes in a ready confession—but only after theirs had met, briefly. He didn't know the language. But he knew that people didn't frivolously curse in some foreign language at a moment of real frustration. He made a mental note to ask Daneka later for a translation, if he could somehow recreate the sound of the words. At the same time, he looked again at the woman and registered a fact: she, at least, was not American—as he'd suspected earlier.

They moved on and found a whole row of vacant seats on the other side of the cabin—in fact, one row of seats facing another, all vacant—and sat down opposite one another. They both looked out the window in silent longing for the ferry to get underway.

After a few minutes, a group of five or six young women arrived at their location.

"Är det ledigt här?" ("Is this seat taken?") one of them asked, looking at no one in particular, yet apparently quite certain that *some* answer would alight upon her ear from *some* benevolent source or another.

"Ja... det är det," ("No, it's not.") Daneka said. The tone and pacing of her answer suggested to Kit—whatever the girl may've asked, and whatever Daneka may've answered—that she wasn't overwhelmingly pleased at the prospect of sharing her relative privacy with an unruly bunch of strangers—to boot: young, female and attractive. Ultimately, it didn't matter whether she was pleased or displeased. The girls all sat down on the long banquette next to her, opposite Kit, then stowed their knapsacks under their seats and settled in for the ride.

From Kit's perspective, each seemed to be attached to a CD player as if by umbilical cord. Player-placentas fed in whatever particular nutrients each girl required. They were all in private wombs, seemingly indifferent to their surroundings, intent on nothing more than sucking in the next bit of musical pabulum. A great invention, he thought, the CD player. And even greater: earphones—for *all* concerned.

"Den här låten är det!" ("My favorite song!") one of the girls suddenly screeched out in rapture, apparently trying to communicate something or other to the other little hawks alongside her, all of whom were lost in their own sonic delirium. Her body began to sway to the rhythm of her particular nutrient. Kit felt embarrassed—not just for her, but for her entire CD-enslaved generation. She started: first to lip-synch, until it simply wasn't enough; then to sing along with the lyrics. She was as tone-deaf as a turnip. At the same time—even Kit could recognize the butchered vowels and consonants—the language was clearly not hers. And yet, she insisted upon declaring her love to some unseen Apollo in, of all things, French.

"Voulez-vous coucher avec moi, ce soir...?" ("Do you want to sleep with me this evening...?").

The irony—the utter irony. Here he was on the Baltic Sea, thousands of miles from home and, at least in his mind, in a deeply romantic—or tragic, or at least Baltic—setting. He was a simple boy from a simple state, from the comparatively simple United States. 'Pacific Ocean' had meant little more to him than a necessary trip to the West Coast to make some quick cash. To a certain Portuguese explorer of the early sixteenth century, however, 'Pacific Ocean' had been an invention—two words to describe to an old world a body of water and a horizon far beyond any western horizon they could possibly imagine.

Kit now tried to visualize another explorer—the Spaniard, Balboa—standing at the far side of the isthmus as he first looked out upon Magellan's "peaceful sea." He next looked at the girl opposite him and tried to imagine what far-distant ear on what far-distant continent would strain for the threnody of her pitiful Siren song. He blinked; looked again; tried to fathom why he'd thought all of this would somehow be different from what he might find in any small town in America.

Daneka, apparently, had had enough. She abruptly stood up and, without a word to Kit, walked to the nearest exit door. He watched her profile pass from window to window as she walked towards the bow. At the same time, he heard—then felt—the rumble of engines down in the bowels of the ferry. Stasis now stripped while Kinesis dressed; only their shared hangar of Inertia remained constant.

Chapter 53

As the ferry prepared to land at Ystad, the girls opposite Kit hastily gathered their belongings and then departed, *en masse blonde*, in the direction of the stern. The ferry maneuvered itself through a 180° turn, then reversed engines and slowly backed in towards the wharf. Kit went out to the hurricane deck for a smoke and to get his first view of Sweden—the landmass, home to the blond mass. He stepped up to the railing and watched the captain complete his maneuver. As the ferry moved into its berth, Kit felt the engines throttle back, pause, then start up again. The churn of water beneath the ship's stern provided the otherwise invisible evidence of propellers behaving like brakes. At the same time, the weathered hands of the ferry's deckhands assisted, on board and on land, in the last part of the docking and in bringing the ferry to a safe standstill, weaving heavy ropes through fairleads and around cleats. They performed their practiced choreography as delicately as any ballet, but in the certain knowledge that a misstep or lost slipper could, in an instant, crush a man to mincemeat between seawall and ship.

Kit continued to survey the scene from his position on the hurricane deck. He saw Daneka standing alone at the bow and looking out to sea; saw passengers on the ferry eagerly waiting to disembark; saw, in line with the others, the American family with the mother of unknown origin; also heard, through the general din, her voice inveigh against the gangly girl of straight, blond hair and a not-unpleasant demeanor.

"Ophelia! *Listen* to me!" The combination of ear-phones and blank expression suggested a deathlike indifference to both the entreaty and its pathetic source.

The girl was not listening to her mother any more than the boy was—now; earlier; maybe ever. This mother might have better luck moving a wall, Kit thought—the shrillness of her voice might cause at least a few molecules of brick to crumble. As if the woman could sense she was being watched, she turned her head in Kit's direction and stared directly back at him. Their eyes met and locked. Even at that distance, Kit could see their soft, tired greenness. The strain he'd noted earlier disappeared for an instant as she seemed to forget—in the uncritical stare of this stranger—her children, her situation, her certain mortality. Head, neck and body started to turn back to all three, but her eyes wouldn't leave his—*couldn't* leave his—and so, shared instead a last moment of quiet communion; accepted a silent benediction; returned a salutation and a last goodbye—and then abruptly turned away.

Although Kit was certain he'd never see the woman again, he was equally certain he'd never forget this singular communion of eyes—that her green stare would be fixed in his visual memory as surely as the smell of fresh cut grass was fixed in his olfactory memory, as the sound of the single Danish word Daneka had whispered the first time he'd entered her was fixed in his aural memory, as the feel of the hair on the nape of her neck each time he'd kissed her off to sleep was fixed in his tactile memory. And that he would take *it*, along with all of the others, to the grave.

The last of the Swedish passengers disembarked. The ferry, Kit calculated at a glance, had been relieved of easily two-thirds of its human and vehicular cargo. The same practiced hands that had brought the ferry into its docking station unleashed it, coiling heavy hemp rope in piles beside thick, landlocked pylons. The ferry's propellers turned just enough to move it forward, though not enough to result in a disturbing wake. The ship moved out to sea and, Kit surmised, in the direction of Bornholm. He turned his head away from the Swedish mainland. Daneka still stood at the bow. She was facing him directly and—Kit noted with enormous relief—smiling. He took her smile as a desire for reconciliation, walked to the stairs joining hurricane deck to main deck, and descended to stand beside her.

She put both arms around his waist. "Hey there, sailor boy."

He looked at her. As the ferry turned up the RPMs and headed out to sea, breaking through waves and sending saltwater spray into both their faces with each return of the bow to the surface of the water, he looked hard at her. However tenuous her genetic tie to the Vikings of old Denmark, something deep within her responded to the pounding of the waves, the breaking of the surf, the forward trajectory—always out, out and away; always searching for new lands, new adventures, new challenges and conquests, always something new. She couldn't help herself—it was in her blood. The thrill of novelty and uncertainty were to her a necessary fix. So long as there was sea, she would never stick to land; so long as there were storms, she would eschew shelter; so long as there was security, she would be a breaker of chains.

He loved her—and, in that instant, resolved to drop, once and for all, any expectation or even wish that he might one day tether her ambition to his. The choice, he knew, was not, had never been, would never be, his.

"How long now till we arrive at—?" He hesitated to say the name of the village, knowing he'd butcher its pronunciation.

"Rønne?" she asked with another smile. "Even less time than it took us to get from Copenhagen to Ystad. Now, c'mon, darling. Let me hear you say it. R-ø-n-n-e. The 'r' is like the French 'r,' and the 'ø' comes very close to the German 'ö'—you know, 'o' with an umlaut. Now pucker up those little lips and say it—R-ø-n-n-e."

"R-ø-n-n-e," Kit tried. He thought he'd succeeded, but he also knew that Daneka was a perfectionist. And so, it came as no surprise to him when she reached up with one hand and squeezed his cheeks together.

"Almost, but not quite. Let's work a bit on that 'ø,' shall we?

Try as he might, it all came out sounding too much like the dipthong 'œ' in 'Gœthe' for her satisfaction. If the German 'ö' was as close as he'd ever get to the Danish 'ø,' so be it; as long as he could make himself understood, he was happy. Daneka's perfectionism, he figured, was her problem.

"Well, darling, we'll just have to exercise. At least you've got the 'r' down like a real champion."

"Like a real *champignon*, you mean," Kit said through a smirk.

"Yes! From now on, you'll be my *champignon*." She snuggled up to him. "And when do you think we could have our next breakfast of *champignons*?"

He reached down with the tip of his finger and touched the tip of her nose. "Just as soon as we can rinse the salt off that delightful little proboscis of yours."

Daneka's mouth opened slightly just as her eyes half-closed. She just as quickly opened them again and began looking around mischievously—for what, he wasn't certain. He, himself, made a quick survey of their immediate surroundings. There was no one else on the deck with them, no faces peering out from behind the windows of the main cabin, and no one on the hurricane deck. The captain's view from just above the handrail enclosing the navigating bridge, however, was unobstructed—and so, presented an obstacle. Daneka seemed to reach the same conclusion at the same instant. An obstacle for her, however, merely represented a challenge. Her eyes made a more thorough inspection of the deck on which they stood, then seemed to hone in on a target. She walked over and picked up a nylon tarp—then returned to Kit, opened it, draped it around Kit's shoulders and her own.

"We need to try to stay dry," she said with a smirk. Her sudden awareness of a condition that had clearly not bothered her in the least since their ferry had left Copenhagen was one that Kit found amusing—and so characteristically 'Daneka.'

She'd solved one problem, only to be confronted by another. The tarp had grommets, but no cord; hence, no way to secure it—another challenge in need of another solution.

"Hold these ends together, will you, darling?" Kit did as she asked, keeping both Daneka and himself thoroughly concealed from the neck down. He sensed Daneka stooping over slightly and reaching down for something, then finding it, then shifting her weight from one leg to the other. She rotated both of their bodies 45° so that Kit's back, shoulders and head presented a screen between her and the windows on the navigating bridge. She then brought her hands up and out from under the tarp just under Kit's. With one hand, she pinched two of the grommets together; with the other, she threaded the pair of holes with some material whose provenance was still a mystery to Kit. Only when she'd managed to get the material through the grommets and had begun to tie a knot in it did Kit understand her ingenuity: in lieu of cord, she was using her panties.

Is there no end to this woman's inventiveness? he wondered. *Why would I even bother to look at other women—for whatever reason? Not only has she thought through and overcome two foreseeable obstacles. She's also anticipated a third in the form of a fine silk barrier—and promptly removed it.*

Apparently satisfied with the security of her work, Daneka turned around to face Kit, then stepped back slowly until her back was up against the handrail. Unknown to him—but apparently not to her—there were two footrests hard-welded precisely where the starboard and port sections of the ferry met at the bow. She stepped up onto them so that her face was on a level with his face, her feet perhaps three or four inches higher than his feet. He felt her hands underneath the tarp as they undid his belt buckle, pulled down his zipper, pushed his jeans down to his knees, then reached for the waistband of his shorts. She smiled at him a third time as she blindly, yet expertly, overcame the final obstacle—his shorts—and slid them down to join his jeans.

He felt those same hands as they hoisted up her skirt, then took him and guided him in. He slid into her easily as she placed her lips on his. Another pair of lips pulled him on, in, and up. Only once he was fully inside her did those lips cease pulling.

Kit could do virtually nothing from his standing position but stand. From her slightly raised position on the footrests, however, Daneka could bend—then re-extend—her legs several inches. The tent-like structure of the tarp gave them the necessary cover. To an outside observer, they appeared to be stationary. On the inside, however, Daneka would take complete possession of the mechanics facilitated by her four or five inches of flexibility. She became mistress of a vertical movement almost too sublime for two mere human bodies to withstand as she rose up, then settled back down again. And again and again.

In the absence of a natural partner to inform her rhythm, she found the rhythm of the sea and of the ship's blunt movements upon it. As the ferry would rise on a swell, she would slide down on Kit. As the ferry would slide back down on the other side of that same swell, she would rise. Occasionally, the ferry would slam; she would slam with it.

Whether it was ultimately the slide or the slam was no one's fault, least of all the sea's—to which swells came naturally and abundantly. On the last but one, Daneka's body rose up and slipped accidentally off Kit. They fought frantically, if blindly, to find each other again. Just as she felt him start to enter her, the ferry slid down the backside of a swell and into a particularly deep trough. She mimicked the ship's movement, raised her feet up off the footrests, encircled his chest with her arms and grabbed his hips with her thighs. His hands immediately slid down under her to lend support. Relieved of much of the burden of her own body weight, she had only that of her legs to worry about—and stomach muscles strong enough to keep them suspended almost indefinitely. She released his hips, spread her knees as wide as she could, pushed her abdomen up against his, and came. When she felt him come just seconds later deep inside her, her vaginal muscles became a bellows, an accordion, clenching and unclenching, drawing in air, and him, and then expelling the air again—and seemingly drawing him deeper in with each contraction.

Daneka buried her face in Kit's neck so as to muffle the sound. With no place to bury his face, Kit gritted his teeth.

When they'd both calmed down enough to see their situation and their surroundings with greater lucidity, it was not shame or embarrassment they felt, but only the tightness and *right*ness of their love. Their faces and lips awash in salt spray, their hair hanging in wet and scraggly strings, they kissed with a passion that would've done honor even to Balboa—and the captain's salute in the form of a long blast from the ship's horn did absolutely nothing to deter or dampen that passion.

These Danes, Daneka thought. *They love to watch almost as much as they love to do.*

Disassembling their little tent proved to be no challenge for someone as talented as Daneka. She simply worked in reverse, as if she'd memorized every maneuver from the moment she'd first spied the tarp—and ran the film back to front. On the matter of the obstruction that had not long ago existed in Kit's shorts, but which had conveniently disappeared, she improvised. What had formerly been hard, dry and stubborn was now soft, wet and malleable. She swiped her hand once across his lower abdomen like a squeegee, then made an 'O' ring out of thumb and forefinger for the same purpose but on another part of him. She then brought her hand up through the opening in the tarp out of which their two heads were sticking, licked it, and suggested with a gesture to Kit that he do the same. He did.

She put her lips on Kit's again, forced them open with her own and tickled his tongue with hers in a long, liquid kiss. The captain acknowledged this second kiss with two short blasts from his horn. Without releasing Kit's mouth from her own, she reached back down, then brought her entire arm out from under the tarp and gave the captain the 'okay' sign with thumb and forefinger.

She and she alone celebrated the knowledge that she'd just used the same thumb and forefinger as an 'O' ring to a somewhat more sublime end.

The tarp having been returned to its original location, Kit and Daneka having returned to their original state of dress, the continents not having shifted appreciably in the course of Kit's and Daneka's minor tectonic rumblings, and the captain, if amused, still holding to his original course, the island of Bornholm now came into view for all parties. Small fishing boats flying miniature Danish flags bobbed here and there over the wake of the *Villum Clausen* as it progressed into port at Rønne. The captain once again executed a 180° turnabout in bringing the ferry to its docking station, and a different—if equally masterful—

set of deckhands delivered the ship to a secure berth.

Kit and Daneka walked back to the main cabin to retrieve their luggage, then disembarked with the remaining passengers. Rønne was a village: hence, the lone service station doubled as the lone car rental agency and was within walking distance of the docks.

Daneka took care of the paperwork while Kit got the car and loaded their luggage. Within minutes, they were off and driving down a two-lane boreen up and around the perimeter of the island.

It was late afternoon by the time they reached Svaneke. Perhaps because the village was on the windward side of the island, any remnants of fog had long since blown off. The sky was a clear, if muted, blue. The colors of the other houses in Svaneke—half again the size of Rønne—were likewise muted: flax and goldenrod; ochre and jonquil. Kit didn't wish to take this as an omen. It was what his growing knowledge of Daneka had prepared him to expect. To be muted was, quite simply, in the Danish conception of things—even in high summer.

Chapter 54

"I'll get the bags. You go in and turn on the lights."

"Thank you, darling.

Kit took their luggage out of the car and put it on the ground. This, he decided, was a Camel moment. *If you can't have the Lucky you love, love the Camel you're with*, he thought to himself with a chuckle. He took one out, lit it, then sat down on what appeared to be a dry-stone wall to look for a long moment at Daneka's cottage. 'Storybook' was the word that came immediately to mind.

He hadn't yet seen enough of the local architecture to know whether it was authentically Danish or something more eclectic. She might've bought it as a "fixer-upper"—or she might've had it designed according to whim, had it then built for her and her alone. In any case, he thought it more beautiful than any Mainline or Greenwich mansion, any Upper East Side townhouse or Brooklyn Heights brownstone, any Great Neck or Bedford Hills estate—than any Italian villa, even, in Porto Fino or along the Lido.

He would, in an instant, gladly give up every place he'd ever known for the chance to live here with her. Without her, he knew it would be nothing but an old piece of gingerbread. But with her? Like living in an adult candyland. They could perhaps, if she still wanted, make babies—little Danish roustabouts, roughnecks, maybe a poet, a dancer— or both. He didn't care. If they raised a family of herring hucksters—that, too, would be fine. Or if she didn't want any children, he wouldn't make it an issue. He'd continue as a photographer and she could do anything she wanted—or nothing at all. She'd already made more than enough money to retire on, and he could support himself. After all, a man of modest means didn't require a great deal. But they'd be rich, wealthy beyond anyone's wildest dreams—including their own—in having just each other, this house, and a bed. Not to mention the sea in front and the stars above.

Kit looked out at this quiet, silver sea—the 'Baltic' by name. It was not the Atlantic from Camden, Montauk or Rio; the Pacific from Mendocino or Viña del Mar; the Indian from Madras or Goa or even from Toamasina on the coast of Madagascar; not the Arctic from Fontur on the coast of Iceland, or from Myggebugten on the coast of Greenland. Nor was it the Caribbean from Cartegena; the Tasman from Auckland; the North from Aberdeen

- 281 -

or, just across the way, the Norwegian from Bergen. Still less, the Caspian from Baku; the Black from Sevastopol; the Adriatic from Dubrovnik; the Mediterranean from Genoa, Ajaccio or Malaga; and certainly not the Aegean from almost any Greek island he could think of.

It was, quite simply, the Baltic. To the south of them lay Germany and Poland; to the east, Lithuania and Latvia; to the northeast, Estonia—beyond that, Finland; and directly above: big, burly Sweden. It was a lot of geography to try to comprehend at a glance. And right in the center of it all, solipsistically speaking, stood Daneka's cottage.

The structure had an old English feel to it: a thatched roof, which looked to be authentic; few windows, and each pair deeply encased in a bulging sill and jamb that looked to have been fashioned out of pumice, limestone or some other crushed stone, then reinforced, perhaps, by metal lath. To all appearances, however, there was not a gypsum block, piece of particle- or plasterboard in sight. Flanking each pair of windows and hanging from wrought iron hinges, a pair of wooden shutters, the grain barely visible, but the struts running vertically—obviously heavy with age and warped. From a distance, the window panes themselves looked to be hand-blown and laid out within an intricate latticework of lead piping. The geometry of the glasswork looked almost *fin de siècle*. Odd, Kit thought, in a structure clearly centuries older.

Just as he was admiring the latticework of one window in particular, he noticed a pair of hands behind, barely visible, the light on them refracted and heavily distorted by the internal bubbles and thickness of the ornamental glass. A tiny flame flickered slowly into view. The same picture came to him an instant later from the next window, and then from the next. Daneka was obviously lighting candles—although the sun this close to the Arctic Circle would still not be setting for hours.

The weathered wisteria-blue of the shutters set off perfectly against the faded sunflower-yellow of the cottage walls. Blue and yellow—the national colors of that behemoth directly to the north. *Perhaps there is* indeed *something else she likes about Sweden,* he thought. The irony didn't altogether escape him.

He next looked at the landscape. Here, he reasoned, he might actually be able to make a contribution. He knew nothing about native flora or growing seasons, but there was always the Internet and the USDA to help him out if she had a computer and a connection.

He'd simply have to confirm the zone. The island was at about 55° north on a latitudinal line running through the middle of the province of Labrador and just above the bottom lip of the Hudson Bay. He figured this location for Zone Two. What he'd have to study up on, however, was the microclimate of a place like Bornholm. But they had time—a whole lifetime if she'd allow it; a good week if she wouldn't. Either way, he concluded that further mental doodling on gardening, hardiness zones, microclimates and geography could wait. Daneka might consider sudden disappearances or even an extended absence *her* rightful prerogative. He knew better, however, than to assume that prerogative for himself.

He picked up their bags and walked to the front door—an impressive structure, probably of heavy oak or walnut and modeled on a typical Dutch door with independent upper and lower halves. The mid-section of the entablature was of solid stone with a date chiseled in: 1636—one nice, round century older than his family's house in Radnor. *A 'fixer-upper?'* he chuckled to himself. This cottage had first been 'fixed up' when Rembrandt, Van Dyck and Velázquez were still actively painting, Corneille writing, and Harvard College barely settled on its foundations.

The cornice, header and jambs were of some wood Kit didn't recognize, heavier even than oak or walnut and of a grain almost as exquisite to his eye as a woman's body. He couldn't resist the temptation to touch it—and consequently did so. The upper and lower panels, traditionally of wood in a front door, mimicked the glass and lead latticework of the windows, even if the color of the glasswork in this case was a diluted version of the shutters and walls of the cottage. A single blue, oval-shaped pane stood in the center of each panel, surrounded by a *Jugendstil* mosaic of the most subtle amber Kit had ever seen. The threshold and weatherboard—he finally noted as he prepared to open the door and step in—were solid, dove-gray flagstones.

He pushed down on the door latch. From its aged and pimpled feel, he concluded it might pre-date even the construction of the cottage. The hinges, bolts and lock were of identical wrought iron—hence, probably fired, forged and hammered by the same blacksmith, then polished to an artisan-acceptable finish by the same whitesmith.

As he entered, he immediately noted the wide wooden floorboards and heard Daneka's footsteps overhead on what he supposed would be identical flooring. A candle in a tarnished brass holder burned in each window, while three more burned in each of two lead sconces to either side of the fireplace. Footsteps around the perimeter of the room above him, punctuated by an occasional pause, suggested to his ear that she was on the way to completing her task on the second floor. The cottage, in short order, would resemble the houses he'd seen many times in Vermont—his only point of reference—throughout the long winter months. Perhaps, he thought, Vermonters had learned the custom from some of the state's early Danish settlers.

He next noticed that the fireplace stood dark and empty. Would she allow the extravagance of a fire in mid-summer? He resolved to take their bags upstairs to ask—and made his way to the stairway.

As if the front door, windows, walls and floors weren't already sufficiently sublime, the staircase announced its magnificence in the only language old, dead wood could speak—namely, imperial silence. The newel post, alone, was a work of exquisite beauty; Kit was certain he'd never seen another like it. Inlays within inlays—he counted six different kinds of wood at a glance, though couldn't even have begun to identify them—absorbed or reflected light, each at its own particular frequency. The balusters were clearly hand-cut and of yet another kind of wood. The handrail appeared to be of the same wood as one of the inlays in the newel post: dark, majestic, and badly in need of a dusting. Both stringers were clearly of common pine, but of a grain suggesting that the particular tree from which they'd been taken was nothing less than patrician. The same was true of the treads and risers.

The crown jewel of the stairway, however, was to be found in the risers themselves. Set into each was a triptych of eggshell-colored ceramic tiles. Then, on each tile and painted in fine but sparse detail—whether worn off by age or intentionally omitted by the artist, it was impossible for Kit to tell—he discerned country scenes and characters from what he could only imagine was the Denmark of a much earlier epoch. Some artisan (or artisans) had, he surmised, spent many long hours firing and glazing those tiles. Some artist (or artists) had then spent just as many long hours painting them. Some craftsman (or craftsmen) had finally spent as many long and careful hours again mounting them into the risers, which a carpenter (or carpenters) would then have put into place quite possibly while holding his—or *their* collective—breath.

He mounted the stairs with a care he normally took only for his camera, then went looking for Daneka in one of the rooms. He noticed, as he looked through two of the three doorways he came upon, that lighted candles already stood in the windows. It was only through the third doorway that he saw her—busy with lighting her last candle—and then walked in.

"Darling!" she said. Whether surprised, shocked or pleased, he wasn't certain. The way she raised her hand to her breast, however, suggested he'd caught her in a deep reverie. "I'm *so* happy to see you. I thought maybe you'd run off with one of the wood-nymphs."

Kit chuckled. "No. As a matter of fact, I haven't seen a soul. I've just been admiring your cottage."

"You like it then?" she asked, as if there'd ever been a question in anyone's mind about its likeability. Still, Kit thought—and certain recollections, reflections and connections suddenly struck him almost dumb—she had to hear it; she had to have the obvious confirmed yet one more time.

"Yes, Daneka. It's nothing less than magnificent."

She smiled like a satisfied child. Daneka, however, was an adult. Some irreparable damage—Kit now allowed himself to conjecture—must've been done long ago to her fundamental self-esteem. Some *one* or some *thing* had kicked out the bottom. He knew that his affirmation—that any *single* affirmation he or anyone else could offer—would ultimately make no difference. The barrel was bottomless; the bottom itself, gone. She'd always be a seeker of compliments in one form or another, and none of them would ever be sufficient to restore that bottom.

"It's adorable," he added. The reinforcement, he knew, was pointless; the first compliment had long since leaked out; there was already nothing left to reinforce.

"Oh, it's just a little getaway is all—a little *pied-à-terre* for me when Manhattan simply becomes too much. That, and a month in the summer—usually mid-July to mid-August, though we're early this year, thanks to you." With this, she walked up to him, put her arms around his neck, stretched her head and mouth up to his ear.

"How about a little fire, fireman? One in here and one downstairs—while I take a quick shower to wash off the salt. Whatever I miss, you can lick off." She said the last barely above a whisper. Kit wondered whether the cottage walls had ears, or whether Danish bedrooms—like Danish trains and Danish train stations—were also quiet zones.

"Deal." He was happy. He hadn't even needed to prompt her where a mid-summer fire was concerned. "And our stuff?"

"Oh, let's not worry about that for now. We'll have more than enough time to unpack," she said as she removed her arms from around his neck, walked over to a hamper in the corner of the room and began to undress, dropping one article of clothing after another into it. Kit watched her. She seemed, initially at least, to be unmindful of his watching—but only initially.

"Darling, don't you want to get to work on those fires?" she asked, suddenly covering as much of her body as she could with both hands. *She can't possibly be self-conscious about her nudity at this stage*, Kit thought to himself. *Maybe she's just teasing.*

But as she'd watched him watching her, Daneka had had her own silent thoughts. The candlelight, she knew, showed her body and face to best effect. There was, however, also still too much direct sunlight coming in through the windows. It was more light than she wanted him to see her by in her present state: tired, stressed, premenstrual, post- much more coital than she'd known in a long time, and consequently fearing—if not yet actually feeling—a urinary tract infection coming on.

"Be a darling now, darling. Run off and make us a fire or two. By the time you're finished, I'll be washed and ready for as much watching as your little eyes can stand. 'Promise."

For the first time in as long as they'd been together, Kit was surprised to discover that he had no difficulty disengaging his eyes from her almost naked body. A moment earlier, he'd been watching her intently. But this time, he knew the impetus was merely his professional curiosity. He'd felt no arousal, no excitement, no sensation of any kind. He'd simply been studying the way the light fell upon her. What it showed him was probably more than either of them wanted him to see.

It fell, it seemed to him, like a brief sun-shower upon a stretch of arid, cracked land. This sun-shower, he realized, could not restore that land to its former fecundity. A torrential rain could not restore that land to fecundity—former *or* future. No amount of water could return that sere piece of land to what it might've once been before years of neglect or maybe the opposite of neglect—too *much* attention and too much of the wrong kind—had eaten and beaten much of the life out of it.

And yet, he thought, women who wouldn't grow old gracefully were one of life's more unpleasant facts: the vanity of the leisure class catered to by plastic surgeons who'd long since traded in their scruples for a summer bungalow in the Hamptons or a *chacra* at the Punta del Este while the children of Magaburaka and Sarajevo went limbless.

Almost as distasteful was the sight of those ageing bodies in clothes more appropriate to a teenager. In New York and Los Angeles, Rio and Buenos Aires, dowagers like bad wax figures on parade. Whenever they crossed his path, he'd actually look away.

Occasionally, very occasionally, he'd come face to face with an older woman who wore her lines proudly: laugh lines, or lines from crying, weeping, fighting illness. A woman who knew to cover her breasts because she'd once used them for their intended purpose—who'd suffered chapped nipples and the inevitable sag that resulted from the tug, the pull and play of a greedy infant or a whole brood of them.

Kit wondered about Daneka—whether she'd one day sacrifice the prize of breast-feeding to her vanity. Looking at her now, he hoped she wouldn't. He wondered, too, whether she'd age gracefully, allowing gray and gravity to do their work, yet without ever losing pride in her ageing body and never stooping to compete with younger women whose only edge might well be their youth. Or would she be one of those women who'd encourage men's leers—and who'd continue to call them out with breast-hugging T-shirts and hip-hugging jeans—until those same men, once perhaps indifferent, might then react with annoyance or even outright disgust?

He cut his reverie short. She was right. She'd understood this rude fact. *This* time, here and now, she shouldn't have allowed him to watch her undress by direct sunlight.

As Kit turned away, Daneka realized what had just happened. She was no mind-reader, but she didn't need to be: she had intuition and experience. The combination had given her wisdom. Wisdom rarely brought deliverance with it; on the contrary, it too often brought pain. She heard the sound of Kit's footsteps diminish as he descended upon the staircase, then disappear altogether as he opened the front door and went outside to collect kindling and wood for the fires. There was an old rocker next to the hamper—a rocker that had been in her family for three generations. That rocker, with its soft, repetitive rhythm, had no doubt served its dual purpose many times: on the one hand, to put babies to sleep; on the other, to take away some portion of the pain of an ageing, abandoned woman. She dropped to the floor the last article of clothing she'd held only a moment earlier as cover. That cover, she knew, was needless—a false modesty, a silly relic. She walked to the bedroom door, closed and bolted it—then walked back to the rocker and sat down.

The tears came slowly. Self-pity was not a refuge in which Daneka often took cover. Self-pity, she'd realized many years earlier, was the land of the lost. She'd been lost—once, briefly, as a girl of fifteen. She'd been forced into a dark tunnel—and then just as forcibly abandoned. She'd allowed herself a few hours' self-pity, had then fought her way back out into the light and sealed off the tunnel for all time.

She would allow *no* man—not Kit or any other—to make her feel that way again. Just this once, however, and close to the source, she'd let herself unstop the tunnel for a brief glimpse back down inside. She would, just this once, allow herself the luxury of self-pity—for a couple of moments while he gathered wood and made a fire.

At the same time, she knew she'd never again let him see her undress by full daylight.

Chapter 55

The next morning, Daneka rose early. She'd reached a conclusion or two during an almost sleepless night following a subdued fireside chat, a light supper, half an hour in front of the fire, and then bed. Bed, in this case, had meant sleep—or at least an attempt at sleep. Kit had had no problem falling off immediately. Daneka, however, had never really found hers.

She'd decided, among other things, that she would never again let his head find hers on the same pillow the morning after—*any* morning after. Rather, she'd get up and out of bed before he even stirred, would shower and dress, would then hide what lines she could with make-up well before his eyes opened to find those lines. She might, if she were able to rise early enough and consistently, undertake some form of aerobic exercise—maybe a daily swim down at the "Y" on 93rd Street. Whether or not she'd be able to manage it first thing in the morning, every morning, was not the critical point. Consistency was. A daily regimen was what she needed—and one that she'd stick to.

Surgery? A radical solution, certainly, but not entirely out of the question. She'd have to think long and hard about it. Maybe she'd run the idea by him and see how he reacted. Botox, in any case, was a quick—if also temporary—fix. There were plenty of players right there in the neighborhood who could do it. For Botox, she didn't need to run off to Stockholm, Geneva, Rio, or even Beverly Hills. On Manhattan's Upper East Side, access to a Botox solution was as easy as going to the corner pharmacy for cough syrup. She'd already heard of a good one right there on Fifth Avenue at about 77th Street. An hour's treatment, and she'd be right back out the door like a shiny new Chevy—or Volvo, she thought to herself sardonically—and then back in once a month for a tune-up.

In any case, age was not something she was going to give in to. They hadn't been together for even six weeks, and already the spell was wearing thin—if it hadn't, in fact, already worn through. Kit might or might not be the one; that wasn't really the point. But he and he alone had re-awakened something in her, and she wasn't about to let it go dormant once again.

Sex was something she could get anywhere, anytime. Cyber was safe, immediate, as often and for as long or short as she was in the mood. She was good with words and even with handles—of which she had half a dozen. She knew how to dip into a chat room with any one of her pseudonymous handles; study the banter; lure someone into a private room if that someone—he or she—struck her fancy; make herself come quickly and as many times as she needed; maybe let the other have his or her own little thrill; then leave—all of it nice, clean, efficient, and commitment-free.

There was the *other*, of course, for those times when cyber simply wasn't enough. She shuddered. She hadn't thought about it even once since she and Kit had left New York. That said something about him, certainly, and about this thing they had—whatever it was. Sex with him had been about more than just orgasms, and she hadn't known at first what to make of it. The feelings and sensations he aroused in her were simply alien.

There had, of course, been that one time, many years before, in Riverside Park.... Entirely anonymous. Also with a younger man. She chuckled inwardly at the swift and sultry memory of it: in like a lion; out like a lamb. It had occurred, she recalled, also in the month of March.

And yes, there'd been many in between—some of them memorable; some of them forgotten within minutes if they even registered to begin with; a few, unfortunately, even less substantial than the drips, drabs and drops they'd left behind in the sheets.

It was different with Kit—perhaps because she was older, somewhat wiser, her life less cluttered. Okay, maybe not entirely uncluttered; there was still Annemette.

Annemette—who'd brought them together in the first place and was the reason Daneka had picked up a copy of the *Village Voice* following an ordinary working lunch with Robert. Annemette, who was also the reason she'd dialed a number almost randomly and based on no better information than the odd combination of "portraits and landscapes." What a thing—serendipity.

She'd have to get around to the matter of Annemette with him sooner or later. Annemette still mattered—mattered a lot. Kit would do fine for what Daneka had in mind. He'd be perfect for the shoot—as he was perfect for her, she mused, in so many other ways.

Kit woke up with a start. It wasn't anything in particular that wrenched him into consciousness—nothing, at least, that he could immediately put a finger on. And then it struck him: it was *nothing* and *no one* he could immediately put a finger on. Where the fuck was she? As she had so many times before, she'd simply vanished. *Why, every time we're beginning to make some kind of progress, does she simply up and disappear?* He was about to get out of bed and go looking when he settled back, instead, to think. Something had happened the day before—something probably neither of them wanted to acknowledge openly—but it had happened nonetheless. He knew and suspected she did, too. All right—so the novelty had worn off. It was bound to go sooner or later, and he was frankly happy to have it gone. Now, he reasoned, they could finally get down to the *real* work of building a relationship.

Work was—in Kit's mind—what made love real, sustainable, vital, the thing for which he lived. He didn't play at photography; he worked at it. The harder he worked, the better he got—and the more he loved it. Why should his love for this woman—or hers for him—be any different? Nobody's born with an innate talent or knowledge of how to love. The only thing we're born with—the only innate knowledge—is an instinct for survival. Everything else is learned, acquired, mastered over time. Then, let circumstances strip away every acquisition and render all learning meaningless, the only thing still left would be a killer instinct to survive. A man would miss his acquisitions, but he'd get over them. He'd miss not being able to put to good use everything he'd learned, but he'd get over that, too. Survival was the only thing he wouldn't merely allow himself to miss. For that, he'd fight. Let anyone threaten that survival, he'd fight—as would a woman.

But what is survival without love? Little more than an opportunity to consume and pollute. To leave nothing behind but junk, the detritus of a wasted and worthless life. Every living thing consumes; every living thing shits and pisses and sloughs off dead skin cells. In that respect, we have nothing over a mere bacterium. Our special talent, our goodness, our *godliness* resides in only one thing. And the work of that one thing—the *real* creation of it—was about to begin.

He'd wanted to declare it to her symbolically once before—perhaps too symbolically, he now realized, and not sufficiently concretely—with his gift of a lichen. Here and now, he'd do it concretely with the gift of a garden. A garden that would, for the rest of her natural life, shout to her eyes on a thousand summer days and whisper to her nose on as many summer nights: *'No man ever had a deeper love for a woman than I do for you. No man ever wanted to meld his soul with a woman's more than I do mine with yours. No man ever sought, or came to know and dared to call a woman his one and only mate—more than I do you.'*

Chapter 56

Kit went downstairs and found Daneka in the kitchen—showered, made-up and dressed. Her reception was cool—standoffish even—as he walked up to give her a morning kiss.

"Sleep well, darling?"

"Yes. And you?"

"Wonderfully," she lied.

"Look. I'm sorry if I fell aslee—."

"Don't be. I, too, was bushed," she lied again. The ensuing extended pause let each of them know the extent of the other's dissimulation. "Coffee?"

"Sure. Thanks." Daneka set to work on the coffee immediately. "What would you like to do today?" Kit asked.

"Well, if you wouldn't mind, I'd first like to go see my mother. Then, if the weather clears up—or even if it doesn't—I'd like to show you my special place."

"I thought *this* was your special place. You mean you have *another* special place here on the island?"

"I do."

"Would you like to give me a little hint?"

"Nope."

Kit stood up, walked over to Daneka, put his arms around her waist from behind and leaned down to her ear. "And if I kiss it out of you?"

"You can certainly try, darling."

Kit pushed the hair up off the nape of Daneka's neck. She obligingly tilted her head forward so as to give him easy access. As he covered it with little kisses, she purred. The tiny hairs on the nape of her neck felt to his lips like mink. He'd never smelled a live mink before, yet he imagined—perhaps irrationally since minks were feral and not in any way known for exceptionally fastidious hygiene—that the smell of one would be as much a gift to the nose as their pelts were to the skin—and as her smell was now to him and his nose.

There'd been only one other woman's neck in his life that had felt to his lips and smelled to his nose as exquisite as Daneka's—and then, it had been only a fleeting smell and touch. He'd thought about it—and about that other nape—from time to time over the years, though not once, until now, since he'd first met Daneka. It was usually, and oddly, always towards the end of February that he thought of her, or whenever he'd stumble onto a patch of ground fog. Maybe it was the anniversary of that evening—he really couldn't remember when it had taken place. Or maybe it was the ground fog in the park—he had only a vague recollection of the conditions under which it had happened. But he had a very concrete memory of mink.

As he continued kissing Daneka's neck, he peeked around the side of her head and saw that she was smiling. He felt a little guilty—but no more than a little—as he brushed the nape of this woman's neck with his lips and stroked it with the tip of his tongue while indulging in the memory of the other....

At the time, and in his own mind, he'd called her a minx—supplying the "x" as a place-holder for the name he never learned. It had been only a few minutes. Then she'd vanished from his life forever, leaving no trace of herself but the smell, taste and feel of the nape of her neck, which he suspected now—though he had no inkling then—he'd carry to his grave. He'd felt the other, too; had then smelled and tasted it as soon as he'd gotten home. He'd even postponed showering for almost a week so as to be able to revisit the smell and taste of her every night after he'd put the lights out and climbed into bed. But his own unwashed smell eventually overpowered the olfactory trace of her; he found himself at an increasing distance from the next body in the classroom or on the subway—anywhere he walked where other people were present; and so, he'd had to shower and wash the last of her scent away.

In the years in between, there'd been many women and many smells, all of which had simply become a blur. It was the smell of her neck alone that remained in perfect isolation in his olfactory memory. And that smell was one which, once logged, he'd kept ever since as the scent of 'minx.'

The smell, taste and feel of the nape of Daneka's neck struck him as somehow similar—though all of it a brushstroke older. It hadn't occurred to him until now, but then he'd never made the connection. Perhaps her smell was why he'd initially been attracted to her. Funny, he thought, that a photographer should be drawn to a woman by the olfactory and tactile rather than the visual.

"Ready for your coffee?" she asked.

"Yes, thank you." She poured it out into a cup and gave it to him, then grabbed a small pitcher of heavy cream from the refrigerator and brought it over to the kitchen table. "You've already been out grocery shopping, I see."

"Yes, just a starter kit, really. We'll shop in Rønne for some real stuff." She held the pitcher up and began to pour. "Tell me when."

He waited a couple of seconds. "When." She returned the pitcher to the refrigerator. "Do you mind if I take a quick shower before we go to visit with your mother?"

"Not at all, darling. Take your time. She's not going anywhere."

"Care to join me?" he asked, trying to make the question sound, if not exactly scintillating, at least not as perfunctory as he knew it was—to *both* of them.

"Oh, thanks for the invitation," she said. Her lips tried to simulate a smile, but fell flat in the attempt. "I've already had mine. I'll just clean up in here a little while you finish your coffee and then take your shower."

Kit watched her as he continued sipping. He'd never actually seen her engaged in this kind of activity before. Estrella—her housekeeper—probably did most if not all of the cleaning for her in New York.

She was, he thought, as exceedingly thorough in this as in everything else. He wondered at what point 'exceedingly' would become 'excessively' or even 'obsessively' as he watched her go over some of the same spots three and four times. But he kept the thought to himself as he hurried to finish his coffee and rid himself of the sight of this unnatural spectacle. He finally stood up, poured the last of his coffee down the drain, placed the cup in the sink, and was about to go upstairs when she stopped him.

"Darling," she said in a tone that signaled to him immediately that she had some corrective measure in mind. "We do it this way here. First, we rinse out our cup, like this"—she turned on the cold water and rinsed it out, then held it up for him to see—"and then we put our cup into the dishwasher, like this." She opened it and pulled out the top tray. She then put the cup down in the rear corner of the tray, just so, and pushed the tray back in—also, just so. "And then we give the sink a last little scrub and rinse in case all of the coffee didn't make it down the drain the first time around. Okay?"

"Yes, Daneka. Okay."

"Would you care to try it yourself one time?"

"No, Daneka. I believe I've got the motions down now. Thanks."

"Good. Then there won't be any misunderstandings about this in the future, I take it."

"None."

As he made his way up the stairs, Kit found himself wondering for the first time what it actually might mean to work for this woman. Not on a one-off project—even *he* could do that. But nine to five, Monday through Friday, with Christmas Day and two weeks off in August. He suspected the question of the 'right' or 'wrong' way to do a thing never really entered into discussion; rather, that there was simply 'Daneka's' way. You either learned it—quickly and absolutely—and then discarded your own silly notions of what might work in a given situation, or you didn't. If you didn't, you found employment elsewhere—with no further need for instruction.

As he showered, he forced himself not to think any more about it, but rather to let thoughts and dirt, dead skin cells and dislodged strands of hair, soap and shampoo run down the drain.

After he'd rinsed himself off to his satisfaction, he rotated the shower knob a full 360° to make sure he'd left no trace of himself behind.

Chapter 57

Thirty minutes later, Kit was showered, shaved, combed, brushed and dressed. As he descended upon the stairway, he noticed for the first time the framed portrait sitting on the mantle. Daneka was just at that moment walking out of the kitchen—hands wringing, dishtowel still clinging.

"Is that, by chance, a picture of your mother?" Kit asked as he gestured towards the mantle. Daneka's eyes followed Kit's over to the same spot.

"Yes. That's *mor.*" He walked over, picked up the frame and studied the portrait. She was an attractive woman, he thought, and he could see the immediate resemblance: the same smile, the same short-cropped hair, the same well-defined lines in the jaw and nose. The portrait was a black and white—and so, revealed nothing about her eye or hair color. She wore a heavy-knit white sweater with some kind of traditional Scandinavian design just below the shoulder; underneath that, what looked to him like a gray, V-necked pullover or jersey; and beneath that, a black undergarment of some kind. He looked at her portrait and could now easily envision Daneka in twenty years—they looked *that* much alike.

"She's a very becoming woman."

"She'll be very pleased to hear you say that, darling."

"How good is her English?"

"Oh, my. *Rather* good! Where do you think I learned *my* English? At finishing school?" she said this time with a wink.

"C'mon. Let's go. I'm dying to meet her."

They jumped into the car and started out across the island. Daneka seemed to Kit to be genuinely excited. She scooted up close to him and rode with one hand inside his shirt—something she hadn't done since Portugal—occasionally pointing out some of the landmarks on their way around the island. Kit knew they must be getting close to the village when she pointed to a cemetery and mentioned that most of her extended family was buried there.

"Except for *mor* and me, of course."

"And is that where you, too, want to be buried one day?" Kit asked.

"Yes. Right alongside *mor.*"

"That'll be nice. Finally, once again, between mother and father—where every child ultimately longs to be." Daneka's mood suddenly seemed to darken. The next words out of her mouth had clearly lost something of their previous star-light, star-bright tone.

"No. *Mor* will lie in the middle. That's where she belongs." Kit didn't press the point, as Daneka's attention was suddenly drawn to a picturesque little building of faded yellow wood siding and dark green window and door frames. "And that," she now pointed excitedly, "was my first schoolhouse!"

This, Kit realized, was Rønne. It was every bit as delightful as Svaneke—though clearly more of a town than a village. They drove into the heart of it—past the wharf where their ferry had landed the day before, past various little shops—until she directed him to turn off the main road and down a little country lane, all cobblestone. Kit squeezed their car past a tractor or two. Farmers nodded; horses chewed. Kit spotted a couple of little girls in pinafores and long, golden braids, both of whom were playing—or so he imagined—the Danish equivalent of hopscotch. Daneka saw them at the same moment and rolled down her window.

"*Hallo! Er I dem, jeg tror I er? Er det virkelig lille Nina og lille Karen, som er blevet så store?*" ("Hello. Is that who I think it is? Is that little Nina and little Karen now grown so big?")

The girls sidled up to the car cautiously. Then, however, they recognized Daneka, and all prior wariness was unleashed to the wind.

"*Daneka!*" they both shouted and reached in through the car window to stroke her face and hair. "*Hvor er det længe siden! Er du kommet for at besøge fru Sørensen?*" ("What a long time it's been! Are you now here to visit Mrs. Sørensen?")

"*Ja, jeg er. Ved I, om hun er hjemme?*" ("Yes. Do you know whether she's at home?") Daneka asked.

"*Ja, selvfølgelig er hun hjemme. Hun er* altid *hjemme!*" ("But of course. She's *always* at home!")

Kit had no idea what this exchange was all about. But it never failed to impress him to hear little children speaking easily in a language he couldn't understand—or, even more, one he himself might be struggling with.

"*Nå, lille Nina og lille Karen—øh, jeg mener STORE Nina og STORE Karen! Vi ses igen snart.*" ("Well, little Nina and little Karen—oh, I mean BIG Nina and BIG Karen—we'll see you again soon.")

Whether prompted by something Daneka had said to them, or merely curious—as their conversation with her now seemed to be at an end—they both looked past her at Kit, then looked again at Daneka, then back at Kit, then at each other, then giggled and ran off arm in arm in sweet delectation of their secret.

"The house is just up the way there, darling," she said, pointing at a structure that looked to Kit as if it might've come straight out of an eighteenth-century painting. "You can park right in front."

When they pulled up, he saw that the house was indeed—if not as storybook in quite the same way as her own—a perfectly preserved relic of an era that could only have produced fairytales and other stories of wonderment. He looked at it and tried to imagine how such a home would've informed Daneka's consciousness, how it would've enriched her imagination just as surely, and to the same—though inverse—degree that a tenement building in East New York or the South Bronx would surely have impoverished another child's imagination. He looked at Daneka. She was indeed a remarkable character in all respects. But he now had his first real clue as to at least one source of that character, and of those to whom she was ultimately indebted for making it possible.

They stepped out of the car and walked up to the front door. She could, Kit knew, simply have opened the door and walked in. Instead, she knocked.

When the front door opened and a woman stepped out into the light, Kit thought he could be looking at an older sister—the resemblance was *that* uncanny. Any doubt was put to rest, however, as soon as Daneka spoke.

"*Goddag, mor.*"

"*Hallo, Daneka.*"

They stared at each other for a long moment. Kit could sense that Daneka wanted an embrace, but that she couldn't bring herself to initiate one. Her mother finally leaned into her, placed her hands on Daneka's upper arms, and gave her a peck on both cheeks. If Daneka expected or wanted a warmer homecoming from a woman she hadn't seen in over a year, it would not be her mother's to give—at least not today.

"*Mor, det er Kit, min—.*" ("Mother, this is Kit, my—.") She stumbled. Perhaps she'd never really considered, at least in Danish, what to call him. Her 'boyfriend?' Her 'beau?' He wasn't her 'betrothed.' And yet, the other epithets seemed awkward, silly at her age. Or perhaps, she realized, she was simply too embarrassed in front of her mother to call him anything at all.

Mrs. Sørensen came to Daneka's rescue. "Your Prince Charming. And if Kit doesn't speak Danish, I don't think we should, either." She extended her hand and a smile. "How do you do. Welcome, Kit, to Denmark and Rønne."

Kit was bewitched—at least as bewitched as he could be by a woman twice his age. Whatever she'd chosen to withhold from her daughter in their greeting of seconds earlier was clearly something she was prepared to give, and give unstintingly, to a perfect stranger. He took her hand in both of his—something he'd never done in his life. And then she spontaneously joined her other hand to her first. They were all hands and fingers—like a ball of happy little baby eels brought back from the brink of extinction.

She next reached up and grabbed his chin; turned his face to one side to inspect his profile; turned it to the other to see the other half. She then turned to Daneka and allowed herself one last communication in Danish: *"Han er jo en ren Adonis. Hvad vil han med dig?"* ("He's an Adonis. What's he doing with *you?*")

Kit had no idea what she'd just said. He looked at Daneka for a clue and couldn't believe his eyes. Her own welled up as if someone had just slapped her. Her lips quivered as she tried desperately to smile. "Desperately" was the only word that occurred to him at that instant.

Mrs. Sørensen turned back to Kit. "Please come in."

Kit and Daneka both walked through the front door. The living room was beehive dark. The sun's rays fought maniacally with one another to climb in through windows the size of bookends. The panes had probably not been washed in years. The lucky ones that *did* manage to climb through were immediately sequestered in shadowy corners, crannies, nooks and—Kit now noticed—books: a private library-full of them. Kit had never seen such a vast collection of books outside of a public library. They lined shelves; were stacked on the floor and on tables; continued in stacks all the way up the staircase. He wondered whether there was any order to them and made a quick study of the shelves of one of the floor-to-ceiling cases. For the second time in the space of less than a minute, his credulity was challenged by what met his eyes.

There were titles and names he recognized from philosophy, theology, history and mythology in this one case alone. Many of the titles contained the 'ø' he'd only recently come to love as much as any man could love a letter of the alphabet—and so he guessed they were in Danish. But there were others—many others—and their myriad accents told Kit he was standing in a house whose mistress danced at *all* the balls of Europe, even if only in her bedroom slippers.

He inspected a second bookcase. Once again, an assortment of accents stood atop proud letters of the names of the greatest writers of *belles letters* in the canon of Western literature. He even saw a few in Cyrillic, which piqued his polyglot pride.

"Скажите, вы говорите по-русски?" ("Do you speak Russian?") he asked with lips that seemed poised to dance at one of her balls if only she'd extend a hand.

"Да, конечно! А вы, кажется, тоже?" ("But of course. And you apparently do, too.") she answered—her own lips like toes long stiff and frozen, but now not. *Now,* uncurling inside dance slippers at the first whispered hint of a waltz.

"А Deneka? Она говорит?" ("What about Daneka? Does she speak it?") he asked, but then suddenly realized he was allowing some mental shutter to open on the light of a small cabal with—of all people—Daneka's mother.

"Отвечу коротко: нет," ("In a word, no,") she answered—and they both shared a conspiratorial chuckle.

Daneka was not amused. She of course wanted Kit and her mother to get along. But did they have to hit it off quite so famously and quite so quickly—and, apparently, at her expense? Her mother could speak Russian and flirt with any old sailor who wandered into port—but not with *her* partner!

"Are you two quite finished?"

"Indeed, we are, Daneka. Kit, why don't you come into the kitchen with me and help put together a little tea party? I was thinking about something … wonderlandish. We could use a Mad Hatter. Right, Kit? So you, Daneka, are cordially invited."

Kit looked at Mrs. Sørensen, then at Daneka, then back at Mrs. Sørensen again. Daneka, he observed, was not looking at anyone or anything except her toes. Meanwhile, she kept her arms crossed tightly across her chest—a bulwark against any other battering rams her mother might now choose to assay with.

"I'd love some tea," he said simply as the two of them disappeared into the kitchen.

Daneka walked upstairs to her former bedroom and found it exactly as she'd remembered it. Her mother had changed none of it over the years—a fact for which Daneka was truly grateful. There was security and safety in it against all the possible monsters in the world save one. That one may indeed have struck; but only once—and would never strike again. That was one fairytale whose ending she was only too happy to have read, to have shut the book on for the last time, to have put on a high shelf—and then, to have relegated to 'for never more.'

She looked at her former collection of books, and her eyes scanned the names of the wordsmiths of her youth: Aesop and Homer, Ovid and Virgil, H. C. Andersen—the complete works, of course—in Danish; Astrid Lindgren's *Pippi Långstrump* series in Swedish; the Brothers Grimm, E. T. A. Hoffmann and Adelbert von Chamisso in German; Jean de la Fontaine, Guy de Maupassant, Prosper Mérimée, Saint-Exupéry, and Balzac's entire *Comédie humaine* in French; Charles Dickens, Jack London and Mark Twain in English; Chekhov, Turgenev, Gogol, Krylov—even Pushkin and Lehrmontov … but in Danish.

Unlike her mother—Daneka knew—she herself would never again be asked to dance at a European ball. She'd outgrown the slippers of her youth and had, for better or worse, chosen to make her home between the Rivers Hudson and East. She'd chosen comfort—the thrum of air conditioners in summer and the bang of central heating in winter. As she sat down on the bed, it came upon her like a thunder-clap out of a perfectly blue sky: she couldn't remember the title of a single book in her own library in New York.

She sat, head in hands, for the next five minutes. Outside her bedroom window, the sun shone. Inside her head, however, dark clouds went on gathering.

Chapter 58

She heard Kit's footsteps as he mounted the staircase. She stood up quickly and looked at her face in the mirror for smudges, telltale evidence of any of her private struggle, then dabbed her eyes just before he reached the door. As he entered, she gave him a smile that he immediately recognized as forced. But he appreciated that whatever she was struggling with, whether hers alone, or something with her mother—and so, with a much longer history—was something they could work on together. Later.

"Tea time, Daneka," Kit said as he put his arms around her. She allowed herself the luxury of his embrace for several seconds, but then gently pushed him away.

"Shall we, darling?"

They walked slowly back downstairs and through the living room, at the far end of which—and just out of sight of the front door—was a small dining area looking out into a greenhouse. As this was summertime, the door leading into the greenhouse was open; the glass roof to that greenhouse, rolled back. Kit noticed that every available space had been devoted to assorted herbs and flowers, all of which had clearly benefited from the hand of a knowledgeable and loving gardener. He now wondered whether he might also have a willing partner for what he intended at Daneka's place in Svaneke—or if not a partner, at least an advisor. He walked out into the greenhouse in order to absorb from close up the colors and fragrances of the flowers and herbs. Daneka, however, simply sat down.

Mrs. Sørensen brought a tray in from the kitchen on which she'd laid out three cups and saucers; a plate piled high with what looked to Kit—he remarked as he wandered back in from the greenhouse—like the Danish equivalent of scones; some clotted cream; and an assortment of jams, jellies and marmalades. The 'leading man' in this culinary spectacle of many-colored and variously-textured players was a rectangular block of butter of an unassailable golden hue. He looked at it, looked at Daneka, then fixed in his mind that this color would forever after be known to his visual memory as 'Daneka gold.' He couldn't, he thought, find a more fitting way to memorialize it and her. But that was Kit—to whom color, light and lichens were everything.

"Are you also a gardener, Kit?" Mrs. Sørensen asked as she began to set out the plateware.

"Well, I don't know that I'd describe myself quite *that* way, Mrs. Sorensen. I'm really a photographer—that's what I do for a living. I'm just a dabbler when it comes to gardening," he said as he helped her distribute cups and saucers.

"He's both, *mor*. And he's very good at both." Daneka, of course, had no way of knowing whether Kit could even tell the difference between a hosta and a honeybee. But she'd decided that he was *her* knight in shining armor, and that she was going to sing his praises to whatever receptive ears she could find. Mrs. Sorensen marveled that Daneka should defend her man so vigorously: this was something she couldn't recall ever having seen in or heard from her daughter.

"Your prince is awfully proper, Daneka. Do you mind if I insist that he call me by my first name?"

"Not in the least, *mor*."

"Then please, Kit. Let's be done with this 'Mrs. Sørensen'—or even with this 'Mrs. Sorensen'—okay?" she said as she set out the tea pot and a pitcher of cream. Kit blushed at her Anglicized rendition of her own name—in clear imitation of his less than valiant effort. She extended her hand a second time. "Just call me 'Dagmar.'" Mercifully, Kit thought, she didn't also Anglicize the sound of her first name, but gave it the full Danish glottal thrust—something he could comfortably replicate. He put his hand back out.

"Thank you, Dagmar. And please—just call me 'Kit.'" They both laughed. Daneka's eyes wandered to the ceiling as she wondered whether it might put an end to their little jokes.

"Well. Now that *that's* out of the way, let's eat, drink and be merry—and no longer morbid, okay Daneka?"

"*Ja, mor*. Whatever. But let's please be more careful in assigning proper credit for this so-called 'morbidity,' shall we?"

"'*Morbidity*?'" No. I was just trying to be motherly. In the same way you've been trying over the last few years to become increasingly daughterly. Daughterly? Kit, can one say 'daughterly' in English—even if that doesn't quite describe my Daneka to a 'T?'"

The sarcasm wasn't lost on Daneka. "I've been very busy, Mother. My job takes huge chunks of my time."

"Yes, I quite understand that, my dear Daneka. 'Daughterly' is not always easy to manage. And speaking of 'daughterly,' how's Margarette?" Daneka shot a quick glance at Kit. "You know 'motherly' is one thing. You can take it or leave it. '*Grand*motherly,' however, is something I feel *I* have a right to for as long as I'm still alive. Do you think I might be allowed to see my granddaughter more than once every couple of years?"

Her glance veered away from Daneka and towards Kit—and she suddenly realized he didn't have a clue. "Kit has never met Margarette?" she asked in a tone of disbelief. Kit's gape suggested to her that the news was even more incredible. "Does he even know she *exists*?"

Kit was helpless at this point to intervene on Daneka's behalf.

"*Åh gud, Daneka! Hvad drejer det her sig om?*" ("My God, Daneka! What's this all about?")

"*Vi har bare ikke haft lejlighed til at tale om hende endnu, det er alt. Det er faktisk Annemettes fortjeneste, at vi lærte hinanden at kende. Jeg bestilte ham til at fotografere hende.*" ("We haven't yet had the chance to talk about her, that's all. It's actually thanks to Annemette that he and I got acquainted. He's going to photograph her.")

"*Jeg ville ønske, du ville lade være med at bruge det rædsomme navn!* ("I *do* wish you'd stop using that wretched name!") I'm sorry, Kit. This is terribly rude of my daughter and me. I seem to have opened a little Pandora's box here," she said, giving 'Pandora' a distinctly Danish pronunciation.

Yes, Mother—you *have* opened one, thanks very much." Daneka reached over and put her hand on Kit's arm. "Darling, I'm sorry. I've been wanting to tell you—but the moment for that discussion was just never at hand. Thanks to my mother," she said glaring at Mrs. Sørensen, "it now is."

"But why all the mystery?" Kit asked.

"She's the project. The reason I went looking for a photographer in the first place."

"To take pictures of *her*? Why don't you do it yourself? You obviously know how to handle a camera."

"I can't. I've tried. She won't sit for me. I don't know why. She just won't." Kit stared at her, still trying to fathom the irregularity of it all. As if there weren't already enough unknowns about this woman, here was one more—a mystery child.

"When can I meet her?"

"Just as soon as we get back to New York. Promise."

"Well. I'm glad *that's* settled!" said Mrs. Sørensen. "Perhaps I'll send along a picture of myself to remind her—but with you, Kit. That way, I'm sure it will actually get to her and not be left under some breakfast table at Tiffany's. Are we ready for our tea now?" she asked as she picked up the pot and a strainer.

With her eyes focused on something elsewhere in the room, Daneka pushed cup and saucer with a dismissive finger in the direction of her mother. Mrs. Sørenson held the pot poised over Daneka's cup, then poured tea for Kit and for herself and promptly put the pot back down on the table.

"*Du kan selv skænke din forbandede te!*" ("You can serve yourself your own damned tea!") In almost the same instant, she dropped her scowl and smiled at Kit. "So tell me about this photography, Kit. What do you like to photograph?"

"Mostly naked women, mother," Daneka interjected.

"Young ones, I hope." She then glared directly at Daneka, who was still staring off into space. "Young, *firm-bodied* ones, no doubt. And with some cause bigger than themselves. Women who—if they have children—actually spend time with those children, listen to them, take them outdoors to play with other children. Who don't leave them locked up behind closed doors, and who—."

Daneka abruptly stood up from the table. "Thank you, *mor*. It has—as it always is—been lively and entertaining. Kit?"

The tension in the room had reached a level that even Kit found intolerable. He was certain he'd like this woman. He wanted to spend more—*much* more—time with her. But today was clearly not the day. *Perhaps again during the week,* he thought as he stood up.

"I'm sorry, Dagmar. I'd hoped we could discuss my plans for Daneka's garden. Perhaps another day? I'd really like your help."

"You're not, I hope, both her lover *and* her gardener, Kit!"

"*Mor!*" Then, instead of trading any further insults with her mother, Daneka chose to exit, turned abruptly on her heel and walked out the front door.

Kit leaned down to give Mrs. Sørenson a kiss on the cheek. She leaned her face up and returned the kiss. "I'm sorry about all of this, Kit. It doesn't usually get this bad—at least not right away. Maybe by the next time we see each other, Daneka and I will have sorted out our differences and will be able to carry on a civilized conversation."

"Please don't apologize. I understand. I, too, have parents. Or rather, they have me."

"Yes, and I'm sure you're a source of unending pleasure to them."

"Well—."

"I'm sure of it. Okay—go now. You probably already know Daneka doesn't like to be kept waiting." They exchanged a quick glance of shared understanding. It was obviously something they both knew all too well.

Chapter 59

Kit walked out to the car and found Daneka already seated and belted in. He could see she was trying not to cry, but quick swipes of a tissue told him her efforts were falling on deaf cheeks.

"Daneka, come over here," Kit said and pulled her to him once he'd settled into his seat. As she scooched over, she made some effort to restrain her sobs, but otherwise none to conceal the hurt behind them.

Kit knew his greatest use to her right then would simply be to *be*—not to withdraw; not to tell her it was all right; not to insist the pain would go away. He knew that nothing would be worse at that moment than withdrawal; that it would never just be 'all right'; and that the pain would have to recede into some quiet place where pain lives in all of us. But he also knew it would never simply go away.

They sat for a good five minutes. Kit could imagine the same scenario right inside Mrs. Sørensen's front door, though without benefit of a comforter. He wished he could split himself in half. But he couldn't—and so, he had to choose. However much he might have wanted to comfort her mother, Kit's allegiance at that moment had to be to Daneka.

Eventually, she stopped. As she rummaged unsuccessfully through her purse for a another tissue, Kit put his hand inside his shirt, bunched the material together in five fingers and offered it up to Daneka without a word. His gesture this time needed no instruction set. She put her nose down and blew—then laughed and threw her arms around his neck.

"I love you, darling. You *and* your snotty shirt."

"Just don't ever mistake it for a potty shirt," he said. "I'll allow it to wipe your nose any day of the week. But don't ask me or it to wipe your ass."

"No. I won't. However, I wouldn't mind in the least if you kissed it once in a while," she said with a smirk.

"In that case, bare it."

"*Here?* In front of my mother's house? Are you kidding?"

"Okay. Not here. But just as soon as we get back to your place. Deal?"

"I'm not sure I can wait that long."

"I'm not sure I can, either. What do you suggest?"

"Drive!" Daneka said. "Drive on, Charon!"

"Where to, my lovely?"

"To Hades. Where else? To burn. Though not just yet."

Kit stared at Daneka. She stared back, then slowly undid the top three buttons of her blouse, reached in and pushed the strap of her bra off one shoulder. "Fuel for your fire, fireman."

He leaned down and opened his mouth. Daneka took a breast out and teased his lips with the nipple. Each time Kit lunged forward, she retreated—but not too far. Not too far at all. Only far enough, really, to keep her nipple poised on his lips. He eventually closed his eyes and stopped lunging. She continued to move the nipple back and forth across his lips until it hardened. Meanwhile, her breath began to come in little bursts.

"Now, drive like the devil!" she said as she put her breast back inside her bra.

Kit made a U-turn and accelerated up the country lane—conscientiously on the lookout, however, for errant tractors or hopscotchers in pinafores. Once they'd reached the main road, she gave him further instructions.

"Let's not go home just yet. Let's go to my special place."

At that precise moment, the sun came out—apparently also in the mood to play. Daneka directed Kit this time not around the periphery of the island, but rather straight across it. Cow pastures and open fields ceded in short order to ever denser foliage. The sun would occasionally peek through the overstory, but only for a quick burst.

"Will you at least tell me what this special place we're going to is called?"

"Of course, darling. We're in it. It's called the forest of Almendingen."

"You want to do the primordial in a forest primeaval?" Kit snickered.

"Only if you do it first. You show me yours. Then I'll show you mine."

"Is there any *special* place within this special place?" Daneka was about to answer, but stopped herself when another, more mischievious idea occurred to her.

"Yes, darling," she cooed. Let me show you." She took Kit's hand and guided it slowly up the inside of her thigh. Today, and quite by coincidence, she was wearing silk. She next reached between her legs with her other hand in anticipation of the arrival of Kit's hand and pulled her panties to one side. Today, she thought to herself, there would be no impasse, as they were way past the point of discovery. If Kit was going to stake her for his queen, he would find her an obliging guide, a grateful slave even. As she considered the notion of herself as a slave to Kit's passions, she felt his fingers prowl along her thigh. Even before she felt her wetness, she could smell herself in the car. Kit could, too.

As his fingers reached that spot she'd wanted them to reach, she lay back against the car door and spread her legs. She guided one finger in; then another; then a third. Kit was content. She, however, was not. She pressed in a fourth, then grabbed his wrist and fixed his hand to the spot. With her free hand, she began to caress herself. She closed her eyes and leaned her head out the window. Little darts of sunlight would occasionally strike her face. The quick warmth of those darts was easily upstaged by the slow glow she felt burning between her legs. She was now, she knew, on fire.

She climaxed—this time, without shame. They'd come far since their first day in Positano. As if to reinforce the point, Kit slowly withdrew his hand and put it into his mouth, one finger at a time. He next reached out, took her hand and placed her index finger in his mouth. At the sight of him sucking on the finger she'd used to caress herself, she did something she'd never achieved through a simple visual stimulus: she came again. Instantly.

When Daneka regained her composure, she looked out the front window and realized they'd driven past the point at which she'd meant them to stop and get out. She giggled.

"Sorry, darling. I guess I got a little distracted. That, or too much sun."

"Yes. Probably too much sun."

"Would you mind turning around?"

"Not in the least." Kit brought the car to a stop and executed a three-point turn. Once he'd brought the car back up to full speed again, he turned to Daneka.

"Oh, it's not more than a mile or two back. I'll let you know when we're getting close," she said as she reached over and put her hand between his legs. "Are you feeling terribly frustrated, darling?"

Kit didn't hesitate. "Yes."

"Oh, my darling. I'm *so* sorry."

"Will you make it up to me?"

"I will—promise. Oh, it's just up there on the right," she said as she pointed out through Kit's half of the windshield. "But let's not park directly in front. I don't want anybody else to discover my little secret. Instead, why don't you pull up about a hundred yards and park on the left-hand side of the road?"

"Yes, ma'am," Kit said and started to tip an imaginary cap. Daneka, however, arrested his arm in mid-salute.

"Oh, *stop* that! Are you making fun of Ron?"

"Well, maybe just a little. But that's only because I like him," Kit said as he brought the car to a halt and turned off the engine.

"Good. Then you like both Ron and Estrella and you *clearly* like my mother. Now if it turns out you also like Annemette and Grace, we're home free."

Kit had apparently missed the mention of Annemette. "Grace? Who's Grace?"

"She's my closest female friend," Daneka said opening her car door. You absolutely *have* to like Grace. If not, well, I'm afraid there's no hope for you, no love for me, and no charity for either of us. Let's just call it the 'Edict of Grace,' Reverend Luther"

"I'll do my best—even if I have to pretend."

"Thank you, darling. I knew I could count on you." They walked across the road into a clearing, then started out down a rough path.

"What does she do, your Grace? Is she a work buddy? A colleague?"

"Oh, no, darling. Grace doesn't work. She doesn't have to. She married well."

"Lucky girl. What, then, does her husband do?"

"He doesn't. He did once. Just enough to leave behind a small fortune. But he's dead."

"Did she marry him for love or money?"

Daneka came to an abrupt halt and squared off—hands on hips in a pretense of annoyance. "Why does it always have to be one or the other? Can't a girl just fall in love in *spite* of a guy's money. Ya know, just ignore the diamonds as he's picking out a big one?"

"What's up with diamonds, anyway?" Kit asked as he glanced down and noticed mushrooms, the occasional fern and mounds of emerald green moss to either side of the footpath. "Why not, for instance, a lichen?"

"A lichen? What's up with lichens?"

"Look down, Daneka. Look around you. What do you see?" Daneka scanned the immediate environs but offered no comment. As they walked on in silence, Kit began to wonder whether he'd made a serious error in judgment in his choice of a gift for her from California. Clearly, she hadn't noticed it on the coffee table before they'd left New York. Maybe he could just quietly sneak it out when they got back.

At the instant he saw it, he realized that her designation of the spot as her 'special place' had been an understatement. He didn't have a word in his vocabulary to describe it. It was almost too perfect to be natural.

In a clearing of not much more than two or three body lengths in any direction, a bed of velvet-soft moss—pure *Polytrichum*—tiptoed up to a sheer and jagged granite wall. Here and there in the moss carpet, tiny poppies peeked through. Map lichen—*Rhizocarpon geographicum*—spotted the granite wall like forests made for Lilliputians. Water dropped down the face of the wall and dripped into a tiny pool. Kit looked into the pool to gauge its depth, but couldn't discern a bottom. The water was blacker than any black he'd ever known. Emerald bridal gowns of liverwort—*Conocephalum conicum*—covered trunks of trees surrounding the clearing while their branches wrestled in wraiths of *Isotheciium stoloniferum* the color and texture of lime-green lace. Oddly, a single piece of lava rock—covered in dark green *Grimmia* moss—was lodged in among the granite boulders.

Kit saw how the various greens played with the sunlight—which, by some uncanny trick of nature, managed to penetrate the overstory here and nowhere else—and then descend, thanks to airborne spores or perhaps just dust particles, like golden spotlights.

He turned to Daneka. The smile on her lips as she regarded him admiring the location told him she wouldn't need to ask him this time whether or not he liked it.

"I used to come here as a little girl and dream. I've never brought anyone else here. Until now, that is." She turned and faced him squarely. "And even when I was a little girl—well, maybe no longer *so* little—one of my dreams was that I'd one day do what we're about to do. I just didn't know with whom—until the Boathouse, that is. Until that first kiss—or maybe only the second."

"You knew *that* long ago?"

"I suspected it. And the reason I ran from you that night was that it scared me. I'd never felt that way, that quickly, before. Do you remember what I said to you when we made love that night?"

"I do. It was the first Danish word I'd ever heard."

Daneka smiled. "Yes. And it was the only time in my life I'd ever said it—at least in that context. And do you know what I was thinking when I said it?"

"No."

"I was thinking of this space and of both of us in it. Doing what we're—."

Before he'd even had time to savor the thought, Kit watched as Daneka kicked off her shoes, pulled her dress over her head, unsnapped and threw down her bra, and stepped out of her panties. She no less efficiently unbuttoned and took off his shirt, untied his laces and removed his shoes and socks, unbuckled his belt, and then removed his jeans and shorts—the last in one smooth yank.

She next lay back on the moss and brought him down on top of her, wrapped her legs around his, did the same with her tongue, and let him slide easily inside.

Other than the setting, nothing was particularly remarkable about this act of love. What *was* remarkable was what next—and for the next ten minutes—greeted his eyes: namely, that she never once closed hers.

As they moved into their easy rhythm, she looked at him—eyes to eyes, eyes wide open—and he knew for the first time that it was really *him* she was making love to and not to some fantasy fuck.

When they concluded and she came just a second or two before he did, the second most remarkable thing happened: she spoke to him in Danish. *"Jeg elskar dig,"* ("I love you.") she said with her eyes open, looking at him, looking into his eyes. And then she said it over and over again.

To every one of her declarations, he provided an echo in English. He, too, said it with his eyes open—looking at her; into her eyes—over and over again.

Chapter 60

Kit and Daneka lay in the same position for several hours and made love twice more. The only sounds they heard during the entire afternoon were those of their own passionate declarations, marginally punctuated by the drip of water trickling down the granite wall and splashing into the pool.

As if by mutual consent, they decided to get up and dressed only once the sun's rays had disappeared entirely from the overstory. It would be light, Daneka knew, for another several hours. They were approaching the summer solstice, the longest day of the year. In Denmark, the sun would finally dip below the horizon only after ten o'clock, maybe later. If lucky, they might also get another celestial surprise sometime this week, but she wasn't about to make any promises. In all of the years she'd lived in Denmark, even she had never seen the *aurora borealis*—the Northern Lights.

They drove at a leisurely pace back to Svaneke. That they'd forgotten to buy groceries in Rønne never once occurred to either of them. The village seemed deserted as they entered, and Kit thought its inhabitants had probably all retired to an early dinner.

"I'll make us a little light supper, darling," Daneka said as she closed her car door. "Why don't you, in the meantime, make us a fire."

"Deal."

"Oh, *damn!*" she said as she suddenly stopped dead in her tracks. "We never went shopping. Are you terribly, terribly hungry, my darling?"

"Nah," he lied.

"Would it be okay if I made us a soup from whatever I've got in the cupboard? I'll just run over to the general store and pick up some bread. We've got wine."

"That sounds about perfect."

Kit took out a cigarette and lit up as Daneka walked off in the direction of town and slowly disappeared from view—but not without appreciatively noting how she'd give her hips an exaggerated swing and occasionally glance back over her shoulder with a provocative smile.

Kit was no child: he'd been in and out of love before; had known long, lonely nights and heartbreak; had been the cause of some to others. He also knew that Daneka was, relatively speaking, little more than an acquaintance, and that anything could happen—and probably would happen—in the coming weeks, months and years to test the mettle of their love. He contemplated for the first time whether it was still too early to propose marriage to her. He wanted nothing and no one else in the world—except maybe his Lucky Strikes. She, he knew, would be sufficient for his entire happiness. She'd declared her love for him on several occasions—even that very afternoon, spontaneously, in her own language.

What, then, were the obstacles? Money, of course. He didn't want hers, but could he ever really make her believe that? Those who had, he knew, were always suspicious of the true motives of those who didn't. This was the curse of being wealthy. How could he convince her that money meant nothing to him—and least of all, *her* money?

Then, too, there was her need for the high life, for what amounted to a prosthetic umbilical cord through which she could suck in her daily regimen of flash and glitter. He could be content anywhere with her—but most especially here in Svaneke. Could she, with him? Somehow, he doubted it. He suspected she needed New York the way a junkie needs dope, and that there'd simply be no way to wean her from the city. They might go crazy from the pace, the demands, the unending and countless ways in which it could abuse people even as it charmed them. He'd leave it in a second if she'd agree to come away with him. If she wouldn't, then he'd stay and be content to grow old and ragged. But at least he'd grow old and ragged with her—and that was all that really mattered.

Perhaps the garden and his hands could convey to her what his words and mouth could not. Maybe the effort and promise of beautiful springs and summers forever after would be enough to persuade her to stay with him here.

He looked around and immediately began to make a more detailed survey of the grounds and to scope out the project. Never—or at least rarely—had a thing so excited him. Not even his photography. He'd plan it like a canvas and let his soul be the brush. The result, he was certain, would convince her.

Chapter 61

Two fires burned in two hearths: Kit's doing. Two fingers burned when she distractedly reached out over the stove while thinking about where *his* fingers had been that same afternoon: Daneka's doing. Two flames flickered in two hearts: their mutual doing.

He now sat in front of another kind of fire, sketching—if only in his mind—when he heard an expletive from the kitchen, jumped up out of his chair and and went in.

"What happened, Daneka?"

"Oh, just a silly thing. Not paying attention to what I was doing." She held up the two offended fingers for his inspection. He gave them each a kiss, then went to the refrigerator.

"Butter or ice cubes?"

"Oh, butter for sure."

"Here, hold out your fingers," Kit said as he, in turn, held out the block of butter. She did, and he smeared the block over the burns. "Does that mean no dessert tonight?" he asked.

"Nothing of the kind. It just means you'll have to pay particular attention to these two little wounded soldiers."

"'Will do—promise." I'll just have to devise a plan."

They sat down to a simple supper after Daneka had first set out and lighted candles in each of the downstairs windows and in the two sconces over the fireplace. In the meantime, Kit opened a bottle of *Echezeaux*—expense had clearly not figured in Daneka's choice of a wine—and poured them each a glass.

"To you and to your wounded soldiers," he said as he raised his glass.

"To you and to your wickedly wonderful tongue," she answered as she pulled out her chair, sat down and raised her glass to meet his.

Their supper consisted of something with morrells and barley she'd poured out of a package and added boiling water to. In addition to a baguette, she'd brought back a bunch of radishes and a jar of cornichons, a wedge each of Danish Fontina and Dutch Gouda, a couple of tins of Corsican sardines, half a pound of the local herring, and a variety of fruit—

peaches, strawberries, bananas. The calories were light; the taste, colossal.

"You know, don't you, that the way to a guy's heart is through—."

"His stomach, darling. But of course. *Every* woman knows that!"

"Actually, I was going to say his nose," Kit said as he downed a sardine.

"And what we *both* really should've said—if we want to be entirely honest with each other—is through his head. The little one, that is. Though sometimes there's not really much of a difference between the two," she added as she tore off a piece of bread.

"And the way to a woman's heart?"

"Why, through *her* head of course."

Kit picked up a second sardine and added a radish to make it a mouthful. "Do you think I could have a go at your garden first thing tomorrow? I've got it pretty well planned out. I just need to have a look at the soil, see if it needs some compost, worms, or anything else."

"Absolutely, darling."

"And you think you can find what I'll need—if I need anything—in Rønne?"

"Certainly. I'll be going there tomorrow anyway—and probably every day this week. I think my mother and I need to do some fence-mending. You just give me your daily grocery list, and I'll get what you need at the local garden supply shop. There's a good one in Rønne—though nothing here." Daneka finished her soup, stood up and took her empty bowl into the kitchen. He heard her rinse it off, then open the door to the dishwasher, pull out the rack and carefully place the bowl inside. He wondered whether she'd also expect him to retire each bowl or dish or plate at the instant he'd cleared it; or whether he could wait until he'd finished his meal, maybe even sit for a leisurely moment at the end of it and have a cigarette—outside, of course.

He didn't have to wait long to find out. Just as he was taking the last spoonful of soup, she came through the door, picked up his bowl and soup spoon and returned to the kitchen—where he heard her execute the same series of tiny tasks.

Was it merely a coincidence, Kit wondered, that her compulsive cleaning seemed to start whenever the subject of her mother somehow entered into the conversation? He didn't yet have enough data to reach even a tentative conclusion, but he made a mental note to continue observing her whenever her mother's name should come up in one of their discussions. In the absence of discourse, he knew he wouldn't be able to infer anything at all. He wasn't, after all, a mind-reader. But maybe there'd be instances enough for him to reach an educated guess.

Daneka came out of the kitchen and sat back down. She took another sip of wine, then helped herself to some of the fish.

"So which do you prefer, darling—herring or sardines?"

"Anchovies."

"Really? And why's that?"

"One of the guys at the studio—a production assistant—is gay. He helps dress and undress the models. I remember he once said—and I quote: *"All* women's cunts smell like anchovies. Even the beautiful ones." Ever since that day, anchovies have been my favorite fish."

"Indeed."

"Yup. He has a good eye for his work. He just doesn't have the right nose for it."

"And to you, darling? What do they smell like to you?"

Kit looked down at the bowl of fruit she'd set out on the table. "Strawberries. Peaches. Bananas. But mostly strawberries. Maybe it's in their choice of douche."

"Or maybe it's what they—or their guys—put in there before they put something else in there. Know what I mean? I once had this guy put a strawberry inside me if you can believe it," she said with a smirk as she reached for some fruit.

Kit felt himself blushing as he thought back to their evening at the Boathouse. "Ever have a banana?" he teased.

Daneka harrumphed. The combination of conversation and wine was clearly having its desired effect. As Kit emptied the bottle into both of their glasses, Daneka broke off a last piece of bread for herself and a second one for Kit. "Shall I cut us some cheese, darling?"

"Yes, please."

They ate their cheese in silence. When they'd finished, it was Daneka who broke that silence.

"Now about dessert…".

"What about dessert?" Kit answered. He noted she wasn't immediately rushing off to rinse the empty dishes and load the dishwasher.

"I trust you've been planning it as hard as you've been planning my garden. At least I hope so!"

"The garden's a no-brainer. But as for desserts, I'm running out of ideas. I think I'm going to have to brush up on my *Kama Sutra* first thing once we get back home."

"Oh, darling! We've only just gotten *started!*" she said with just the hint of a grin. She still hadn't touched the empty dishes, he noted. At the same time, her mischievous little smile got him thinking about newer possibilities.

"Let me see those wounded soldiers."

Daneka extended her hand and added a pout. "Another kiss?" she asked.

"Of sorts." Kit stood up from the table and picked up Daneka's napkin. He stepped around behind her chair, rolled the napkin into a long strip, then brought it up to her eyes and tied it around her head.

"Oh, dear," she said almost too gleefully. "Something with a bit of kink?"

"Shush."

"And me, a little mink?

"Shush."

"Brought back from the brink—of extinction?

"Shush. Once and for all!"

"Yesh, Sir."

"Shush again or I'll gag you." This time, Daneka said nothing—but grinned foxily. She was now blindfolded—and so, at Kit's entire command. He took her by the same hand she'd just extended and pulled her out of her chair, then led her over in front of the fireplace.

"Raise your arms."

She complied. He first took hold of her dress and pushed it slowly up and off—then flung it across the room to the couch. She now stood only in bra, panties and grin. He unsnapped her bra, rolled the straps off her shoulders and down her arms, then threw it in the direction of her dress. Next, he knelt down and took the waistband of her panties between his teeth. He considered tugging them down, but then decided against haste. Instead, he'd first explore with his tongue the little blond hairs descending from her navel.

She inhaled sharply. He next pressed his face up against her belly as his teeth worked her panties down, then pushed his nose into her at the instant at which the tip of it locked on her labia. His nose repeatedly nudged her up and down until any vestige of friction had been lost to a perfectly oiled wall of soft, warm flesh. Beside herself with sensation, Daneka reached around and pulled his head harder into her, at the same time allowing her feet to inch apart.

Kit abruptly stood up.

"*Darling!*" she moaned. "*Please* don't stop."

"Shush!" he ordered once again. He walked to the dining room table and picked up his napkin. He then returned to stand behind her, took hold of both wrists, brought them around to the small of her back and bound them with the napkin. Her mouth dropped open—and stayed open—as he returned to his original spot in front of her, reached between her legs and inserted three fingers. She obliged by moving her feet another few inches apart.

He then brought his hand up to just below her nose, paused, and ran his index finger along her upper lip. At the smell of her own sex, Daneka's nostrils flared. He dropped the tips of the same three fingers to her lower lip and ran them from one end to the other and back. She opened her mouth wider. He inserted the three fingers up to the knuckle. He could feel her breath coming back out at him, over his fingers, in short, urgent bursts.

He knelt down and again took hold of her panties with his teeth, also again inserted his nose. This time, rather than up and down, he moved it from side to side, extending each time her inner lips. He noticed that what covered his nose was also running down the insides of her thighs. He'd barely started—and yet, the bondage, blindness, and silence were all apparently working together to move Daneka into another dimension.

He decided the panties had to go—and so, pulled them down over her thighs, knees and calves with his teeth. One foot was already poised two inches off the ground by the time he got to her ankles, and he slipped her panties first over it, then immediately over the other.

She now stood naked before him as he sat back and admired her body against the reflections of fire- and candlelight.

Rather than return to touch her with finger, nose or lips, he began quietly to undress himself. He wondered whether the suspense of not knowing exactly what he was up to, where and how she would next be touched, might have a pleasurable effect on her. In quick answer, he saw her legs come together, saw one rise up tightly against the other as if the viscous surfaces of both her inner and outer lips could—by means of pressure and pressure alone—somehow relieve the pulsing within. He watched her, fascinated by the desperation of her effort; then decided that it just would not do. He went to the cupboard and found two more napkins. When he returned to her a moment later, she was still seeking relief.

He devised a strategy, then looked around for tools. He spotted an ottoman and two heavy armchairs—exactly what he needed. He picked up the cushy footstool and moved it directly in front of Daneka, then dragged the armchairs to their respective positions about three feet below and at a 45° angle to the outside of the footstool. Next, he reached behind her, took hold of the napkin securing her wrists, and moved her to the center of the triangle formed by stool and chairs. With his free hand, he gently pushed her to the ground so that her breasts and belly lay on the ottoman while her knees rested on the floor.

Yes, Kit knew that a mushroom was just a toadstool, and that an ottoman would lose no sleep in being called a mere 'footrest' or 'footstool.' But Daneka had once turned 'toadstool' on its head by referring to it as a *'champignon.'* Moreover, as this was now her abdomen he was dealing with, 'ottoman' or even 'hassock' struck him—at least in *his* head— as the logical choice to describe the creature comfort to which he'd just strapped her down.

He let her lie in this prone position, to wonder in silence, while he tied napkins to the legs of the two armchairs. Her gasp was audible when he then reached up to take one ankle, extend her leg and bind the ankle to the chair. By the time he'd finished with the second, her first gasp had evolved into a low moan. With this maneuver, he'd removed both the temptation and her ability to gain relief from the caress of one thigh against the other.

He stood up and inspected his rigging. She was quite secure now, entirely immobilized: the picture was almost perfect. He gathered together all of the pillows he could find in the living room, ran upstairs to their bedroom and retrieved the pillows from their bed. Bondage was one thing; discomfort another. He came back down and piled the pillows he'd taken from their bed one on top of the other and moved the lot under Daneka's head. He found that four were sufficient for her neck to lie at a comfortable angle. He took the other, smaller pillows he'd found on her couch and placed one each beneath her knees and feet. Then he took the remaining pillow he'd brought down from upstairs, doubled it over and slipped it between the ottoman and her pelvis. This had the immediate effect of raising her abdomen another six inches and straining the ties at her ankles almost to the threshold of pain. But only *almost.* He then walked to the dining room table, picked up the bowl of fruit, returned to where Daneka's head lay, and sat down to unpeel the banana.

"Time for dessert," he whispered.

"May I talk now?" she asked in what sounded to Kit more like a rasp than a voice.

"You certainly may *not,* darling. I need your mouth, tongue and teeth for something else right now."

A low laugh came back to him by the same route her question had taken. She then puckered her lips in anticipation of having them filled with something other than fruit.

"No, darling, you've first got to *earn* your banana." He picked up a strawberry, pulled the stem off and placed it right in the center of her puckered lips. As she gently closed her lips on Kit's fingers and the fruit, he released it, then withdrew his hand after having first massaged her gums for a moment with thumb and index finger. "One for you, one for me," he said as he pushed a strawberry to the side of the bowl.

There were a dozen altogether, and he fed her six in exactly the same way.

"Oh, dear—we're fresh out of strawberries!" he said as he fed her the last of her portion. He took one of the two peaches in the bowl and split it in half, removed the pit, and fed it to her—followed by the second half once she'd swallowed the first. "All right now. I think you've been a very tidy little girl and have earned your banana. There's only one problem with *this* banana. You can't eat it."

Daneka first grinned, then obliged Kit once again with a pucker. He took the fruit in his hand and began to rub the tip of it over her lips. At the first touch and before she actually caught the scent of it, she lunged forward with her mouth. She immediately realized, however, that it was indeed a banana, and her eagerness gave way to a grumble. When Kit next began to insert and withdraw the fruit from her mouth, however, he could only marvel at her dextrousness. Her teeth didn't once touch the smooth flesh of the fruit, while her lips worked their usual magic. It excited him almost as much to watch her with the banana as it would've excited him to be in its place.

He eventually withdrew the banana altogether. "Well, darling. I believe it's now *my* turn." She grinned and puckered her lips into a perfect 'O.'

He, however, picked up the bowl, stood up, walked down to the ottoman and sat back down. He had six remaining strawberries, one peach, one banana—and a fair idea of how he might employ each of them. One after the other, the six strawberries went into Daneka, then into Kit's mouth. He split the single remaining peach, smeared the open faces of it over her exposed vulva, then popped them into his mouth. The peach juice could certainly account for *some* of the wetness of the pillow on which Daneka's breasts, belly and lower abdomen rested—but only for some of it. And neither the strawberries nor the peach could take entire credit for the swollen condition of her outer lips, the rhythmic pulsing of her inner lips, or the fact that both sets of lips had long ceased their natural inclination to close.

He put just the tip of the banana inside her to see how she'd respond. If ever he'd thought Daneka could no longer surprise him, he was about to be disabused of that fatuous notion. He pushed it in about an inch, then stopped. She took it out of his hand and, by the sheer strength and determination of her vaginal muscles, sucked in all but a couple of inches. A first view of the icy cliffs of Antarctica could not have thrilled him more: it was majestic and wonderful at once—and she, a miracle.

He grasped the portion of the fruit that was still visible and pulled it gently back—but not entirely—out. With about an inch to go, her muscles began to contract once again—and the banana to disappear with the effort. She and Kit continued this trick for only a few minutes, as the fruit was beginning to lose its firmness. He took it out entirely. And ate it.

He then unbound her ankles, unbound her wrists, took the napkin away from her eyes and kissed her as he'd kissed her once before at the Boathouse. "Let's go upstairs, darling," he said. His wish coincided perfectly with her own. He grabbed the four bed pillows and followed her up the stairs. She walked to the bed and lay down immediately on her back. He climbed on top, kissed her once more on the mouth, then moved his mouth down between her legs.

What met his tongue was the sweetest, most exciting fruit punch he'd ever tasted.

She came long and effortlessly in his mouth. Denmark was a quiet country—and so, from the neck up she came into a pillow. He then climbed on top once again, entered her, and within seconds released all of the pent-up energy of the previous couple of hours. She came immediately again with him; and this time, it was his mouth that muffled her screams.

Several minutes later, he rolled off. "Darling," she whispered. "Would you be horribly offended if I douched? I'd love to keep all of it right there until morning. But the yeasty beasties, you know—I'm sure they'd have a field day."

He kissed her forehead. "Always thinking, aren't you, my little mermaid! Of course, I wouldn't be offended. Please," he said indicating the door to the bathroom.

When she came back five minutes later and slid back in under the *duvet*, he curled up behind her and kissed the nape of her neck. Any further oral declarations of love at this point would've been superfluous. The *fact* of it to both of them was crystal clear—and plain as punch.

Chapter 62

When Kit awoke the next morning, it was to gray skies and warm but womanless sheets. He got out of bed, dressed, went downstairs, and found her in the kitchen.

"Morning, darling. Sleep well?"

"Yes. And you?"

"Very well, thanks." He waited to see where and how the conversation would next go. Would she mention anything about the previous evening? Would she, perhaps, pay him the kindness of a compliment? No. Stone silence from a statue with a sponge. "Any coffee, Daneka?" More silence. Maybe, Kit thought, she'd misunderstood him. Maybe she'd thought he was asking whether they should start a coffee plantation in Africa. Meanwhile, she continued scrubbing the counter.

Kit stood up, walked up behind her and took her wrists. "Coffee?"

"Oh! Sorry, darling. I didn't hear you." She took a cup and saucer down from the cabinet. Kit sat back down in his chair and looked out the window. Denmark—he thought—could certainly be a drag. He wondered whether anyone had ever thought to name a shade of gray 'Denmark Dreary.' He looked back at Daneka and saw that she'd gone back to her scrubbing. He stood up again to get a better angle—to see *what* it was she was scrubbing. There was nothing. The spot was spotless.

He decided to risk making his own coffee and opened the door to the refrigerator.

"What are you looking for, darling?"

"Uh, the coffee. Beans. Grind. Anything that suggests caffeine."

"I really think we should be drinking more milk. Why don't you have a glass of milk instead?"

"'Milk' doesn't quite satisfy my yen for caffeine." he answered.

"Oh, all right." She pushed him aside rather less than lovingly. He shrugged and sat back down. He watched her reach in and grab a tin of coffee, set it on the counter, then grab her sponge again and begin to wipe down the shelves in the refrigerator.

"Coffee, Daneka? *Caffè?*"

"Yes, yes. I'm getting to it."

Kit decided this was a good time for a smoke. The scene was just too bizarre, he thought. He stepped outside the front door and lit up. It was drizzling. *Drabby old Denmark.* But then he thought again as the nicotine finally lit a fresher, happier fire in his brain. *Today is a day for gardening. What more could a guy want?* He took another drag and decided to walk around the property. There it was—exactly as he'd sketched it out in his imagination the evening before—before everything else, that is. He saw what looked like a toolshed and opened the door. Sure enough: shovels, rakes, trowels—even a Japanese weeding knife. Daneka was nothing if not thorough—at least in her acquisition of the *implements* of gardening. He inspected her tools more closely and discovered that most of them had never been used. That, or she'd been so careful and thorough in their clean-up, they just looked as if they'd never been used. Well, this was one thing he was about to change; they'd get a good workout over the next several days.

He closed the door and continued to survey the property, then reached down and dug up a handful of earth. The soil was good: neither too sandy nor too loamy—just the right combination of both—and so, he wouldn't need to trouble Daneka with picking up compost. He also wouldn't need to trouble himself with thoughts of how he was going to pay for it.

They hadn't yet discussed the issue of money for plants and whatever else he might need to do the job. He was hesitant to bring it up—as he was hesitant to bring up the topic in connection with anything else they did together—but he knew he really couldn't afford it. He was already stretching his overdraft privileges to the breaking point, and it was she who'd picked up most of the tabs along the way. It was just a different life-style, a different perspective, a different capacity for living the good life—even if they both knew how to live it in abundance.

He hoped she'd bring the matter up and allay his anxiety, that she'd simply acknowledge he was a capable if penurious gardener—and so, not really able to give her more than the gift of his hands, his love and some talent. He decided to return to the kitchen in order to see whether she'd made any progress with the beans.

When Kit opened the front door and walked in, he was quietly pleased to see she'd indeed put a pot of water on to boil, had ground the beans, had even poured the ground coffee into a filter. At the same time, he was less pleased to see she was still scrubbing the refrigerator—that she'd moved on from the shelves and was applying all of her energies to the walls. Kit gave them a cursory glance: they defined 'clean.' If she was still finding spots, he was at a loss to know where.

"I wonder whether you wouldn't mind helping me with the living room today," she said without looking up from her scrubbing. "I think it needs a thorough cleaning."

"I thought you were going to visit your mother, Daneka. We have a whole week to clean. I was really looking forward to getting started on the garden."

"Oh, I'm going all right, darling. I just thought we could straighten things up a little bit. You know—a little dusting here, a little vacuuming there." The pot had begun to whistle. Daneka, apparently, didn't hear it, as she had her head and shoulders in the refrigerator so as to get a closer look at the spot she was scouring into oblivion. The hyperbole came naturally to Kit at that instant, as the whole place reeked of cleaning fluids and disinfectant. He stood up and turned off the gas, then filled the coffee filter to the brim.

"Look, I've got an idea. Why don't you just finish up there and I'll take care of the rest, okay? You go see your mother and I'll clean up the living room and bedroom myself. The kitchen looks pretty much done to me—except for my cup and saucer, which I'll be sure to rinse off and put into the dishwasher when I'm finished."

"Oh, this kitchen's *filthy!*" she said. "I could spend five days on it alone! But if you really wouldn't mind?"

"Not in the least. Why don't you just put that sponge down and run on up to powder your nose before you leave? I'll have my coffee, then get straight to work on the rooms."

"Well, if you really don't mind," she said more to the back wall of the refrigerator than to Kit. At least, he thought, the view of her ass was pleasant enough to contemplate— even if the reason she was flashing it was rather less so.

"There!"

Finally she quit, re-emerged from the refrigerator and rinsed off her sponge. Kit filled the coffee filter back up, then watched it drain. It was less painful to watch water run through coffee grinds than to watch Daneka rinse her sponge—and both actions were taking about the same length of time.

"Why don't I show you where I store all of my cleaning utensils, and then I'll walk you through what needs to be done in each of the rooms?"

"I already know where you store your cleaning utensils, Daneka, and I can probably figure out for myself what needs to be done." Kit was stoically trying to keep a level voice— at the same time, trying to understand all of this from inside *her* head.

"You do?"

"I do."

"Well, in that case—"

"Yes. Now, go powder. Everything's in good hands here. I promise. I think you'll be delighted at what I can accomplish with a mop and a pail of soapy water."

"Oh, just let me show you where I keep the pails and which one I use for the floors, which one for the bathroom, which one for the kitchen—"

"I know where you keep your pails, Daneka. But if it's important to you that I use a particular one for the floors, perhaps you should point that out to me."

"Oh, but it *is*, darling! We can't be mixing our germs now, can we?

We just played sexual Star Trek with a fruit basket twelve hours ago, and now she's worried about a couple of kitchen germs ending up on the bathroom floor? Kit was beginning to wonder how far into Daneka's head he'd have to reach to find the circuit breaker: this particular horror show was turning really, *seriously* horrid.

She finally finished rinsing out her sponge; placed it carefully next to the sink; aligned it with the side of the basin; dried off her hands with a dish towel; folded the towel carefully and put it back on the rack to dry; stepped a few feet away and looked back at the rack; returned to it to adjust the corner of the towel perhaps half an inch so that its edges were in perfect alignment with the horizontal edges of the rack; stepped away and looked back again. Kit was relieved to see that she now seemed satisfied with its revised position. At the same time, he again felt an urgent need to step outside for a second cigarette. Daneka left the kitchen and walked up the stairs.

When she came out the front door ten minutes later, he was on his fourth cigarette and second cup of coffee. Wanting her out of his sight was a feeling Kit had never had about Daneka, and it disturbed him. *If only we can be apart from each other for a few hours,* he thought, *perhaps this feeling will simply disappear.*

"Darling, anything you need me to pick up in Rønne?" she asked as she opened her car door and climbed in.

"No, not a thing. I've got everything I need to get started. I'm sure that preparing the beds will take me the better part of today."

"Oh, I don't want you to spend *that* much time on them, darling. Just put the pillow cases out to air and hang the duvet out the window. When I get home, I'll show you how to make them up."

"Sure thing." Kit was crushed. She either hadn't heard him at all, or had clearly misunderstood him. He began to wonder whether this matter of making her a garden—like the gift of the lichen—was simply all in his mind. "Have a nice time with your mother, and please give her my warmest regards."

Daneka started the car and began to back out. Her only acknowledgment of Kit's request was a half-smile that seemed to come out of some other toolshed of little-used tools.

Chapter 63

With her gone, he could breathe again—and did: lustily, creatively, *freely*. He would also work fiendishly over the next several days to find some way to convey to her, in the form of a free-flowing garden, what he felt—even if it might eventually be to no avail.

The routine was always the same. He'd wake up to empty sheets, find her cleaning in the bathroom or somewhere downstairs, and would then somehow manage to get her out of the house. Once she'd left, he'd set to work: clearing the beds; turning soil; planting—mostly seeds, but also some plants she'd brought back from her mother's greenhouse. They'd managed to reach a compromise—seeds would do just fine, she'd insisted, as the two of them weren't going to be around anyway to appreciate the flowers. Seeds, of course, were cheaper than plants from the garden center in Rønne; the plants she brought from her mother's, cheapest of all. He might not see the product of his labors—at least not until next spring, but that, too, was all right.

He'd retire his tools each day at about the same time, careful to wipe them down as she'd shown him. Then he'd turn his attention to some other task she'd set out for him to do inside the house and try to complete it just in time for her arrival. Daneka wasn't lazy, nor was she using him to do jobs she really didn't want to do. Quite to the contrary: she always re-did them when she returned, usually far into the evening, sometimes far into the night.

The dinners they now had together were functional affairs. It wasn't that she was cheap. She wasn't. She never failed to bring something fresh and tasty back from Rønne. They'd eat well—entirely to Kit's satisfaction—but in silence; would then retire their empty plates to the kitchen, rinse them, set them in the dishwasher, and run it. The dishwasher became their evening music.

She taught him how to load it—how to set each plate, glass or cup just so; how to lay each piece of silverware in the top rack and with the tines all pointed in the same direction for maximum efficiency. She taught him how to make her bed—she never called it "our bed"—but by the fourth morning, he still hadn't quite learned her way. And so, he gave up and would simply put the duvet and pillow cases out to air, then assist her when she got home at the end of the day. She made the bed; he simply handed her the bits with which to make it.

When he assisted at all, he usually just held, handed, or awaited further instructions. They'd both reached the same conclusion early on: he simply couldn't learn to do it the way she wanted it done—and so, "no way" was preferable. Sometimes, mercifully, she'd dismiss him from watching, waiting, holding, handing—and he'd go outside for a smoke. Since she hated inefficiency, she'd invariably attach some little task to his trip downstairs: take out the garbage; return a tool that wanted returning to the toolshed; fetch a tool that needed fetching from that same toolshed; unstick a window that needed unsticking from the outside. She never once asked him to chase a moonbeam, lasso a star, go for a midnight swim, take an evening walk, or even just talk.

Wine was always served with dinner—good wine—but she now handled the pouring of it, as he couldn't seem to keep the last drops from running down the outside of the bottle. She kept the bottle next to her—as well as the cork, which she assiduously returned to the bottle after each of them had had two glasses. It was better this way, she reasoned: they'd sleep more soundly, be more productive, rise earlier and more refreshed each morning. She was right of course—in this, as in so many things—and Kit knew it. He'd retire to a smoke, but only after having first removed, rinsed and stacked his empty plate, then been handed the garbage, some tool, or some instruction. Daneka would also then retire—to a task.

Occasionally, they'd make eye contact across a candle. But the contact was fleeting—almost like an accident.

Occasionally, he'd say a word—but her terse, usually monosyllabic response would result in a stillbirthed conversation.

Occasionally, when she returned from her mother's by early evening, she'd glance at his work in the garden. She might say a word. Then again, she might not. He eventually stopped asking, anticipating, seeking her approbation. He simply wanted to complete the task and retire the tools—after, of course, first cleaning them to her satisfaction.

When they retired each night to bed, she'd leave one candle burning in the window. This particular window faced west, towards Rønne—and beyond it, New York. He'd curl up behind her, his lips half an inch from the nape of her neck, but not quite touching it.

He'd stare at the candle either until it burned out, or until sleep overcame him—usually the former. In that same window, he could see the reflection of the face next to his on the pillow: her lips closed; her eyes always open—at least until his no longer were, or until the flame had burned out.

On the fourth evening, after dinner, Daneka announced that it was time for them to return to New York. She was right, of course. She always was, and Kit knew it. The work in the garden was finished. There'd be nothing more to do until the following spring—if there even were to be another spring. She'd just tidy things up around the cottage, she said. Would maybe even pack their bags so that they could get an early start the next morning. She'd already called from her mother's house and made the reservations. The flight would leave from Copenhagen shortly after noon. That would give them plenty of time—if they got up early enough—to visit with her mother one last time; return the car; take the ferry to the train; take the train to the airport; check in.

Kit retired his empty plate, wineglass and silverware to the kitchen; rinsed them; put the plate and glass in the dishwasher—just so—and laid his silverware in the top tray, with the tines all pointing in the same direction. Daneka handed him the garbage. He took both it and his cigarettes outside for a smoke.

He noticed—or maybe it was only in his imagination—that the days had begun to grow shorter in just the space of the week they'd been in Denmark. It was not yet even nine o'clock, and already he sensed that night was moving in upon them. If there was a shimmer from the western sky, there was none at the opposite horizon. Kit looked directly overhead as he put a lighter to his cigarette. The sky was cloudless, stars too many to comprehend at a single glance—or maybe even in a lifetime.

He heard the sound of a vacuum cleaner from inside the cottage. He'd heard it many times that week, but only now did it sound to him more like keening than humming. There was, he knew, no more dirt or dust—not to speak of crumbs—to be had.

As he continued to look up at the sky, a celestial maelstrom abruptly met his gaze. He wondered whether he was hallucinating, whether the sadness he felt had released some strange endorphin.

Or was this the thing he'd read about so often, but had never seen? An explosion of multi-colored lights skittered across the sky—over and over again and never once repeating the same pattern. It was like some cosmic Fourth of July celebration with rockets and fireworks shooting off from somewhere below the horizon, reaching out into depths he couldn't see—still less fathom—then dissipating, slowing disintegrating, then finally falling back to Earth like piles of powdered sugar. It was the thing the Romans had called Aurora; the Ancient Greeks, Eos; the Vikings, a false dawn; and the moderns—at least those who preferred science over poetry—a display of the electro-magnetic forces of…etc.

These, then, were the fabled Northern Lights.

He would now have liked—just as he would've once liked, in Rome—to have Daneka by his side. It was again a moment of miracles—and she was missing in action. He felt the conflict like some distinct, internal electro-magnetic field, but without the powdered pay-off. He sat down on the ground and crumpled up like the useless vagrant she'd apparently already decided he was. The vacuum cleaner continued to keen in the background. The Northern Lights continued to flicker and fall in the foreground. And with them, his hopes.

Chapter 64

They rose early, just as she'd suggested. They then showered—separately; and dressed—indifferent to each other's bodies. Finally, they loaded the car in silence and locked up the cottage.

Kit bade a quiet *adieu* to the toolshed after first whispering an even quieter thanks. He knew the gesture was absurd, but he also knew this toolshed would have to stand outside in the cold all winter long with no one to open it, no one to wish it a goodnight or a good morning, no one to pay it any kind of attention at all. Scandinavian silence would be hard on a pine toolshed, he figured. But then, Scandinavian pines—which would've known silence from birth to buzz saw—were conditioned to that kind of silence. He could probably learn a thing or two from this toolshed—if one could learn anything at all from old, dead wood.

He got in behind the wheel, turned the key in the ignition and backed out.

"Bye-bye, house," Daneka said almost sing-song. "See you next summer." Maybe she wasn't so different from him after all, Kit thought, even if any mention of spring had clearly not figured into her 'goodbye.'

"Shall we go across the island or around it?" he asked, hoping she might want to drive one last time with him through the forest, maybe even stop off briefly to visit her special place.

"Oh, it makes no difference to me. You choose."

It's an opportunity, Kit thought to himself. *No time to dally.* He turned the car in the direction of the forest and accelerated. It was another sunny day—until, within minutes, the overstory was eating up the sun's rays and leaving them in dense shade. Although he'd seen the location only once, some of the stands lushly looming over the road already looked familiar. Meanwhile, Daneka rummaged through her purse—looking at, crumpling, then discarding various slips of paper. Kit knew it was now or never.

"Wanna chuck wood?" he asked, but it seemed to him that his voice somehow floundered, like a broken buzzsaw, on the last word.

"Huh?" she said. "Oh, fuck!"

"What's wrong?"

"I can't find the damned picture of my mother—the one she wanted me to take to Annemette."

"Maybe it's in one of your bags."

"Maybe. But if I left it behind, she'll be furious."

Kit saw a second opportunity. *Maybe*, he thought, *this one is providential.* "Why don't I just pull over, and we can look through your bags?"

"You don't mind? I hate like hell to lose time. This is so *stupid* of me!"

"I don't mind at all, darling. We've got more than enough free time to lose." Funny—he thought to himself—his using the D-word. Then it suddenly hit him: he hadn't heard her say it to him in days.

Seconds later, he spotted the exact spot at which they'd parked days earlier—and pulled over to the side of the road. He wondered whether Daneka would say anything. She did.

"Why don't you pop the trunk and I'll go check. You don't have to get out. I'll only be a minute."

He did as she requested, then sat gazing out the window at the clearing on the opposite side of the road. He no longer wondered whether she'd notice their location and suggest a last visit to her special place. He already had his answer.

He heard mumbled grunts and curses enough to know she wasn't finding what she wanted. When she returned to her seat, her tone suggested more than mere disappointment.

"Damn it! Damn it! *Damn it!*"

"Darling, if you'd like, I can turn around and we can go back to the cottage to look for it."

"It's all because of the clutter. If the place weren't always such a mess, I'd know where things were and wouldn't misplace them!"

Kit wondered whether 'always' might be some thinly veiled reference to the five days he'd been a guest. As for 'clutter,' he could remember once, immediately after a shower, when he'd laid his towel down on the bed while he looked for a clean pair of boxer shorts. She'd swooped in like a hawk and returned the towel to its particular rack in the bathroom. He'd wondered at the time whether any hint of moisture might've escaped out onto the bedsheets and whether she'd demand that he now strip the bed and put the sheets out to dry. He wanted to avoid having to hear a direct order and was about to ask when she came back out of the bathroom, bent down to inspect the sheets herself, ran her hand a couple of times over the spot where he'd dropped the towel and apparently decided it wasn't worth the trouble.

He never again repeated that particular mistake. For once, he'd learned to do it *her* way.

"No, no. We haven't got the time. Let's just continue to my mother's place. Maybe she's got another photo."

Kit started the car up again and looked back through his rearview mirror—first for oncoming traffic, then just to get a last look at the clearing—swung out onto the road and accelerated to the legal limit. Daneka, he noticed, was wringing her hands, repeatedly scratching some spot on her arm until it actually began to bleed.

"Oh, *damn* it!" she said as she rummaged through her purse for a tissue. She found one, touched it to her tongue, then blotted the raw spot on her arm.

They continued on until Kit spotted a marker at the side of the road indicating their arrival at the outskirts of Rønne. Rather than engage Daneka in conversation, he decided to review, in reverse, the visual memory of the first and only time he'd driven out from Rønne to Svaneke. As he'd heard nothing from her so far, he assumed he was on the right course.

"Where are you going, Kit?"

"To your mother's house. Where else would I be going?"

"Was it your plan to take the scenic route, perhaps take one last spin around town before maybe—but only *maybe*—ending up at her place?"

Kit stopped the car; took the keys out of the ignition amd handed them to her. "Here. You drive. I think I'd rather walk. Rønne's a small town. I'm sure I'll find the house sooner or later," he said as he started to open his door.

"Oh, don't be ridiculous! Just slow down and watch where you're going. I'll give you directions. Now please drive."

Kit put the key in the ignition and started the car back up. His thoughts turned to Ron, her driver, and he discovered a newer respect for him; considered whether his tic of tipping an imaginary cap might be something more than a mere artifact.

"Where to from here?"

"Instead of turning right, which you were just about to do, turn left. We'll take it from there once you've made the turn." Kit realized she was now going to spoon-feed him the directions as if he were a child. He turned left.

"This is the main road. Continue on it until I next tell you where to turn."

He had an urge to strangle her—to rip her fucking head off and stuff its mouth, like a pig's snout, with a banana rather than an apple—then roll it down the 'main fucking road' like a knobbly soccer ball. Instead, he resorted to humming "Dancing in the Dark." He hated hummers. Fortunately for both him and Daneka, he didn't get further than a few bars. "Oh, stop that, will you! It's such a shit-for-brains piece of Americana!"

"Would you prefer I hum *Daneka Does Denmark*? Hmmm? Did you, by the way? Do most of Denmark, I mean. Is *that* why you moved to New York? Just ran out of doable Danes? Who'd already run out of bananas?"

She slapped him. Hard. He stopped the car and turned to her slowly.

"I may have deserved that. If so, I now offer a formal apology. But let's understand something right here and now, Ms. Sørensen. Nobody, but *nobody,* slaps me or anyone I know—not even you. You may've noticed that up until now—and even when you were dressed to kill in only a blindfold and napkin ties—I haven't, didn't and would never lay more than a feather on you—or maybe a champagne kiss. I don't *do* that—not in jest, not in fun, and certainly not in anger. What you do after bedtime stories and lights-out is your business. Just don't include me in any of that shit."

"And what exactly do you mean by *that?*" she asked, her mouth almost frothing.

Kit quickly got himself under control. He'd lost it—he knew that—and could lose her as well if he didn't choose his words carefully. At the same time, the thing was finally out. He needed right now to deal with it rather than try to stuff it back into some bag of unsolved mysteries. He took a breath and held it, then proceeded cautiously.

"For as long as I've known you, you've had this tendency…this habit…this penchant for disappearing. I first noticed it in New York, of course. Nights in particular. But your doorman, what's his name?"

"The Fitzgerald has a number of doormen. Am I supposed to know which fucking doorman you have in mind?"

"The one who was working the nightshift that early morning I came up. You

- 336 -

weren't in. By the time I'd gotten back from my walk in the park, you—"

"You mean Mr. Kelly. Michael Kelly?"

"Yeah, that must be it. But let's forget him. He's not worth spending time or words on—other than to say that he's a genuine prick who knows *almost* how to keep his mouth shut."

"And what precisely do you mean by *'almost?'*"

"'Almost' meaning that, like most guys, you rub his prickly ego long enough, he sings. You outta try him out the next time you're looking for a facial."

Daneka's hand flew back. But then she caught herself—and it.

"Oh, you know that word, do you? Must be all that quality time you spend on the Internet—increasing your word power. Not everyone in Christendom knows the difference, by the way, between a facial and a *facial,* darling."

"Are you and my mother by any chance in league together?" she growled. "What's the deal anyway? You have some kind of mutual admiration thing going? She with her pink fucking carnations, and you with your purple piccies? It's a shame the two of you don't work on a Website together. The color scheme would work wonderfully. Very complementary colors, pink and purple."

"I don't know, Daneka. I'm afraid that cum-sucking pink faces on purple plush just wouldn't pull in the traffic—so we'd never have the pleasure of *your* visit."

Each was breathing heavily following this volley of insults in an all-out effort to fatally wound the other. If they didn't pull in the reins—and pull them way back, soon—Kit suspected one of them was going to get seriously hurt in the exchange.

He decided to throw in the glove. It wasn't exactly a truce he was proposing; he just wanted to lower the temperature a few degrees.

"Let me get back to your doorman."

"What about him?" Daneka hissed. Kit realized she was still in battle mode and not at all prepared to step down. He withdrew the glove.

"Well, dear, he sang—*metaphorically* speaking." Kit let the word slip out like a mongoose on the prowl for a napping cobra. "You know how it is with these Irishmen— they can't help themselves. It's in their fucking nature."

"Is this little story actually going somewhere, or is it your intention to tell me a saga? Because if it's a saga you intend, I've already heard just about as many as I can stand. I grew up on sagas, Kit. I don't need to hear another one just now."

"He explained to me that morning—very Irish of him—that you like to 'walk the dog.' And that yours being an 'old dog,' you sometimes take a little longer to 'walk' it. Now, I happen to know you don't own a dog. So if Mr. Kelly tells me you're out 'walking the dog,' I get his meaning."

"The little Mic fuck. I'll deal with him tonight."

"Ethnic slurs don't exactly become you, darling Daneka."

Daneka reared up her head—which, at this point, was seething.

"Listen to me, Kit, and listen well. I don't care what some fucking doorman has to say about me and my doggie habits. If he says I like to take long walks with my dog—or with anybody else's for that matter—if he has pictures of me and fourteen dogs—or as many donkies—and they've each got a dick up my ass ... if I then tell you it's a lie—that the pictures are phonies, fakes, digital tricks—who're you gonna believe, me or the pictures? Huh? Be very careful how you answer this one, Mr. Addison. *Very* careful."

Daneka was hyperventilating. Kit had long ago realized that sooner or later his little white lies would add up and either come crashing down on his head, or necessarily coalesce into one big black lie. This was it: he either wiped the slate clean and started over with her, or he lied. Either way, he knew, they were finished—and that there'd be no second spring for him in Svaneke. There'd be no reward for his labors. If he told her the truth, there'd be only a ten-hour trip back to New York in Scandinavian silence—and a lichen to retrieve. If he lied, he—unlike the lichen—wouldn't want to exist just for the sake of existence—at least not under *her* kind of sun. They might push on for a few weeks, a few months even. But he, inside, would be dying—and she, intentionally or not, would be killing him. He looked at her. He looked deep into eyes that seemed already to have glazed over as they looked back at him. And he lied.

The glaze miraculously disappeared. She smiled her Daneka smile and put her hand on his arm. Her hand felt warm; his own arm, to him, ice-cold. "Let's go then, shall we, darling?" she murmured. Kit started up the car. "The turn is just up there on the left."

Kit moved the car forward. Within seconds, he saw the cobblestone lane they'd taken at the time of their first visit to her mother's place and turned into it.

The same tractors stood at attention in exactly the same attitude of country kindness of five days earlier. Disconsolate, Kit considered how wrecking balls in New York in as much time could easily have made a train station disappear; how lives could've been disrupted if not deleted; how deals could've been struck; how the foundation could already have been poured for a new luxury high-rise for those on easier terms with cold cash. All you needed was the kind of people who could spoon-feed directions to make it happen quickly, efficiently, on their kind of clock—namely, with hands of steel and a rock-steady tic-toc—and no desire to split hairs over truths or consequences.

He spotted two slightly familiar little girls in pinafores and golden braids. Daneka rolled down her window as Kit brought their car to a stop.

"Hej, piger! Hvad har I for i dag?" ("Hi, girls! What're you up to today?")

"Hej igen, Daneka. Ikke noget særligt. Vi leger bare," ("Hallo again, Daneka. Nothing special. We're just playing.") said one of them.

Then the other started to explain. Kit inferred, from the elaborate way in which she acted it all out with hands and feet that she was talking about their game. But she also apparently stuttered, couldn't seem to find the words fast enough, and was growing increasingly frustrated.

Daneka, he noticed, was once again wringing her hands, even if in her lap and out of everyone's sight but his. He looked at her face. The muscles in it—strained tight as those of a beaten fighter—staggered in an effort to maintain her smile. She was a pugilist struggling to stay alive—fighting her opponent, but also herself and everyone else in the arena.

The girl noticed it and thought that she, herself, was the cause. A stutter and an occasional, mangled syllable turned into word porridge as she began to cry and hug herself, rocking up and down from the waist. The other girl, incapacitated, looked on in horror, then also began to cry. The first looked at the second, then looked down at the road between her shoes where she saw that she was making a puddle, though not of tears.

She ran off, and the second followed. Daneka scratched the raw spot on her arm, which started to bleed again—and yet she continued to scratch.

Kit drove on slowly until he spotted Mrs. Sørensen's house, then pulled the car over and parked it. He turned off the engine and took the key out of the ignition. Daneka then spoke to him as if out of a crypt.

"You go ahead. I'll follow in a minute."

Chapter 65

Kit walked up to the front door and knocked. A woman answered. He'd seen her only once before, but Kit had a reliable visual memory. And yet, as he looked at this woman standing before him, he thought there was only the ghost of a resemblance between her and the woman he'd seen a week earlier.

"Hello, Kit. Is Daneka not with you today? Is she perhaps out walking the dog?"

The coincidences were beginning to make Kit skittish. Or did she, too, know or suspect something about Daneka's after-hours peccadillos? He wasn't sure he wanted to probe—not now, not here in what had fixed itself in his mind as a special place even before he'd first seen Daneka's 'special place.'

"Hello, Dagmar. She's in the car—resting. She'll be in shortly."

"Resting at this hour? She should get more sleep. Even dogs, once in a while, need a little respite from the night. Please come in," she said as she pulled the door open and craned her head and neck up to give Kit a kiss on the cheek. "Can I make you a cup of tea or coffee?"

"Tea would be nice. I've already had my quota of coffee for the morning."

"Daneka's coffee? Pffa! That's not coffee. That's cow piss. Let me make you a *real* cup of coffee."

Kit chuckled, though he didn't like the sound of what was brewing—even if she hadn't yet put the water on to boil. Perhaps, now that they were alone, he could discover what was really going on between Daneka and Dagmar. He probably didn't have much time and would have to come to the point quickly, directly. He followed her into the kitchen.

"Can I ask you something, Dagmar? Something rather rude, rather direct—something that may be none of my business, but which I need to know?"

"Of course," she said as she spooned three mounds of freshly ground coffee into a filter. "*I* have no secrets to keep. Life's too short for secrets—too precious *and* precarious. Secrets, if you really want my opinion, are an incredible waste of time and energy—as much for those keeping them as for those trying to figure them out."

"What's up between you and Daneka?" Kit asked bluntly. "This antagonism, this hostility, I mean."

"What's at the core of hostility between *any* two people, Kit? History. Sometimes chemistry, biology, even anatomy. But in my experience—" she began with a coy smile that, because of its familiarity, left Kit feeling a bit weak in the knees "—chemistry, biology and anatomy usually lead either to armistice or to something a little less antagonistic, if you know what I mean."

"Though not ... always to ... happiness," Kit stuttered, but only because Dagmar's smile had so distracted him from the topic. The smile first; but also how she bent her neck *just so*: he'd seen that smile and that angle once upon a time. The combination struck him as something out of a fairytale—and now just as fabulous. He looked back out through the kitchen door into the living room. How had he missed it the first time? Candles were burning everywhere.

"History," he repeated—and the word had a whole new meaning for him. It wasn't just history between nations and peoples or religions and philosophies that drove the world to madness and mayhem. It was, in microcosm, also family history. And if each family had its own unhappy history, Kit reasoned, then the sum of those histories might ultimately add up to a general malaise in the human condition—particularly if part of that condition was a shitty climate.

"Have you ever read Hegel, Kit—or our own Søren Kierkegaard?"

"No, I haven't," he answered, turning back into the kitchen and stepping up to the counter. At least not Kierkegaard.

She placed a maternal hand on his hand. "Promise me you'll read him—at least a little something—before we next meet." Dagmar then looked Kit straight in the eye. "And we shall meet again, Kit. I promise you," she said patting his hand. She removed her hand but not her stare as they both heard the front door open and close. "We're in here, Daneka—in the kitchen," Mrs. Sørensen announced as she finally let her eyes fall away from Kit's.

He could hear the approach of footsteps. They sounded tentative, wary even. When her face finally appeared in the frame of the doorway, he was struck once again by the resemblance. The difference between these two faces could be counted in years only. The mother's face was the daughter's face—and both seemed to have weathered unnaturally, savagely, in the storm of the previous five days. Whether it was the revelation of new truths or the further concealment of old lies that had done the damage, he couldn't know. He had only the hard evidence of their faces, of the expressions they exchanged when they greeted each other, of the tiredness in both their voices, of the despair, desolation and loneliness each had bequeathed to the other in the space of those five days.

Kit's mind suddenly shot back to his first trip, as a young child, to the Philadelphia zoo. He remembered, in particular, seeing a pair of big cats behind the iron bars of adjoining cages. Having exhausted every other means of threat at a big cat's disposal, they stared at each other—but their pupils told the truer story. It was not their caged fight that had done them in, but something with a much longer history....

Out on the savannah, before their capture, they could easily have coexisted. In fact, they *had* coexisted—for years. Had found mates. Had raised litters of cubs who played with one another in pretend-fight, pretend-hunt, though never venturing out of sight of one lioness or the other. The two lionesses had hunted together, had shared prey and domesticity, had even groomed each other when their mates were elsewhere for days at a time—doing whatever mates did when they were away for days at a time.

Until, that is, the snares found them—and soon after the snares, the poachers; and with the poachers, trucks and cages. Their cubs, meanwhile, had run behind bushes at the first incursion of machinery. From this leafy vantage point, they watched, trembled, then growled their pitiful little lion cub growls as men's hands surprised them from behind; picked them up by the tail; dropped them into canvas bags—never to see lionesses, or their savannah playground, or even Africa, ever again.

As mothers heard the screams of their kidnapped cubs, their paws, in snares, clawed the air for poachers' blood—scratched and clawed as if the air itself could be made to bleed and pay for this unnatural crime. As the air gave them no satisfaction, they broke their snares. The first showed how it could be done; the second followed her example. They both then ran to their screaming cubs. They ran as no gazelle could run, as even no cheetah could run. They ran like sprinters whose hearts were halfway to breaking from the stress of the sprint—never mind the cubs—until a feathered dart shot from an elephant gun found them both in mid-sprint and knocked them to the ground like a pair of punctured baloons.

The rest, Kit knew, was history. And all of that history could now be read in two pairs of pupils: in the pupils of caged lionesses then; in the pupils of Daneka and her mother, now.

"I was just making Kit a cup of coffee. Would you like one as well?"

"Sure, Mother." Daneka walked out of the kitchen and sat down at the table in resignation. She was now well beyond sighs as she let her eyes wander out to the greenhouse where they stayed in fixed and empty contemplation. A few minutes later, Kit arrived with her cup and a pitcher of cream.

"Tell me when, darling," he said.

She shifted her stare to watch him pour the cream in a steady stream into her coffee. Mesmerized by the flow, however, she said nothing.

"Darling?" Kit said.

"Yes," she said with a sharp intake of breath. "That's good. Thank you."

Daneka was still stirring her coffee when her mother came out of the kitchen and sat down. After a long moment of silence, Mrs. Sørensen reached over and put a photograph in front of Daneka. It was, apparently, the picture Daneka had been looking for in the car. She'd left it not in the cottage, as she'd thought—but here, in her mother's house. That her mother was willing to remind her of the fact, albeit without commentary, Kit saw as a peace offering—as did Daneka.

"I'm sorry, *mor*. I shouldn't have been so forgetful. I was distracted. Forgive me."

"There's no need to ask forgiveness," Mrs. Sørensen said without even a hint of recrimination in her voice. "I took it out of your purse yesterday when you weren't looking," she lied. "I wanted to look at it one more time—to decide whether it was the right one for Margarette."

Daneka appeared thankful for the reprieve. Whether or not her mother's version of events was true, she was clearly grateful she wouldn't be made to pay. Kit noticed that her lower lip was beginning to quiver. As much as he might've wanted to console her in this instant, he felt it was not *his* opportunity, but her mother's. As if reading his thoughts, Mrs. Sørensen rose up out of her seat and came to her daughter's side. She then knelt down and took Daneka's hand in her own.

"My girl," she said. "My poor baby girl."

For Kit, watching the spill of someone else's pain or grief was not a spectator sport. He stood up and went upstairs to Daneka's former bedroom. As he walked up the stairs, he heard the sobs begin—as well as the Danish. The only word he recognized—as Daneka repeated it over and over again—was 'mor.' Kit stepped into Daneka's former room and sat down on the bed. He wondered what happy stories this bed and these walls could tell—but also, when and where it had all gone wrong. He looked up at her bookcase, at the names and titles along the spines. He recognized all of them, thought how different the contents of this bookcase were from what she had in New York, and how—.

His eyes had wandered to the top shelf where he saw a single video cassette. He stood up and reached for it. The title was in English; the face of the woman on the cover quite familiar. She looked lovely in her black dress, single string of pearls, black hair swept up from a swan's neck, and foot-long cigarette holder. But then, to Kit, she'd always looked lovely—even without all the accoutrements. He wondered what particular fascination this woman—and this movie—might've had for Daneka as a young girl. Maybe he'd still get a chance to ask her; maybe not. But now, he also understood just how deeply her mother could dig. Dagmar Sørensen was a smart woman. But as with all smart people, she could combine intelligence with ruthlessness, and the result—if she wished to launch it—could be a stinger missile to the soul. *"Breakfast at Tiffany's"* indeed, Kit thought. He would never again be able to hear Audrey Hepburn's rendition of "Moon River" or walk past the building on Fifth Avenue without remembering this relic—this piece of New York and Americana—in a little girl's bedroom in a cupcake of a house in a fairytale village on a remote island in the Baltic Sea.

He put it back exactly where he'd found it; pulled out, at random, one of the tomes in a collection of books by the same author—and whose name stood out clearly, embossed in gilt: H. C. Andersen. The text was in Danish—and so, to him, unreadable. The illustrations, however—all by Vilhelm Pedersen and Lorenz Frølich—were unmistakable. He was able to leaf through and see some of the faces and scenes he'd first seen in his own childhood. There was Karen, of "The Red Shoes"… the ungainly, gray cygnet of "The Ugly Ducking"… Little Tiny in the story of the same title, asleep in her walnut shell … the steadfast tin shoulder … the little match girl … the wild swans. And then he saw her: the little mermaid. With the ubiquitous billboard ads for the Disney-animated version of the story as his only recent point of reference, he'd forgotten how authentically beautiful and sad one little mermaid could look. He could tell from the smudges on the page that a child's fingers had turned it many times; had held it while touching the cheeks of the mermaid and the eyes *just so*. He couldn't look any longer—and so, promptly closed the book and put it back on the shelf.

He glanced one last time around Danek'a bedroom, then walked out and back down the stairs. At the base, he peeked around the corner and across to the niche where he'd left Daneka and her mother sitting. Mrs. Sørensen had, in the meantime, moved her chair around and placed it next to her daughter's chair. Daneka's head now lay in her lap as Mrs. Sørensen stroked her hair.

Kit sat down on the bottom stair and waited. This was not his moment, or his place, to intrude. He'd wait. However long it might take, he'd wait. His own timekeeper was now a clock without hands. If Dagmar could somehow bring Daneka back into the light, he'd make time do his bidding—for both of them.

Chapter 66

I t wasn't too long before he began to hear pleasant murmurings from the other side of the room, and he looked up to see the two women embracing. Never had he been happier to see a pair of arms around Daneka—happier even than when those arms had been his own.

As he walked over, Daneka saw him immediately and extended a hand. "Group hug?" she asked with an ironic smile.

"What the fuck is a 'group hug?'" Mrs. Sørensen asked, intentionally giving the 'r' a strong Danish trill to indicate she really had no idea what they were talking about. Both Kit and Daneka bent double in laughter. In all the years they'd known each other, Daneka had never heard her mother say 'fuck.' She was actually surprised her mother even knew the word. Although he'd not been privy to their conversations in Danish, Kit found it almost unimaginable that Dagmar would swear in *any* language. To hear her pronounce 'fuck' as if it were just *any* old word struck him as supremely amusing.

"Did I say something funny?" she asked, looking genuinely surprised.

In answer, Daneka threw her arms around Kit's neck, reclined her head on his shoulder and smiled back at her mother. "Isn't he a darling?"

Mrs. Sørensen hesitated only a second, then raised an instructive pointer finger. "As a darling, he's daring. As daring, he'll do. Too bad he's not Danish—or Winnie the Pooh." Kit stared at Dagmar. There was clearly much more than a mere physical resemblance between her and Daneka.

"Brava, mor!" ("Well done, Mother!")

"Maybe in exchange, you'll bring Margarette the next time you—" she paused, looked at Kit and took a deep breath, then looked back at Daneka "—and Kit come back to visit."

Daneka lowered her eyes and said nothing.

"When, Dagmar, will you come to visit *us?*" Kit barked spontaneously in the warmth of the moment, forgetting what he'd discovered only an hour earlier—and then he suddenly remembered again. "I mean, when will you come to visit Daneka and Margarette?"

As if she'd actually been present at the earlier rages and even now understood Kit's internal struggle, Dagmar looked directly first into Daneka's eyes, then into Kit's. "I'll come to visit all *three* of you just as soon as Daneka invites me."

"How about in the fall, *mor?*" Love becomes me in the fall. That's what Kit's always telling me, anyway."

Kit's eyebrows shot up. "I am?"

"Well, you haven't been really—not yet. But you will be very shortly. When the first leaves start to turn—that's when you'll tell me." Kit wondered, in addition to everything else, whether she was also clairvoyant. If so, then she must know they were good for at least one more season.

"Well," Mrs. Sørensen sighed. "It certainly has been an instructive visit, wouldn't you say, Kit?" Kit took her hand in his as all three of them stood up from the table.

"Yes, it has been—that, and much more. I hope we can do it again soon."

"So do I, Kit. So do I. If not here, then maybe in New York."

They walked to the front door and stepped outside. "Brrrrr!" Mrs. Sørensen said as she pulled her shawl tightly about her. The weather had changed dramatically. The sky was gray, and there was a noticeable dampness in the air. It was just beginning to drizzle—the same kind of weather, Kit considered, that had greeted them upon their arrival. *Drab and dreary Denmark,* he thought. If there was one thing about Denmark he wouldn't miss, it was the weather.

"Goodbye, *mor.* I'll call you as soon as we get back. I'm sure you'll still be up with your Heidegger at that hour."

"No, I'm actually with Husserl at the moment—though not willingly. My, but I hate these Austrians! He and Wittgenstein seem to take pleasure in being difficult for the sheer pleasure of being difficult."

"Okay. Then with your Husserl."

Mrs. Sørensen embraced Daneka one last time before Daneka started off towards the car. She next embraced Kit and slipped something into his pocket.

"What's that, a 'Go directly to jail/Do not pass Go' card?" he chuckled.

"That's the picture of me Daneka again forgot. Please—for my sake—make sure it gets to Margarette."

"I will. I promise. And I truly, *truly* hope to see you again soon."

"You will, Kit—but whether sooner or later depends upon Daneka. We'll see each other again in either case. I guarantee it. Goodbye for now, Kit. If you were Danish, you could be Hamlet. I'm afraid, instead, you might be Macbeth. Either way, *adieu, sweet prince.*"

Chapter 67

They drove off in silence. Kit pulled up to the dock and dropped Daneka off with the luggage. He then returned their car to the rental agency and paid for it with a credit card that was already beginning to feel like a warrant for his arrest. He joined her just as the *Villum Clausen* was pulling into harbor, watched the men perform their tasks like the experts they were, watched the passengers disembark. *Only five days ago*, he thought. It was a lifetime—yet had the ring of a death knell.

Kit and Daneka boarded and found an empty space on the starboard side of the ferry. She looked out the window; continued to look when the ferry pulled out of its berth; then looked some more—in fact, looked out all the way to Ystad. Kit sometimes looked with her, occasionally glanced across the aisle at a tall, rather attractive girl, early-twenties, with long blond braids and a book. The girl occasionally looked back over the book at Kit when she sensed his eyes were on her. He craned his head once to try to read the title; she instead rotated the book and mouthed the title: *Nio Månadar (Nine Months)*. He smiled by way of thanks. She smiled back by way of … he wasn't sure.

When the ferry arrived at Ystad, she got up and started to pull on her knapsack. Whether she was genuinely struggling with it or only wished to show a perfectly pert pair of breasts to best effect, Kit couldn't be certain. In any case, he felt obligated to lend a hand. He stood up and grabbed the bottom of the knapsack—safer, he thought, then grabbing a strap. He wasn't sure where his hand and head might end up.

She got the business with the strap straightened out and turned around to face him. "*Tack själv,*" she said. He'd heard the first word often enough to know what it meant; the second half, however, was a complete stranger to him. He decided a simple nod would be sufficient.

"*Adjö,*" she said to him smiling once again, but now back over her shoulder as pert breasts pushed on towards land. *Must be a fun country*, Kit mused. The '*adjö*,' in the meantime, had sounded much like '*adieu*.' This was his first real Swedish word, and he decided he'd pocket it for future reference. One never knew when a simple Swedish 'goodbye' might come in handy.

Kit and Daneka spent the remainder of the trip from Ystad to the Danish mainland in silence—unchanged by so much as a syllable for the duration of the train ride from there to Copenhagen—and arrived at *Kastrup* mid-morning with more than enough time to get to the airport. Maybe it was this fact, and this fact alone, that finally prompted Daneka to speak.

"Darling, we've got a few minutes to spare. Would you like to see *den lille havfrue*—the little mermaid? We can leave our stuff in temporary storage here at the train station and walk there easily enough."

"I'd love to," Kit said—happy for the respite from the long silence. He thought maybe she'd lost her voice—or left it behind in Rønne—and was quite relieved to hear it again. They started out towards the harbor. And since Daneka clearly knew the way, Kit was content to let her take the lead.

"Do you know her story, by the way? Of the little mermaid, I mean."

"I believe so," Kit said, "although it's been a while." He began to search his memory banks, and she let him search in silence as they continued to walk.

"I remember that it starts with the description of the Sea King's castle—pearls in roofs of shell, walls of coral and windows of amber, all in a world of blue—or something to that effect." He looked up briefly as if seeking a word or maybe just a nod of encouragement, at least of acknowledgment. He got none, but continued anyway.

"The Sea King—. The Sea King was a widower, I believe, and lived with his mother, who took care not only of him, but also of her six granddaughters—the sea-princesses. The youngest was the prettiest. Unlike the others, she cared for only two things: her marble statue of a handsome young boy and the rose-colored weeping willow she'd planted alongside it. From her grandmother, she learned about ships and towns. That same grandmother promised her she'd be allowed, on her fifteenth birthday—as each of her sisters would be allowed on their own fifteenth birthdays—to swim up to the surface and sit upon a rock, and from there to watch the great ships sail by.

"Meanwhile, year after year, the youngest had to listen to her sisters' stories. Year after year, she became more and more eager to reach her own fifteenth birthday—and with it, the opportunity to sit on that rock. 'Pride must suffer pain' the old lady said to her when her fifteenth birthday finally arrived and as she was attaching oysters to the little mermaid's tail. When she then rose up to the surface, she was greeted by the sight of a single, large ship

- 351 -

on which people were celebrating. As she looked in through the portholes, she saw singing and dancing. At one point, she also saw a handsome young prince with coal-black eyes and jet-black hair."

Daneka looked appreciatively at Kit—*her* prince of almost coal-black eyes and jet-black hair—as he continued to narrate the story.

"At one point, the ship set sail, ran into a terrible storm and broke apart. Everything and everyone went overboard—including the prince. At first, she was happy because she thought she'd now have him all to herself. Then, however, she reflected. Humans, she knew, couldn't live underwater. Consequently, she decided to risk life and limb to find him in the wreckage. She dove deep into the sea where she finally spotted him, eyes closed, sinking. She brought him back up to the surface and kept his head aloft until morning, letting the waves take them where- and however the waves would.

"By morning, they'd come within sight of land. The prince's eyes were still closed—and so, the little mermaid took him to shore and laid him out on the beach, then went back into the water to wait and watch. Soon, a number of young girls came to the beach and found him. He eventually opened his eyes and then left with them—ignorant of his *real* rescuer. The little mermaid, now even sadder than before, swam back down to the sea castle. She told her sisters nothing—and continued to say nothing to anyone as she returned each night over the coming months to the place on the beach where she'd laid the prince out. She found consolation only in her garden and with the marble likeness of another handsome prince.

"She eventually told one of her sisters... who told another... who knew someone... who knew where the prince kept his castle—and took her to see it. From that time on, she went every night—to see the castle, of course, but also to see the prince, who liked to sit on the beach in the moonlight.

"She overheard many stories from fishermen about the prince's benevolence—and she grew fonder of him, and of human beings, by the day. She asked her grandmother, who'd spent a great deal of time up above, and who consequently knew all about humans. Her grandmother explained that mermaids lived much longer than humans, but that when they died, they merely became ocean foam. Humans, she explained, had a body that died and then turned to dust. But they also had a soul, which lived on forever. The little mermaid asked how she might win such a soul. Her grandmother explained that there was only one way to acquire it—and that it was through the never-ending love of one man.

"She resolved to seek the help of the Sea Witch, who lived in a house made of the bones of shipwrecked humans. In exchange for her voice as payment, the Sea Witch prepared a draught that would replace her tail with legs—and then the Sea Witch cut off her tongue.

"The little mermaid, now and forevermore mute, took the draught and swam to the prince's palace, crawled up on land and drank it. The pain was so great, she swooned, fainted and remained unconscious until morning. When she awoke, the prince was standing next to her. She was naked—and so, hid herself in her long, thick hair. The prince asked the little mermaid her name and also where she'd come from—but she couldn't answer as she had no tongue, and therefore no voice.

"In the coming weeks and months, he came to love her and would take her everywhere with him—but he loved her only as a child and not as a potential mate. Without that kind of love, of course, she couldn't win an immortal soul—and, as the Sea Witch had instructed her, would die the day after he married another.

"Finally, it was decided that the prince should visit the daughter of a neighboring king. He traveled over sea with the little mermaid to the king's castle, where he was greeted by the sounds of trumpets and merry-making. After a week's celebration, he finally met the king's daughter. Believing her to be the woman who'd saved him from certain death that one stormy night at sea, he resolved on the spot to marry her.

"At dawn on the prince's wedding day—and so, the day on which she was to die—the little mermaid stood at the railing of the bridal ship and looked out to sea, where she saw her sisters. In exchange for their hair, the Sea Witch had given them a dagger, which they now instructed the little mermaid to plunge into the prince's heart. When his warm blood then fell upon her feet—her sisters explained—they'd grow together into a tail, and she'd once again be able to return to the sea as a mermaid.

"But she loved the prince even more than she loved her own life. She hurled the knife into the sea and jumped in after it—believing she was jumping to a certain death. She was indeed transported, but it didn't feel anything like death. Instead, she felt that her body was rising higher and higher out of the foam. When she finally asked where she was, the answer she received came from the daughters of the air. They told her, as a mermaid, that she couldn't win an immortal soul; alternatively, but only as a human, that she would first have to gain the unconditional love of another human. 'On the power of another hangs your eternal destiny,' they said. Like mermaids, daughters of the air didn't possess immortal souls, either. They could win one, however, through good deeds. They'd watched her sacrifice for her prince. They'd seen her devotion. And so, they'd allow her to become one of them and to win an immortal soul—but only, like them, after three hundred years."

Kit was out of breath. Daneka looked at him with genuine admiration. "You have an extraordinary memory, darling. You remember far more of that fairytale than even I do—and I must've read it a hundred times. You also have a talent for story-telling. You could be that, you know—a story-teller. You could still do your photography, but you could first be a teller of stories. It's a worthy ambition—and a rare talent."

Kit blushed. He couldn't remember the last time she'd paid him a direct compliment, if ever. The heat of his blush was like a warm bath; the wash of it, heavenly. In the meantime, they'd arrived at a four-lane highway and had to cross over and into a park by means of a pedestrian walkway. Kit could see the harbor and a wide expanse of water not far from where they now stood. He then saw, just off the seawall, a large rock and a bronze figure sitting on top of it and staring out to sea.

They walked to the seawall and peered out at the figure of an ageless little mermaid who'd known—Daneka next told him—probably more attacks of vandalism than any other statue in the world—save those, collectively, of Lenin and Stalin. What—Kit wondered—was there about this little mermaid, this bronze water nymph, that could possibly incite vandalism? It simply made no sense to him. Could Daneka explain it?

She attempted a grim smile as she asked him: "Kit, you know Andersen's version of the story. But do you know the other version—the NC-17 version?"

"I didn't know there was one."

"Oh, but indeed. I don't know that it's ever been published, but it's very much alive—and lives in the hearts and nights of many, *many* women."

"Would you tell me that version, Daneka?"

She looked hard at him. "Are you certain you want to hear it? Because I can assure you that once you do, you'll never look at this statue again, never hear mention of the fairytale again, never even hear the name of H. C. Andersen again—in quite the same way."

Kit looked at Daneka and noticed, as he'd noticed only one other time, how quickly her face could age when it lost its smile and when the laughter went out of her voice. She was looking at him now, and it was as if someone had chiseled years of grief into her eyes. "Yes, darling, tell me that version."

Daneka fixed her stare once again upon the bronze statue in front of them.

"In the NC-17 version of the story, the characters looked very much like Andersen's characters. The little mermaid was not, however, one of six sisters—she was an only child. The Sea Witch was in fact not a witch at all—at least not in the beginning. She was a simple mermaid married to a simple merman who, while he may've thought he was the Sea King, was just a merman—with a simple merman's foibles. He had, if you will, a tail of clay.

"One day, he and the mermaid decided to make a baby. That baby is the little mermaid. Already in her infancy and toddler years, she's unquestionably the most beautiful, the most graceful, the happiest and therefore the most delightful merbaby in the kingdom. Merman and merwife—now merfather and mermother—are ecstatic at their good fortune. With each passing year, she becomes only more of what she'd been the previous year—until, that is, she approaches mermaidenhood."

Daneka paused in her storytelling—which allowed Kit to observe that she'd abruptly shifted tenses from the simple past to the present, and he wondered what significance that might have for this alternative version. He also found the "mer-" prefix a tad cloying. But his eye told him what his ear could not—namely, that her insistence upon this peculiar prefix had the force of a mantra. That she was not unintentionally using it so much as *it* was quite intentionally using *her*. To what end was something he still needed to discover.

"Do you know, Kit, what happens to mermaids when they enter mermaidenhood? They may have tails instead of legs. They may swim underwater rather than walk on land. But otherwise, they're very much like humans. They have hormones—just like humans. They throw a teenager's tantrums—just like humans. And, just like humans, they feel desire.

"The little mermaid is now no longer feeling little. She wants very much to become a merwoman and to find her own mermate. It's something her mother—later the Sea Witch—can quite understand. It's something the would-be Sea King, however, cannot even think about, much less tolerate.

"As this little mermaid is on her way through mermaidenhood to becoming a merwoman, she begins to slip out every night after dark to swim by the light of the moon. Before long, she finds a merboy with coal-dark eyes and jet-black hair who's on his own way to mermanhood. They do what mermaids and mermen do—by the reflected light of a moon casting beams far above the surface of the ocean, but whose same beams are magically magnified by the refraction of the water. They also do it deep within their own chosen house of coral—over and over again—until, that is, one night when the Sea King follows her out. She's been doing it for so long now, she no longer thinks of being cautious and doesn't once look back to see whether someone might be following her. Consequently, she doesn't know that on this particular night, she has a stalker—and that that stalker is her father.

"As is her habit, she finds her way quickly to the coral bed and dives down deep. Her stalker stops and watches from the top of the coral shaft through which she's descending, then sees that she's joined by a budding merman. Her stalker proceeds cautiously—just far enough behind so as not to be seen, just close enough so as not to lose them from sight—until the mermaid and the budding merman come to settle in a coral cove on the sandy floor far below. He can't actually see their bodies, which are partially hidden inside the cove. But the moon casts long shadows. Occasionally, too, their tails come into view. He notes that those tails are never more than the width of a dorsal fin apart."

Kit noticed that Daneka's telling of the story had been reduced to a monotone. At the same time—and although he couldn't look directly into them—he sensed her eyes had glazed over in that all-too-familiar way. He liked neither what he heard nor what he saw, but it was too late to stop her.

"The stalker watches the two lovers until he can watch no longer. Then, in a fury, he leaves and returns home, but says nothing to his merwife.

"Towards the end of the next morning, and under the pretext of needing to do a bit of coral fence-mending, he manages to get the budding merman to accompany him. You see, Kit, the would-be Sea King knows that budding mermen need sleep to restore their mermanhood—and so, has allowed this merman to get *all* the sleep he needs. As they approach the edge of their coral colony, beyond which all merfolk—young and old, male and female—know it's dangerous to swim because of sharks, the would-be Sea King urges the budding merman on. He knows precisely where he wants to go because he's been there once already this morning—to *break* the fence. The budding merman is wary, but he doesn't dare show it. He eventually wants to ask the Sea King for his daughter's hand in marriage, and he now needs to demonstrate one of his many manly virtues: courage.

"At last, they find the broken piece of fence. It's a vertical piece of coral a good inch in diameter. The break is clean, though the tips of the two broken halves are jagged and razor-sharp. The budding merman thinks to himself that this can have been caused only by some very large, very angry, or very hungry fish. They must first gather seaweed—the would-be Sea King suggests—to bind the break. The Sea King is in no rush. He is, instead, methodical, precise, exacting and patient.

"They both swim off in opposite directions—though always within the protective barrier of the coral reef separating them from the open ocean in which, they both know, danger lurks. They each then return with an armful of seaweed. The Sea King, only too willing to acknowledge the budding merman's greater strength, convinces him to do the harder business of pulling together and binding the two jagged ends of the broken coral fence. He—the Sea King—will meanwhile hold the seaweed and feed it to the younger man as needed to make the repair.

"The budding merman struggles in vain to get the two ends to budge. The Sea King instructs him on how he can achieve greater leverage with his tail if he first places himself - *between* the broken shafts. This makes no sense to the budding merman, but he doesn't want to question the wisdom of the older man—his future merfather—and so, he positions himself as instructed.

"The Sea King lunges and slams the young merman down with all his might, impaling him on the lower shaft. It goes straight through his abdomen and out his back—he's now simply a piece of bait writhing at the end of a spear. Little bubbles escape his mouth as he screams, but he's quickly losing strength, consciousness—and most importantly for the Sea King—blood. Our would-be monarch, meanwhile, works quickly to bind the merman's wrists and ankles to the coral fence. He knows that within minutes, sharks will smell blood and come to do more than merely sniff. It will be a riot of teeth, and the Sea King doesn't want to be caught anywhere in the vicinity of sharks crushing bone and tearing merflesh to frenzied bits.

"His job done, he swims home to his castle, where he is once again and *finally* the undisputed Sea King. That night, he follows his daughter out to her rendezvous. She pauses momentarily, tail all a-flutter, at the point at which she normally meets her budding merman—a merman, however, who buds no longer. She decides he must've grown impatient and swum on alone to the sandy bottom. She goes down blindly, frantically. The Sea King chases her. When she gets to the bottom and discovers that her lover is not in the cove, she turns around and looks back up the watery shaft. That's when she comes face to face with the Sea King, who promptly wrestles her to the sand.

"None of this takes much longer than a minute. It's not counsel or advice the Sea King now wants to give. What he wants to give—and so *does* give—doesn't require counsel, advice or more than a few heinous seconds.

"They return home, though not together.

"The next day, she stays longer in her seaweed bed than even an especially tolerant mermother thinks appropriate. The mother goes in, and when she comes out half an hour later, she's no longer a mermother or even a merwife. She's a Sea Witch.

"The Sea Witch finds the Sea King repairing his throne of whale- and shark-bones, which he hasn't sat on comfortably in a long time. He sees her coming—but sees, too, that she's not exactly sporting a picnic basket. He stands up and moves behind the throne in case she cares to sit upon it. With super-merwoman strength, the former mermother—present Sea Witch—tears one of the bones out of the throne.

"He leaves and never comes back. Sea Witch and mermaiden live together not so happily for a while. Then, when the mermaiden becomes a full-fledged mermaid, not so happily ever after at all.

"You see, the mermaiden then went looking for her father—he was, after all, *still* her father. At first, the Sea Witch tried to discourage her from looking—but Sea Witches are deal-makers; and so, the mermaiden consented to a deal. She let the Sea Witch cut out her heart in exchange for keys to all the wrong places in the kingdom, and Daneka went looking night after night after night."

Kit was shaken—especially by her last declaration. She couldn't possibly have made this story up on the spot. There'd simply been too much data for him to absorb in listening to it even to venture a guess at secondary meanings. If it was representative or symbolic, what—he wondered—was it representative or symbolic *of*?

"You like that story, Kit?" Daneka asked rhetorically. "I didn't think so. It's not a very likable story. And besides, I don't tell stories as well as you do—which is why I pay other people to write them. I simply make deals and then approve the lay-out."

"Daneka—"

"Oh, don't worry, darling. I'm not in the least offended. Listen, we'd better get going. I'm not concerned that we'll miss the plane or anything like that, but you know me—punctuality is next to godliness."

They walked back to the station in silence. They collected their bags, took an inner-city train to the airport, presented their passports and tickets, went through airport security and passport control and then on to their gate—in silence. Daneka bought a magazine, sat down and began to flip through the pages, all in absolute silence.

Kit was beginning to wonder whether they'd ever talk again.

Chapter 68

When the announcement to board came over the public address system, Daneka closed her magazine, got up and went to stand on line without a word to Kit. The silence, he thought, was becoming almost unbearable. When he went to join her on line, he discovered that a few people had managed to get in between them. He decided—rather than ask permission to step ahead and join his partner—to wait and see whether she'd make the request herself.

He needn't have waited; she never once looked back.

By the time he got to his seat, he was grateful to see they'd at least be sitting next to each other. If he couldn't speak to, touch, or look directly at her, he could at least smell her. She'd taken the aisle seat this time—maybe, he thought, the other would make her feel too claustrophobic. *Is she now that, too?* he wondered. On the other hand, maybe she felt something coming on; wanted easier access to the lavatories; didn't want to have to excuse herself each time and ask him to get out of his seat to let her get by. *Yeah, maybe that's it,* Kit thought—suddenly relieved. He hadn't really known her that long. Maybe she was premenstrual and hadn't wanted to say anything. That would explain the mood swings of the last couple of days, her crankiness—towards both him and her mother.

The last passengers where filing in, most of them speaking in English, though he noted some Scandinavian language or other now and again. He pretended to leaf through his in-flight magazine. *Fucking pabulum. Why didn't I at least bring a book? Why? Because I thought I might actually have a partner for conversation for the next six or seven hours—that's why.* Jesus! *Does this mean I'm going to have to converse with myself all the way back to New York?*

Before he could answer his own unhappy question, he heard a couple of feminine French voices. *Frenchwomen on an American airline flying from Copenhagen to New York? How odd.* He looked up as the voices got closer to where he and Daneka were sitting. One of the women looked familiar, though from some other context—he couldn't put his finger on it. The problem was the clothes—he couldn't place her in those clothes. He suddenly wondered whether he'd slept with her at some point in his life—and so, never seen her clothed. Then he saw her smiling at Daneka, who was quite clearly smiling back—all trace of premenstrual syndrome having suddenly vanished. *Maybe Daneka's slept with her!* he thought bitterly. *But then how and why would she look familiar to <u>me</u>? It's all too fucking complicated* was his final thought as he went back to his in-flight magazine.

The captain's voice came over the public address system—all cheery, confident, bubbly American, just a slight Southern drawl. *Why do all airline pilots sound as if they come from Texas?* he wondered while quite intentionally turning off his brain—since he couldn't plug his ears—to whatever it was the man was saying. "Can't they at least speak standard English?" he mumbled to himself, thinking he was only *thinking* the question—which he was—though he'd neglected to first check the volume control on that thought.

"What was that, darling?" Daneka asked.

"Oh... Nothing... The pilot... That's all."

"He's quite charming, don't you think? I mean the way he welcomed us all on board, welcomed us to New York—'a little prematurely,' he added—ha-ha, and then welcomed any and all of the unescorted ladies on board back to his place for a little nightcap, tee-hee—'also somewhat prematurely,' he added—and then extended a very special welcome to the two flight attendants from Air France who were joining us today— unescorted, ha-ha-ha, except by each other."

Kit found Daneka's laugh particularly grating. He didn't find pilots in the least bit funny. But now, at least, he knew who the woman was—their attendant on the flight from Paris to Lisbon. The *Veuve Cliquot* cocktail waitress with Air-fucking-France. No wonder he hadn't recognized her. Then, lips, mouth and breasts had all been properly buttoned-up in a uniform. This woman, however—the one who'd just passed them in the aisle with smiles especially for Daneka—was wearing a blouse unbuttoned nearly to her navel. The only thing separating her from her escort trailing directly behind was a bit of skin, bones, lungs and lace. The lace—even Kit had noticed in the couple of seconds before the escort had passed out of view—seemed to reveal more than it covered up—and seemed perfectly coordinated in color and frills with the garter belt his eye zeroed in on as she walked by, but only because the slit in her dress opened up almost as high as the unbuttoned buttons reached down. He liked the way the French could dress for success when they weren't working.

He felt a headache coming on just as their plane lurched backwards thanks to the gentle nudge of the little four-wheeler tugboat that helped the bigger craft out of their bays. He hadn't had a headache in years—and so, wondered whether it might be too much French, too much Danish, too much Texas drawl—or some revolting cocktail of all three.

"Have you got a couple of aspirin by chance?"

"Oh, no, darling, I don't," Daneka lied. "My poor darling. Have you got a headache?" she asked, unbuckling her seatbelt. "Let me go ask one of the attendants. I won't be a minute," she said, already out of her seat.

"But you can't—"

Kit wasn't sure how much time had passed when he heard the captain announce that their plane was next in line for take-off, then asked everyone to make sure their seatbelts were securely fastened. He glanced back; she was nowhere in sight. He assumed, then, that she'd found a seat elsewhere—at least for the duration of the take-off and until they were ready to begin leveling off at twenty-five or thirty thousand feet. How convenient! How *fucking* convenient!

Ten minutes later, Daneka was walking back up the aisle towards her seat with something in hand. She paused for a pensive moment, then continued on.

A few seconds later, she was standing next to Kit with the door to the overhead bin open. He heard a zipper, then heard the sound of something he couldn't quite identify. He looked up, saw her tapping something into the palm of her hand, heard the distinct snap of plastic against plastic. She sat down all smiles and—Kit noticed for the first time that day—with a newly acquired southern exposure of her chest just in time for the cooler winter weather. Or maybe, he thought, she'd just found it a bit stuffy in the cabin. It happened sometimes. People not used to flying might find it difficult to breathe—might just spontaneously start reaching for cramped collars, too-tight ties, bothersome buttons—anything just to get some air. *Given how flushed her face is, that must be it. But at least she's got the aspirin.* "Roche" he read on the tab. *French fucking aspirin.*

"You didn't by chance think to bring back any water with this, did you? A little something to wet also *my* whistle?" Kit said as he noticed the sheen on Daneka's lips.

"Oh, darling, I'm so sorry," she said, and he thought he detected just the hint of something like champagne on her breath. "Shall I go again?" she asked—and Kit mused—

like a Golden Retriever straining at the leash.

"No, that's okay." He popped the pill and swallowed, then gave Daneka his best facsimile of a smile. "I'm a little tired. A little headachey. I think I'll try to sleep."

"That's a wonderful idea, darling!"

Kit thought again of the Golden Retriever—namely, that she'd never so much resembled one as at this moment—and one with a belly just dying for a rub. He wondered at what point she might start drooling.

He forced himself to close his eyes. The world—at least *his* world—was spinning out of control. He didn't particularly care for scenes in public places. All he really wanted at this moment was to fall asleep and shut it all out—which is what he promptly did.

Daneka continued to leaf through her magazine, occasionally glancing over at Kit to try to determine whether he'd fallen asleep. At the same time, she was being pulled back towards the galley as if she had a stomach full of filings while someone in the rear held a giant magnet.

At one point, the French flight attendant walked up the aisle in the direction of the cockpit. Daneka peeked around the seat in front of her to see the attendant first knock, then open the door and disappear within. She knew that this kind of thing was strictly prohibited except to working attendants, wondered how the woman had managed to pull it off and for how long she'd be allowed to remain inside.

Daneka's curiosity was satisfied a brief twenty minutes later.

As the attendant walked back—no worse for the wear, Daneka noted, even if somewhat disheveled—her eyes met Daneka's as soon as the attendant entered the tourist-class cabin. The reciprocal stare held steady as she walked. She dropped an arm to her side and, at the moment she passed Daneka and Kit, let her fingers run the length of Daneka's arm from wrist to elbow.

Daneka felt a delicious little *frisson*. Whether or not Kit was asleep, she simply couldn't wait any longer. She quietly unbuckled her seatbelt, just as quietly stood up, then walked back and arrived at the galley just in time to see the attendant open one of the lavatory doors and disappear behind it. When Daneka got to the door, she read *'Unoccu-*

'pied' and immediately got the message. She opened it and stepped inside, then threw the bolt. If it had been unoccupied a moment earlier, it now no longer was.

"*Et votre ami?*" ("And your friend?") the attendant asked, though in her tone it was rather difficult to distinguish whether she was suggesting a *ménage à trois* or simply wanted to reassure herself that he wouldn't come barging in at an inopportune moment.

"*Il dort,*" ("He's sleeping,") Daneka answered as she slowly rotated and pulled the hair up from the nape of her neck. "*De toute façon, la chose—c'est finie. Il ne le sait pas encore, mais tant pis. Il s'en rendra compte plus tôt ou plus tard.*" ("In any case, the thing's finished, he just doesn't know it yet, but too bad. He'll get the picture sooner or later.")

Just before the attendant put her lips to that nape, she whispered into Daneka's ear: "*Qui dort, dîne, n'est-ce pas, mon trésor? Et qui va à la chasse, déguste à sa place.*" *

"*Sans doute, ma fleur, sans doute.*" ("No doubt, my sweet, no doubt.") Daneka whispered back into a French ear before reaching a hand behind, then slipping it down and inside the garter belt of another excited little Golden Retriever rutting for a rub.

Some beavers—Daneka now thought to herself through the *soupçon* of a smile—*are just so* eager!

---

* The first part of this is simply a French proverb: "He who sleeps, eats." The second is a pun involving another French proverb ("Qui va à la chasse perd sa place")—which, in modern American English, would be the equivalent of "Ya snooze, ya lose"—that plays off the first proverb and would be rendered, in rough form: "the *active* hunter enjoys the *present* spoils."

Chapter 69

Kit remained fast asleep almost from the moment he'd taken the aspirin until the moment their plane touched down on at JFK. Daneka had happily eaten both of their lunches, then both of their dinners. She'd initially left only their desserts—but had then made a snap decision to take them and her napkin elsewhere. By the end of the trip, she was on a first-name basis with virtually all of the attendants, male and female, working or off-duty. With the pilot and co-pilot, however, she'd merely exchanged telephone numbers and email addresses. That contact could wait; it wasn't her style to compete with the controls of a 747.

Just before they landed, she decided to celebrate the trip with a split of *Veuve Cliquot*. Kit was still asleep; she hated to drink alone—and so, she didn't. She also took advantage of this last run to the lavatory to check that her clothes were presentable; her make-up fresh and precise; her hair combed. If rambunctious playtime had cost her a button or two along the way, that was the cost of doing business with a fun-loving Hansel or Gretel. If one or the other wanted to share a little nightcap before retiring to more mundane matters, and if Kit was still asleep—well, then, she certainly had nothing against a post-prandial romp. As she inspected her face in the mirror, she couldn't remember when her cheeks had looked more naturally flushed and youthful—a reflection of just how she felt: youthful.

Kit, meanwhile, was jarred out of his sleep as soon as tires hit the tarmac.

"Where are we?" he mumbled.

"We're home, darling! Home at last. I think I've read every magazine on this plane since you fell asleep. So many stories. I'm all read out!"

Kit looked at her. *Some people certainly travel better than others. I probably look like fucking death warmed over. She, on the other hand, looks absolutely stunning. My God, how does she do it?*

The captain's voice came over the public address system once again to thank the passengers and welcome them all—officially this time—to New York. He wanted to add his special thanks to the flight attendants from Air France who'd gone above and beyond. He'd been led to understand that one of the passengers had been air-sick during the flight and had had to make a number of trips to the lavatory. While the crew had been particularly solicitous of this passenger's comfort, the flight attendants from Air France had also made a

- 365 -

significant contribution.

Kit noticed that Daneka had been listening intently and trying hard to suppress a smirk throughout the captain's speech. He wondered what it all meant—whether she'd been aware of any of it or had simply been concentrating so hard on her reading she'd been ignorant of the predicament of a sick passenger.

"Did you get any new names?" he asked. The question seemed to startle her.

"New names? What do you mean 'new names?'" she asked.

"You know—authors' names, for future publications. From the articles you read."

"Oh," she laughed. *A bit too hard*, he thought. "A few, yes. But of course I'll first have to run them by the fiction department to see if any of these names have a history of publications. We're not really in the habit of *discovering* new writers, you know. We leave that to the likes of *Granta*."

Kit wondered at the emphasis on 'discovering.' He already had an answer to the question of the additional emphasis on *Granta*. She apparently hadn't forgotten—nor would she be willing to forget—his earlier *faux pas*.

"Kit, darling, you must be famished. Why don't we grab a cab back to town, drop our bags off at my place, then find some little bistro in the neighborhood. I believe there's one just a couple of blocks south of 96th Street on Madison Avenue. What do you say?"

"If you wouldn't mind."

"Not in the least! I'm starving!"

"But didn't you eat anything on the flight—while I was sleeping, I mean?"

"Oh, no. I never touch airline food. You never know what the kitchen staff has been up to." She lowered her voice to almost a whisper. "I frankly don't know whether these attendants ever wash their hands after they've used the facilities. They're just in and out—like a revolving door. You'd think they'd be a little more hygienic—at least with their hands."

Kit had no idea what she was getting at. It sounded to him like some bizarre personal rant—but what prompted it was a complete mystery to him. *No matter*, he thought to himself. *We're going to dinner—and* that's *a hopeful sign.*

Their plane pulled up to the gate, and passengers patiently disembarked. Kit and Daneka went through Passport Control, then descended to the Baggage Claims area. As bags began to roll out, he saw the French flight attendant arrive at the other side of their carousel. She seemed, thankfully, to be completely oblivious of both him and Daneka. He turned his attention once again to the carousel, eager to collect their bags and be underway, and saw their first bag as it came out on the conveyer belt.

"There, Daneka." he said, pointing. "That one, I believe, is ours."

"If you wouldn't mind, darling, I'm just going to make a quick run to the Ladies' Room, okay? I'll be back in a jiff."

"Sure, no problem." He was still watching for their bags, half of which had already arrived, when he looked again across the carousel. The flight attendant was nowhere to be seen, although her traveling companion, still standing there collecting bags just as he was, now looked up and directly at him. If ever he'd seen a Mona Lisa smile in his life, this was it. 'Enigmatic' was the word that came to mind. He smiled back, but his smile didn't feel quite right to him. It was an odd sensation—as if someone else were forcing a smile onto his face that he just didn't feel. The woman looked away quickly, as if embarrassed, and he went back to watching out for their bags.

As the last of their luggage made its way to him on the carousel, he caught sight of Daneka standing just behind him. She was opening one of her bags, slipping something into it that she held tightly in one hand while she fumbled with the zipper with the other. A hint of whatever it was peeked out from between her fingers. It looked powder blue, shiny—like silk. In any case, Daneka's hand slipped inside the bag and whatever she was holding disappeared from sight. She withdrew her hand and once again pulled the zipper shut.

Kit grabbed the last bag and loaded it onto their luggage cart. As he wheeled the cart around to start off in the direction of Customs, he looked across one last time at the Air France flight attendant's traveling companion with whom he'd stumbled into a smile moments earlier—and saw not only her, but also once again the attendant.

They got through Customs easily and were welcomed home by the official—Kit always found this little courtesy somehow endearing—then made their way out to a taxi stand where they were already next in line for a cab. They loaded their luggage, then climbed into the back seat as Daneka gave directions to the cabbie. Within seconds, they were off in the direction of Manhattan. Whatever had moved her to resume conversation with him at one point in the airport had now, once again, *removed* itself—and so, they rode in silence.

Chapter 70

As their taxi pulled up in front of The Fitzgerald, a doorman rushed to the curb to open Daneka's door. To Kit's chagrin, however, he noted that it wasn't Michael Kelly: he'd been hoping to see Daneka aim some of her heavy artillery at another target for a change.

This other doorman greeted her warmly, nodded in Kit's direction, then went immediately to the trunk of the taxi to retrieve their luggage, which he dutifully carried up the stairs and into the lobby. Daneka slipped out of the back seat and went straight to the elevator, and Kit realized this fare was going to be his. Luckily, he'd kept some bills in reserve—just enough, with two singles left over, to cover the fare and tip. He paid and got out.

There were a couple of bags still in the trunk—both his. He pulled them out and slammed the trunk shut, then walked into the lobby where the doorman was busy moving Daneka's bags to a luggage carrier. She was nowhere in sight, and Kit concluded she'd already gone up. He thanked the doorman, added his own bags, wheeled the carrier to the elevator and called for it. Within seconds, the elevator arrived and the doors opened. He pushed the carrier in and squeezed in after it, then hit the button for the thirteenth floor.

As Kit and the carrier began to ascend, he was struck by a disquieting thought. It was not in his nature to snoop, but he suddenly had an irrepressible urge. He stopped the elevator in mid-ascent, unzipped one of Daneka's bags and reached inside for something baby blue with a shine to it. He found it first with his fingers. Silk, for fingers, had a language of its own that rendered eyes redundant.

If, at this moment, he could've ordered a mass arrest of moths for conspiracy, he still would've considered the task only half done. The other half demanded a house-arrest just a few floors above him.

Kit took the panties out of her bag. He didn't know whether Daneka owned a pair of baby blues, but he somehow doubted it: they wouldn't have coordinated very well with her eye color. He looked at the tag on the inside. *Nettoyer à sec* (Dry clean only) it instructed without benefit of an English-language translation, but he didn't need one. He wouldn't be going to the cleaners anytime soon; nor, he concluded, would he allow himself to be taken there again anytime soon—not by *anyone.*

He put the French panties back inside Daneka's bag and started to withdraw his hand when he suddenly felt something else, small and plastic. As he pulled it out, he heard a rattle inside. His eyes then fell upon a prescription label made out to Daneka Soerensen. **Take as needed for sleeplessness. Do not exceed two tablets in any 24-hour period.**

What the fuck was *this* all about? She'd never mentioned problems with sleeping. And then a second thought hit him. He opened the plastic container and looked more closely at the tablets. The blue Roche signature was on all of them. These were the "aspirin" she'd given him on the plane. No wonder he'd slept like a dog and then felt disoriented upon waking. She'd fucking well drugged him to sleep.

Kit was about to put the container back into her bag when his eye caught sight of something else. He took the lid off again and emptied the contents into his hand. All but two tablets said 'Roche,' and those two said 'Bayer.' Sure, he thought: Bayer—as in *aspirin.* She'd clearly gotten them after all, but had then changed her mind and given him sleeping pills. She'd obviously wanted him to sleep—and sleep hard. The question was why? The answer now suggesting itself to him was not a particularly palatable one. It smacked of Mr. H. C. Andersen's fairytale—but of the *alternative* version.

He dropped the plastic container back into her bag and zipped it up tight, then re-started the elevator. When he arrived at the thirteenth floor and stepped out, he saw that her door stood slightly ajar. Fresh flowers in the crystal sconce at the right side of the door suggested that Estrella had been taking good care of things in Daneka's absence—even if a certain bouquet of fresh flowers hadn't been recently misted.

With one of his bags, he prodded the door open. At the same moment, he heard Daneka flush the toilet in the bathroom off her bedroom and realized that she in all likelihood hadn't heard his entrance. He put the first bag down quietly and used it to prop open the door, then held his breath as he heard her walk across the room, open a drawer, close it, then walk a few more steps. He next heard the sound of her computer booting up and decided the moment was opportune to take off his shoes—which he did before placing them noiselessly in the coat closet. Finally, he heard Daneka activate her tape machine. The robotic voice gave back date- and time-stamp as she listened to her phone messages.

She'd apparently forgotten him completely and didn't once come out to the living room to see whether he might be around or need any help. The taped messages were difficult to decipher from his vantage point. Only the last one clearly registered as that of a male.

As he continued bringing their bags in through the door, he heard her footsteps cross the bedroom floor once again, then heard her pull out a chair. He couldn't know which one it was until he also heard the sound of her fingers on a computer keyboard.

So much for dinner! So much for 'famished.' Is it really so *important to her to check her email and phone messages?*

He decided, rather than interrupt her, to sit down and read—if he could find a book worth reading. His eyes scanned the titles and authors' names until he saw one he recognized: *The Painted Bird*, by Jerzy Kosinski. He pulled it off the shelf and opened it. The book creaked—suggesting to him once again that it, too, had likely never been read. But that was rather beside the point, he now realized as he saw a personalized inscription on the first page and read it: "To Daneka, my daring demoniac: Flying with you on your trapeze"—Kit noted that the writer of this particular inscription had underlined the word— "was the high-wire act of a lifetime, with all the thrills and spills of a season. Keep falling, darling; it becomes you." Jerzy.

Why did this business about 'fall—or falling—becomes you' sound familiar? Kit racked his brain to find a context. Daneka's mother came briefly into focus, but it was all too vague. There'd simply been too many other images in the meantime.

He sat down and started to read—or rather, to try to read. But the sound of Daneka's tapping—not to mention the occasional word she said to herself as she tapped— was proving to be too much of a distraction. He decided to take a shower after having first put the book back on the shelf.

As he turned away from the bookcase, his eye caught sight of the lichen still sitting in the center of the coffee table. He'd have to remember to take it with him when he left. He'd rather eat it, he decided, than leave it behind.

Kit opened up one of his bags, took out his travel kit and a clean pair of boxer shorts, then walked back to Daneka's bedroom. It wasn't until he'd actually opened the bathroom door and turned on the light that she looked up from her screen.

"Oh, hello, darling. I didn't hear you come in." Kit waited an instant to see whether there might be any additional words of endearment. There were none.

He closed the door, then ran the water as hot as he could stand it. He stood for twenty minutes with his face directly under the shower nozzle, got out, dried off, shaved and brushed his teeth. He'd do without dinner—not, however, without pajamas.

He put his shorts on, brushed his hair and opened the door. Daneka was still typing, typing, typing like a maniacal midtown secretary. He turned off the lamp on the night table, slipped in under the covers and shut his eyes. Sleep, however, didn't come. The sound of Daneka's locomotive fingers, however, did—especially how she seemed to type the last bit of punctuation of every email with an audible flourish before sending it off.

Perhaps three-quarters of an hour—or maybe a full hour—later, he wasn't sure, he heard her shut down the computer after having concluded her session with a little late-night surfing. On which beach or beaches and on what size or shape of wave, he didn't know and didn't really care to know. He heard her go into the bathroom, start up the shower, stay under the water five or ten minutes, get out and then brush her teeth. She emerged a moment later in a terrycloth bathrobe and with her hair up in a towel. Behind him, he could hear her briskly drying her hair, then brushing it. Finally, he heard her untie the terrycloth knot—feather-soft; heard her place it and the towel over the back of her chair; heard her turn off her night light; heard her finally settle down into darkness under the covers.

Under other circumstances, this would normally have been a moment of rapture for both of them. Kit had no idea what the direction of Daneka's thoughts or intentions might be; he knew only his own—and it was on sleep. The thought of touching her—any part of her—filled him with almost as much revulsion as it did dread. As he was contemplating the apparent impasse at which they'd once again arrived, he felt Daneka move up behind him and drop her hand over his chest. He then felt it descend slowly. She was apparently in the mood to play. He wondered whether she'd also provide him with a courtesy set of blindfold and napkin ties.

He noticed he was now becoming erect—and hated his own body's automatism. He turned over on his stomach and let her hand fall away, heard her sigh, then felt the sheets stir as she turned her back to him.

Kit lay still for a long time. He heard the shudder of church bells down the street tell him just how long he'd lain in stillness; counted first two chimes, then one more an hour later. Shortly before three o'clock, he heard Daneka's breathing become heavy and regular. As quietly as he could, he slipped out of bed, collected his clothes and walked to the living room. Once out of range to interrupt her sleep, he dressed, opened the front door and moved his bags into the hallway, then took his shoes from the coat closet, stepped outside and closed the door.

Clearly forgotten, the lichen continued its ten thousand-year-old struggle for existence, in silence, in the center of Daneka's coffee table.

This might or might not be the last night—or just half-night—he would spend in her bed. In any case, he didn't intend to spend it there when he could spend it just as sleeplessly in his own bed half a city—and about a million miles—away.

Chapter 71

The elevator arrived at lobby level, and Kit pushed the luggage carrier and his bags out through the door. As if this night were not already sufficiently dismal, the face he now saw was that of The Fitzgerald's first and truest blackguard: Michael Kelly. *They deserve each other*, he thought. *They're made of the same sticky stuff.*

The doorman watched Kit as he wheeled the carrier over to its prescribed location just behind his console. He was apparently quite busy with some personal transaction or other—too busy to lend Kit a hand, though he had no apparent problem lending commentary.

"Out walking Mrs. Sorensen's dog, son? Or still just trying to track her down by her scent?"

Kit had heard the 'son' very distinctly, but wasn't about to fall for the ruse. "No, *Mr.* Kelly. I'm not doing either of those things. I don't walk dogs. I'm not a dog-walker. And as for her scent, I believe I found that a long time ago."

The doorman smirked. "Yes, t'would appear you did, son. T'would appear you did indeed."

"It's actually quite easy to track when she gets a little excited."

"Well, now, son—."

"The name's 'Addison,' Mr. Kelly. Charles Addison."

"Well then, Addison. You wouldn't now be suggestin'—"

"I'm not suggesting anything at all, Mr. Kelly. I believe you'll come to know Ms. Sorensen's true scent for yourself just after sunrise. Much pleasure may it give you." Kit next took his two bags off the carrier and walked to the front door—then paused and turned around. "Tell me, Mr. Kelly. Have you found your personal savior yet? Have you come to Jesus in your heart? 'Cause if not, I'd really recommend it sometime between now and dawn."

With that, Kit walked out the door, turned left and walked the hundred feet to Park Avenue. Once there, he crossed it and continued on down towards Lexington where he descended into the subway, pulled out his last two dollars and bought a Metrocard. The days of dallying for brass tokens, he knew, were done. He didn't need to pretend otherwise—not to himself and not *for* anybody else.

He struggled through the turnstile with his bags, then turned left on the platform and walked to the end. He decided at this hour and carrying two pieces of luggage that he'd just as soon do most of his walking underground. No need to tempt the natives of the East Village with thoughts about what he might have stashed inside.

The Number Six local arrived just as he got to the end of the platform. He boarded the empty last car and put his bags down in front of a seat reserved for the elderly and disabled. He was feeling neither, but the competition for space was not particularly stiff at that hour. He then opted to stand and look out the rear window of the car as the train released its brakes and began to move out of the station. Within seconds, they were at 86th Street—the Hunter College stop. Her 96th Street exit already looked like something on a distant and fast-deteriorating canvas. He wondered—as the doors opened, then closed, and the train again undertook its southerly journey towards Brooklyn—whether he'd ever again have a reason to travel up to this part of the island.

As his train pulled into the Astor Place station, 14th Street/Union Square was as far north as he could see. Ninety-sixth street was already as good as gone.

He got out, walked to the exit and climbed the stairs to street-level. If there was still noise and activity about, Kit was unmindful of it. He walked south and east to his apartment building, climbed the stairs to the front door and opened it. He then climbed another five sets of stairs to his apartment, opened the door, entered and turned on a light. It was exactly as he'd left it—including the prints of Daneka still hanging from the clothesline.

He dropped his bags on the floor, went to the refrigerator and took out a beer, then pulled a chair up in front of the clothesline and sat down. Over the course of the next few hours and until sunrise, he made occasional trips either to the refrigerator to replace an empty bottle with a full one, or to the bathroom to replace a full bladder with an empty one. Otherwise, he simply let his eyes roam back and forth along the clothesline.

When Daneka awakened, it was neither to an alarm clock nor to sun's rays streaming in through the window. She awakened spontaneously, on her back, and stared at the ceiling. When the church bells began to ring, she counted them with her fingers in the air: *"en...to...*

tre...fire...fem...seks...syv...otte. Eight o'clock," she said out loud. She dropped her arms to her sides. Only then did she turn her head to see whether Kit's was still present on the neighboring pillow. It, of course, wasn't.

She promptly got out of bed, showered and brushed her teeth, dressed, made herself a cup of coffee, picked up the telephone and dialed a number she knew by heart. After a couple of rings, someone at the other end picked up. "I've been away. I'm coming down." She didn't identify herself; she didn't need to.

Kit stood up as he heard the bells outside his window begin to chime. He counted to eight in his head as he slowly and deliberately began to take down the photos of Daneka and put them all in a pile on his work desk. When he arrived at the last—the one he'd taken of her at the Boathouse just as she'd pushed her dress off her shoulder and was rubbing what appeared to be a bruise—he decided to study it more carefully. He hadn't, until now, looked at it closely—thinking at the time that the bruise was probably some injury she'd received from falling luggage. With what he'd recently learned and now suspected, however, he had reason to question his original supposition.

He left the photo hanging and resolved to have the negative cropped and enlarged. He wanted to take a closer look at this bruise, and there was only one shop he knew of that could do it the way he needed it to be done.

Chapter 72

K it arrived at Duggal's on 20th Street and Fifth Avenue just as the doors were opening for business and after he'd stopped at a local ATM. His account was running on fumes or less, well into overdraft territory, and Kit knew he needed to get back to work. Fast. This might be an extravagant expenditure, but it was one he required—at whatever cost.

"Morning, Yoon," he said even before he'd reached the counter just inside the front door.

"Morning, Kit," said the woman behind the counter over the rim of her coffee cup. She took a sip and then asked. "What can I do for you today, my prince?" She paused momentarily over the coffee cup and studied Kit's face more carefully. "Or should I say my 'knight of the mournful countenance?' What's up, Kit? You look dreadful."

The two knew each other well. The first time they'd met and Kit had learned her name, he'd announced: "You are my morning, Yoon and night!" From that point on, he'd been treated to a flat twenty-five percent off rate-card. From that point on, he'd also stopped shopping elsewhere.

Kit didn't bother to address her last remark, and Yoon knew better than to persist. "Crop this to just below the tit and then feed it to the enlarger, will you? Make me a poster."

"Which tit, Kit?"

"The one just below the black and blue road sign."

"You took this shot for some rough trade rag?"

"Rough trade, yeah. But no rag."

"What's a sweetie like you doing out in the rough stuff, Kit?"

"Just playing on through, Yoon. Just putting to the moon."

"They don't get any better than you, Kit, when it comes to putting."

"They do, Yoon. But they gotta be Tigers."

"*Tigers*—check that. By when do you need it?"

"I'll wait."

"It's a rush job then?"

"Rush? Like Christmas, Yoon."

"Not *like* you, Kit."

"I'm not myself, Yoon."

"Check. Give us thirty?"

"Thirty's good. I'll go grab a bagel. Want one?"

"You're a doll. That's more like the Kit I know. Sure. Poppy seed with a schmear of cheese and chives. Twice toasted."

"Check. See you in a couple or five." He walked out the door and across the street to a deli where he ordered coffee and a couple of bagels—two of a kind, to go. He was out of the deli in three minutes with a pair of toasted, then back through the door at Duggal's. He was home now, and once again in his element; and so, it was time to pick up the pace. *High* time. Paris and Portugal were already light-years away; Italy, an illusion; Denmark, a dreary dream.

Yoon greeted him with a smile as he handed her the bagel.

"How's the work coming along?" he asked.

"Fine. Just a few more minutes now. Nice lighting on that one. You do it?"

"All natural, Yoon. Camera did the shoot. Nature did the light show. I just punched the clicker."

"I know better, Kit. I see some shit in here from time to time. Your stuff? Never stinks."

"Thanks."

"Pretty lady, by the way. That is, till we cut most of her out. Older model?"

"Not a model at all. More like a mannequin. Body's a great hanger, but it lacks a soul."

"Too bad. Lady like that oughta have a soul."

"Check that, Yoon."

Their banter had gone on just long enough to let the technicians do their job. One of them brought the poster-sized enlargement of Daneka's shoulder out to the front counter and placed it down in front of Kit and Yoon.

"*Whoa!*" Yoon said. "*Ouch!* Nasty little bugger. She a boarder?"

"Surfer," Kit said. "Likes a rough sea and big waves. Likes to ride 'em right into the jetties where she parks her board by moonlight." Kit looked at Daneka's injury. It was decidedly not luggage-inflicted. He could even see four little gouge marks where someone had spared her only a thumb.

"Nice work, guys. How much do I owe?"

Yoon took out her calculator, added eight and three-quarter percent for Mayor Mike, then subtracted thirty because Kit was Kit and not Hizzoner. "Twenty-eight even," she said. Kit was relieved he'd been left with lunch money. He gave her thirty; she gave him back two and a second smile.

"Thanks, as always, for the great work."

"*Mon plaisir, Monsieur* Addison IV," she said with an exaggerated American accent.

"They may tell you you're French, Yoon, but you're really just looney. Toodles," Kit said.

"Ta," Yoon answered.

Kit was out the door, up to Fifth Avenue, where he turned right, turned right again at Nineteenth Street where he found the front door to his studio. He glanced at the elevator and then bounded up the steps. Rachel met his smile with one of her own.

"Howdy, stranger!" Long time, no see. How was Europa? Still old?"

"Old and dreary," Kit answered.

"Hmmm. So tell me, *Monsieur Bon Vivant*. When are you coming back to work? Or *are* you?"

"Today," Kit answered. "If there's any work, that is."

"You're in luck! Clown #1 just called in complaining of some kind of a bug. He sounded hungover to me, but you know how it is with #1. The shoot's in half an hour. Fashion princess for *Vogue*. Wanna take it?"

"Perfect! Thanks, darl—. Thanks, Rachel." Kit made a mental note to excise the D-word from his vocabulary. "I owe ya."

"Pizza's always a plus."

"With pepperonis?"

"You know, Kit, for an *old* guy, you still got a pretty decent memory."

"For an *old* guy, Rachel, I still got lots of decent parts! You'll just have to take my word for it."

"Check that, Kit. But let's not go there."

"Didn't intend to, Rachel, but you left the door wide open."

"Hah! I know you're itchin' to get inside my bobby socks, Mr. Addison, but this chick doesn't roll 'em down for *old* guys."

"'Not my lucky day, I guess. Oh, well. Maybe on my birthday."

"Yuk! By then, you'll be one year *older!*"

They both laughed. Kit liked Rachel and Rachel liked Kit. But that was as far as it went for either of them. "What time did you say the *Vogue* gig starts?" he asked just as the elevator door opened and a ravishing blonde stepped into the room.

"Goot morningh," she said with an accent that sounded like a street urchin she'd adopted for the day only. "I'm named Eva. I haf a shoot scheduled for eleven o'clock." She gave 'scheduled' an Oxbridge pronunciation. Kit and Rachel both delighted in the irony.

"Yes, Eva. We were expecting you. And this is Kit, your photographer."

"I am very pleased to make your acquaintance, Kip," she said.

"And I to make yours, Eva. Whenever you're ready, we are, too."

"Oh, just gif me a pair of minutes, please." She turned to Rachel. "And the green room? It would be where?"

"It would be there," Rachel said, pointing down the hall.

"Sank you."

"No, sank *you!*" Rachel said. She winked at Kit as the blonde walked off. "Good luck with *that* one!" she whispered.

"Not a Dane, I hope."

Rachel pulled the girl's headshot from the file and looked at her bio on the back. Running her finger down past a long list of credits, she found what she was looking for. "Swede," she said. "Same thing, I guess."

"No, quite different," Kit answered, now with some actual authority. "Okay. I'm off to get prepped. Please give me a call once the snow princess has been prepped."

Kit walked back to his cubicle and found it exactly as he'd left it—including the framed portrait of Daneka looking back at him as unabashed as the day he'd taken the shot—though now with considerably more backstory. He put the poster away. He might or might not look at it again. In any case, it wouldn't really be necessary, as the image was burned into his brain.

Ten minutes later, Rachel called. Eva was ready—as was the set. He walked back to the studio and greeted his crew. After an absence of some length, handshakes to the guys and kisses to the girls' cheeks weren't at all inappropriate, and he distributed them freely. As he was doling the last of them out, she walked in wearing sky-blue—and very little of it. *Blue*, Kit thought, *must be the color of the week.*

As he pulled out his light meter and went to work, Kit wondered whether a word for 'modesty' even existed in the Swedish language. From what he'd seen—and was seeing again now—he didn't think so. *Must be a fun country*, he thought.

Towards evening, Daneka returned home to find her bags still unpacked and Kit's still gone. Apparently—she thought to herself—he wasn't planning to return anytime soon. Funny. He was a hard one to predict. *I wonder if it was something I said*, she mused.

As she thought about it, her eyes started to blink and her arm to itch. She scratched it—kept on scratching it as if it might contain the answer. She kicked off her heels and sat down on the sofa. She didn't really want to unpack—not now. She had a whole evening in front of her for that. And so, she sat … and scratched. *But I really have to do something about these eyes,* she thought. She got up and went into her bathroom to look in the medicine closet. With one hand, she turned bottles and little plastic containers around in order to read the labels; with the other, she scratched. It shouldn't have been difficult to turn, read and scratch at the same time, but her eyes kept blinking. She couldn't quite focus. She couldn't think clearly. *Goddamn it!* she thought—and then she said it out loud. Her arm had started bleeding again. She put her mouth to her wrist at the spot where it was bleeding, sucked up the blood and spat it into the sink—but it was coming out too fast. She'd simply scratched too deep. Drops of blood started to splatter on the floor.

"God*damn it!*" she screamed. *Okay, get a grip, girl. Bandage first. The floor later.* She reached again into the medicine cabinet, unthinking, with the bleeding arm. The blood ran down and into the sink. She started to knock containers out of her way as she looked for the sterile gauze. Some of them fell into the sink; others, to the floor—where they broke and spilled their contents. The floor was now a mess of blood, broken glass and pills—as was the sink.

She forced herself to think clearly. She opened the door beneath the sink—there it was, still in its original wrapping. She used her teeth to bite through the thin plastic; spat the bits into the sink; used her teeth and one unbloodied hand to unwind the gauze; laid it across the open wound and began to wrap her arm. This seemed to work. She rinsed the blood off her arm and hands, then looked around for a towel. There was one hanging from the rack on the far wall, but she couldn't risk walking across the floor with all of the broken glass.

With the cleaning sponge that Estrella—*Where the* fuck *is Estrella, anyway?*—had left at the end of the bathtub, and which Daneka was just able to reach without having to step out onto the floor, she was able to clear a path among the blood, glass and pills. She could now once again maneuver.

In short order, she had the floor cleaned up.

The activity restored a sense of self-control, but she was exhausted and wanted to take a shower. First, however, there was the matter of a call to Annemette—that much she could manage.

She picked up her cordless phone and dialed the number. As the phone rang at the other end, she wandered from her bedroom, down the corridor and into the living room. She heard a voice at the other end, then spoke up.

"Annamette, it's Mama."

Coming back to her through the receiver was a voice both happy and sad—slow and with a great deal of effort, as if it were difficult for the speaker to string simple words together in a sentence.

The involuntary blinking had long since stopped. Now, however, another involuntary action occurred—and in reaction to the voice. Tears. She put her hand over the receiver so that her daughter would hear none of it, but the tears flowed in a torrent. Until she abruptly realized she'd just been asked a question—and that the question awaited an answer. As she struggled to regain her composure, her eyes strayed over the coffee table and settled on the lichen.

"Oh, it was great. I loved every minute of it."

Kit had finished his shoot, and it had been a long day. Eva had been good—even if a tad temperamental—and her occasional peevishness had made it difficult to get the job done as efficiently as he might've liked.

He was, however, grateful for the work. Work meant income. In a city like New York, if there wasn't cash flowing in, it was gushing out. In New York, there was no such thing as stasis where money was concerned. At the same time, the job had kept his mind off Daneka—and just such a distraction was what he most needed right now.

The job was finished, however, and his mind had no place else to wander. He walked back to his cubicle, saw her picture and picked it up. He unraveled the poster and studied it. *Fuck this!* he thought.

He stopped off to hit Rachel up for an advance out of the petty cash box. It was empty, she told him, but then reached into her own purse without hesitation. "Will a twenty get you where you need to go?" she asked.

"A twenty gets you pizza with pepperonis for life," Kit answered with a look of genuine gratitude. "Thanks a mill'." He grabbed the bill, then ran out of the building and down the stairs. A cab stood curbside as a passenger was just paying her fare and getting out.

"You free?" he asked the driver.

"Yeah." Kit got in. "Where to?"

"East Ninety-sixth Street, between Park and Madison. I'll tell you where to stop when we get to the block."

"You got a preference?"

"Huh?"

"Park or Madison? They both go uptown. Doesn't matter to me."

"Park. It reminds me less of Madison."

"Huh?"

"Never mind."

They rode in silence. Once they'd gotten across town to Park Avenue South, the cabbie managed to get his car in synch with the traffic lights. They were uptown in record time. Kit gave the cabbie a ten-dollar bill and told him to keep the change.

"Thanks."

"Don't mention it."

"Good choice, by the way."

"Huh?"

"Park."

"Oh, yeah. Experience."

Kit walked into the lobby of The Fitzgerald and past the doorman's console. "Can I help you, Sir?" the doorman asked.

"No, you can't. But maybe you can help your colleague, Mr. Kelly. I suspect he'll be needing some help pretty soon."

"Uh, Mr. Kelly was asked to take indefinite leave as of this morning, Sir." Although this doorman didn't recognize Kit, it was obvious to him from Kit's pair of remarks that he'd been a prior visitor. The doorman let him pass.

Kit opened the elevator door and walked in, then pressed the button to the thirteenth floor. *Lucky thirteen* he thought to himself for the first time. *Has to be one of the few buildings in New York with a thirteenth floor.* In most buildings, floors went automatically from twelve to fourteen.

The elevator arrived. He got out and walked to her front door, then rang the bell three times to allow more time to pass between rings. Nothing. He banged on the door. Nothing. He banged again—harder. Nothing from inside, although a neighbor opened her own door and peeked out.

"Can I help you, son?"

In this case, 'son' didn't offend Kit in the least. He had a pair of grandmothers her age, and this form of address under the circumstances was consequently familiar—and welcome.

"I'm looking for Daneka Sorensen. I have reason to believe she's inside, and that something may be—." The woman studied Kit for an instant.

"Yes," she said. "I think I've seen you here before. Mind you, I'm not nosy," she lied. "But I believe I heard Miss Sorensen talking to someone on the telephone just a few minutes ago. She was out all day—probably at work. But then she came home about forty-five minutes ago. She sounded upset and made a telephone call. I haven't heard anything since."

Kit made a mental note to befriend this woman. She could probably tell him quite a bit about Daneka's 'dog-walking habits.'

"Would you happen—," he was about to ask her if she might have a key. Until, that is, the woman quite 'serendipitously' produced one herself.

"Why don't you try this?" she suggested. "I'm sure she wouldn't mind—you being a nice young man and all."

"Thank you very, very much, Mrs. —?"

"Parker-Bradford," the lady said as she extended a hand. "Rosie Parker-Bradford. Just 'Rosie' to friends, mind you. I don't generally keep tabs on my neighbors, you understand. I'm frankly too busy just keeping tabs on *myself!*" she giggled. "But in Miss Sorensen's case, I make an exception. She seems to have a pretty busy night life, and I rather like to stay up with the times—if you know what I mean. I can't stay up with the owls anymore and I certainly can't stay up with her, but I keep an ear out just to make sure everything's all right."

"And I'm sure she's very grateful for that. Everyone should have such a guardian angel," Kit added with a smile. He opened Daneka's door and handed the key back to her. "Thanks again."

"Well, you just call again if you need anything." Kit looked briefly over her shoulder as she took the key. He noticed a glass standing bottom up on a table next to the wall separating the elderly lady's living-room from Daneka's. No, of course she didn't "keep tabs." She just liked to listen. And if a water glass helped her to listen better, well, then— who was *he* to find fault. Kit was suddenly thankful they'd never had sex in the living-room.

From the front door, he could hear the shower running. *That would explain why she didn't hear me ringing or knocking,* he thought. He walked back and peeked around the corner of the bathroom door. There she sat, hair wet, in terrycloth robe, on the edge of the bathtub. Kit reached in and turned off the water. She didn't react. He pulled her up and into the bedroom. She didn't resist; instead, she started to untie her belt.

"Don't bother," he deadpanned.

She dropped her hands, then walked—very precisely—to her vanity, where she sat down, picked up a hairbrush and attempted, listlessly, to brush the tangles our of her hair. He gave her a minute, during which he studied her lifeless and repetitive movements, then noticed the bandage on her arm. When she showed no sign of stopping, he walked over and took the brush out of her hand. She didn't object. He pulled her up out of her chair, and her robe fell open. That's when he noticed.

"*Jesus*, Daneka! What's *this?*" he said as he pushed the robe off her shoulders and let it drop to the floor. She registered nothing, made no effort to cover herself up, no effort to hide the multiple bruises from the base of her neck clear down to her knees. In places where her skin was not red or purple, it was stretched, lined or waterlogged. She looked as if she'd aged twenty years since he'd last seen her naked. Her nipples were raw, her breasts scratched. He turned her around. She didn't resist. Welts lined her buttocks and upper torso, and the backs of her thighs showed what looked like teeth marks. "I want to know. *Now!*"

"Oh. Those. I fell off my bicycle riding in the park," she said as she picked up her robe.

"You don't *have* a fucking bicycle, Daneka! Come clean with me right fucking now or I'm history. *We're* history."

"I thought you—and we—already were. I thought maybe you'd just come back for your little houseplant. Or to see if I'd joined the daughters of the air like a good little mermaid."

"Stop fucking with me, Daneka!"

"Oh, is that what we're doing?"

"Where were you today? I called here several times," he lied. "I called your magazine," he lied again. "They didn't even know you were back in town. Your P.A. told me you were still in Europe. I looked up Ron's number," he lied a third time, "and I called him. He thought the same thing as your P.A. Where the fuck were you?"

With each mention of a new avenue of investigation, Kit noticed that Daneka's face had turned a brighter shade of red. Perhaps she was actually ashamed. If she had a conscience, he could still reach her. Without a trace of it, he knew, the case was hopeless. He held his breath.

"You did *what?*" she screamed. He had his answer. "Who gave you permission to call my place of work? Who gives you permission right now to ask me anything at all? My life-style and I don't require your particular approval, Kit. Who the fuck do you think you are anyway? Some little two-bit photographer and petty landscaper with a fondness for strawberries and kinky bananas is what you are! *Fuck you, Kit!*"

Her mention of bananas now made him feel acutely ashamed. He would never forgive himself for that. At the same time, he understood her tactic and had no intention of letting it—and her—succeed. He might not be able to help her back from the brink, but he was not going to allow himself to be insulted and belittled at the same time.

"How easily we've gone—and how little time it's taken us to get there—from 'fuck me' to 'fuck you,'" he said.

"Yeah, fuck you! Fuck you! *Fuck you!*" she screamed through a spray of saliva.

"You forgot to add 'harder,'" he said at the same level tone.

She swung. He saw it coming, however, and grabbed her wrist in mid-swing. Unfortunately for Daneka, he grabbed it hard—and it was the injured wrist. She cried out in pain.

Although he was at that moment livid and wanted to give back as good as he was getting, it hadn't been his intention to hurt her physically. She sat down on the bed in apparent agony. He took her arm with one hand and unwrapped the gauze with the other. When he saw the wound, he remembered the exact circumstances that had produced it in the first place.

He went to the bathroom, took a fresh washcloth off the shelf and put it under cold water. He then wrung it out, returned to her side and applied the cloth with a firm but gentle pressure to stop the bleeding. He would've liked to offer an apology, but decided against it.

After a few minutes, Daneka put her hand on Kit's and left it there. It might—he realized—be the last time she'd ever touch him with anything like affection.

Chapter 73

Daneka began her story slowly, calmly, as seemingly detached from it as she now was from everything and everyone else. If Kit appeared to be unmoved by her narration, appearances in this case were not an attempt at dissimulation. That's not to say that he was unmoved by the tragedy of it, but rather that he was unmoved by the *meta*-tragedy, by whatever it was that had compelled her to keep this story a secret for so long. He also suspected it might not be altogether true.

"I have a daughter—Annemette. You know that already. She lives in the West Village. She doesn't go to school. I pay for her tutoring—she's essentially home-schooled, though not by me. At an early age, I had her at Trinity. She lived with me. Trinity was the ideal place for young children, and she was happy there. While the other kids got smarter, however, she didn't. It became apparent that she wasn't going to succeed at Trinity.

"I found a studio apartment for her in the West Village and moved her in. I visit with her three, four times a week—usually for dinner. When my mother comes to visit, she always stays with her. She says she prefers Annemette's place—and Annemette's neighborhood—to mine.

"The first call I make from work every day is to her. Often, too, the last call."

"And her father?" Kit asked. "Where is he?"

"Dead. He died before she was born."

"Suicide?" It was a risk, but Kit was willing to take it. If he could somehow get her to trust him, he still felt there might be a way back.

Daneka didn't even raise an eyebrow. "No. He died a natural death. He was much older. He was also quite wealthy by Danish standards. That's how I managed to get out of Rønne and come here to New York. I had enough to pay for college and then two years of J-School—and to keep an apartment up on Amsterdam not far from the campus."

"But why the secrecy until now? I don't understand. I also don't understand why you call her 'Annemette' while your mother calls her 'Margarette.' Is 'Annemette' some kind of pet name?"

"You'll understand better when you see her."

"Then let's go."

"Tomorrow's soon enough. As a matter of fact, we can do the shoot tomorrow if that works for you."

"*Now*, Daneka!"

She looked at him and knew, at a glance, that her options had run out. "Okay, fine. Let's go."

She called Ron. "Be here in fifteen minutes. We'll meet you downstairs." That was it. No "how-do-you-do." No "nice to hear your voice again, Ron." Just "be here." Kit hoped she paid him well.

Daneka threw on a pair of jeans—no frills or make-up. They took the elevator down, walked out and past the doorman, then arrived curbside just as Ron did. She gave him the destination, nothing else.

Traffic at that evening hour was heavy as they traveled down Fifth Avenue. As soon as he got to 79th Street, Ron turned right into the park, crossed it and came out the other side. He then continued on over Central Park West, Columbus, Amsterdam, Broadway and West End. When he reached Riverside Drive, he turned left and headed downtown.

Fifteen minutes later, Ron turned left again at 14th Street and drove into the Meat District. Even with the windows up, it smelled beefily obscene. 'Carnal' was the word that next came to Kit's mind as he surveyed the odd juxtaposition of warehouses and whorehouses, the bright reds of fresh sides of beef alternating with the soft reds of lights behind curtains suggesting an equally meaty commerce—if not quite so fresh. The entrances to some of the clubs were either gaudy well beyond bad taste or simply sinister in their depravity. As if it were possible to excel in this too *excellent* sea of black and red, one locale in particular looked as if it might even smell bad. Or maybe it really did—and Kit was made aware of the smell only because Ron seemed to have slowed down as they approached it. There was no neon or other sign to announce its mission or purpose—just a distinctly brutish-looking doorman standing in front. To Kit, the man looked as if, in childhood, sunshine had never been this boy's companion.

Kit noticed that Ron was looking at Daneka in the rearview mirror as if expecting to get a signal of some kind from her. None came. He continued on for another block and a half.

"This is good, Ron," she finally said.

He pulled the car over not to the curb—there was none here—but to cobblestones running down and merging with the asphalt. Kit looked down and noticed a pool of water—black as night, but with a distinct, *sub rosa* tinge of red as if the secret of its coloring might be hinted at, but not openly divulged. Ron drove through it and brought the car up on dry land. Kit opened his door, and both he and Daneka stepped out.

She led him up to the front door after the two of them had mounted a chipped cement stoop. She rang the buzzer—two short rings, followed by one long ring, followed by another two short ones. Kit assumed it was some kind of secret code she and Margarette—or Annemette—used as a signal.

His assumption was confirmed when the buzzer on the inside of the front door sounded and the door sprang loose from its electronic latch. Daneka pushed it open, and they ascended three flights of stairs to the top floor. A single, bare, fluorescent bulb illuminated each floor except the top one, which might've been entirely dark but for the light leaking out from under an apartment door.

The door opened just wide enough for one curious eye to peer out. Satisfied that that visitor was the same one who'd just sent an encoded signal from downstairs, the door opened further. Kit saw a face and heard a voice.

"Mama!" the voice said. Kit thought it was the loneliest sound he'd ever heard.

The girl whose voice he'd just heard opened the door wide enough for the two of them to walk through. In the dim light, Kit looked hard at her and decided that she was, in fact, no girl at all, but a woman not too much younger than he. *How's that possible?* he wondered.

He made a quick survey of the room before he sat down. It was bare except for the essentials: one table; two chairs; one sofa more the size of a loveseat, but clearly not serving that purpose; a single bed in the corner of the room—a single pillow upon it—a single lamp standing next to the bed and serving as the only source of light for the entire room. Windows which might otherwise look out onto a street and therefore offer some source of light—at least during daylight hours—were boarded up with cardboard.

Before he could think too hard or long about any of this, his attention was arrested by the sounds coming out of the mouth of this girl-woman: slow; deliberate; barely audible. Daneka's answers were also slow and deliberate, though clearly audible. Kit realized with a start that this girl-woman—this daughter of Daneka, this long-withheld secret, this "Margarette" to one and "Annemette" to the only other women remaining in the Sørensen family—was severely retarded.

Kit collapsed onto one of the two available chairs and listened to the labored way in which Daneka explained to Annemette-Margarette that she and Kit would return the next morning without fail, bright and early, to take her to his place in order to take her picture. Upon hearing the mention of Kit's name, the girl looked up and noticed his presence for the first time. It was just a brief acknowledgment, however, before she ducked again behind her mother and grabbed her around the waist.

The girl implored her mother not to leave—not yet. Daneka continued to comfort her—but with words and gestures, Kit thought, more suitable to a small animal. The petting eventually achieved its desired result: she calmed down. But not before Kit, taking advantage of Daneka's distraction, was able to slip the picture of Dagmar out of his wallet and put it, face down, on the table. Daneka then managed to walk her daughter to the bed and get her to lie down. Once supine and so, no longer quite able to keep her arms around Daneka's waist, she put the thumb of one hand into her mouth and the other hand between her legs. Daneka continued to stroke her hair until she eventually fell asleep.

Daneka signaled wordlessly to Kit that they could now leave. They slipped quietly out the door, and she tested the knob to make sure it had locked from the inside.

Once back outside, and as if by mutual consent, they walked. Ron followed at a distance and drove at a pace mimicking their own, with only parking lights illuminating the car's forward motion and an occasional street lamp illuminating their path. Daneka announced she wanted some supper, and they stopped in at a small restaurant off Bleeker Street. She ordered a hamburger, very rare, with raw onions. Kit ordered a glass of white wine. They didn't talk.

At the conclusion of their meal, Daneka was the first to speak. "Shall we go?"

"Yes, let's."

She got up from the table, handed Kit her credit card and walked out the front door. Kit paid the bill and signed the credit card receipt, then followed her out to where Ron had parked the car. Daneka already sat in the back seat, her door open. Kit ducked down and stuck his head in, but found himself at a loss for words. Instead, he returned her credit card and added the receipt.

"Aren't you getting in?" she asked.

"No. I think I'll walk."

"All the way to 96th Street? Don't be ridiculous."

"No. All the way to St. Marks Place. It's just a few blocks across town. I'm going home."

Daneka looked at Kit with a kind of dumb curiosity for a few seconds, then closed the door. "The Fitzgerald, Ron," he saw rather than heard her say just before the door bolted shut.

Chapter 74

Kit walked—lost once again in this newer miasma of contradictions, all stinking even worse than the offal of the meat district he'd just left behind. That there was no way back for her was now clear. If she could treat her own daughter this way, how much worse could she treat him? The answer wasn't something he even cared to contemplate. Only one thing drove him now: self-preservation. He was in deeper than he'd ever been; deeper, he considered, than he'd likely ever be again. One didn't just dismiss a love affair like this—unless one happened to be a woman named 'Daneka.'

He crossed Fourth Avenue onto Astor Place, then walked on across Third Avenue to the brief expanse of Cooper Square and on to St. Marks Place. Once home again in the East Village, he picked up his pace as he walked past familiar brownstones and eventually arrived at his own. He bounded up the stoop past the same three squatters he'd seen there roughly three weeks earlier. The stoop to his building had apparently become their favorite hang-out. The same sweet-smelling Goth of a girl gave him the same sweet smile; he gave her his own in return. Maybe one day, after all. But just not today.

He bounded up the stairs to the fifth floor, opened the door to his apartment, stepped in and turned on a light. If he was going to brood, Kit decided, he'd brood constructively. Straightening up—hardly one of his favorite activities—was long overdue; he'd barely touched the place in almost a month.

He first checked to see whether there was anything rotting in the refrigerator or bathroom. There wasn't. He then took down the only photo of Daneka still hanging from the clothesline and put it on a pile of things he wanted to take to work the next day. This subtraction was followed in short order by the clothesline itself. A few other odds and ends and—an hour later—he was ready for a shower and bed.

Just before turning in, he opened the window to a full moon. It wasn't the Northern Lights, and moonbeams over Manhattan were hardly powdered sugar. But they'd do for now.

Daneka, in the meantime, had long since arrived home. Finally spared the distraction of a constant lover, she could be diligent in preparing for her first day back to work. There'd be lots of matters to attend to, and she wanted to get them all organized as quickly as possible. In her bedroom, she first made a list of tasks—each of which she intended to check off just as soon as she'd accomplished it. Cleaning or straightening up was not on the list; Estrella had already seen to that. She looked around to determine whether there might be some item Estrella had overlooked, noticed two and wrote them down. She read the list over to herself. When she finished, she stood up, clapped her hands once, then commenced with her first task.

She walked to her nightstand and picked up the picture of Kit. As she started to disassemble the frame, intent upon removing and then shredding the picture, she dismissed the activity as too time-consuming. Instead, she simply dropped picture and frame into the trash, then went back and checked the item off.

She next went into the living room, picked up the lichen and took it into the kitchen. She opened the door beneath the kitchen sink to pull out a garbage bag, reconsidered, then turned on both the water and the garbage disposal. The ten-thousand-year growth of lichen was ground up and gone within seconds. She washed and rinsed her hands, dried them on a dish towel, then returned to her bedroom to check off the second item. "Done!" she pronounced to herself with evident satisfaction.

Within a couple of hours, Daneka had accomplished her tasks, had checked them all off, had then shredded the list. She showered, took her terrycloth robe off the hanger, thought again, walked over to her computer and booted it up as she arranged the robe like a seat cushion. A little playtime before bedtime was in order, and the robe would absorb any effluent.

Twenty recreational minutes later—all submissions responded to, all emissions evanesced—she logged off, crawled in under the covers and went immediately and soundly to sleep.

Further down the island, Kit couldn't find his way to sleep quite so easily. He glanced at his alarm clock for confirmation just as he heard church bells chime out four o'clock. The necessity of self-preservation was one thing; the accomplishment of something as simple as sleep, quite another.

Chapter 75

Daneka rose early—and at the precise instant Kit finally managed to fall asleep. Moments after showering, she called Ron and asked him to be waiting outside in thirty minutes. Yes, she explained, she was getting an early start—her first day back to work after an absence of a little over two weeks.

When she walked out the front door of The Fitzgerald, the car was already waiting curbside. So was Mr. Kelly's replacement—another Michael—with a smile, a salute and an open back door. Daneka nodded a greeting to The Fitzgerald's newest employee and glided into the back seat without breaking stride. Ron put the car into gear, crossed Madison and then turned left into Fifth Avenue. At that early hour, there was bustle, certainly, but the traffic lights on Fifth were all synchronized to keep a fleet of chauffered limos moving without interruption. The power brokers of New York needed just enough time to peruse the major stories in *The Wall Street Journal*. They didn't require the inconvenience of extra stops and starts to catch up on the rest of the world in the *Post* or *Daily News*. Daneka was in the publishing business—and so, her paper of record was of course *the* paper of record. At the same hour, the readers of esoterica could be counted on to have their news-hunting noses in *The Observer*—and the readers of exotica, to have theirs in *The Voice*.

She looked over the front page of the *Times* as her car sped southward the fifty-four short blocks to 42nd Street—short indeed, she thought, but marble- and granite-hard in cash, convertibles, and other cash equivalents. She looked up ten minutes later as her car passed the Pierre on the left, then the Plaza on the right. Front doors were still shut tight on Bergdorf's and Tiffany's as those two monuments to commerce also passed by seconds later in a blur. One day soon, she thought to herself, she really should arrange to have breakfast at Tiffany's—and she'd make sure it was accompanied by a brisk bottle of *Veuve Cliquot*.

At 42nd Street, Ron turned right—leaving Grand Central behind and passing under the peripheral gaze of stone lions in front of the New York Public Library, followed by Bryant Park on the left. Up past the granite sweep of the W. R. Grace building, followed by the now Disney-kitschified stretch of 42nd Street between Sixth and Seventh Avenues, she could already begin to smell the approach of Times Square and her home away from home.

Ron pulled the car up in front of her building. As Daneka opened the door and was about to step out, she noticed an outstretched hand, then looked up into a familiar face. Robert, her always ready and reliable Art Director, assisted her out and up in one smooth motion.

"Welcome back! We've missed you," he said, all chivalry and smiles.

"Oh, but it's nice to *be* back!" She ducked once again into the car. "Usual time, Ron?"

"Yes, ma'am," he said. She was gone—leaving Robert to close her car door and catch up to her in time to open the building's front door. She glided through as unimpeded by glass as her car had glided unimpeded by traffic or traffic lights, then paused only long enough at the elevator to let Robert catch up once again.

"Going my way?" she asked, bending her neck at *just* such an angle. It was—Robert now thought to himself—one of the many things he adored about her.

"Yes, ma'am, I do believe I am," he said, extending a gallant arm, which she took before the two of them crossed the threshold. As the elevator ascended—stopping now and again to allow other passengers to get off—she questioned him about work. He knew better than to ask her anything about personal matters—especially in such a public place—and waited until they'd stepped off at the top floor.

"So, how was the trip?"

"The first week was mostly business-related. Then I spent a week with my mother, and of course that was delightful. We're such a pair, she and I. More like sisters, really."

"Don't we wish we could all say that about our parents!" Robert replied with a groan.

"Believe me. I know how fortunate I am."

"Well, it's certainly nice to have you back!"

"Thank you, Robert. Let's try to have lunch again this week or next. I never did find that photographer I was looking for. And so, maybe you can help me after all."

"I'll be happy to," Robert said before walking off in the direction of his office.

Kit awakened several hours later—unrested; disoriented; despondent. He wondered about the shoot with Margarette: would it still be on, or was that little project—like everything else—already old news? He thought he'd wait an hour to see if she called.

He needn't have wondered a second—much less waited an hour.

He eventually collected his things and went off to his studio. Upon entering, he greeted Rachel with a brief nod, then walked stone-faced back to his cubicle.

Rachel was young and hip, but not insensitive. She wondered whether her remark of the previous day had wounded him in any way. She liked Kit too much to tolerate the thought. It was almost lunchtime. Maybe she, for a change, would buy the pizza. She scrounged down in her purse to see what she had left between now and payday. It wasn't much, but she'd gladly give up dinner in exchange for some peace of mind.

She left the studio and went to the corner pizzeria where she bought two slices with pepperoni and one iced tea with a pair of straws—then returned, dropped her purse at her station and went back to Kit's cubical. He was sitting hunched over, his hands under his chin, staring out the window. She tried, as noiselessly as possible, to extract his slice from the bag; but Kit heard the rustle of paper and turned around.

"What's this, Rachel?"

"Oh, nothing much. Just a little snack is all." She looked at Kit and saw something in his eyes she'd never seen there before. *My God*, she thought. *He's not going to cry, is he?*

"Oh, Kit. Please, *please* tell me it's not because of what I said yesterday!" Kit looked at her in confusion, then thought back to their brief dialogue of the day before. That she might think her flippant remark about his being an 'old guy' would be the cause of his despondency both amused and impressed him. *How different two women can be*, he thought. He realized he should lighten up a bit, that he wasn't alone in the world, that he had a responsibility to not infect others with his sense of loss.

He stood up and did something he would otherwise never have considered doing as either possible or appropriate: he embraced Rachel. For the first time in his life, he had a paternal interest in another human being … and it made him realize he might not be wrong for the role one day.

Rachel, for her part, came to a similar realization. She'd always liked Kit—but as an older colleague and sometimes, even, as a kind of mentor. She'd had other men's arms around her from time to time, but those arms had had a different interest, a different objective. They'd embraced her differently, and what she'd felt in response to that kind of embrace was also quite different.

She allowed herself to wallow in the warmth and security of Kit's embrace—and then the tears came, which she couldn't have anticipated, didn't know she had, but now didn't want to stop. These were not cold, lonely tears, but the contrary—and they felt wonderful on her cheeks.

She didn't want to let go of this man. He—and his embrace—felt too good. Eventually, however, she did. When she next looked up at Kit with happy eyes, she was also desperately in need of a tissue. Kit put his hand inside his shirt, scrunched up the material, then put it to her nose. "Blow," he said.

And blow she did.

Chapter 76

At the end of the workday, and feeling much better than when he'd arrived that morning, Kit decided he'd accomplished enough. There was only one thing he still needed to do before leaving, and that was to unpack and put away the items he'd brought from home in a plastic bag. Everything else could wait.

He hauled up the bag and began to lay things out: papers, letters, receipts, knick-knacks—and the picture of Daneka. Perhaps, just for the sake of sentimentality, he'd buy another frame with his next paycheck and set the picture up on his desk—at least until there was someone else's picture to put in place of hers. He wasn't, after all, already too old to have a girlfriend. As he was giving the black and white print one more glance before putting it away, a model walked by his cubical, paused, then leaned in over his shoulder.

"Hey, I've seen that woman before," she said unprompted.

Kit turned to her. She was—like all of them—quite stunning, even if a little dicey-looking for a model. "You have? You're sure?"

"Sure I'm sure. I saw her just yesterday. I didn't have a shoot and I wasn't in the mood for Molière—so I went out to scrimmage."

"What? You saw her in the park? You saw her playing *football?*" Kit laughed. "Nah, not this one. There's only one contact sport this one plays—and she doesn't scrimmage."

"Uh, *duh!* I don't play either. I was speaking metaphorically." Kit looked at her more closely. He'd known some sharper tacks in his day, but never one who could pull a metaphor out of her hip pocket like a spare licorice stick.

"Where are you from? Boise?"

"Barnard, darling. The college, that is—not the town. I'm a campus flower. Have to be until next year—my senior year."

"And before that? Home, I mean—where your parents live."

She stepped back, fluffed up her hair, then pushed her jeans down to a point just south of decent, north of anatomical.

"Staten Island, doll—born and bred." Kit stared at her for a long moment. His first acquaintance with a model from Staten Island. *That might explain the slightly saucy look. But Barnard? C'mon! Time for a litmus test.*

"How many squares would a square root wreck if a square root wrecked for a reason?"

She didn't even blink. "Nope. 'Don't wanna chuck. You're an *old* guy. I don't chuck with old guys—unless, well, they also happen to be loaded—and I don't mean with fourfold roots. I mean with enough payola to give *me* adequate and sufficient reason. Now," she said coyly, "we might not chuck, but we can always argue—epistemologically speaking, that is."

She'd demonstrated her credentials for both Staten Island and Barnard in fifty-plus words. "Where did you say you saw her?"

"I didn't."

"Oh, so now you *didn't* see her?"

"I didn't say that, either. I said I saw her. I didn't say where."

"Okay. So, do I have to *pay* you to get that info?"

"No. Just be nice. Make believe I'm from Boise. Can you handle it?"

"I can and I will. Promise. I'm sorry. It's been a rough couple of weeks."

The model looked again at Daneka's picture. "No doubt. That—as I recall—is the way she likes it." Kit suddenly wasn't entirely sure he wanted to learn what this woman might be able to tell him. However, his curiosity had to be satisfied—cost him what it might.

"Would you please tell me where you think you saw her?"

"'You sure you can deal with it? You look young to me." Kit's age, they both knew, was up on hers by at least a decade.

"You just called me an *old* guy."

"You're an old guy to me. But you may be a tad young for Nate's."

"Nate's? What is Nate's?"

"A club. A private club. *Very* private."

"What kind of club."

"Not a country club, darling. *Ohhh*, no."

"Do you have a name? Mine's Kit. So, please don't call me 'darling.'"

"Just call me 'Nove.' That's what I'm called at Nate's. You got a problem with 'darling?'"

"Nove? What kind of name is 'Nove?' Yes, I do."

"To the rest of the world, my name is Evon. But at Nate's, everything is backwards. What's your problem with 'darling?'"

"What's up with 'backwards?' Don't worry about my problem. It's *my* problem."

"I have no idea. I asked once. They told me Nate had a thing for palindromes. I didn't figure it was my business to set them straight on definitions. I don't go to Nate's to educate. I go there to *get* educated."

"And what kind of education is that?"

"You'll have to find out for yourself. It's not like they put out a syllabus or anything. They expect their customers to pay before they play."

"And the price to play?"

She rotated slowly and pushed her rear end provocatively out at him. Her jeans were still riding at half-mast and covered only what fell below the dimples. The contours of her buttocks were set off like a nice pair of parentheses by a bit of floss that resembled a thong—but in name only. "For me?" She left the answer to be inferred from a little slap she gave herself on one of the contours.

"Where's it located?"

"In the Village."

"The Village is a big place."

"Be nice. Remember?"

"Sorry. Where, more precisely, in the Village?"

"The meat district. On 13th Street. Don't look for neon or a billboard. Just look for a doorman. Big, ugly guy. I think he also bounces. There's a brass plate next to the door. It sorta says 'Nate's'—except that the 's' and the apostrophe are at the head-end rather than at the ass-end. Either they're totally illiterate, or it's Nate's idea of a palindrome."

Kit smiled. "Thanks. You've been very helpful."

"No prob. And the next time you need a lady to ride a leopard, lemme know. I generally get $1,500 an hour, but I'm worth it. The camera doesn't give a fuck about either Staten Island or Barnard. And *I* know how to work the spots off even a leopard."

"I'm sure you do, Evon. I'm sure you do."

Chapter 77

Kit decided to go on foot. The location of this club—if it was the same one he now had in mind—was only five or six blocks away. There'd probably be an entrance fee of some kind and it wouldn't be trifling: the more exotic the venue, he knew, the higher the price. He'd no doubt exceed his overdraft privileges and have to pay a penalty, but he needed an answer.

He headed down Fifth Avenue and stopped at the first available ATM, from which he withdrew three hundred in crisp twenties, then stashed them in his pants. When he got to 13th Street five minutes later, he turned right into longer blocks and numbered avenues. In a matter of fifteen minutes, two stark things met his gaze at a distance not diminished by twilight: the first was Daneka's car; the second—and a block further west—the club, or at least a token of it: the club's doorman. Kit looked to his right and thought he recognized Margarette's apartment building, though there was little to distinguish one set of bricks from another in this part of the Village. He continued walking. As he approached Daneka's car, he noticed Ron in the front seat with head bowed—either snoozing or reading, Kit thought. In any case, if Ron had seen and recognized Kit at a distance, he was now choosing not to acknowledge him.

The doorman came into sharper focus as Kit left the vehicle behind. He realized it was parked—*perhaps strategically?* he wondered—halfway between the club and what he believed to be Margarette's building.

He looked more closely at the doorman, who sported a scowl, two-day-old growth and a long coat, the color of bishop's purple. *How appropriate*, Kit thought. He also noted the coat was badly in need of a clean, especially from the waist down. He was a bull of a man—a bull who apparently spent too much time in the mud—or whatever it was that besmeared and bespattered his overcoat.

Kit glanced past the man to the front door and saw the brass plate Evon had spoken of—polished to a high gloss, with letters in black *bas-relief*. He saw the name "Nate," but it was keeping some awkward company, the meaning of which Kit couldn't even begin to decipher. It was either gibberish or Gaellic—Kit didn't know which. But if Gaellic, he thought, maybe Nate was related in some way to Michael Kelly. Hell, maybe even this doorman was related to Michael Kelly—and of the same Irish stock gone raffishly to seed.

He decided to try to bluff his way in and reached for a shiny brass door handle.

"And just where the fuck you think *you're* going, clown?"

"In," Kit answered.

"Not here you're not. This club's private. No kids allowed—unless they've got the right credentials."

"And what might those be?" Kit's question elicited a smirk from the doorman that made 'evil' sound like a nice word.

"Tits and ass for starters. A good pair of lips for finishers."

"And if I can't offer either?"

"Then you're shit outta luck. Cause I don't care dick about dick."

"Well, then, maybe you could just help me out with a little information," Kit said, reaching into his pants pocket. "You see, I'm trying to find my mother. I think she may be in there—'walking the dog,' so to speak."

Kit noticed the doorman reach inside his own coat at the same instant. The doorman withdrew his hand again only after he'd seen what Kit was reaching for. A low rumble greeted Kit's ears, and he wasn't sure whether the source of it was the subway or the doorman.

"Your mama got a pussy? Or are you it?" he asked.

"My *mama* flicks off fuckers like you just for kicks," Kit answered.

"That so?" the doorman sniffed. "Could be. We get a couple of elderly ladies here from time to time. The price of admission? If they come alone—as they usually do—they gotta eat me first. I'm tellin' ya—even young pussy can't compete with an older lady's lips— especially when she's desperate to get through that door. The older ones know how to suck like a shop floor vac."

Whatever thoughts Kit might've once had about doormen on the Upper East Side, he now realized there was a whole species at an evolutionary level far below them—and that he'd just met one sparkling specimen.

"Well, you see, my mother's still got all her front teeth, so I doubt she's had the pleasure."

"Oh. Still got her teeth, has she? Well, then, she'd most likely not be on the inside.

Cause by the time I'm finished with 'em, they're lucky if they still got their molars."

Kit saw his opening. "You mind, then, if I just take a peek?"

"Gotta become a member first."

"How much are we talking?"

"A hunderd." Kit counted out five twenties and handed them over. He then reached again for the door handle. "Hold on there, kid. Not so fast. Membership may have its privileges, but who said one of 'em gets you through the door?"

"What are you talking about? I just paid you for that privilege."

"No, not really. You just paid the annual dues, so now you're a member. But there's still the matter of a cover charge to open that door and get a peek."

"And how much would the cover charge be?" Kit spat out.

"If you wanna get nasty, maybe you can't afford it. You wanna be nice? I may be willing to discuss price."

"And how much, Sir, might the cover charge be?" Kit asked mock-politely.

"Much better. Cover charge is another hunderd."

Kit counted out five additional twenties and gave them up. As he then grasped the door handle and was about to open the door, he wondered for an instant what sort of childhood could produce an animal like this one.

"Peek only, remember?" the doorman said.

"What the fuck are you talking about? I just paid you a hundred for membership and a hundred to enter."

"Oh, no," the doorman laughed. "You paid to peek. You wanna *go* inside? You gotta have a ticket."

Kit was finding it increasingly difficult to keep his rage under control. "So where do I purchase a ticket?"

"You don't purchase. You bring."

"Huh?"

"A ticket's a little lady. A chick. A pussy. No guy gets inside without one. Club rules. Strictly enforced."

"You might've told me that right up front, fucker. It's clear I didn't come here with a date."

- 403 -

They stood at an impasse—until, that is, serendipity waved to Kit from a distance. He looked over the doorman's shoulder and saw Evon walking up the street in their direction. She wasn't carrying groceries or even a purse to pay for them. He waited in silence until she arrived. She assessed the situation in an instant, then spoke directly to the doorman.

"I'm his ticket," she said before giving Kit a kiss on the cheek. She then opened the door, walked in and let the door close behind her. The doorman looked on as she glided right on through and out of sight, then looked back at Kit.

"Your lucky fucky day, kid."

"Yeah. Like you say—my 'lucky fucky day.'" Kit was about to reach again for the door handle when the man leaned down and stopped him with an outstretched paw.

"What's your name, kid?"

"What's it to you?"

"Just trying to be helpful is all. Just trying to give you some 'inside' before you *get* inside."

"Name's 'Kit.'"

"Well then, if you wanna remain—as they say here—'nonymous, you tell 'em 'Kit' on the inside and they'll turn it around to 'Tik.' You want folks to call you by your real name, you tell 'em on the inside your name's 'Tik.' They'll turn it around to 'Kit.' Your choice." And then he stood back up and smirked again before delivering a spoonful of his own lackluster wit. "Tick," he said. "Blood-sucking tick. Go suck some, sucker."

Kit turned away, grasped the door handle, then glanced once more at the brass plate next to it and read "Enola niaga ecno s'nate." *Sure enough. Either gibberish or Gaellic.*

Kit all but reeled back on his heels at the assault on his ears. The place was so dark and clinical-smelling, hearing was the only sense he could make immediate use of. The music sounded otherworldly—hideous if not downright hellish. As his pupils adjusted to the darkness, he stepped forward. Something or someone—he couldn't *see* anything, but now, at least, he could feel—shoved something into his gut. A second something or someone screamed into his ear: "Take your clothes off and put them in the basket."

He hesitated, but a hand he could now make out directly in front of his eyes snapped its fingers. The fingernails, Kit noted, were long and painted day-glo-pink. The finger-snapping was not in syncopation to the music, but was rather a clear command for action—an order to strip, fast and final. Kit hadn't just spent two hundred dollars to stop now. What he wanted to know was somewhere up there in front of him—he could see the shimmer of strobe lights from around a bend—and if he had to strip to get to it, so be it.

He took his clothes off and dropped them into the basket, then handed the basket back. He was ready to move on, but the hand stopped him, reached down and began to masturbate him. However distasteful the whole scenario may've been to him, the hand knew what it was doing—and it wasn't long before it had achieved its objective. A second hand, nails this time painted in purple, approached his penis with something that looked like a cock ring with a number attached to it. *So this is how they match clothes with customers,* he thought.. *How perfectly swift.* As both hands worked to get the cock ring in place, Kit wondered how they handled the women—then decided he'd rather not think about it. The hand signaled to him that it was finished.

Now barefoot, he could feel the floor. It was warm and clammy, as was the air. A few steps further on, a new voice assaulted his ear. "What's your name?"

He opted for anonymity. "Kit." And then he spelled it so there'd be no misunderstanding. "K—I—T." He felt yet another hand slide between his legs to verify gender. A third hand came up to his chest with an artist's paintbrush and day-glo paint—blue. *How nifty. Blue for boys. Pink, no doubt, for girls.* He watched as the hand holding the paintbrush wrote out "Tik," then spun him around and wrote the same—he assumed—on his back. He wondered whether he'd shortly see "Akenad" scribbled across a pair of too familiar breasts—or whether she'd be in the driver's seat and he'd consequently see the same scribbled across an otherwise anonymous back.

The hand finished and waved him on.

In the meantime, his eyes had adjusted entirely to the darkness. As he walked slowly down a long corridor, he could just barely make out an opaque black curtain hanging at the end. The strobe effects were almost completely swallowed up by the heavy black material, but there was a crack where the two halves of the curtain met, and Kit could see through it. The light on the other side was as blindingly bright as the music was deafeningly loud. Both were repulsively repetitive.

When he finally opened the curtain and stepped through, sight, sound, smell and feel all combined to produce a taste in his mouth like metal. He had, he realized, bitten his own tongue, and the result was the onset of nausea.

He saw bodies everywhere, writhing like snakes at the bottom of a too-small pit. The strobe made their movements appear spastic, made what might be smiles appear to be sneers. It was as if both Dante and Bosch had colluded in one small enclosure, and Kit's feet felt as if they were standing in a swamp.

At the head of the room was a raised stage. Through the strobes, he could just barely make out the bodies of one—or maybe two—women, and several men. The men were converging on the woman—and yes, there *were* two women, but Kit could see that the second was also converging on the first—seemingly from all directions. Their motions were too furious for Kit to make out names, although all chests and breasts clearly sparkled with the day-glo of identification. He tried to focus on the pink lettering, but breasts and backs were moving too fast for him to get a fix. He tried, instead, to focus on faces—but with no greater success.

He thought he saw—but maybe only imagined—the face of a young girl with green scales painted around her eyes, a mermaid's scales; he then thought he saw in the same figure—but maybe only imagined—an older woman, with weary intelligence instead of scales etched into rather than around her eyes; he finally thought he saw—but maybe only imagined—an old hag, a witch—in the very same woman. And then he knew he was merely hallucinating because all of the men resembled Neptune or Poseidon—less the characteristic trident.

He approached the stage stepping over bodies on the floor in front of him, up against columns to either side of him, hanging from cages overhead. He tried again to focus on the woman, but she was in the throes of something repulsive and menacing. He saw what he suspected was a name painted across her back and tried to focus on some of the letters before another body blocked his view.

The volume and the tempo of the music abruptly increased. The woman looked out from the stage with a leer for an appreciative public. He thought he recognized the face, for an instant, but then his brain—or maybe just his imagination—went into shock and blocked out the vision. He turned away and walked back towards the entrance with little or no regard for the flesh he was trampling, possibly bruising, and which apparently had as little regard for being trampled and bruised.

As he parted the curtain, he removed the cock ring with its basket number and looked for a pair of hands in the dark—with either pink or purple day-glo-painted fingernails—to offer the ring to, found a pair and promptly exchanged it for a basket. Without pausing to get dressed, he walked to the front door and exited. It was nighttime, and the street was empty except for parked cars—several of them limos—and a doorman dressed in a bishop's purple overcoat. The last sound he heard as he ducked into an alley to put his clothes back on was the rumble of a man's laugh—echoed by the rumble of the subway beneath his feet.

He dressed quickly, then headed out in the direction of home—a million thankful miles away.

Chapter 78

Kit resolved to wait her out—to wait, if necessary, until hell froze over. The weeks passed, but he heard nothing. And so, he concentrated on his work—and assumed she was doing the same. He really didn't want to think about what she might be doing when she wasn't working.

As frequently happens when the mind and body are at odds over a course of action, one or the other has to suffer the consequences. In Kit's case, it was his body.

He had little appetite and began to lose weight precipitously. He slept badly, if at all—and so, his eyes began to resemble dark caverns. Most conspicuously to himself—but also to others around him—the stress of not knowing, of not understanding, and of not being able to find resolution to his incomprehension began to show itself in his hands. He thought at first it was just the change of seasons. Fall had arrived in New York—and with it, the colder, drier weather.

He looked down at his hands and felt like an old man. No matter what he put on them—or how much—they would dry up within seconds. He could literally watch the lotions disappear into the pores. He might go through an entire jar of petroleum jelly in a day. It didn't matter. Fissures opened up between his fingers, then in his palms, and might start at any moment to bleed. He took to wearing beauty gloves at work so as to hide the state of his hands from the models—also to keep the blood off the equipment. Whenever the blood began to seep through, he'd put on a second pair of gloves over the first.

His clothes became ill-fitting, but he could easily hide what lay beneath. It was at times almost impossible to keep his eyes open; at others, impossible to close them. Still, the worst of it—because the most visible at least to him—was in his hands.

Almost three months had passed since he'd last seen her, since he'd *really* come to understand what she'd meant by 'Scandinavian silence.' The condition of his hands had deteriorated accordingly—as if they, in their sorry state, could somehow communicate his loneliness. If not to him, because he simply wouldn't acknowledge it, then somehow to her, in the form of a silent prayer she might finally understand. Kit was now at the point where he preferred to call in sick rather than show up on a set, only to have people gawk at him, too embarrassed to ask either about the gloves or about the clear evidence of something terribly wrong inside of them.

Today was Friday. Thanksgiving was less than a week away, and he'd be spending it in Radnor with his parents. They would, of course, ask about her—and he, of course, would tell them. At the same time, they'd see and ask about his hands—and he'd have to explain that, too. As he walked in circles from bed to kitchen and back again—he hadn't been to work the entire week—he realized the afternoon was fading into twilight. In just the same way, he knew that Friday would fade into Saturday, then Saturday into Sunday, then on and on without differentiation. Each day would be equal to the other, and each would be equally meaningless.

He had to act.

He left his apartment and walked to the subway station, then descended to platform level and took the Number Six uptown. He could've changed over to the Express at 42nd Street, but he was in no particular rush. The important thing was that he was finally doing something.

When his train arrived at 96th Street, he got out, ascended to street-level and walked west into a setting sun. The air was more brisk than normal, even for that time of year, and the wind kicked up acorns and leaves that the street-cleaners had not yet removed. Looking into the distance and out beyond Park, Madison and Fifth Avenues into Central Park, he noticed the maples had all put on their various costumes of fall foliage. The *palmatums* from Japan, China and Korea, in particular, were a wash of reds—from salmon and carmine to crimson, claret and fire; of yellows—from amber and straw to Paris and yellow madder; of purples—damson and dahlia, raisin, solferino and wine; and of oranges—from carnelian and carotene to burnt sienna and ochre. The more native *saccharums* and *saccharinums* were equally brilliant in their variegation, if somewhat less refined in the structure of their lobes and leaves.

Kit had already come to the conclusion in Denmark that he'd miss her in spring—and that they'd likely not have another together. But it was the fall above all other seasons, when nature symbolically bled into its second death, that he'd hoped would be theirs to share. At least once. Fall was *his* season—the season of his birth—and the time he least wanted to be alone. Not because the isolation made him feel lonely; but rather because the sublime beauty of the season was simply too great to be deprived of the company of another with whom he could share it. The colors; the chill in the air; the smells of desiccating leaves and burning chestnuts; the anticipation of winter—this was the season when his skin would otherwise come alive and burn for the nearness of another. Now, however, it was—like the leaves—dying.

The sun was just setting behind the maples in the park and rolling out a long, golden carpet down 96th Street as he arrived at the The Fitzgerald. The doorman, whose face Kit recognized only vaguely, mercifully made no effort to stop him. Kit entered the elevator, pushed the button for the thirteenth floor and ascended.

He stepped out, noticed that *someone* had recently misted the bouquet of fresh flowers in the crystal sconce next to the door, and rang the doorbell. After several seconds, he heard *someone's* footsteps approaching from the other side, then the sound of a chain jangling as *someone* slid the latch back. He next heard *someone* turn the knob, which released the latch lever and moved the bolt out of the lip. When the door finally opened, that certain *someone* standing before him was Daneka.

She stepped back and allowed him to enter, then looked down at his feet and asked him to remove his shoes. As he bent down to untie the laces, she closed the door and returned to her bedroom without a word.

Kit followed a moment later to find her seated in front of her computer. She didn't look up from the screen, but simply continued to pound away at the keys. Kit observed her in silence for a full minute, then finally spoke up.

"Daneka, is this it?"

Her answer after a pause was toneless—almost robotic—as she continued typing. "I'm not sure I understand what you're asking."

"Is this the end of the line for us?" Kit's question was followed by another, longer pause during which Daneka offered nothing in return.

"Do you think the world really gives a fuck about your magazine or my photography? It doesn't, Daneka. Life will go on without the two of us. Your magazine will survive you. Photography will survive me. The only thing that matters—and I grant you, even *it* matters very little, except to the two of us, or at least to me—is our love. The world can get by easily enough without it. But I can't—at least not at this moment.

"I'll survive this break-up. You'll clearly survive it. But every little break-up in love is a break-up in the only thing that makes life worth living. There's nothing else of any real consequence, Daneka. Not your magazine. Not my pictures—."

Although she'd finally stopped typing, Daneka didn't take her eyes off the screen.

"Listen to me," Kit continued. *"Please.* Just once—and maybe for the last time. You're not the only one who aches. I'm not the only one who aches. We're just a pair of, of—."

She looked up at him as if he'd just poured liquid *kitsch* into her ear. He caught the look and understood what it meant; also understood his error; also, finally, understood that he was trying to break through a wall that could simply not be moved—not now, not ever.

"Goodbye, Daneka. If you have nothing to say to any of this, then goodbye."

He waited five more seconds, then slowly walked down the corridor to the front door, collected his shoes, opened the door, walked out of her apartment and out of her life, he knew, for the last time.

Daneka refrained from typing long enough to hear the elevator doors open and close again. What greeted her then was silence. Estrella had gone home for the weekend; there were no children or pets about; there was no music, radio or television playing in the background. Even the sound of traffic outside her window had died. There was only silence—her own Scandinavian silence. Her fingers, poised moments earlier in mid-air over the keyboard, dropped to her lap as she lowered her head soundlessly to her chest.

Chapter 79

Kit decided to walk the eighty-seven blocks from East Ninety-sixth Street to his own little nest on the Lower East Side. The Lower East Side, he knew, was a place of aspirants. Many would fall out along the way; many would eventually move to Long Island or New Jersey once the scales tipped in favor of space and animal comforts over the relative weightlessness of raw aspiration and ambition. They wouldn't need to be pushed or even nudged. They'd know when it was time to go.

Kit wasn't yet ready to scrap all of his aspirations. Tonight, he'd allow himself to grieve. He'd grieve, of course, first for himself—but he'd also grieve for their larger loss. He believed he'd found his mate; she just hadn't found hers. And there, as they say, was the rub.

It would take him an hour and a half to walk the distance a subway train might cover in fifteen minutes. He was glad he'd decided to walk, as the physical effort would make the emotional loss seem somehow more manageable.

He stopped for a moment and allowed himself to muse upon a certain afternoon of many years earlier along the banks of a certain river: the Moika; and upon a certain Russian town: then, Leningrad; now—and as it had once been—St. Petersburg. He remembered looking out over the River Moika as he could now have looked out—had he cared to walk a few blocks further east—over the East River. But he didn't care to. At the time, the Moika had meant life; now, in contrast, the East would mean only deterioration.

Here and now, he decided, he'd return to those magical moments along the Moika.

That afternoon with Svetlana had concluded—as all such afternoons *must*—and he'd left the apartment they'd borrowed for a few hours' tryst and walked towards the bus-stop. As he walked, he heard a single male voice accompanied by a guitar. He approached and listened. This, then, would be the only real souvenir he'd leave with, would be the saddest thing he'd ever heard. It might've been the circumstances; it might've been the male voice or the lone guitar; it might've been St. Petersburg or a thousand different things. He didn't know. He didn't even know at that point who Yesinin was—much less Yesinin's poem—although he was about to find out. The world he'd comfortably known was about to come undone, and the undoer of that comfortable world was, of all things, a poet.

He'd stood and listened, and he believed nothing would ever equal that moment and that experience.

He was wrong, of course, as youth is often wrong. Twelve years would first have to pass. The equal of the pain he'd felt that early evening along the Moika was now present as he walked down First Avenue towards home. Tonight, he decided, he'd celebrate a kind of anniversary of pain.

At St. Marks Place, he turned left. When he arrived at his address less than a minute later, he greeted his three squatters. They were, he decided, becoming something like human kudzu. As he mounted the steps, she stopped him again. She was, even Kit had to admit, attractive—the Goth elements notwithstanding. *Too bad*—he was on the verge of thinking— until she stopped him short with a familiar Slavik accent.

"Good evening, stranger." Kit looked hard at her and wondered if she might be Tatiana of the next-door consignment café, the neighbor he'd never met.

"*Вы русская?*" ("Are you Russian?") he asked.

"*Да,*" ("Yes,") she answered—she was Russian. That much was certain. *Сто процентов.*" ("One hundred percent.") Neither of them blinked.

"*Бесспокойной ночи,*" ("Then *un*goodnight,") Kit answered.

"*Бес*—?" she answered. *Почему бес*—?" ("*Un?*' Why '*un?*'")

"*Потому что…*" ("Because…") and then he let it drop. She shouldn't be expected to share his grief. She didn't need to know why he'd just wished her an *un*goodnight. "*Как тебя зовут?*" ("What's your name?") He at least wanted to know her name, though he wasn't certain what difference it would make.

"*Надежда,*" she said. "*А тебя?*" ("Nadeshda. And yours?")

"Kit," he answered. "*Меня зовут* Kit." ("Mine's Kit.")

"*Мне нравится,*" ("A pleasure,") she said with a smile that allowed Kit, once again, to admire her dental endowment. This time, he was the one who leaned down and kissed her cheek. Ironic, he thought, to be kissing the cheek of a woman named 'Hope.' She tilted her cheek up to be kissed, and Kit could see that she closed her eyes at the moment his lips found it.

"Спокойной ночи," he said. ("Goodnight.")

"Спокойной ночи," she answered. ("Goodnight.")

He continued up the stoop and opened the front door, then took the stairs one by one to his fifth-floor apartment. It was entirely dark inside except for a few moonbeams trying to squeeze in through soot-covered windows, a couple of which he now opened. As if it had been sent to him as a gift, in error, he stared at a late-season harvest moon only partly concealed by the dark silhouettes of water-towers on the building next to his. It was enormous, pale orange, and as round as a perfect pumpkin. The reflected light was sufficient to show him everything he needed to find in his one-room apartment.

He went first to the refrigerator to find the bottle of Tokai he'd bought months earlier in the off-hand chance that Daneka should change her mind and show up one day unannounced. He took down a single wineglass, then reached in and pulled out his little mermaid of a corkscrew. *"Den lille havfrue,"* she'd said. "How cute," she'd added.

He cut off the top of the metallic cap, then inserted the corkscrew into the cork and worked the screw down into the bottle. The little mermaid's arm once again allowed him to pull out the cork with ease. Her hand once again fit snugly onto the glass lip of the bottle. As before, he pulled slowly and carefully, and the cork came out in one, smooth motion.

He poured himself a glass. He wasn't working at the moment—and so, he decided, he'd allow himself a glass or two.

His stereo system stood next to the open windows. He went to his closet and pulled down a box of LPs, then thumbed through them until he found what he was looking for: *Клён ты мой опавший (Maple, You Are My Falling),* by Alexander Podbolotov. Podbolotov's wasn't quite the voice Kit had heard that early evening along the Moika, but it would do.

He took the record out of its jacket, placed it carefully on the turntable, found the track and dropped the needle down gently.

Single strings of a single guitar started up out of silence, but with a background blush of balalaika. Podbolotov's voice introduced itself as if from out of a back alley—or perhaps from out of a hotel room just large enough for one dismal occupant. Kit took a long sip of the Tokai, then sat down on the widow sill.

Ты жива ещё, моя старушка?

Жив и я. Привет тебе, привет!

Пусть струится над твоей избушкой

Тот вечерний несказанный свет.

He looked down, took his gloves off and realized how profusely his hands were now bleeding. He reached for an old T-shirt he spotted on his work desk and picked it up for the purpose of stanching the flow of blood. That's when he saw it—and stared at it from his position on the sill as he listened to the next stanza of Podbolotov's song and Yesenin's verse.

Пишут мне, что ты, тая тревогу,

Загрустила шибко обо мне,

Что ты часто ходишь на дорогу

В старомодном ветхом шушуне.

It was his one attempt at translating verse—something he'd written to her six weeks earlier in a burst of energy and melancholy—and then promptly forgotten to send, just as he'd forgotten to retrieve the lichen. He picked it up, but continued to listen to Podbolotov's original rendition in Russian.

With his eyes fixed on the piece of paper in front of him, but staring at it blindly, as the combination of Podbolotov's voice and his own private reverie had him temporarily transfixed, Kit was unaware that neighbors were gathering at windows below him and across the way, turning off their television sets or radios or stereos and shushing their children. Kit couldn't have known that none of these neighbors spoke Russian, that none of them had ever even heard of Yesenin—much less read his poetry. Consequently, none of them would've known that the poet had written this poem in a hotel room in St. Petersburg—not with pen and ink as was fashionable at the time, but with his own blood, on the wall, just after he'd slit his wrists.

И тебе в вечернем синем мраке
Часто видится одно и то ж:
Будто кто-то мне в кабацкой драке
Саданул под сердце финский нож.

Ничего, родная! Успокойся.
Это только тягостная бредь.
Не такой уж горький я пропойца,
Чтоб, тебя не видя, умереть.

Я по-прежнему такой же нежный
И мечтаю только лишь о том,
Чтоб скорее от тоски мятежной
Воротиться в низенький наш дом.

Я вернусь, когда раскинет ветви
По-весеннему наш белый сад.
Только ты меня уж на рассвете
Не буди, как восемь лет назад.

Lost in his private ruminations, Kit also couldn't have known that Nadeshda, on the front stoop, heard the music only too clearly, understood the words perfectly, and knew much of Yesenin's poetry by heart—a heart that was now torn by a grief that was not hers, but which she knew belonged to all of them. She'd never read Donne in the original. But she had the heart of a Russian, and she understood with that Russian heart that "no man is an island." And so, in this moment, this near-stranger's pain—as well as Yesenin's more distant pain—became hers.

Не буди того, что отмечталось,

Не волнуй того, что не сбылось,

Слишком раннюю утрату и усталость

Испытать мне в жизни привелось.

И молиться не учи меня. Не надо!

К старому возврата больше нет.

Ты одна мне помощь и отрада,

Ты одна мне несказанный свет.

Так забудь же про свою тревогу,

Не грусти так шибко обо мне.

Не ходи так часто на дорогу

В старомодном ветхом шушуне.

The song came to an end. Kit got up from the window sill and was about to pick the record up in order to put it back in its jacket. He took another sip of wine and decided, instead, to allow himself one more reverie before retiring the LP back to his closet. This time, however, he'd also read his own translation as he listened to Podbolotov.

He dropped the needle and waited for the melody to start up again before sitting back down on the window sill.

Before bothering to look at his own efforts on paper, however, he looked east in the direction of a harvest moon, Queens, Long Island, the Atlantic Ocean, and Europe ... and he thought of their first hotel in Paris, of the bathroom plumbing and of the couple he'd watched making love across the way ... of the pool in Cabo de São Vicente and of a burning sunset over the Atlantic as he and she looked west ... of Rome, of her silhouette standing behind French doors as he looked up from the *piazza* ... of Positano, of a borrowed fisherman's boat out in the Gulf of Salerno ... of the beginnings of a garden on a tiny island in the middle of the Baltic, and of a 'special place' in the middle of the forest on that same island.

He then looked down and began reading his modest attempt at a translation of

Yesenin's brilliant and evocative verse.

Hallo one last time, dearest mother of mine,
    I trust that you're keeping my bed
as white as our birches; as starched as our pine;
    as clear as our sky overhead.

The rumour now runs: my old mother misses
    some devil—apparently me.
That devil, in truth, remembers her kisses,
    her ratty old coat and her tea.

Some evenings, I'll wager, the vision's perverse:
    a tavern; your boy in a brawl
with sailors whose cunning eviscerates; worse:
    his verse scuds to blood on the wall.

Now pause for a moment to think this one through;
    and tell me I've failed to comply
with wending what may not seem homeward to you,
    but *is*, with a kiss, on the fly.

I think rather not—and trust you'll make haste
    to give this old rumour the lie.
The truth is I'm homesick and don't want to waste
    one swinish night more in this sty.

In spring, I'll come running back home to your arms
    outstretched, bearing handfuls of sage,
if you'll just relinquish those motherly charms
    that can't come to grips with my age

and leave me to suffer my hedonist's binge
    on wine-baited women and song,
the better to serve them my head on a fringe
    of lace—as they've asked all along.

But please don't suggest that redemption and grace
    can somehow be gotten by prayer;
you are the steeple I mount for the chase,
    the blue-ribbon prize at the fair.

So, empty your pail full of nettles and needs,
    and don't let our cabin grow cold;
then strip your decrepit old coat of its beads
    and hang it outside to be sold.

In his concentration, Kit couldn't have known that all activity and foot-traffic on the street below had come to a halt; that even the rappers had turned off their boom boxes and now stood listening; that as distant as this rhythm, this music and this language were from their own experience, they, too, felt it with an unaccustomed poignancy.

In her perfect understanding, Nadeshda could be of no help to any of them—least of all to Kit. While she understood with both her mind and her heart that each of them was simply "a piece of the continent," she knew, too, that every man's grief was ultimately his own. As she sat down on the stoop and put her head in her arms, she would've gladly—as her name implied—taken all of their collective grief upon herself. But she couldn't. She had looked into Kit's eyes; had felt his lips upon her cheek; had smelled him up close. He was in pain—that was clear—but he'd survive. He had the smell and the feel of a survivor. It would only be a matter of time, she knew, and of hope.

Chapter 80

The next day, Kit got up at his usual hour. He showered, shaved, brushed his hair and teeth, dressed, grabbed his camera and a scarf—then walked, rather than bounded—downstairs and out the front door. As he walked west along 8th Street, he tied a tight knot in his scarf to cover the front of his neck against a chill autumn wind.

The knot was indicative: tight—suggesting caution, experience, the weariness *and* wariness of age. It was a brisk day towards the end of November, with clear skies and a bright sun. A day, Kit thought, for work. And so, he headed out towards the "N" or "R" line to take him uptown to Madison Square.

At the intersection of Third Avenue and St. Marks Place, as he heeded the pedestrian signal and waited on the curb for a green light, he observed a limousine heading south. As it sped past, Kit glanced at the car, then at the license plate—the digits were a wash—then noticed a head and a bob of straight auburn hair against the headrest in the backseat. The figure inside, Kit believed, was that of a woman.

This was not to be the last time he would see a woman from a distance and be deceived by the illusion. In the days, weeks, months—and then years—to come, his world would be haunted by likenesses of Daneka: hurriedly through rear windows of passing limousines or taxis disappearing around corners; looking straight out from behind a sea of faces in a packed elevator just as he arrived and the doors closed; or making last-second exits from a subway car before he, and it, pulled out of sight—however unlikely it might be, he knew, that she'd be taking a subway. It would always be the same. It couldn't be. She was long gone. In a city of eight million, there would be hundreds of Daneka look-alikes. She would have aged anyway, while he was stuck with the image of an ageless woman. And yet, he would always look until the limousine or taxi or subway was out of sight, or until the elevator had actually begun its ascent. If both he and the woman were on foot, he'd run to the corner. If the woman were then still visible, he'd run to a point just beside her and attempt a sideways glance to convince himself that no—this one also wasn't Daneka.

And yet each such instance was only the beginning. He'd subsequently find himself trapped for a good part of the remaining day in reviewing the details of their affair, item by item, event by event, each item and each event holding him in the muck as he tried, in vain, to pull himself out. But the memories were like a stubborn grapnel anchor, each bill holding fast to the bottom no matter how hard he pulled or twisted.

Chapter 81

Spring, ten years later

It was a glorious day towards the end of April—in many respects, identical to the one on which a certain camera had made accidental contact with the front bumper of a certain limousine traveling south along Lexington Avenue a decade earlier.

Kit, now graying at the temples but with nothing even remotely gray in the same fiery dark eyes, was visiting his mother in Radnor. His father had died years earlier and had been buried—and so, allowed, finally, to join the other Charles Wesley Addisons in all of their knickerbockered splendor—in the cemetery just up Fletcher and off to the right down Upper Gulph Road.

Kit was in Radnor on a mission: he'd promised his mother he would construct a pond for her garden. She wanted, she'd told him, to hear at least the sound of running water through the last of her remaining days. They'd finally decided to put it just off the kitchen terrace, right alongside a moss garden he'd already constructed for her many years earlier.

Over the years, he'd had a number of assignments abroad. From each, he'd never failed to harvest and return with a lichen or some kind of native moss—and then carefully, lovingly, to incorporate the new addition into the moss garden. The lichens and moss were, of course, for his mother; but they were also for this other woman who sat with his mother on the terrace leading off of a colonial house where they both sipped their morning coffee. Mrs. Addison—Kit's mother—read the *Philadelphia Inquirer*. On paper. The second Mrs. Addison—Kit's wife—read *The New York Times*. On a palmtop. Others had read and signed a certain declaration not far from this house whose construction pre-dated even that document by some forty years. On parchment.

The second Mrs. Addison taught young children—as much her avocation as her vocation. She and Kit had two of their own, both toddlers, with whom he now played in the middle of a yard spreading out over several acres at the corner of Fletcher and Brower.

As he was alternatively inspecting the grade of the land and watching that his children didn't wander too far out of sight, the second woman approached him, palmtop in hand. Kit noticed a pained expression in her eyes and he wondered what kind of news she might be bringing him.

"What is it, Nadeshda?" he asked as he abruptly stood up. She handed him the palmtop. Once his eyes had adjusted to the tiny print, he saw the headline in bold: **Managing Editor Found Dead, Alone, at Home.** Next to the announcement was a picture. Kit recognized the face immediately and took out a cigarette.

He sat back down on the grass to read the article. The cause of death would remain unknown pending an autopsy; the body of the deceased, by request of next of kin, would be sent to Denmark for burial. *The Times* had spelled the final destination "Roenne." *The Times*, Kit decided, still had no special feelings for any vowels or consonants but its own—and apparently found nothing particularly sexy about 'ø.' Even Daneka's last name—Kit lamented—had been *Times*-sized to 'Soerensen.'

Leading their two toddlers by the hand, Nadeshda came up behind him just as he was finishing the article. He stubbed out his cigarette and felt a hand on his shoulder. He put his own on top of it, finished reading the last paragraph, then looked up into his wife's eyes.

His were dry. Hers, however, were beginning to mist over. She would cry for both of them, as only a Russian could. In answer to his unspoken question, Hope simply nodded. Once.

Meaning 'yes,' of course, he must go.

Chapter 82

"**S**o, Kit, you have come to help me bury Daneka. I thought you might. I knew almost the first moment I laid eyes on you that you were someone I could count on—that *both* Daneka and I could count on."

"And if Daneka and I had been able—." At the sight of Dagmar Sørensen, now also ten years older and stung by that singular grief that only parents of lost or prematurely dead children can know, Kit stumbled. "You and I wouldn't now be standing here. Instead, we'd be burying *you*. Forgive me."

"My forgiveness is not necessary. You are quite right. I would be the one in the ground now, and the two of you would be dancing on my grave."

"Dancing is not what we'd be doing, Dagmar. Not on your grave or anywhere else."

"I would have insisted upon it!" she said as she limped along with a smile. "For my own amusement. Daneka was never much of a dancer. I assume you are not either. You were alike in that regard—as you were in so many other ways. And so, I would have insisted that you two dance on my grave for *my* sake."

Kit squeezed out a smile of his own. "I, too, thought we were very much alike. I guess you and I both guessed wrong."

"Not wrong, Kit. Your differences were very small. Your obstacle—your impasse—was the narcissism of those small differences."

"The *what?*"

"It's not important—just a Freudian thing."

"A Freudian thing is the reason I'm now here to help you bury Daneka rather than here with her to bury you? I'm sorry, but you've lost me."

"Never mind, Kit," Dagmar said with a wave of her hand. "I want you, instead, to come with me on a journey. I want to tell you a story—a true story. Often, Kit, truth is stranger than fiction. This tale in particular is one with historical antecedent. I know. I read a lot. Well-read, Kit, doesn't necessarily mean well-liked—trust me on that. But at my age, friends are here today, dead and gone tomorrow. I prefer to read."

"You're losing me again."

"Sorry. I was saying—."

"You were saying, in so many words, that 'but for the grace of God—'."

"Yes, I suppose I was—in so many words. I'm the one who should be in that coffin and going into the ground. We would all be happier. That's how even I would have preferred it. Help me to do this thing that now must be done, and then we shall talk. There are reasons for everything in this world, Kit. And I shall very shortly try to help you understand those reasons—to help both of us."

Her burial place was a small churchyard just down the road from her mother's house—the cemetery Daneka had pointed out to Kit the only other time he'd visited Rønne. He and Dagmar went there now on foot. On the tombstone, he saw her name: Daneka Sørensen— and the dates: 24 *februar* 1960—25 *april* 2014. Kit then read, beneath her name and dates, an inscription in English:

> *Here ends the nightmare;*
> *to curds turns the cream.*
> *I'll never reprise it—*
> *nor with it, the dream.*

Alongside the stone was the head and neck of the Virgin Mary, a replica of Michelangelo's *Pietà*, waiting to be put into place as a headstone.

It was nearly dusk when the service concluded. Daneka's coffin was lowered into the ground, last flowers and symbolic handfuls of earth thrown in after it, the hole filled up with dirt, the headstone cemented to the tombstone. Kit and Dagmar walked back to her cottage together. Two months away from the first day of summer, late afternoons on the island of Bornholm were still arrestingly chilly. Mrs. Sørensen asked Kit to make a fire while she went into the kitchen to brew a pot of tea.

He had a small fire burning when she returned with a tea tray set for two, which she then placed down in front of him. While Kit poured for both, she lit a dozen candles around the room—which flickered like fireflies in the small, dark interior.

Once she'd finished lighting her candles, Dagmar settled back into her rocker facing the fireplace. It was quite dark where they sat—but for the candlelight and the fire Kit had just made. Both of them sat for a moment in silence, mesmerized by the flames, until Kit finally broke the silence.

"The inscription on her tombstone. How did it get there?"

"She requested it—a month ago. I don't know where it came from. She sent me the request and asked, should anything ever happen to her—'before her time' is how she put it—that I honor her last wishes. One was the inscription. A second was the headstone, the *Pietà*. I'm not sure of its significance, although I remember that when we first took her as a young girl to Rome, she stood as if transfixed before that statue and stared at it for a long time. Then,"—at this point Mrs. Sørensen angled her own neck *just so*—"she bent her neck in imitation of the Virgin and simply held it. The third wish—which you didn't see today because I haven't yet found someone to drive me out to the forest of Almendingen—was for a lichen to be placed upon her grave. You probably don't know that following your one and only visit here to the island of Bornholm, Daneka began to take a very keen interest in lichens and mosses. She even constructed a moss garden at her cottage in Svaneke." Mrs. Sørensen chuckled and shook her head. "She became something of a fanatic about lichens and mosses. She would collect them wherever her business travels took her and would then bring them back to Bornholm and attempt to plant them in her garden."

Without thinking, Kit reached for his pack of cigarettes, pulled one out, put it between his lips and was about to light it when he realized his *faux pas*. "Excuse me," he said. He stood up and started towards the front door. "I need some air."

Mrs. Sørensen stood up from her own rocker, took Kit gently by the wrists and sat him back down. She then went into the kitchen, got an ashtray and brought it to him.

"There's no need for you to go outside, Kit. I'm not my daughter." She stated the last with a sad half-smile, and in that moment Kit understood that she perhaps knew a great deal about the grown-up Daneka who'd left the island decades earlier. He sat back down, grateful for her permission to stay indoors next to the fire where he could remain warm.

"Do you know anything about Danish history, Kit?" She didn't wait for his answer. "No, of course you don't. Why should you? Ours is what the Germans once called 'the little country.' Our national history is not remarkable. It is, like any national history, a story of the collective, of the universal. Leave that to the Germans and to their Hegel. Have you, since we last met, read Kierkegaard, Kit?" Once again, she didn't wait for his answer. "For

Kierkegaard, existence was a matter of free choice.

"But I don't want to talk philosophy tonight," she said, cutting herself off with an abrupt wave of her hand. "I want to tell you a story. A personal history. I mention this idea of Kierkegaard's only because I agree with it—and because I think this personal history I'm about to tell you is one even he might have liked." She got up again from her rocker and stirred the fire. "So let us first talk a little geography and a little history.

"I don't want to insult you, Kit. But I know that Americans generally don't have much patience with things like geography and history. We Europeans have no choice. Geography, in particular, affects everything we do. Do you know what country lies directly below ours?"

"Germany. And a piece of Poland, I believe."

She smiled. "Exactly, Kit. I'm impressed." He blushed.

"And history. Do you know why the year 1940 is important to us Danes?"

"I'm afraid I've forgotten."

"In 1940, the *Bundeswehr* marched into and over Denmark—and into and over Holland and Belgium, Luxembourg and Norway—just as it had marched into and over Poland the year before. But that's war. That is a collective action. Individual action, individual choice is where I start my story—or rather, where I start my mother's story as she told it to me. You see, I was not yet on this planet at the time of the German invasion."

Kit took a deep drag on his cigarette and sat up straight in his chair.

"These other Danes—the ones before me—knew about Hitler's *Endlösung* ("Final Solution") for the Jews long before the rest of the world did—or at least long before the rest of the world chose to acknowledge it. You know, perhaps, that all Danes wore armbands in solidarity with the Jewish people. But here, on Bornholm, the islanders did much more than that.

"I believe you know of our little forest here in the middle of the island, Kit—the forest of Almendingen. Daneka used to take long walks in that forest when she was a girl." Mrs. Sørensen smiled. "I think those long walks helped to nurture her thinking skills. Unfortunately, people these days—and yes, Daneka, too—do not seem to have the patience or the stamina for long walks and quiet, thinking time."

Kit also smiled as he thought for an instant back to their one visit together to the island and to their love-making in the same forest. "Yes, I know the place. And yes, I unfortunately agree with you."

"The people of Bornholm built an underground shelter in that forest, Kit. They took as many Jews from the mainland as their network could smuggle out. The islanders kept them there for several months. It was not home, by any means, but it was safe—for a while, at least. I say 'them,' but the Jews and the Danes were the same at that point—just as they would be in the end.

"One day, a German soldier found them, and they thought—how do you say it in English?" Dagmar paused as if scratching her brain for the precise phrase. "Ah, yes—they thought 'the gig was up.' That was because they did not know he had been watching them for some time. He knew all about their shelter and their network. And yet, he had never interfered."

Kit's expression suggested he was thoroughly confused by this story: both by the content, which contradicted everything he'd ever heard or read about the behavior of the Germans in the war, but also by her purpose in telling it—which he couldn't yet discern.

"I see that you are a little surprised," Mrs. Sørensen said. "Allow me to continue."

"Please do."

"My mother didn't know why he chose her, of all the people there were to choose from. At the very instant he walked up to her, she thought she would be the first to die. Instead, he took her arm, very respectfully, and walked her off into the forest. When they found a place far enough away and where the others could not hear them, he stopped her. He saw that she was trembling and he put a hand on her shoulder. '*Nein*,' he said. '*Es ist nicht meine Absicht, Ihnen zu schaden.*' 'I don't wish to harm you,' is what he said.

"He then asked her if she understood German, and she told him she did. For the next quarter of an hour, he explained to her that he had been watching them—and her in particular—every day for some time. He admired what they were doing. He hated what he and his country were doing—to the Jews, certainly, but also to the Danes, and to much of the civilized world. He told her he had not been born into this world only to become what he called *ein Todesportier*—a porter, a *janitor*, of death. He wanted to live. He wanted others to live. And now he wanted to help them.

- 428 -

"Nothing could have surprised my mother more, as you can well imagine, Kit. He told her he would bring what he could, *whenever* he could, from his own supply depot. And he did just that. For the next several months, he brought things—food, mostly—every day. He risked his life. As Kierkegaard would have said, he proved his existence through his individual action.

"They became lovers. I know that this fact may sound risible to you, to think of an old lady in that way. But she was not always old. She—like me—had once been a young woman, a woman of desires, the kind of woman Daneka was to you ten years ago. And yet, for a Danish woman who had not seen even her twenty-years birthday, to be the lover of a German soldier was… I don't know if I can make you understand how it must have torn her heart to love this man who spoke the hateful language of the enemy.

"You can guess the rest, as it is in the nature of living, loving things to perpetuate themselves. One day, she became pregnant. She knew she couldn't tell him, that it would have been his end. He was as much in love with her as she was with him, and he was full of life. He would not have been able to keep the secret, and his own happiness would have been his betrayal."

Mrs. Sørensen got up from her rocker and stood for a moment in front of the fire with her back to Kit. Then she turned around and faced him again. "That's often how it is with happiness and love and wanting deeply, *deeply* to live and let live. Those things are hateful in the eyes of many men, however much they may claim the contrary. And not just in war, Kit. No, in times of peace, too. We pay tribute to love and life—all of us. But what most of us really teach our children is hate and fear and slow death. In schools, certainly. But also at home and by our example—so that we can eventually return to war—our more *natural* state.

"I'm sorry. I said no philosophy, and here I am—." She paused for a moment before continuing her story. "She didn't need to worry. A few days later, her father—my grandfather—found them in the woods and immediately saw what they were up to. Then he kept watch for several days over her and her German lover. He watched that German lover of hers bring food to the shelter. He saw the many Jews they'd hidden in that shelter come up for a few minutes each day for fresh air and a few precious seconds of sunlight.

"One night, after he had been watching for several days, he confronted her. He told

- 429 -

her that she was a disgrace to him, to her mother, to the Danish people, to all humanity, to human dignity itself. That she was lower to him than the whores of Copenhagen. And then he raped her.

"The next day, that same father who was now her violator, the proud Danish patriot and protector of human dignity, the man who would not allow the word *tysk* or *Tyskland* one second in his mouth—in any of their mouths, his hate of all things German was so great—went to the German compound and reported everything he had seen.

"One German officer and several soldiers followed my grandfather out into the forest. As my mother's lover opened the hatch to the shelter that day, the German soldiers came out from behind the trees and surprised him. He did not resist. He told them he was proud of what he had done, of what the people of Bornholm had done. He told them that he was, himself, ashamed to be a German soldier. And then he did an odd thing. He took an armband out of his pocket, as if it had been there all along for just this moment, and he put it on. The armband had on it—what else? The Star of David. Then he looked his commanding officer directly in the eye, and said: *'Auch ich bin Jude.'* 'I, too, am a Jew.'

"This, as you can well imagine, infuriated the officer. He ordered his soldiers to line up everyone in the shelter. And next to the Jews, to line up the Danes. My grandfather protested. He said his daughter, my mother, should be spared—after all, he had led the German officer to the shelter and to this soldier who was a traitor to the German cause.

"The officer simply told my grandfather to stand in line with the others. Then he ordered the lover of my mother to shoot all of them. Not in the back of the head, as was usual. But face to face, and between the eyes. To let those eyes see how one *Jude* kills another.

"This lover first stepped up to my mother. What to her were the softest, bluest eyes in all the world now looked once again, and for the last time, into hers—into her own Baltic-blue eyes. She told him she forgave him. That she understood it was not his will. He took one long, last look at her, turned abruptly around to face his commanding officer, put the gun into his own mouth and pulled the trigger.

"There was a moment of confusion. With bits of his brains splattered all over her face and body, my mother became delirious. She had the feeling she was somewhere outside of herself, watching all of it from a cloud receding speedily up and out into the sky.

"The German officer stepped forward and ordered his soldiers to shoot all of the Jews and all of the Danes—including my grandfather. Then he marched off, and the soldiers agreed among themselves to spare my mother. She told me she never knew why, but that she suspected they'd known the secret all along. In this case, they, too, risked their own lives by disobeying an order.

"Somehow, she got home. Somehow, she survived. Her own mother did not. Her mother died a few days later—perhaps of a broken heart—though my mother never revealed what her father, the husband to her mother, my grandfather, had done to her and to her lover.

"And then, somehow, several months later, she delivered a girl. I am that girl. It is why my name is Dagmar—which is as much a German name as a Danish one."

Kit's head was spinning as he took out another cigarette, and Mrs. Sørensen looked at him with sympathy. "I'm afraid, Kit, that I've told you only the beginning of the story. Could I have one of those, too?" she asked, pointing to his pack of cigarettes. He extended the pack, then half-stood up out of his chair to light it for her.

"My mother never married. She raised me alone through the years following the war. She did so by running our home as a kind of Bed & Breakfast for tourists—Danes, mostly, from the mainland. Occasionally, a haughty Swede or two who seemed to mistake our island for one of their own—perhaps because it lies so close to Sweden—and who in any case seemed to think our house was for their very *neutral,* very exclusive Swedish pleasure."

The venom Dagmar had just attached to the word 'neutral' did not escape Kit's attention.

"Over the years, little by little, the Germans also discovered this island and our particular Bed & Breakfast. They came often to the island of Bornholm. Perhaps because of my mother's experience of the war, perhaps because of me—I do not know—but she did not feel towards Germans the way most Danes did then and still do today. She met everyone—German, Swede, Dutch, it did not matter—without prejudice, and then waited to see how they would prove themselves. She would not act with the collective, and she would not treat her country's former enemies collectively. She exercised her free will, her *choice.*

And she taught me to do the same."

Kit noticed how Mrs. Sørensen seemed to withdraw into herself as she next spoke. "And I taught Daneka—at least I thought I did. But perhaps I did not spend enough time. Somehow, after she had left Denmark and had lived for a while in New York, she seemed to change. I do not know why. I do not know if there is something about New York, or if it is …was … just Daneka. It was very small at first, but it was there. I saw it even in the way she treated you, Kit—yes, even you. It troubled me because I sensed when I saw the two of you together for the first and only time here ten years ago, that you, too, felt it. And that if it did not destroy you first, it would sooner or later destroy your love for her."

Kit suddenly wished he had tried much harder to reach Daneka through this woman. It might've made a difference; it might not have. There was a great deal of history between these two women which he couldn't know or even guess at. What could he have done even if he'd known? In any case, their story—his and Daneka's—was just another little history, now and forever buried beneath a head- and tombstone.

Mrs. Sørensen interrupted his reverie. "One German family in particular had been staying with us the first month of summer, every summer, for many years. They had a son, Olaf, who had been my playmate all of those years. And then, in the summer of my eighteenth year, that playmate and I fell in love. Just as my mother had, I exercised *my* free will, *my* choice, and Olaf and I did what young lovers do.

"Luckily, I did not become pregnant. But my mother knew it was only a matter of time before I would—with Olaf, or with someone else. She did not wish for me the same fate she had suffered. Raising a child alone, poor, keeping house for other people. And so, she quickly found me a husband." Daneka's mother smiled in a slightly self-mocking way. "A kind man, who happened also to be rich—at least she *thought* he was rich.

"We started off well enough, and my first and only child was born the following winter, on February 24, 1960. That baby was Daneka."

Kit took out a third cigarette and lit it.

"Daneka was—how do you call it in English?" Here, she put a fist to her mouth in a studied portrait of thought. "I think the word is 'spitfire.' Yes, that is it. She was a spitfire! She never needed me for anything. She took the world as she found it and converted it to her will. When she could not get the lessons or find the books she wanted here on Bornholm, she organized her own correspondence courses. Yes, *really!* Can you believe it? She was ambitious. Far more ambitious than I had ever been. Some might even say that she was calculating, although I would never allow myself to think of her in that way.

"As it turned out, my husband's fortune was diminishing just as the ambition of Daneka was augmenting. As his fortune and fate seemed to darken, so, too, did his mood. The only thing that seemed to give him real happiness was his daughter. Certainly I did not.

"With ambition, Kit, often comes precociousness. Was Daneka precocious? Yes," she said with a self-deprecating chuckle, "even more than I was. She had a first lover at fifteen—at least I think it was her first, although older men had already begun to look at her years earlier in ways they do not usually look at young girls. I noticed it. My husband did also—and he tried desperately to hold onto the little girl who was still his daughter.

"But she did not want to remain a little girl. She did not want to remain that because she could *not* remain that. As much as she wanted the affection of her father, she also could not keep down those things—those thoughts and actions—that come naturally to girls once they cease being little girls.

"It is perhaps a great challenge for most men. For many, it is simply too great—especially if they are unhappy with their wives or with themselves. I speak of the challenge of watching a daughter grow into a woman, and of letting her grow, and change, and ultimately go off into the arms of another man. Some can do it, no doubt. Most struggle with it, but manage to overcome their desires—or at least to keep them under control. Some, however, do not.

"It was in the fifteenth year of Daneka that my husband and I had our first serious difficulties. Our finances may have had a lot to do with it. But I think it was also because he knew he was losing Daneka to the world outside. That summer, our little island of Bornholm had a visit from a family from New York City. We had occasionally had visitors from America before, but never from New York City. They were different. Big and boisterous and full of the kind of confidence that is quite foreign to anything we know here in Denmark. And Daneka was smitten.

"They had a boy—very handsome, very lively. You reminded me a bit of him, Kit, when I first met you, although he wasn't so quiet, so contemplative, as you. When he spoke or gestured, you knew that he was going places—that he would be a great success in life.

"He and Daneka became lovers. My husband was beside himself. With jealousy? I don't know. I prefer not to think so. But sometimes fate is in the genes. And when there is a fateful disease in the past of some family—no matter how quiet or how many generations it may take—it always seems to find a way back into the present of that same family.

"The father of Daneka, my husband, found them together one night—exactly as the father of my mother—my grandfather—had found her with her German lover. Whether it was rage, or jealousy, or temporary insanity, my husband did to Daneka later that night what the father of my mother had done to my her."

Kit involuntarily sprang out of his chair. He needed air, badly, and he went to the front door and out into the early evening darkness entirely unaware of his motions.

He didn't know how long he'd been standing there, hyperventilating and looking off to a sun low on the horizon and all but obscured by heavy cloud cover, when he heard the front door open behind him.

When he turned around, he saw two bodies framed in the doorway: one belonged to Mrs. Sørensen; the second, to another woman. It was impossible to know anything more at that distance—with the fire and candles as the only sources of light shining upon them, and from behind.

When he came back in through the front door moments later, the woman was sitting on the floor with her head in Mrs. Sørensen's lap. Daneka's mother was brushing the woman's hair, and the woman was smiling. There was, however, something slightly wrong with the woman's smile. She lifted her head to inspect Kit—as a dog might, out of curiosity, but only long enough to register the scent—and then laid it back down in Mrs. Sørensen's lap. In that instant, a memory flashed before Kit's eyes—just one or two frames in a fast-moving film that was the length of his life.

Daneka's mother put down the hairbrush, leaned over the woman and kissed her gently on the top of her head. The woman looked up at her, smiled gratefully—or was it obediently, or dumbly, Kit couldn't be sure—and then Mrs. Sørensen stood up and lifted the woman gently off the floor. The two of them walked to the staircase and up, Kit assumed, to Daneka's former bedroom.

Eventually, Mrs. Sørensen came back downstairs and sat herself down.

Kit's curiosity was piqued, but he decided to wait for Mrs. Sørensen to provide the answer to this latest riddle at her own pace and in her own good time.

"Daneka was not as fortunate as my mother. We cannot always discern the order of nature—but she has one, no doubt. And she also knows when it is time to put an end to things.

"That woman you just saw is Margarette, the daughter of Daneka. She lives with me now. For how much longer, we don't know, as she has a degenerative disease. But as you can see, she was already predestined from the beginning. The end of Margarette is something both Daneka and I had been reconciled to long before Daneka decided that she, herself, needed to go first. Margarette, as you know, used to live in New York City—alone, down around 14th Street, I believe. I don't know. I haven't been to New York City in years. Daneka always insisted on coming here, sometimes with Margarette, but not always. Margarette was her dark secret."

There are moments in life when the body or the mind or both are so overwhelmed by a present reality that they go into shock and cease to register: the instant before your car slams into another; the seconds—or, if you're unlucky—minutes left to you as the jetliner in which you have been comfortably and horizontally seated abruptly goes into a tailspin, and you realize that you—together with everything in your world—are now fixed vertically, tragically, on an arrow called 'doom' that you are riding straight into the ground.

This was such a moment for Kit, and he had no idea how much time and how many words—or who said them—had passed before he regained a sense of time and place, a memory of the preceding dialogue and a context for its continuation. When he did, gradually, it was only because the two contrasting bits of information he'd just been given were now, finally, beginning to make some kind of sense. The definitive news of Daneka's suicide—from her mother's own mouth—felt like the quick plunge of a dagger. The pain of it was only partially offset by his learning the solution to the puzzle over which he'd never really ceased to agonize.

Almost against his will, Kit leaned forward. "And Margarette's—or rather Annemette's father?"

"As I said before, nature has an order and a logic all her own. In Daneka's case, it was not her American boyfriend whose loving attentions ultimately found her willing egg, but those of her father—of my husband."

Mrs. Sørensen continued in something of a monotone. "The day after the incident, my husband hanged himself. Daneka became comatose. The boyfriend went back to New York City and didn't return the following summer—or ever again. When we discovered that Daneka was pregnant, I wanted her to abort the child. It would not have been difficult here in Denmark under the circumstances. But her pregnancy brought her back to herself, back to life. She believed that her baby was from her lover, not from her father, and so she wanted to keep it. She even named it—Margarette."

"But I thought her name was Annemette," Kit said half in question.

"It is. Margarette means 'pearl' in Danish. Daneka hit upon the name one day as she was rubbing her belly—something she did constantly to polish the thing growing inside her," Mrs. Sørensen said with a sad smile. "When she delivered a baby girl and immediately understood who the true father of that baby was, she chose the name Annemette instead. Annemette in Danish means 'bad pearl.'" And now, for the first time, Kit could discern a touch of bitterness around the edges of Mrs. Sørensen's mouth. "You see, Daneka was smart. She was ambitious. She was precocious. But she could also be… Well, Kit, I will let you provide your own word."

Kit looked down between his knees and stared hard at the floor. He had no words to respond adequately to any of what Mrs. Sørensen had just told him.

"I think you can probably provide the rest of the answers as well as—or maybe even better than—I can. How and why she moved to New York City. How and why she was able to thrive in New York City as she never could have thriven here. Denmark is full of pain and grief, certainly—just like any other place. But because we are so small, because there are so few of us, all of it is necessarily lived on the outside. Unlike in big, loud, boisterous New York City, there is simply no good way to hide it here. In New York City, I would imagine that people suffer many of the same private agonies. Human beings are not all that different the world over. It is what they choose to *do* with those agonies—whether they allow themselves to be overcome by them, or achieve in *spite* of them, or maybe even *because* of them—that matters.

"I think Daneka chose to live in New York City because only there—and not here—was it possible to keep her secrets hidden away in dark places. Until, of course, she just could not any longer—until the power and grief of that secret simply overwhelmed her. At which point she had to come back, even if only in a box. She had to come *here* to find a final, peaceful resting place.

"You, Kit, were at first something of a mystery to me. You were also a great hope. I had always hoped that someone would break through to Daneka. That someone kind, patient and gentle enough would allow her to reveal her secrets—at least to herself—so that she would finally be able to grieve, and accept, and love—that other person, certainly, but first of all herself."

More than at any time in the months in which he'd seen his relationship with Daneka growing colder by the day, more than at any time in the ten years since he'd last walked out of her bedroom and closed the door to her apartment—knowing that he'd never open it again—Kit now felt her absence. It came to him not as a twinge or as a pinch, but as a howling out of some deep pit. He realized for the first time that she perhaps really *had* loved him—that she'd simply been incapable of showing that love for the reasons her mother had now finally made clear to him—and perhaps for many others, too, many of which might find their source and explanation with this very same mother.

As tears welled up in his eyes, they were not tears for himself or for *his* loss. They were tears for Daneka, who'd too rarely allowed herself to cry. But they were also tears for this woman who, in the end, had found mosses and lichens of her own—and who'd apparently discovered the beauty of them; for this woman who'd found that a certain kiss on the nape of a certain neck—namely her own—had meant more to one man than all the world's riches or all the world's sins; for this woman who'd realized that the dream which could've been would never be; instead, that the nightmare which had consumed her in life would continue to haunt her in death—unless and until she put an end to that nightmare by coming home to bury it at its source.

He thought of the passage in Milan Kundera's book he'd only recently read, and yet which had locked itself into his short-term memory: "For the woman who is dead is a woman with no defenses; she has no more power, she has no more influence; people no longer respect either her wishes or her tastes; the dead woman cannot will anything, cannot aspire to any respect or refute any slander…".

Kit rose up out of his chair, put on his winter coat and gloves, pulled his scarf tight about his neck and walked out the front door. It was now indeed cold outside, and he braced himself against the wind blowing in from the sea. He walked back to the cemetery and to Daneka's gravestone, gazed upon the head and neck of the Virgin even as they seemed almost to transform themselves into Daneka's own head and neck.

As he approached her stone bust from the rear, he noticed a pair of moths in the folds of her headdress and raised his hand to brush them away. In that single gesture, at the sight of that single pair of moths, a view—and then a smell—came to him from somewhere deep in his memory. In that same instant, he knew—finally and conclusively—that she'd also been that elusive first one.

As he bent down and put his lips to the back of her stone-cold neck for one last kiss, he closed his eyes and allowed himself to feel the heat of the brand she'd once left in a park called Riverside, in a city called New York, in a pain called eternity. The brand might've lost its burn, but not its scar—he now realized as he whispered "adjö" in the only Scandinavian language in which he'd ever learned the word for "goodbye."

The End

About the author:

Russell's work has been widely published both in print and on the Internet. He believes, with Hobbes, that "life is short, brutish and nasty." He also believes, with Donne, however, that art is long; and that no man is one, entire of itself—either an island or a work of art.

Connect with Russell online:

Twitter: http://twitter.com/Russell538
Facebook: http://facebook.com/profile.php?id=647677735
Amazon Author Page: https://authorcentral.amazon.com/gp/profile
Blogspot for *Trompe-l'oeil*: http://russell-bittner.blogspot.com
Webpage for *Trompe-l'oeil*: : http://www.russellbittner.com/
My Webpage: http://www.indiekindleauthors.com/?page_id=317
My e-mail address: **RussellBittner@gmail.com**

Made in the USA
Middletown, DE
09 January 2024

47474351R00247